The Brutal Art

Also by Jesse Kellerman
Sunstroke
Trouble

Plays
Things Beyond Our Control
3m1w

The Brutal Art

JESSE KELLERMAN

sphere

SPHERE

First published in the United States in 2008 by G.P. Putnam's Sons,
a division of Penguin Group (USA) Inc.
First published in Great Britain in 2008 by Sphere

A CIP catalogue record for this book
is available from the British Library.

Hardback ISBN 978-1-84744-152-2
Trade Paperback ISBN 978-1-84744-154-6

Typeset in Garamond by M Rules
Printed and bound in Great Britain by
Clays Ltd, St Ives plc

Sphere
An imprint of
Little, Brown Book Group
100 Victoria Embankment
London EC4Y 0DY

An Hachette Livre UK Company
www.hachettelivre.co.uk

www.littlebrown.co.uk

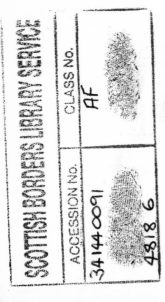

TO GAVRI

True art is always found where we least expect it, where nobody is thinking about it or saying its name.

Art hates to be recognized and greeted by name.

It flees instantly.

–Jean Dubuffet

. . . a mirror of smoke, cracked and dim
in which to judge himself . . .

–The Book of Odd Thoughts 13:15

ONE

In the beginning, I behaved badly. I'm not going to lie to you, so allow me to get that on the table right away: while I would like to believe that I redeemed myself later, there's no question that – in the beginning at least – I lacked a certain purity of purpose. That's putting it mildly. If we're being honest, let's be honest: I was motivated by greed and, more important, by narcissism: a sense of entitlement that runs deep in my genes and that I can't seem to shake, no matter how ugly it makes me feel, some of the time. Part of the job description, I suppose, and part of the reason I've moved on. Know thyself.

Christ. I promised myself that I'd make an effort to avoid sounding like a pretentious prick. I ought to be more hardboiled; I'd like to be. I don't think I have it in me. To write in clipped sentences. To employ gritty metaphor in the introduction of sultry blondes. (My heroine's a brunette, and not the especially sultry kind; her hair isn't jet-black and dripping; it's medium chestnut and, more often than not, pragmatically tied back, workmanlike ponytails or flyaway buns or stashed behind her ears.) I can't do it, so why bother trying?

We each get one story to tell, and we have to tell it the way that comes naturally. I don't carry a gun; I don't get into car chases or fistfights. All I can do is write down the truth, and truthfully, I might be kind of a pretentious prick. That's all right. I can live with that.

As Sam is fond of saying *It is what it is.*

Generally, I don't agree. A more appropriate rule of thumb – for my life, my line of work, and this story – might be *It is what it is, except when it isn't, which is most of the time.* I still don't know the whole truth, and I doubt I ever will.

But I'm getting ahead of myself.

All I mean is that, having lived a long time in a world of illusions, a costume-party world, wink-wink and knowingness and quote marks around everything everybody says, it's a relief to speak honestly. If my honesty doesn't sound like Philip Marlowe's, so be it. It is what it is. This might be a detective novel, but I'm no detective. My name is Ethan Muller. I am thirty-three years old, and I used to be in art.

OF COURSE, I LIVE IN NEW YORK. My gallery was in Chelsea, on Twenty-fifth Street, between Tenth and Eleventh avenues, one gallery of many in a building whose identity, like that of the city around it, has been in flux more or less since birth. A row of stables; a garage for hansom cabs; then a corset factory, whose downfall coincided with the rise of the brassiere. The building lived on, though, subdivided, reunited, resubdivided, condemned, uncondemned, and – finally – rezoned as residential lofts for young artists, some of whom had taken to wearing corsets as a protofeminist throwback. But before the first struggling MFA filmmaker could sign her lease and get her boxes out of storage, the entire art world decided to drag its sagging ass uptown, creating a neighborhood mini-boom.

This took place in the early 1990s. Keith Haring was dead; the East Village was dead; SoHo was dead; everyone had AIDS or AIDS ribbons.

Everyone needed a change. Chelsea fit. The DIA Foundation had been there since the late 80s, and people hoped that the move would redeem art from the rabid commercialization that had metastasized the downtown scene.

The developers, nosing out an ideal opportunity for rabid commercialization, took their newly prime piece of real estate and had it rezoned yet again, and in May of '95, 567 West Twenty-fifth reopened for business, accepting into its white-walled bosom a few dozen smallish galleries and several large ones, including the airy, double-high, fourth-floor space that would eventually become mine.

I used to wonder what the corset-maker or the stablehands would make of what transacts on their former plot. Where horseshit used to turn the air sulfurous and rank, millions and millions and millions of dollars now change hands. So goes the Big City.

Because of the number of tenants engaged in the same activity – i.e., the sale of contemporary art – and because of the nature of that activity – i.e., frantic, jealous, shot through with schadenfreude – 567 frequently feels like a beehive, but a hip and ironic one. Artists, gallerists, assistants, collectors, consultants and assorted flunkies buzz up and down its smooth concrete halls, nectar-heavy with gossip. It's a schmoozer's paradise. There are openings to attend, a sale to scoff at, a resale that makes the first sale look like a bargain – plus all of New York's standard social touchstones: adulteries, divorces and lawsuits. Marilyn refers to the building as the High School, for her a term of endearment. Marilyn was homecoming queen, after all.

There's no lobby, as such. Three concrete steps lead to a steel gate, opened by a numerical keypad, which has about as much thief-stopping power as a twist tie, or perhaps a banana peel on the floor. Everyone relevant knows the code. On the off chance that you'd recently arrived from Mars or Kansas and, never having seen an art gallery before, that you took the first taxi you could find to 567, you would have little trouble gaining admittance. You could wait for an intern to come toddling in, balancing four cups of coffee, all prepared with extreme precision, one for herself and three for her employer. Or you could wait for an artist to show up lugging a hangover and the new canvases he promised eighteen months ago. Or for a gallerist himself, someone like me, getting out of a cab on a cold and windless January Monday, phone pinned between head and shoulder, negotiating with a private party in London, fingers going numb as I count off the fare, filled with a sourceless and dreadful certainty that today was going to be one hell of a day.

FINISHING THE CALL OUTSIDE, I let myself into the building, hit the button for the freight elevator, and savored my solitude. I tended to show up at about eight thirty, earlier than most of my colleagues and a full hour before my assistants. Once work began, I was never alone. Talking to people is my strong suit, and the reason I've been successful. For the same reason, I treasured those few minutes to myself.

The elevator arrived and Vidal pulled open the screeching accordion gate. As we exchanged greetings, my phone went off again. The caller ID read KRISTJANA HALLBJÖRNSDOTTIR, confirming my hell-of-a-day premonition.

Kristjana is an installation and performance artist, a behemoth of a woman: six feet tall, thick-limbed, with a drill sergeant's crew cut. She manages to be somehow dainty and enormously heavy-footed, like a bull in a china shop, except that the bull is wearing a tutu. Born in Iceland, raised all over the place: that's her provenance as well as her art's; and although I admire the work deeply, it's barely good enough to justify the headache of representing her. When I took her on I knew her reputation. I knew, too, that other people were rolling their eyes at me. It had become a point of pride that I'd kept her in line, putting up her most successful show in years: reviewed well and sold out for well above asking, a feat that left her literally weeping on my shoulder with gratitude. Kristjana is nothing if not demonstrative.

But that was last May, and since then she had gone into hibernation. I'd gone by her apartment, left messages, sent e-mails and texts. If she was angling for attention, she failed, because I stopped trying. Her call that morning was our first contact in months.

Cell phone reception in the elevator is spotty, and I couldn't make her out until Vidal hauled open the gate and that huge, panicked voice came bursting across the airwaves at full bore, already deep into an explanation of her Idea and the material support she required. I told her to slow down and start again. She drew in a wet, heavy breath, the first sign that she's about to go haywire. Then, seeming to reconsider, she asked about the summer. I told her I could not show her until August.

'Impossible,' she said. 'You are not listening.'

'I am. It can't be done.'

'Bullshit. You are not *listening.*'

'I'm looking at the calendar as we speak.' (Not true; I was looking for my keys.) 'What are we talking about, anyway? What am I committing myself to, before I say yes?'

'I need the whole space.'

'I—'

'It's not negotiable. I need the full space. I am referring to *landscape*, Ethan.' She launched into a highly technical and theoretically dense discourse on the disappearing Arctic ice pack. She had to show in June, at the absolute peak of summer, opening on the night of the solstice, and she wanted the air-conditioning off – the *heat on* – because that underscored the notion of dissolution. *Dissolfing* she kept saying. *Everything is dissolfing.* By the time she got to post-post-post-critical theory, I had ceased listening, absorbed by the problem of my keys, which had migrated to the bottom of my attaché. I found them and unlocked the gallery doors as she outlined a plan for destroying my floors.

'You can't bring a live walrus in here.'

Wet, heavy breathing.

'It's probably not legal. Is it? Kristjana? Have you even looked into that?'

She told me to go fuck myself sideways and hung up.

Knowing that it was a matter of time before she called back, I left the phone on the front desk and began my morning routine. First voicemail. There were six from Kristjana, all between four and five thirty in the morning; God only knew who she had expected to reach. A few collectors wanted to know when they could expect their art. I was currently running two shows: a series of lovely, shimmery paintings by Egao Oshima, and some of Jocko Steinberger's papier-mâché genitalia. All of the Oshimas had presold, and several of the Steinbergers had gone to the Whitney. A good month.

After phone came e-mail: clients to touch base with, social machinery in need of grease, arrangements for art fairs, arrangements to look at new work. Much of dealing art consists of keeping one's plates spinning. A friend of mine in the business wrote to ask if I could get ahold of a Dale Schnelle he lusted for. I replied that I might. Marilyn sent me a macabre cartoon one of her artists had drawn of her, depicting her as Saturn eating his children, à la Goya. She found the image delightful.

At nine thirty, Ruby showed up, coffees in hand. I took mine and gave her instructions. At nine thirty-nine Nat arrived and resumed typesetting the catalogue for our upcoming show. At ten twenty-three my cell phone rang again, a blocked number. As you'd imagine, most of the people I liked selling to had blocked numbers.

'Ethan.' A voice like flannel; I recognized it immediately.

I'd known Tony Wexler all my life, and I considered him the closest thing I have to a father that I didn't despise. That he worked for my father, had worked for him for more than forty years – I'll leave the psychoanalysis up to you. Suffice it to say that whenever my father wanted something from me, he sent Tony to go fetch.

Which had happened with increasing frequency over the last two years, when my father had a heart attack and I didn't visit him in the hospital. Since then I'd been getting calls from him, through Tony, every eight or ten weeks. That might not sound like much, but given how little communication we'd had prior to that, I had lately come to feel a tad assaulted. I had no interest in bridge-building. When my father builds a bridge, you can bet there's going to be a toll on it.

So while I was pleased to hear Tony's voice, I didn't especially want to know what he had to say.

'We read about the shows. Your father was very interested.'

By *we* he meant himself. When I started at the gallery nine years ago, Tony got himself subscribed to several of the trades; and unlike most art-mag subscribers, he reads them. He's an authentic intellectual in an age when that term has come to mean nothing, and he knows a shocking amount about the market.

He also meant himself when he said *your father*. Tony tends to pin his own sentiments on his boss, a habit designed, I believe, to conceal the absurd fact that I have a closer relationship with the payroll than with the man who sired me. Nobody's fooled.

We talked art for a little bit. He asked me how I felt about the Steinbergers in the context of his return to figuration; what else Oshima had planned; how the two shows communicated. I kept waiting for the request, the sentence that began *Your father would like.*

He said, 'Something has come to my attention that I think you should know about. Some new work.'

It's always open season on art dealers. Quickly one develops strict submission policies. In my case, impenetrable: if you were good, I would find you; otherwise I didn't want to hear from you. It might sound elitist or draconian but I had no choice. It was either that or face the endless pleading of acquaintances convinced that if you would take the time to come to their sister-in-law's best friend's husband's half-brother's debut show at the

Brooklyn Jewish Community Center you'd be bowled over, converted, dying to showcase their genius on your obviously bare walls. *Et tu*, Tony?

'Is that a fact,' I said.

'Works on paper,' Tony said. 'Ink and felt-tip. You need to see them.'

Warily, I asked who the artist was.

'He's from the Courts,' Tony said.

The Courts being Muller Courts, the largest housing development in the Great State of New York. Built as a postwar middle-class utopia, drained of its founding intent by white flight, it holds the ignominious title of most crime-ridden area in Queens; a blight on an already blighted borough; a monument to wealth, ego and slumlordship; two dozen towers, fifty-six acres and twenty-six thousand people. Bearing my surname.

Knowing that the artist hailed from that hellpit awakened a sense of obligation in me, one that I had no right to feel. I didn't build the damn thing; my grandfather did. I wasn't responsible for its poor upkeep; my father and brothers were. Nevertheless I began to rationalize. There wasn't any harm in having a look at this so-called art by this so-called artist. Provided word didn't get around that the Muller Gallery had flung open its doors, all I stood to lose was a few minutes of my time, a sacrifice I would make for Tony. And he had a decent eye. If he said a piece had merit, it probably did.

Not that I intended to represent anyone new. My roster was full. But people like to have their good taste confirmed, and I supposed that even Tony, who I considered the picture of self-composure, was not immune to the need for validation.

'You can give him my e-mail address.'

'Ethan—'

'Or he can come by, if he'd like. Tell him to call first and use your name.'

'Ethan. I can't do that.'

'Why not?'

'Because I don't know where he is.'

'Who.'

'The artist.'

'You don't know where the artist is?'

'That's what I'm telling you. He's gone.'

'Gone where.'

'*Gone* gone. Three months he misses rent. Nobody's seen him. They start thinking he might have died, so the super opens the place up, but instead of finding the tenant, finds the drawings. He had the good sense to call me before tossing them.'

'He called you directly?'

'He called the management company. They called up the tree. Believe me, there's a reason it got this far. The work is out of this world.'

I was skeptical. 'Drawings.'

'Yes. But they're as good as paintings. Better.'

'What are they like?'

'I can't describe them.' An unfamiliar note of urgency came into his voice. 'You have to see for yourself. The room itself is essential to the experience.'

I told him he sounded like catalogue copy.

'Don't be snarky.'

'Come on, Tony. Do you really think—'

'Trust me. When can you come?'

'Well. It's a busy couple of weeks. I'm going to Miami—'

'N-n-n. To*day*. When can you come today.'

'I can't. Are you kidding? Today? I'm in the middle of work.'

'Take a break.'

'I haven't even gotten started.'

'Then you're not interrupting anything.'

'I can come up – next Tuesday. How about then?'

'I'll send a car for you.'

'Tony,' I said. 'It can wait. It'll have to.'

He said nothing, the most effective rebuke of all. I held the phone aside to ask Ruby for a slot in my schedule, but Tony's voice came squawking from the receiver.

'Don't ask her. Don't ask the girl.'

'I'm—'

'Get in a cab. I'll meet you there in an hour.'

As I gathered my coat and bag and walked to the corner to pick up a cab, my cell phone rang again. It was Kristjana. She'd done some thinking. August could work.

TWO

All twenty-four Muller Courts towers are named for gemstones, a stab at elegance that misses its mark by some distance. I had the driver circle the block until I spotted Tony waiting for me in front of the Garnet unit, his tan camel-hair coat vivid against the brick, sniffing distance from a heap of trash bags bleeding into the gutter. Above a concrete awning fluttered the three flags of country, state and city, and a fourth, for the Muller Corporation.

We entered the lobby, overheated and fumy with institutional floor cleaner. Everybody in uniform – the security guard inside his bulletproof kiosk, the handyman prying off baseboards near the management office – seemed to know Tony, acknowledging him out of either cordiality or fear.

A reinforced glass door led into a dark courtyard, hemmed in by Garnet behind us, and on three sides by the Tourmaline, Lapis Lazuli and Platinum units.

I remember once asking my father how they could have named a building Platinum, which even I, at age seven, knew was not a stone. He didn't answer me, and so I repeated myself, louder. He kept reading, looking supremely annoyed.

Don't ask stupid questions.

All I wanted to do from then on was to ask as many stupid questions as possible. My father soon declined to look up at me when I approached, finger crooked, mouth full of imponderables. *Who decides what goes in the dictionary. Why don't men have breasts.* I would have asked my mother but she was already dead by then, which might help explain why my questions so irritated my father. Everything that I did or said served the same purpose: to remind him that I existed, and that she did not.

At some point I figured out why they chose Platinum. They ran out of stones.

Seen from high above, the courtyards from which Muller Courts draws its name look like dumbbells. Each consists of a pair of hexagons, four sides of which are residential towers and two of which taper into a rectangular stretch of community property – the bar of the dumbbell – that features a playground, a small parking lot and a grassy patch for sitting when weather permits. Between them, the various courtyards also contain six basketball hoops, a volleyball net, an asphalt soccer field, a swimming pool (drained in winter), a handful of unkempt gardens, three small houses of worship (mosque, church, synagogue), a dry cleaner and two bodegas. If your needs were simple enough, you could get by without ever leaving the complex.

As we crossed the hexagon, its towers seemed to loom inward, weighed down by air conditioners painted in pigeon shit. Balconies served as overflow storage for decrepit furniture, moldy carpet remnants, three-legged walkers, charcoal grills abandoned in mid-assembly. Two kids in oversized NBA jerseys played a rough game of one-on-one, driving toward a basket whose broken rim drooped at a thirty-degree angle.

I pointed this out to Tony.

'I'll write a memo,' he said. I couldn't tell if he was being sarcastic.

The so-called artist lived in the Carnelian, on the eleventh floor, and on the way up I asked Tony what efforts he'd made to get in touch with the man.

'He's gone, I told you.'

I felt uneasy waltzing into a stranger's apartment, and told Tony as much. He assured me, though, that the tenant had forfeited all rights when he stopped paying his rent. Tony had never misled me in the past, and I didn't think him capable of doing so. Why would the thought have crossed my mind? I trusted him.

Looking back, I might have been a tad more careful.

Outside the door to C-1156, Tony asked me to wait while he went in and cleared the way. The entry-hall fixture didn't work, and the rest of the place was very crowded; he didn't want me to trip. I heard him moving around inside, heard a soft thud and a muttered oath. Then he emerged from the gloom and pinned an arm across the door.

'All right.' He stood back to allow me in. 'Go nuts.'

BEGIN WITH THE MUNDANE, the squalid. A narrow entrance opens onto a single room, no more than a hundred and twenty square feet. Floorboards worn down to the bare wood, dried out and shrunken and splitting. The walls waterstained and pricked with thumbtack holes. A dusty lightbulb, burning. A mattress. A makeshift desk: inkstained particleboard balanced on stacks of cinderblock. A low bookcase. In the corner, a white enamel sink, archipelagoed with black chips; underneath, a single-burner electric hotplate. The windowshade permanently down, unable or unwilling to retract. A gray short-sleeved sport shirt on a hanger hooked around the bolt of a heat pipe. A gray sweater draped across a folding chair. A pair of cracked brown leather shoes, soles pulling away from uppers, making duckbills. A doorless bathroom; a toilet; a sloped tile floor with a drain underneath a ceiling-mount showerhead.

13

All of this I saw later.

At first I saw only boxes.

Motor oil boxes, packing tape boxes, boxes for computers and printers. Fruit crates. Milk crates. 100% REAL ITALIAN TOMATOES. Boxes lining the walls, tightening the entryway by two-thirds. Smothering the bed. Tottering in stacks like elaborately vertical desserts; on the sink; in the shower, crammed in up to the ceiling; boxes, bowing the bookcase and bricking up the windows. The desk, the chair; the shoes crushed flat. Only the crapper remained exposed.

And in the air: paper. That rich smell somewhere between human skin and bark. Paper, decaying and shedding, wood pulp creating a dry haze that eddied around my body, flowed into my lungs, and burned. I began to cough.

'Where's the art?' I asked.

Tony squeezed in beside me. 'Here,' he said, resting his hand on the nearest box. Then he began pointing to all the other boxes. 'And there, there, there, and there.'

Incredulous, I opened one of the boxes. Inside was a neat stack of what appeared to be blank paper, sour yellow and crumbling at the corners. For a moment I thought Tony was playing a joke on me. Then I picked up the first page and turned it over and everything else disappeared.

I lack the vocabulary to make you see what I saw. Regardless: a dazzling menagerie of figures and faces; angels, rabbits, chickens, elves, butterflies, amorphous beasts, fantastic ten-headed beings of myth, Rube Goldberg machinery with organic parts, all drawn with an exacting hand, tiny and swarming across the page, afire with movement, dancing, running, soaring, eating, eating one another, exacting horrific and bloody tortures, a carnival of lusts and emotions, all the savagery and beauty that life has to offer – but exaggerated, delirious, dense, juvenile, perverse – and cartoonish and buoyant and hysterical – and I felt set upon, mobbed, overcome with the desire to look away as well as the desire to dive into the page.

The real attention to detail, though, was concentrated not in these characters but in the landscape they populated. A living earth, of wobbling dimensions: here flat, there exquisitely deep, inflated geographical features, undulating roads labeled with names twenty letters long. Mountains were buttocks and breasts and chins; rivers became veins spilling purplish liquid nourishing flowers with devil's heads; trees sprouting from a mulch of words and nonsense words; straightrazor grass. In some places the line was whisper-fine, elsewhere so thick and black that it was a miracle the pen had not torn straight through the page.

The drawing pushed at its edges, leaching into the murky air.

Electrified, unnerved, I stared for six or seven minutes, a long time to look at a sheet of of $8^1/_2$-by-11 paper; and before I could censor myself, I decided that whoever had drawn this was sick. Because the composition had a psychotic quality, the fever of action taken to warm oneself from the chill of solitude.

I tried to place what I was seeing in the context of other artists. The best references I could muster at the time were Robert Crumb and Jeff Koons; but the drawing had none of their kitsch, none of their irony; it was raw and honest and naïve and violent. For all my efforts to keep the piece orderly – to tame it with rationality, experience and knowledge – I still felt like it was going to jump out of my hands, to skitter up the walls and spin itself into smoke, ash, oblivion. It lived.

Tony said, 'What do you think?'

I set the drawing aside and picked up the next one. It was just as baroque, just as mesmerizing, and I gave it the same amount of attention. Then, realizing that if I did that for every drawing in there, I'd never leave, I picked up a handful of pages and riffled them, causing a sliver near their edges to disintegrate. They were all dazzling, all of them. My chest knotted up. As early as then, I was having trouble coming to grips with the sheer monomania of the project.

I put the stack down and returned to the first two drawings, which I set side-by-side for comparison. My eyes went back and forth between them, like those games you do as a child. There are nine thousand differences, can you find them all? I began to feel light-headed. It might have been the dust.

Tony said, 'You see how it works.'

I didn't, and so he turned one of the pages upside down. The drawings aligned like puzzle pieces: streams flowed on and roads rolled out. Faces half-complete found their counterparts. Then he pointed out that the backs of the drawings were not, in fact, blank. At each edge and in the center, lightly penciled in a tiny, uniform script, were numbers, like so:

$$2016$$
$$4377 \quad 4378 \quad 4379$$
$$6740$$

The next page was numbered 4379 in the center, and then, clockwise from the top: 2017, 4380, 6741, 4378. The pages connected where the edge of one indicated the center of the other.

'They're all like this?'

'As far as I can tell.' He looked around. 'I haven't made much of a dent.'

'How many are we talking about?'

'Go on in. See for yourself.'

I squeezed into the room, covering my mouth with my sleeve. I've inhaled plenty of unnatural substances in my day, but the sensation of paper in my lungs was entirely new and unpleasant. I had to shove boxes out of the way; dust leopard-printed my slacks. The light from the hallway dwindled, and my own breaths seemed to have no echo. The eight feet between me and the door had effectively erased New York. Living here would be like living ten miles below the earth, like living in a cave. I don't know how else to describe it. It was supremely disorienting.

From far away, I heard Tony say my name.

I sat on the edge of the bed – six exposed inches of mattress; where did he *sleep?* – and took in a stomachful of dirty, woody air. How many drawings were there? What did the piece look like when assembled? I envisioned an endless patchwork quilt. Surely they could not all fit together. Surely nobody had that much mental power or patience. If Tony turned out to be correct, I was looking at one of the larger works of art ever created by a single person. Certainly it was the largest drawing in the world.

The throb of genius, the stink of madness; gorgeous and mind-boggling and it took my breath away.

Tony shimmied between two boxes and stood next to me, both of us wheezing.

I said, 'How many people know about this?'

'You. Me. The super. Maybe some of the other people at the company, but they were just passing on the message. Only a few people have seen it firsthand.'

'Let's keep it that way.'

He nodded. Then he said, 'You didn't answer my question.'

'What was the question.'

'What do you think?'

THREE

The artist's name was Victor Cracke.

ROSARIO QUINTANA, apartment C-1154: 'I didn't see him a lot. He came in and out a couple times a day, but I'm at work, so I didn't see him unless I was home sick or I had to come back for some reason, to pick up my son when his father drops him off too early. I'm a nurse. Sometimes I passed him in the hall. He left early in the morning. Or, you know what, he might've worked at night, because I don't think I saw him after six o'clock. I think maybe he drove a taxi?'

ROSARIO'S SEVEN-YEAR-OLD SON, Kenny: 'He was weird-looking.'
  How so?
  'His hair.'
  What color was it?

'Black.' [rubs nose] 'And white.'

Gray?

'Yeah. But not all of it.'

Long or short?

'. . . yeah.'

Which one. Long?

[nods]

Or short?

[rubs nose]

Both?

[nods, makes gesture indicating spikes in every direction] 'Like that, kind of.'

Like he stuck his finger in an electrical socket?

[look of confusion]

JASON CHARLES, apartment C-1158: 'He talked to himself. I heard him all the time, like a party goin on.'

How do you know he was alone?

'I know cause I know. He never talked to nobody else. Unfriendly dude.'

So you never really spoke to him.

'Hell naw, man. What we suppose to talk about, the *Nas*-daq?'

What did he say when he talked to himself?

'He had, like. Different voices.'

Voices.

'You know, different kinds of voices.'

Different accents?

'Like. Like a high one. Yiiii yiii yiii. Then low. Like hrmahrmahrmm. Yiii yiii yiii, hrmmhrmmhrmm . . .'

So you couldn't understand him.

'No. But he sounded mad.'

Mad about what?

'All I hear's him screaming at t'top of his mufuckin lungs. Sounds mad to me.'

He was screaming.

'Sometimes, yeah.'

What about a job? Do you know what he did?

[laughs]

Why's that funny?

'Who's gonna give him a job? I wouldn't.'

Why not?

'You want some crazy-ass crazy-lookin dude running around your restaurant scaring the fuck out the customers?'

Someone said he was a cabdriver.

'Shit. All I know, I get in a cab and it's him, I'm gettin *out*.'

ELIZABETH FORSYTHE, apartment C-1155: 'He was lovely, just a lovely, gentle man. Always he said hello to me when I saw him in the hall or the elevator. He used help me carry my groceries. I may be an old woman – don't shake your head, you don't think I believe you, now do you? Well aren't you a flirt . . . What was I saying? Oh, yes, well, however old I may be, he was hardly in a position to help me, at his age. He lived in that apartment longer than I can remember. I moved in in 1969, and he was already living here, so that should give you an idea. My husband passed in 84. He wanted to leave because he said the neighborhood wasn't the same anymore. But I used to teach right around the corner – at the high school? Math. So we stayed put.'

Do you know how old he was?

'My husband? He was – oh, you mean Victor. Well. Around my age.'
[sees questioning look] 'You're not supposed to ask a lady that, you

should know that.' [smiles] 'Now let me see. Well, I remember on V-E Day, going with my sister to meet her boyfriend, who had just come home from the Navy. She left me alone, right there in the middle of the street, so they could go off and neck. Sally was five years older than me, so you can figure it out. But I never knew exactly how old Victor was. He wasn't too *chatty*, if you get me. It took a while for him to warm up to us. Years, I imagine it was. But once he became familiar with us, we came to see that he was very gentle, not at all the person that he seemed at first.'

How could you tell?

'Oh, well, you should have seen him. You know things about a person the first time you look at them. You just look at their hands. Victor had the smallest hands, like a boy's. He wasn't much bigger than a boy, only an inch or two taller than I am. He wouldn't hurt a fly. And he was very religious, you know.'

Was he?

'Oh yes. He went to church all the time. Three times a day.'

That's a lot.

'I know. Three times a day, for Mass. Sometimes more! I go to the First African Methodist on Sundays, but before I knew Victor I wasn't aware you *could* go that often, that they would keep on admitting you. When you buy a ticket for the movies you can only go to one show, after all. My husband and I used to watch the double features, back when they still had them.' [sighs] 'Well. What was I saying?'

About church.

'Yes, church. Victor liked to go to church. That's where he was headed, darn near every time I saw him. "Where are you off to, Victor?" "Church."' [laughs] 'Our Lady of Hope, I believe that's where he went. It's near here. He had that look that Catholics have, you know the look? Like they're about to be punished.'

Guilty.

'Yes, guilty, but also resigned. And afraid. Like his own shadow might jump up and bite him. I think the world was a bit much for him.'

Does he have a job?

'Well, I'm sure he must have, but I don't know what it is. Is he all right? Has something happened to him? From the way you were talking before, I thought he might have passed, but now you're making it sound as though he's still around. Is he? I haven't seen him for months.'

It's not terribly clear.

'Well, you find something out, you let me know. Cause I liked Victor.'

One more question, if you don't mind.

'Go right on ahead. You can stay as long as you want. But you have to leave at six, that's when my girls come over. We play Scrabble.'

Did you ever hear him talking to himself?

'*Victor?* Goodness, no. Who told you that?'

Your neighbor across the hall.

[makes face] 'He's one to talk, with the music that he plays. He plays it so loud that I can hear it, and I'm half deaf. It's true.' [indicates hearing aids] 'I complain to the superintendent, but they never show up. You know, my husband was probably right: we probably should have left a long time ago. I keep hoping things might get back to the way they used to be. But. They never do.'

PATRICK SHAUGHNESSY, superintendent: 'Quiet. Never complained and I never had a complaint about him. That's the kind of tenant you like to have, although he was so damn quiet you have to wonder how a person could stand to hold it in for so long. When I saw the state of the place, that's when I figured it out. I said to myself, "Patrick, *that's* where all his talk is going." Sight to behold, I tell you.' [spreads hands three feet apart] 'Incredible.'

Yes.

'I said to myself, "Patrick, what you're looking at is art. You can't g'wan and throw it out like it's garbage." I know it when I see it, am I right? You're the art dealer, so you tell me: am I right?'

You're right.

'Right, then. Hey, now: do you think those paintings are worth anything?'

Do you?

'I would think so. I would think so. But you tell me. You're the expert.'

It's impossible to say just yet.

'I sure hope so.'

Do you know where he went?

[shakes head] 'The poor fellah might've gone off anywhere. He might be dead. What do you think, he's dead?'

Well—

'How do you know, you're not the police, right?'

No.

'Okay, then. That's who you should be talking to, if you want to find him.'

Would the police know?

'They'd know better than I would. That's their job, isn't it?'

Well—

'You want to know what *I* think, I think he decided he didn't like it here anymore. Can you blame him? Got his money saved up and went to Florida. That's where I'm going. I'm getting prepared. The nest egg and more coming, I tell you. If that's what he did, then good for him. More power. I hope he has a good time. He never seemed too happy, I will say that.'

Unhappy in what way. Depressed, or guilty, or—

'Most of the time I remember him looking at the ground. Straight down at the ground, bent-over-like, weight of the world 'n'so forth. I used to see him and think that he wanted to look up but couldn't stand what he'd see. Some people might keep quiet but get along fine, cause they don't have anything to say. Him, though. He had a lot to say and no way to say it.'

DAVID PHILADELPHIA, upstairs neighbor: 'Who?'

MARTIN NAVARRO, Rosario Quintana's ex-husband, now moved eight flights below: 'I can tell you what I remember. Wait a minute, though, you talked to Kenny?'

Kenny?

'My son. You said you talked to him.'

Yes.

'What did he look like?'

Like—

'I mean did he look happy. I know what he looks like. He looks like me, you don't need to tell me that. She keeps saying that he looks like *her* father but, trust me, she doesn't know what end it's coming out of. Not a *clue.* So whatever she told you about your guy, you can bet it's wrong. What did she tell you?'

That he was a taxi driver.

'Okay, first of all, *first* of all, that is wrong. No way that guy could drive. He couldn't even *see.* He was always bumping into the walls. That's what used to drive us crazy, because he was always dropping things and bumping into the walls at two in the morning. You should ask the neighbor downstairs, I'm sure they can tell you about that.'

So what was he, then?

'I don't know, but he wasn't driving no taxi. What kind of job does somebody like that have? Maybe he was a bus driver.'

You said he couldn't see.

'Have you ever been on a bus in this city? Maybe he was one of those guys that sold the pretzels.'

He seems a little old for that.

'Yeah. You're right. I didn't think about that. How old was he?'

What do you think?

'He was old. How old did Rosario say he was?'

She didn't say.

'Whatever she said, add ten years. Or twenty. Or subtract. Then you'll have the real answer.'

GENEVIEVE MILES, downstairs neighbor: 'It sounded like he was kicking sandbags up there.'

Her husband, Christopher: 'Yeah, that's about right.'

What does that sound like?

'What do you think it sounds like.'

Like – thumping?

'Uh-huh. Like thumping.'

HOW DO YOU DISPLAY TWO ACRES OF ART? That was the question facing me as I began to claw through the Victor Cracke oeuvre. By our estimate, there were around 135,000 drawings, each on the same type of 8^1/$_2$-by-11 paper, low brightness, cheap and readily found – enough paper to cover 87,688 square feet. We couldn't very well hang the entire piece, unless the government of China decided to lease us the Great Wall.

I advanced a year's rent on Victor's apartment and brought in a photographer to document the placement of every item inside. I hired two temps, whose sole mission was to number the boxes, record their general contents, and haul them down to a truck. After the apartment was empty, I had it scrubbed and vacuumed to clear out the rest of that choking dust. Then the operation moved from Queens to Manhattan, where I set up a makeshift laboratory in a storage facility three blocks from my gallery. With the boxes piled high in one locker, I outfitted the adjacent locker with a desk, chairs, a high-powered surgical light, a plastic tarp that I spread on the floor, cotton gloves, a magnifying glass, a space heater, floodlamps and a computer. Nightly, through the end of winter and all of spring, Ruby and I sat with two or three boxes, sorting their contents as rapidly as possible while still noting pieces of exceptional quality, racking our brains to figure out how in the world to put up a show.

In theory we could have – I don't know – laminated them all. I suppose we could have done that. We could, I suppose, have laid them all out in a field in western Pennsylvania or the Hudson River Valley and affixed them to the ground, invited people to walk around the perimeter, like some big conceptual piece by Smithson. That would have been one option.

But the logistics upset my stomach. Once sheathed in plastic, how well would the drawings align? Standing at the edge of the piece, would you be able to tell anything about its center, a hundred feet away? Was there even a center? What about glare, or wind, or warping? How could I possibly get people to make the drive?

At the same time, I had to acknowledge that shown individually, the drawings lost much of their power. Which is not to say that they weren't still arresting – they were. But splitting them up undermined what I believed to be one of the piece's essential themes: connectedness, the unity of everything.

I drew this conclusion soon after bringing the first box out of storage and laying out fifty or sixty of the drawings. When I had pieced them together, I saw immediately the true nature of Victor Cracke's monumental work: it was a map.

A map of reality as he perceived it. There were continents and boundary lines, nations and oceans and mountain ranges, all labeled in his meticulous handwriting. Phlenbendenum. Freddickville. Zythyrambiana, E. and W. The Green Qoptuag Forest, sending its fingers down into the Valley of Worthe, in which gleamed the golden cupola of the Cathedral Saint Gudrais and its Chamber of the Secret Sacred Heart – KEEP OUT! he warned. Names ripped from Tolkien, or Aldous Huxley. Adding more panels, zooming out, you encountered other planets, other suns and galaxies. Wormholes led to distant parts of the map, alluded to by their numbers. Like the universe itself, the edges of the piece seemed to be speeding away from its unfathomable center.

It was not just a map of space; it was a map of time as well. Places, figures and scenes recurred in adjacent panels, moving in slow motion, like a comic book photocopied a thousand times, torn up, thrown into the air. Walking alongside the piece, reading its repetitions, one sensed the frustration at being unable to record everything, seen and imagined, in real time – the lines on the page always a few seconds out of date, and Victor sprinting to keep up.

DOES ANY OF THAT MAKE SENSE? I'm not sure that it does. Great art does that: it cuts out your tongue. And Victor's art is especially hard to describe, not just because of its size and complexity but because it was so damned weird. Everything was out of whack; everything repeated ad nauseam, giving rise to two unsettling sensations. On the one hand, once you got used to his visual vocabulary – the creatures, the wild proportions – you began to feel a profound sense of déjà vu, the strange becoming familiar, the way jargon starts to sound normal when everyone around you speaks it. On the other hand, the moment you stopped looking at the drawings, you were besieged by jamais vu, the familiar becoming strange, the way a regular word starts to sound wrong if you repeat it enough. I would look up from the drawing and notice Ruby playing with her tongue stud and the sound of it, the glint of it – her whole face – her knees tucked under her – her stark shadowed shape on the locker wall – all of it would somehow seem *wrong*. That is to say: the drawing was so massive and encompassing and hypnotic that it had a hallucinogenic effect, distorting our perception of the real world to the extent that I sometimes felt like Ruby and I were figments of Victor's imagination – that the drawing was reality and we were characters inside it.

I fear that I'm not making sense again. Let me put it this way: we had to take a lot of breaks for fresh air.

SO THAT WAS THE PARADOX I FACED: how to exhibit an artistic Theory of Everything in fragments.

After a lot of thought and struggle, I settled on showing ten-by-ten segments, a decision that yielded 'canvases' approximately seven feet by nine. The gallery could not accommodate more than fifteen or so – or about one percent of the total work. I would suspend the canvases away from the wall, allowing viewers to walk all around them, to see the drawings' luminous fronts as well as their systematic backs, which I came to interpret as a war between Victor's right and left brain.

He had done his best to create a work of art that thwarted the notion of public exhibition; however, I am not easily put off, and I hate to fail once I've begun. In short, I didn't give a damn about the creator's intent.

I told you I behaved badly, didn't I? I did. You were warned.

HE DID MORE THAN DRAW. He wrote as well. A few of the boxes contained thick, faux-leather-bound journals dating back to 1963. In them he had recorded the weather, his daily intake of food, and his church attendance, each category filling several volumes: thousands of entries, many of them identical. The food journal, in particular, was mind-numbing.

TUESDAY MAY 1 1973

breakfast	scrambled eggs
lunch	apple ham & cheese
dinner	apple ham & cheese

WEDNESDAY MAY 2 1973

breakfast	scrambled eggs
lunch	apple ham & cheese
dinner	apple ham & cheese

His meals never varied, with the exception of Christmas, when he ate roast beef, and one week in January 1967, when he ate oatmeal for breakfast – an experiment that must have failed, because by the following week he was back to scrambled eggs, a habit dutifully recorded for the next thirty-six years.

The weather journal, while it varied every day (containing information on temperature, humidity and general conditions), conveyed much the same effect.

They made for dreadful bathroom reading. But I saw a kinship between the journals and the drawings, the same obsessiveness and strict adherence to routine. You could even call it love; for what is love, if not the willingness to repeat oneself?

Whereas the church journal made the idea of a benevolent, present God seem absurd. If you prayed every day, three times a day or sometimes more, wrote down all your rosaries and Hail Marys and trips to the confessional, and yet *nothing changed* – your meals remained the same, the weather kept on being gray or slushy or muggy, just like it always had been – how could you continue to believe? 'Mass' began to sound like just that and no more: a bulk of useless activity that added up to nothing.

Lest you think I was reading too much into the work, let me tell you that I was not alone in finding something awe-inspiring about the journals. They were Ruby's favorite part of the installation, much preferred to the drawings, which she found somewhat overbearing. At her behest I decided to display the journals in their own corner, without explanatory text. We would let people decide for themselves.

We put the opening on the books for July 29. Usually I run shows for four to six weeks. I slotted Victor Cracke in for eight, with a mind to let him run longer if I so chose. We hadn't even touched the bulk of the work, but I simply could not wait to get the pieces up. I called Kristjana and told her that her Arctic ice pack installation would have to wait. She swore at me, threatened me, told me I'd hear from her lawyer.

I didn't care. I was lovesick.

For those six months I barely went out. Marilyn would come by the storage locker after work, bring me a panino and a bottle of water. She'd tell me I looked like a homeless person. I'd ignore her and eventually she'd shrug and leave.

While Ruby and I labored to compile the catalogue raisonné, Nat handled the front end of the gallery. He consulted me on important decisions, but otherwise he had total control. He could have stolen anything he wanted, sold pieces for half off, and I would not have noticed. The lone apostle has a full-time job.

AND THE PROPHET HIMSELF?

To tell you the truth – and here begins my confession – I stopped looking for him. Before very long I thought that I might be better off never meeting the man.

I conducted the interviews excerpted at the beginning of this chapter, as well as a handful of others with people who claimed to have noticed Victor roaming the halls of Muller Courts. All their stories turned out to be fragmentary, anecdotal and self-contradictory. One of the security guards told me that Victor had been a drug dealer. Others suggested janitor, cook, writer and bodyguard.

A physical description proved slippery as well. He was tall; he was short; he was average. He was gaunt; he had a big belly; a scar on his face, a scar on his neck, no scars at all. A moustache. A beard. A moustache and a beard. That everyone remembered him differently made sense; he had never been in one person's presence long enough to leave a distinct impression.

He tended to stare at the ground rather than look you in the eye. On that people agreed.

With Tony's help I learned that Cracke had been a tenant since 1966, and that his apartment was heavily rent-controlled, the monthlies low even for the slummiest part of Queens. Until the time of his disappearance, in September 2003, he had never missed a payment.

There were no other Crackes in the phone book.

Father Lucian Buccarelli, of Our Lady of Hope, had never heard of Victor. He recommended that I talk to his colleague, Father Simcock, who had been around the parish a lot longer.

Father Allan Simcock didn't know any Victor Cracke. He wondered if I had the right church. I told him I could be wrong. He made a list of all the neighborhood churches – a list far longer than I expected – and, wherever possible, gave me the names of people to talk to.

I did not follow up on them.

I am not a detective. And I owed Victor nothing. He could have been dead; he could have been alive. It didn't matter to me. All that mattered to me was his art, and that I had, in spades.

PEOPLE DON'T APPRECIATE the creativity of dealing art. In the contemporary market, it is the dealer – not the artist – who does most of the work. Without us there would be no Modernism, no Minimalism, no movements at all. All the contemporary legends would be painting houses or teaching adult education classes. Museum collections would grind to a halt after the Renaissance; sculptors would still be carving pagan gods; video would be the province of pornography; graffiti a petty crime rather than the premise behind a multimillion-dollar industry. Art, in short, would cease to thrive. And this is because – in a post-Church, post-patronage era – dealers refine and pipeline the fuel that drives art's engine, that has always driven it and always will: money.

These days especially, there is simply too much material out there for any normal person to be able to distinguish between good and bad. That's the dealer's job. We are creators, too – only we create markets, and our medium is the artists themselves. Markets, in turn, create movements, and movements create tastes, culture, the canon of acceptability – in short, what we think of as Art itself. A piece of art becomes a piece of art – and an artist becomes an artist – when I make you take out your checkbook.

Victor Cracke, then, was my definition of a perfect artist: he created and then he disappeared. I couldn't have imagined a greater gift. My very own tabula rasa.

SOME OF YOU MIGHT DEEM my actions ethically squishy. Before you judge me, consider this: plenty of times art has been dragged into public without its creator's knowledge – even against his will. Great art demands an audience, and to deny that is itself unethical. If you've ever read a poem by Emily Dickinson, you will agree.

Moreover, it's not as though I lacked precedent. Consider, for example, the case of the so-called Wireman, the name given to the creator of a series of sculptures discovered in a Philadelphia alley on a trash night in 1982. I've seen them; they're eerie: thousands of found objects – clock faces, dolls, food-containers – cocooned in loops of heavy-gauge wire. Nobody knows who the artist was; nobody knows what motivated him to produce.

We don't know for certain that he was, in fact, a he. And while the question of whether the pieces were intended as art is open to debate, that they were pulled out of the garbage would seem to indicate quite clearly that they weren't intended for public consumption. This misgiving, however, has not stopped galleries from selling the pieces at commanding prices; it has not stopped museums across the United States and Europe from mounting exhibitions or critics from commenting on the work's 'shamanistic' or 'totemic' properties, speculating about its similarities to African 'medicine bundles'. That's a lot of talk and cash and activity generated by what might have ended up as landfill, were it not for a sharp-eyed passerby.

The point is that in creating his objects, the Philadelphia Wireman did only some of the work, and I would argue not the majority of it. He made *things*. It took dealers to make those things into *art*. Once anointed as such, there's no going back. You can destroy, but you can't uncreate. If the Wireman showed up tomorrow and began shrieking about his rights, I doubt anyone would listen to him.

And so I regarded as more than fair my vow that were Victor ever to turn up at my door, I would pay him according to the traditional artist-dealer split: fifty-fifty. In fact, I congratulated myself on my generosity, knowing that few of my colleagues would have made such an outlandish and indulgent promise.

I'LL SPARE YOU THE GORY DETAILS of prepping the show. You don't need to hear about rail mounts and track lighting and the procurement of mediocre pinot. But there is something I don't want to leave out, and that's the strange discovery Ruby and I made late one night at the storage locker.

We had been working for four months. The space heaters were gone, replaced by a series of fans strategically placed so as not to send piles of paper flying. For weeks we had been searching for panel number one, the point of origin. The boxes had gotten mixed up in transit, and we'd start on one that seemed promising – whose top sheet numbered, say, in the low hundreds – only to find that the page numbers went up, not down.

We did eventually find it – more on that later – but on that night it was a different page, from the 1100s, that caught Ruby's eye.

'Hey,' she said, 'you're in here.'

I stopped working and came over to have a look.

Near the top of the page, in slashing letters three inches high:

MULLER

All the warmth went out of the room. I can't say why the sight of my own name terrified me the way it did. For a moment I heard Victor's voice shouting at me over the whirr of the fans, shouting at me through his art, clapping his hands in my face. He did not sound pleased.

Somewhere, a door slammed. We both jumped, I against the desk and Ruby in her chair. Then silence, both of us embarrassed by our own skittishness.

'Odd,' she said.

'Yes.'

'And *creepy.*'

'Very.'

We looked at my name. It seemed vaguely obscene.

'I guess it's reasonable,' she said.

I looked at her.

'He did live in Muller Courts.'

I nodded.

She said, 'Actually, I'm surprised you're not in there more often.'

I tried to resume work, but I couldn't concentrate, not with Ruby clicking her stud against her teeth and that drawing radiating ill feelings. I announced that I was heading out. I must have sounded paranoid – I certainly felt paranoid – because she snickered and told me to watch my back.

Normally, I take a cab straight home, but that night I ducked into a bar and ordered a soda water. As I sat there watching people trickle in, gasping and cursing the sultry night, my uneasiness began to change shape, to soften and turn to encouragement.

Ruby was right. Victor Cracke had been drawing the universe as he knew it. Naturally, the Muller name would loom large.

The bar had a jukebox. Somebody put on Bon Jovi, and the place filled with off-key singing. I got up to leave.

I gave the cabbie directions and sank back into the sticky vinyl. If anything, I reflected, my name in Victor's art could be interpreted generously. I was no intruder. Quite the contrary. I had every right to be there. I was there all along.

INTERLUDE: 1847.

Solomon's cart has many miles on it, and holds the entire world. Cloth, buttons, tinware. Tonics and patent medicines. Nails and glue, writing paper and appleseeds. So many different kinds of items, unclassifiable except perhaps as What People Need. He works a kind of magic, showing up unexpected in some dreary Pennsylvania town, drawing a crowd with shouts and theatrics, laying out his wares, defying the townsfolk's attempts to stump him. I need a hammer. Yes, sir. Glass bottles, about so big? Yes, ma'am. People joke that the cart is bottomless.

He understands much more English than he speaks, and when forced into a particularly heated negotiation he will resort to the use of his fingers. Seven cents? No, ten. I'll give you nine. Okay? Okay.

Everybody speaks bargain.

The same rigamarole applies when he needs to pay for a room, although he avoids that if he can, preferring to sleep outside, in a field or an open barn. Every penny he saves will bring his brothers over that much sooner. When Adolph comes they will be able to earn twice as much money, and when Simon comes, three times. He plans to bring them over in that order: first Adolph, then Simon, and last, Bernard. Bernard is the second oldest; but he is also the laziest, and Solomon knows that they will achieve much more, much more quickly, if they leave him behind for now.

But sometimes . . . when it is so cold outside . . . when he craves the dignity of a roof . . . when he cannot face another night on the dirt, in a pile of hay, bugs crawling all over him like an animal . . . Too much! He caves in, wasting an entire day's earnings on a featherbed – only to spend the rest of the week chastising himself. He is not Bernard! He is the eldest; he should know better. Their father sent him first for a reason.

The crossing nearly killed him. Never had he been so sick, nor had he ever seen so much sickness around him. The fever that took his mother could not be compared to the horrors he witnessed on that boat, people dissolving in piles of their own waste, wracked and groaning bodies, the wet stench of physical and moral failure. Solomon took care to eat alone; against his nature, he did not socialize with his fellow passengers. His father had commanded him to keep to himself, and he obeyed.

Once he saw a woman go mad. Solomon, alone on deck, up from the hold for fresh air, joyous to feel the light rain, saw her come up the stairs, shaky, green, bloodball eyes. He recognized her. The day before she had lost her son. When they pried the body from her arms she had let out a noise that stood Solomon's hair on end. Now he watched her stumble to the bow where she did not hesitate but leaned over the railing and dropped into the churning sea. Solomon ran to where she had existed a moment ago. He looked down and saw nothing but whitewater.

The shiphands came running. *She fell!* Solomon said, or tried to say. What he said was *Sie fiel!* But the crew came from England. They did not understand him, and with his babbling he was getting in the way. They ordered him belowdecks, and when he protested, four of them picked him up and carried him away.

By the time the *Shining Harry* dumped its human cargo at Boston

Harbor, Solomon had been at sea for forty-four days. He had lost twenty percent of his body weight and had developed a painful rash on his back that would persist for months, making his nights spent on the ground all the more miserable.

At first he lived with a cousin, a cobbler, their relation so distant that neither of them could quite pinpoint where their blood mingled. Right away Solomon could tell that the arrangement would not last. The cousin's wife hated him and wanted him out of the house. While he tossed and turned on the workbench that served as his bed, she would tramp around upstairs in wooden shoes. She fed him rotten fruit and made his tea with muddy water and let bread stale before cutting him a slice. He planned to leave as soon as he had enough money and English, but before he managed to get there she came downstairs one night and bared her breasts to him. Early the next morning he loaded what little he had in a burlap pack and set out walking.

He walked to Buffalo, arriving in time for an awful winter. Nobody bought his odds and ends. Chastened, he hurried south, first to New Jersey, then into the heart of Pennsylvania, where he met others who spoke his language. They became his first regular customers: farmers who came to depend on him for specialty items that did not justify a long trip into town, indulgences such as a new razor strop or a box of pencils. He filled his burlap sack to bursting, but soon it could not hold enough to meet his clients' demands, and he got another, one as tall as he was. As his inventory grew, so did his route and his clientele; and despite his limited vocabulary, he revealed himself as an able salesman: quick to laugh, firm but fair, and always aware of the latest trends. The second sack did not last long. He bought himself a cart.

On its side he painted

SOLOMON MUELLER
DRY GOODS

'Dry goods' has always sounded wrong, as some of the items he sells are not, in fact, dry. He merely copied what he saw on the sides of other carts, belonging to other men – the competition. He is not the only Jew walking these back roads.

He knows that he has plenty to be thankful for, having exceeded his own expectations. When he dons his tefillin, he praises God for sustaining him through these dark days and begs for yet more assistance. So much remains to be done. In April he turns eighteen.

WITH ADOLPH'S BIRTHDAY COMING UP, as well, Solomon has decided that the time has come to send for him. In Punxsutawney he starts a letter, in Altoona he mails it. The thought of having his brother with him brings a lightness to his step that carries him humming over the Appalachians, though his cart and back creak with fatigue.

York, Pennsylvania, sounds like the place to treat himself to a night indoors. Though he knows that he really should wait until he *needs* a bed, wait for a night of blistering cold or pounding rain, rather a balmy evening that predicts spring. But what good is life if you cannot enjoy it? He has been prudent, perhaps too much so. Luxury reminds us of the purpose of toil. With his remaining money he will allow himself a taste.

Taverns glow along the main thoroughfare, which is rutted and damp with urine. He pushes his cart and thinks about beer. His mouth waters with the remembered taste of yeast. He misses his home. He misses his sister, who makes the most delicious cakes, tender and light, recipes their mother passed along before she died. The coarse bread and beans on which he currently subsists make him want to weep. He has not eaten meat in four months. The most available – not to say affordable – is pork. That he refuses to touch. He has his limits.

Some of the taverns offer rooms, and when he steps inside one to inquire about vacancies, a wave of hot air and body odor breaks over him.

In one corner a piano roars. Every table is full. He shouts his request at the bartender, who misunderstands and brings him a glass of beer. Solomon considers giving it back, but his thirst gets the better of him. The bartender comes back to collect the glass and offer another, but Solomon shakes his head and points to the ceiling. Upstairs?

The man shakes his head. 'Silver Spoon,' he shouts.

Solomon waves his hands around, indicating *I'm lost*. The bartender walks him to the door and points down an alleyway. Solomon thanks him, unties his cart, and heads for the Silver Spoon.

The alley is dark, spilling onto another wide road. Cicadas fiddle. His limbs feel half connected to his trunk. Perhaps he should stop right here, go to sleep . . . It is tempting. How bad could it be? Then he steps in a pile of dung and, having regained his purpose, goes up the street one way, back down it along the other side. The wheels on his cart have begun to squeak; he should oil them. He finds nothing. Sighing, he heads back toward the alley. Three men approach, singing, their arms linked.

Solomon raises a hand. 'Hello, friends.'

Like one body they veer toward him. They smell like a belch.

'Hello, friends,' says one of the men, and the other two begin to laugh.

Solomon doesn't get the joke, but it would be impolite not to participate. He laughs. Then he asks about the Silver Spoon. The men start laughing again. One asks where Solomon is from.

'Here.'

'Heeeee-ah, huh?' says the same man. His imitation of Solomon's accent is absurd but it strikes everyone as extremely funny. More laughter ensues.

Once they've finished, Solomon tries to repeat his question. But the man – the talking man, the man with the felt hat and the cheeks stubbled black, the one a great deal larger than the other two – interrupts again, asking more questions. While Solomon does his best to answer, he gets tangled up in the net of words, tripping and stuttering, eliciting hoots and howls and backslapping and bringing a purposeful smirk to the man's face.

What happens next is unclear. It begins with a shove; it then becomes a wrestling match, no blows falling but a grunting stalemate, Solomon pinned against the cart, which rocks as the man holds his arms and presses against him, his embrace warm and boozy and almost intimate as he fills Solomon's ears with incomprehensible threats.

Then Solomon dares to resist, and all three of them – like ten men, so many fists and feet they have – converge, stomping. They are too drunk to be methodical, and that is why he lives.

WHEN HE CAN WALK AGAIN, it is with a limp. He considers abandoning the cart and starting over, with a shop, one he doesn't have to carry on his back. He could go back to Boston, back to Buffalo. Nobody bought, but at least they didn't try to kill him.

But no. To begin with, they robbed him blind; how could he open a shop? If he's very lucky, his suppliers will extend him credit; only a fool would loan money to a crippled immigrant with no tangible assets.

There is another reason not to quit: in less than a year, Adolph arrives. The physical damage – the limp, the divots on his face – that cannot be hidden. Spiritually, though, Solomon cannot show himself a broken man. Adolph will drop dead of fright, or else he will flee back to Germany on the first boat. That mustn't happen. For his family's sake, Solomon must show that America still has much to offer – a belief that he himself wants so badly to retain, one he longs for even as it oozes out of him.

He looks on the bright side. Three men beat him; but one man has taken him in, fed him and healed him. That man reads to him from a Bible and, upon discovering that his patient is not a Christian, has spent hours sharing the wisdom of the Lord Savior. Solomon, understanding that this is the price of his recovery, listens politely, noting with interest that the Lord Savior indeed went through a fair amount of hardship. That doesn't make him God, but it does make him a sympathetic character.

One idea that comes to Solomon while he lies in the bed – a real bed! Strange, how agony begets pleasure – listening to tales of the Lord Savior is that he needs to improve his English. *Silver Spoon* he had asked for, except that his Silver came out as *silber* and the Spoon as *shpoon*, clanging shibboleths. If he had been able to speak he could have talked his way to safety. And how much more business would he bring in if he sounded like an American?

As the healer speaks of the salt of the earth, Solomon devises a plan for self-improvement.

Four and a half weeks later he rises up from his bed and limps to the most American place he knows: smoky, impatient Pittsburgh, a town for the up-and-coming, the meshed cogs of industry. Smiling through pain, he peddles his wares to women doing the washing in their front yards. He peddles outside factories and saloons. He forces himself to talk, counting every complete conversation a victory, even if he sells nothing. He asks for help with his pronunciation; sometimes, he gets it. At the end of the day he walks along the riverbanks, reciting whatever new words he has learned that day, going until he feels too tired to continue, at which point he sits down and makes camp. Twice he flees to avoid arrest for trespassing. Though he has stopped putting on his tefillin, he takes a moment to thank God when he reaches safety.

As summer comes to a boil, he improves. With enough effort he will soon sound no different from the men who attacked him. By the time Adolph arrives, they will be unable to communicate! The idea makes Solomon laugh.

One morning he spots a poster announcing the arrival of a new theatrical enterprise specializing in the most dramatic and comedic and thrilling, etc., etc. Normally, he would never waste money on such stuff, but then he considers the educational benefit: in the theater, people do nothing but talk. He can sit and take in the words. He copies down the information on the poster. The Merritt Players open that evening, at seven o'clock, at the Water Street Theater.

THE MERRITT PLAYERS turn out to consist of a single massive fellow draped in a velveteen cape. His beard looks like a horde of skunks has burrowed halfway into his chin, tails wagging as he bellows his lines and wiggles his sausage fingers, sweeping and stabbing for emphasis. His trousers could hold two Solomons, one in each leg.

He performs selections from Shakespeare at a rapid clip, pausing now and then to savor a particular phrase. Try as he might, Solomon cannot keep up. Moreover, he senses that this fellow's diction does not match what one hears on the street. In other words, the show completely fails as a learning tool.

Nevertheless Solomon remains in his seat. He's paid for his ticket, and he intends to get his money's worth.

Over the next hour, against his will, an unexpected thing happens: he falls under the actor's spell. The man has a voice that could stop a train, yes, but he can also sound beguiling and innocent. Though Solomon cannot understand all the words, he hears perfectly the emotions behind them. The man's pain evokes Solomon's own pain; their longings and joys and fears merge, making him feel, momentarily, that he has a friend.

The show finishes and the scant audience gets up to leave, but Solomon remains, unwilling to move for fear of shattering the magical sense of peace and belonging and companionship that he has been so long without – the humanity missing in his lonely, lonely life – remains sunk down in his chair so that the top of his head is invisible to the manager, who closes up without further ado, locking him inside.

When the lights go off and he discovers his predicament, he does not panic. At worst he'll spend the night indoors. Then he remembers his cart tied up outside, and he sets about looking for a way out, groping around in the near dark. All the exits are bolted shut, as is the stairwell to the second floor. Nonplussed, he climbs onto the stage, wanders into the wings. A single shaft of moonlight aids his search, not enough to prevent him from tripping over a pile of sandbags and banging his head against a chunk of scenery, causing it to tip over and nearly crush him. In leaping to safety he accidentally pushes open an unseen door, revealing a stairwell that descends to a dim corridor. There are many doors, all of them locked except the last. Relieved, he opens it and steps facefirst into the actor himself: naked to the waist, pouring sweat, beard unkempt, filthy, a ham hock in long johns.

'By God!' he shouts. 'Who's this!' He lifts Solomon by the lapels. 'Eh? You? You! By God, man, you'd better say something or I'll snap you like a twig! What! What's that! Eh? Man! Speak up! Cat got your tongue?' The man drags him, not unkindly, to a chair, and seats him with two firm hands on Solomon's shoulders. 'Now, what. What, man, what! What's your name!'

'Solomon Mueller.'

'Did you say Solomon Mueller?'

'Yes.'

'Well, well. Well, good, Solomon Mueller! Tell me something, Solomon Mueller: do we know each other?'

Solomon shakes his head.

'Then how is it you're in my dressing room! Mary Ann!'

A fleshy woman in a gingham dress pokes her head through a rack of costumes. 'Who's that?'

'Solomon Mueller!' says the actor.

'Who's Solomon Mueller?'

'Please—' says Solomon.

'Who are you?' asks Mary Ann.

Helplessly, Solomon indicates the stage above them.

'You were here for the show? Yes? Yes? I see! And? Yes? Did you *enjoy* the show?' He takes Solomon by the shoulders, gives him a friendly shake. 'Yes? *Yes??*'

Solomon smiles as best he can.

'You did!' cries the actor. 'Good boy! Did you hear that, Mary Ann? He enjoyed the show!' He begins to shake with laughter, his stomach bouncing and his breasts jiggling.

'Isaac, it's time to get dressed.'

Ignoring her, the actor kneels down and takes Solomon's scuffed, sinewy hands in his own moist ones and says, 'Tell me something, Solomon Mueller: you truly enjoyed the show, yes? Yes? Then let me ask you this: would you like to buy me dinner.'

THE ACTOR'S FULL NAME is Isaac Merritt Singer. As he explains over a meal of potatoes and sausage – which he consumes unaided – Mary Ann is his second wife. He had a first wife, but the show must go on. 'Isn't that so, Solomon!'

'Yes,' says Solomon, happy to agree with anything this strange man says.

Isaac talks about Shakespeare, for whom he does not have enough superlatives.

'The Bard of Avon! The Pearl of Stratford! The Pride of England!'

Every so often Solomon makes an effort to insert a comment, but Isaac's monologue ceases only when he pauses to swallow a length of sausage or to lift his mug. He seems thrilled to have a dining companion, especially when Solomon buys him a second plate of food and a third beer.

'Now,' says Isaac, wiping his moustache of sauce and crushing his hands together, 'tell me something, Solomon Mueller: you're not from around here, are you?'

Solomon shakes his head. Then he sees that Isaac is waiting; his chance to speak has arrived.

Briefly, he recounts his youth in Germany, the boat to America, the success of his business and tragedy of his assault. As he talks, Isaac knits his brows, scoffs, scowls, laughs. Even as a listener he never ceases performing, so that by the time Solomon concludes his tale, he feels as though he has composed a masterwork, akin to Homer.

And, as far as he can tell, he has done it accent-free.

'By God,' says Isaac Merritt Singer. 'That is a fine story.'

Solomon smiles.

'I wouldn't mind listening to a story like that again. I wouldn't mind putting such a story *up on the stage*. I like a man who can tell a story. A man who has a story to tell is a man who's a friend of mine. Eh? Ah! Well' – taking a huge draught of beer – 'I'm glad we've met, Solomon. I think we might become dear friends. What do you say?'

THEY BECOME DEAR FRIENDS.

A friendship driven on the one side by Solomon's loneliness, his desire for talk, and on the other side by Isaac Singer's desire not to pay for dinner. Later, Solomon would estimate that during that summer he spent twenty-five to thirty percent of his income – money he could not afford to spend! Profligate! – on meals with Singer. Or loaning Singer money to patch his trousers, or for a new gewgaw for one of Singer's many children, or for flowers for Mary Ann, or *for no reason at all*, simply *giving* Singer money, *giving it away*, because his friend asked.

Not with a mind toward getting rich does he do these favors. He does them because he needs to give something to someone, and Singer makes him feel unalone.

Nevertheless his generosity comes back to him a millionfold. In 1851, Singer moves to New York, taking with him his family and his wagon and some of the money that he has borrowed from Mueller. There he founds a company called the 'Jenny Lind Sewing Machine Company', a multilayered name. Lind is Singer's favorite singer; naming his company for a singer puts a pun on his last name, hinting as well at his affection for Life in the Theater.

However meaningful, though, the name proves a touch unwieldy, and soon enough people have begun to refer to his machines simply as 'Singers'.

Plenty of people in the United States make sewing machines; by the time Singer's hit the stores, there are four other competing designs. But his is the best, and in a very short period of time, he becomes one of the wealthiest men in the United States – taking along with him Solomon Mueller.

Still, we may wonder *what if.* What if Solomon had never been beaten within an inch of his life; if he had gone back to Germany; if he had not enjoyed the show; if he had declined to pay for dinner. If he knew then – as he found out later – that Mary Ann Singer was not, in fact, Isaac Merritt Singer's second wife, but his mistress; and that she would be the first of many, and that Singer's philandering would eventually force him to leave the country. As a young man, Solomon Mueller had a priggish streak; perhaps he would have disassociated himself from Singer if he had known the truth. Many alternative realities stood between Solomon and the great fortune that became his. Might he have succeeded on his own?

He might have. He worked hard, and he had brains. What else do you need?

ONE OF THE LAST THINGS Isaac Merritt Singer said before he departed for Europe in shame was, 'You remind me of my father.'

This conversation took place many years later, in a drawing room richly furnished, in a home a hundred feet high. By then, Solomon Mueller was Solomon Muller, and Mueller Dry Goods had grown into Muller Bros Manufacturing, Maker of Finest Machine Parts; Muller Bros, Importers of

Exotic Wares; Muller Bros Railroad and Mining; Muller Bros Textiles; Ada Muller Bakeries; Muller Bros Land Development Corporation; and Muller Bros Savings and Loan.

'How so?' Solomon asked.

'You always sounded like him,' said Isaac Singer. 'His name was Reisinger, you know. Did you know that?'

Solomon shook his head.

'Saxony! He spoke German to me until I was five. By God! Uncanny, I tell you, man.' Singer smiled. 'The first time I heard you I said to myself, "Well, now, Singer, that fellow is the very *ghost* of your father!" Ha! Like Hamlet's father, yes? Yes. Well what's the matter, Muller, you look like I shot and ate your dog.'

Solomon explained that he had thought his accent gone by the time they met.

'My friend, you *still* sound like my father.'

Solomon, chagrined, said, 'I do?'

'Of course you do, man. Every time we speak I yearn to see the old bastard again . . . Ha! Well, now. Don't look so sad, Muller, that voice of yours contributes a large part of your charm.'

Solomon Muller né Mueller said, 'I would prefer to sound like the American that I am.'

Isaac Merritt Singer, he of the libido and the fortune and the belly and the laugh, that laugh like a bellowing shiphorn, the siren song of America – he laughed and hammered his friend on the shoulder and said, 'Not to worry, old man. Round here, you are what you say you are.'

FOUR

These days, the idea of an 'opening' has become something of a farce; usually all the work on display has been presold. I decided to buck the trend by refusing to allow any previews or advance sales, and by midsummer I had begun receiving anxious phone calls from collectors and consultants, all of whom I put at ease with assurances that *nobody* was getting preferential treatment. They'd all have to come discover Victor Cracke for themselves.

Marilyn thought I was making a terrible mistake. She told me so at lunch, the week before I opened.

'You want to *sell* them, don't you?'

'Of course,' I said. And I did, not for the money so much as for the legitimacy: by convincing other people to literally invest in my vision of genius, I made my act of creativity a matter of public record. A closely related part of me, however, wanted to keep the drawings all to myself. I always felt pangs letting go of a favored piece, but I'd never felt the possessive impulse as strongly as I did toward Victor – largely because I considered myself his collaborator rather than his sales representative.

I said, 'Whether I sell them now or after the show, they're sold.'

'Sell them now,' Marilyn said, 'and they're sold *now*.'

People had a hard time understanding my relationship with Marilyn. To begin with, there was the question of age: she is twenty-one years older than I am. Come to think of it, that part might not be so hard for women in their fifties to understand.

My less discreet friends, though, tended, when drunk, to point out the peculiarity of my situation.

Newsflash!

She's old enough to be your mother.

Not quite. Were my mother still around, she would be four years older than Marilyn. But thank you; thanks very much. I hadn't noticed that similarity at all, not until you brought it to my attention. I appreciate you keeping me in the loop.

These same friends were usually careful to add (I guess as a means of breaking the hard news to me more gently) *She looks good. I'll grant you that.*

Thanks again. I hadn't noticed that, either.

Marilyn *does* look good, and not just for her age: objectively, she is a beautiful woman and always has been. True, she's had work done. Who around here hasn't? At least she comes by her beauty honestly: Ironton High School Homecoming Queen, 1969. What you see is the result of maintenance rather than a complete fiction.

The southernmost city in Ohio, Ironton bequeathed to its fairest daughter a ferocious ambition and, when she is annoyed, a hint of northern Kentucky drawl, useful both for feigning innocence and for dropping the sledgehammer of Southern condescension. You do not want to make Marilyn mad.

Today her haircuts cost as much as her first car. She has phone numbers for people who don't have phone numbers. I strongly suspect that when she walks into Barneys they press a special button to mobilize the sales force. But any true New Yorker knows that the real measure of success is real estate and what you do with it. Marilyn has succeeded. In the dining room of her West Village town house hangs a de Kooning worth ten times as much as her parents made, cumulatively, in fifty years of honest labor. Her uptown apartment on Fifth and Seventy-fifth affords a generous view of Central Park; and when the sun sets across the island, silhouetting the Dakota and the San Remo, flooding the living room with sweet orange light, you feel as though you are floating on the surface of a star.

You can't take the Ironton out of the girl. She still gets up at four thirty A.M. to exercise.

Her rise on the scene is the stuff of legend. The family of eleven; the arrival in New York, literally on a Greyhound bus; the handbag counter at Saks; the banker buying a birthday present for his wife, leaving also with Marilyn's phone number; the affair; the divorce; the remarriage; the charity balls; the museum boards; the swelling collection; Warhol and Basquiat and disco and cocaine; the second divorce, rancorous as a Balkan blood feud; the jaw-dropping settlement; and the Marilyn Wooten Gallery, opening night, July 9, 1979. I was seven years old.

However random or fortuitous this chain of events might seem, I have always envisioned her planning it all out – on the Greyhound, perhaps, rocketing eastward, perhaps written down in a little Gatsbyesque composition book. MY VERY OWN TEN-STEP PLAN FOR SELF-BETTERMENT, FAME AND FORTUNE.

She found the similarities between selling art and selling handbags to far exceed the differences. And she could sell. The house in the Hamptons, the flats in Rome and London – those she bought with her own money, alimony be damned.

Everyone knows her; she has run with or over everyone in her path. She called Clement Greenberg, the most prominent American critic of the twentieth century, an insufferable asshole to his face. She was the first to show Matthew Barney, whom she still refers to as 'the Boy'. She has capitalized on our culture's penchant for recycling, buying up unfashionable work and then creating, through sheer force of will and charisma, a revival whose profits accrue largely to her. She sells artwork that she does not own, on the assurance that she will own it sooner or later – a practice that got her banned from the auction houses for a time. Again and again people pronounce her dead. Always she ascends, phoenix triumphant in her tailored suit, gimlet in hand, to say *Not quite yit, honey.*

We met at an opening. At the time, I was working the floor for the woman who would leave her gallery to me. I had moved in the art world for a few years by that point, and though I certainly knew who Marilyn was, I had never spoken to her before. I saw her eyeing me through the bottom of her wineglass, and then, in defiance of her own tipsiness, making a beeline for me, wearing her Acquisition Smile.

'You're the only straight man in this room I haven't fucked or fired.'

An auspicious beginning.

People used to describe me as having tamed her, which was ludicrous. We simply met at the right time, and the connection proved so expedient, pleasant and intellectually invigorating that neither of us had any reason to call it off. She is a talker; I am a nodder. We both sold, albeit in very different ways; and though we were both control freaks, we maintained our own private lives, which prevented us from clashing. And although she would never admit it, I think the Muller name plucked a chord of awe inside her. In the pantheon of Old American Money, I might not rate very high, but to Marilyn 'My Father was an Industrial Mechanic' Wooten, I must have looked like John Jacob Astor.

It also helped that we had no expectations of fidelity. That was the unspoken rule. Don't ask, don't tell.

*

'LEAVE IT TO YOU,' she said, forking her roasted-pepper-and-goat-cheese napoleon, 'to find the one who can actually *draw*. I thought that was the whole point of outsider art, that it looked like shit.'

'Who said it was outsider art.'

'You have to call it something.'

'I don't see why.'

'Because people like their hands held.'

'I think I'll let them dangle a bit.'

'You're really lousing this up, you know that?'

'I'm not doing it for the money.'

'"I'm not doing it for the money."' She sat back, wiping her mouth. Marilyn eats like an ex-convict: hunched over, in perpetual fear that her food will be taken away, and when she pauses it's not with satiety but with relief. Eight siblings and you learn to protect yourself. 'You'll never get over your love of pretty things, Ethan. That's your problem.'

'I don't see why that's such a problem. And they're not pretty. Have you even seen them?'

'I've seen them.'

'They're not pretty.'

'They're like something Francis Bacon would draw in detention. Don't listen to me, darlin. I'm just jealous of your margins. Mine, please?'

I handed her the rest of my salad.

'Thank you.' She dug in. 'I hear Kristjana is on the warpath.'

'I had to cut her loose. I felt bad about it, but—'

'Don't. I don't blame you. I had her for a time, did you know that?'

I shook my head.

'I discovered her,' she said.

This I knew to be a lie. 'Is that a fact.'

She shrugged. 'In a way. I discovered her at Geoffrey Mann's. He wasn't doing anything for her. So I rediscovered her.'

'Stole her, you mean.'

'Is it stealing if you want to give it back?'

'I offered to reschedule her show, but she wouldn't listen.'

'She'll live. Someone'll pick her up, they always do. She called me, you know.'

'Did she.'

'*Mm.* Thank you,' she said, accepting her duck from the waiter. 'She pitched her project to me. With the ice? I told her no thank you. I'm not turning off the air-conditioning in my gallery so she can stroke herself off about the environment. *Please.* Make me something I can sell.'

'She used to be a good painter.'

'They all start out that way,' she said. 'Hungry. Then they get a couple of suck-up reviews and next thing they start thinking if they shit in a can it'll be brilliant.'

I pointed out that Piero Manzoni had, in fact, sold cans of his own shit.

'It was original then,' she said. 'Forty years ago. Now it just smells bad.'

I DID CONCEDE MARILYN'S BASIC POINT: Victor Cracke's art didn't fit into any clear category, which made my role in its success – or failure – that much stronger. Part of a dealer's skill, his creativity, lies in surrounding a piece with the correct context. Everybody likes to be able to talk about their art to their friends, to be knowledgeable. In this way one can rationalize spending half a million dollars on crayon and string.

In theory, I had the easiest job imaginable: I could make up whatever I wanted. Nobody would contradict me if I decided to make Victor a dishwasher, a professional gymnast, a retired assassin. Ultimately, though, I decided that the most compelling narrative was none at all: Victor Cracke, cipher. Let people write the story themselves, and they will insert whatever hopes, dreams, fears and lusts they want. The piece becomes a Rorschach test. All art of value achieves this to a certain extent, but I suspected that the scale of Victor's piece, its hallucinogenic totality, would make for a lot of audience countertransference. That, or a boatload of confusion.

I thus found myself answering a lot of opening-night questions the same way.

'I don't know.'

'We don't really know.'

'That's a good question. I don't know if I know that.'

Or:

'What do *you* think?'

At an opening, you can identify the novice by his interest in the work. Gallery people don't bother to look at all. They're there for the wine and crackers, and to talk about who's up or down this week.

'Smashing,' Marilyn said, tipping back her plastic cup.

'Thank you.'

'I brought you a present. Did you notice?'

'Where.'

'There, silly.' She nosed at a tall, handsome man in a slim-cut suit.

I looked at her with surprise. Kevin Hollister was a good friend of Marilyn's, her ex-husband's Groton roommate. Quarterbacking Harvard to three Ivy League titles earned him a spectacularly cushy banking job right out of school, and ever since then he's been on the rise. He lives, you might say, comfortably. His hedge fund is named Downfield.

Recently he had turned his attention from shorting Eastern European currencies to art, a typical Culture Climber, to whom a canvas was little more than an expensive ticket to an exclusive party. I am forever astonished at how men with money and brains – men who control world markets, run major corporations, have the ear of politicians – become dribbling imbeciles in front of a painting. Not knowing where to begin, they run to the nearest source of guidance, no matter how biased or mercenary.

In a spectacular display of poor judgment, Hollister had hired Marilyn as a consultant, giving her what amounted to a private tap on his bank account. Needless to say, she had sold him work exclusively by artists she represented, barking at anyone who tried to step onto her territory. Earlier she had told me, 'He doesn't appreciate that a world-class collection is the product of thought and patience, and cannot be created in one fell swoop. But I'm happy to help him try.'

I'd met him once or twice, but we'd never spoken for more than a few minutes, and never about art. That Marilyn had brought him tonight meant one of two things: she thought Victor Cracke was good, or she considered me and my art no threat at all to her monopoly.

'I'm expanding his horizons,' she said. She winked at me and went to take Hollister's arm.

I worked the room all evening, chatting up the usual suspects. Jocko Steinberger, who looked as though he hadn't shaved since his own opening the previous December, came and spent the whole evening staring catatonically at one drawing. We had a surprise visit from Étienne St Mauritz, who, along with Castelli and Emmerich, used to be one of the premier American dealers. Now he was old, a liver-spotted demigod being wheeled around by a woman in a long fur coat and Christian Louboutin heels. He thought the work excellent and told me so.

Nat brought his boyfriend and they hit it off talking to another dealer named Glenn Steiger, a former assistant to Ken Noland with a dirty mouth and an arsenal of dirty stories. As I passed them I overheard him saying, '. . . tried to buy a canvas from me with forty-eight thousand dollars . . . in one-dollar bills . . . that fucking *reeked* of marijuana . . . fucking *playground* money . . .'

Ruby, her hair in a complex plait, had sequestered herself near the Cracke journals. I'd never met her date before, although she'd spoken of him in the past.

'Ethan, this is Lance DePauw.'

'Nice to meet you,' I said. 'I've heard a lot about you.'

'Same here.' Lance's eyes were bloodshot and in constant motion. He, too, smelled like playground money. 'This is some pretty crazy shit.'

'We've been looking at the food journal,' Ruby said. 'I find it comforting, the way he always ate the same thing. My mom used to pack me lunches, and she'd always give me the same sandwich, cream cheese and jelly. That's what this reminds me of.'

'That,' Lance said, 'or prison.'

We all looked at the food journal for a moment.

Lance said, 'Whack.'

From across the room, Marilyn waved at me. I excused myself and went over to talk to Hollister. His handshake was not at all the masculine vise clamp you'd expect, but dry and wary. I noticed also that he had a manicure.

'We were just admiring this piece,' Marilyn said.

'Good choice,' I said.

'Am I right in thinking this is the center of the piece? Ethan?'

I nodded. 'Panel number one.'

'How biz*arre*,' Marilyn said. 'What *are* those? Babies?'

'They look like cherubs,' said Hollister.

'Funny you say that,' I said. 'That's how we refer to them. "Victor's Cherubs."'

At the center of panel one was a five-pointed star, its dull brown an uncharacteristically muted note in an otherwise lurid palette. Around it danced a ring of winged children, their beatific faces in stark contrast to the rest of the map, which teemed with agitation and bloodshed. Victor had been a very capable draftsman, but evidently these figures had been important enough to him that he wanted to take no chances: they had been rendered with a precision that suggested tracing rather than freehand.

Marilyn said, 'They look – oh, I don't know. Like Botticelli meets Sally Mann. Sort of *pedophilic*, don't you think?'

I raised an eyebrow at her.

Hollister leaned in and squinted. 'It's in remarkably good condition, all things considered.'

'Yes.'

'Did you see the place when it was like that?' he asked, gesturing to a wall where I had hung enlarged photos of the apartment before disassembly.

'I discovered it,' I said. Behind him, I saw Marilyn smile.

'Kevin would like to learn more about the artist.'

'I honestly don't know how much more I can tell you,' I said.

'How would you compare him to other outsider artists?' Hollister said.

'Well,' I said, shooting a quick evil eye at Marilyn, 'I'm not sure *that* I'd call him an outsider artist.'

Hollister blanched, and I quickly added, 'Per se. I'm not sure, per se, that he's comparable to any other artist – although you might be right, then, in calling him an outsider artist, because part of what defines outsider art is its lack of reference.'

Behind him, Marilyn rubbed her thumb and index finger together.

I spooled out a lot of textbook stuff on Jean Dubuffet, Art Brut, the anticultural movement. 'Usually we're referring to work created by prisoners, children and the insane, and I'm not sure that Cracke was any of those, per se.'

'*I* think he was all three,' said Marilyn.

'He was a child?' asked Hollister. 'I thought he was old.'

'Well, no,' I said. 'I mean – yes. No, he wasn't a child.'

'How old was he?'

'We don't know, precisely.'

'I don't mean *literally*,' said Marilyn. 'I mean look at his concept of the world. It's so *juvenile*. Dancing angels? Come on. Who does that? You can't do that sort of thing with a straight face, you just *can't*, and I think it's terribly sweet that he did.'

'Cloying,' said Hollister.

'It might be, except the bulk of it's not like that at all – just the opposite, it's so awful and gory. That's what makes the piece interesting to me, the extremity of the two emotions at work. I think – you can tell me if I'm wrong, Ethan – but it looks to me like there are two Victor Crackes: the one who draws puppies and cupcakes and fairy rings, and the one' – she pointed to a canvas filled with graphic battle scenes – 'who draws decapitations and torture and so on.' She smiled at me. 'What do you think.'

I shrugged. 'He was trying to encompass everything he saw. He saw kindness and he saw cruelty. It's not two Victor Crackes: it's the fault of the world, for being inconsistent.'

Marilyn gestured around the room. 'You can't deny that the work has a crazed quality to it. The obsession with filling in every square inch of the page . . . Only a madman would draw for forty years and stick it all in a box.'

I admitted that my first thought had been as such.

'See, there you go. That's part of its appeal, of course.'

'All I know is it's good.'

'Well, fine, but wouldn't you feel a little less inclined to show it if you knew it was an SVA student's senior thesis?'

'An SVA student couldn't produce anything this honest,' I said. 'That's exactly the point.'

'Now you're sounding like Dubuffet.'

'Fine. I think it's refreshing not to have to think four levels of irony deep.'

'Let's imagine, for a second, that he was a criminal—'

'Hang on,' I said.

'I'm just saying. As a thought experiment.'

'There's nothing to suggest that. He was a loner. He never bothered anybody.'

'Isn't that what they say about serial killers?' she said. '"Wouldn't hurt a fly."'

I rolled my eyes.

'Regardless,' she said, 'the term *outsider artist* seems right to me.'

I didn't really believe that Victor Cracke could be so easily and neatly packaged. But I inferred from Marilyn's expression that she was trying to do me a favor by giving Hollister something concrete to cling to. He was, I gathered, a labels-and-categories kind of guy.

'We can call him that,' I said. I smiled at Hollister. 'For argument's sake.'

He squinted at the canvas again. 'What does it mean.'

'What do you think it means?'

He spent a few moments pursing and unpursing his lips. 'Nothing, inherently.'

We decided to leave it at that.

All evening long I kept an eye out for Tony Wexler. I had sent him an invitation – pointedly addressed to his home rather than to the office. I knew he couldn't come. He never did. He couldn't come if my father had been snubbed, and I invariably snubbed my father, which mooted the whole point of sending Tony an invitation.

Given his interest in the artist, and his contribution to the discovery of the work, I had figured that I'd at least get a phone call. But I'd heard nothing. It rankled a tiny bit. Even the goddamn superintendent, Shaughnessy, showed up, stuffed into a heavy sport jacket that had not recently seen the light of day. At first I thought he was some artist dressed deliberately down, a crude parody of a lower-middle-class wardrobe. Then he waved at me from afar and my memory clicked into place: the smudged glasses, the thick wrists. For the life of me I couldn't figure out why he'd come – or how he had even known about the show. I mentioned this to Nat and he told me that – per my request – we'd sent postcards to everyone I'd interviewed as a way of thanking them.

I was bewildered. 'I said to do that?'

Nat smiled. 'Senile already.'

'I've been living in a bubble,' I said. 'Anyhow I doubt I expected anyone to take the invitation seriously.'

'He did.'

'Indeed.' I felt bad for Shaughnessy, who spent the evening walking around and around the drawings, awkwardly trying to pick up the tails of other conversations. Finally, I went over to shake his hand.

He waved at the canvases. 'Something else, huh? Was I right?'

'You were.'

'I know it when I see it.'

'You certainly do.'

'I like this one.' He showed me where Victor had drawn a bridge – Ruby thought it looked like the Fifty-ninth Street Bridge – turning into a dragon whose tongue forked and grew into the air trails of a jet, which flew into an ocean, which itself became the open mouth of a giant fish . . . and so forth. The pictures tended to nest inside one another, so that every time you had found the largest unit, you discovered, upon the addition of more panels, a more impressive superstructure.

'Wild stuff,' said Shaughnessy.

I nodded.

'So'd you sell any yet?'

'Not yet.'

'You think you will?'

I glanced at Hollister. 'I hope so.'

Shaughnessy licked his lips. 'Hey, lemme ask you something. You think I might be able to get some?'

For a moment I thought I was being propositioned. 'Get some.'

'Yeah, you know.'

'You mean – buy a drawing?'

'Not so much.' He licked his lips again.

'What then.'

'Like a commission.' He smiled. 'Finder's fee.'

In the distance I saw Hollister talking to Marilyn as they headed for the front door. I said, 'You want me to give you one of the drawings.'

Abruptly he reddened. 'It's not like they're yours.'

'Excuse me,' I said, and left Shaughnessy standing there.

Before going, Hollister handed me a card and asked me to call him on Monday. He left a wake; everyone stepped aside to watch him go. They had been tracking him all evening long, eager to learn if he was no longer off-limits as a client.

I turned to find Shaughnessy again and spotted him across the room, furiously stuffing canapés into his mouth. Then he concealed an entire bottle of wine inside his coat, rolled up three exhibition catalogues, and left without saying good-bye.

THE ONE TRUE DARK SPOT on an otherwise bright evening arrived close to the end, when only I, my staff, and a handful of the hardest-core booze moochers remained. Nat, having gone behind the front desk for some promotional postcards, tried to intercept Kristjana, but she blew right past him. He then ran to warn me, but by then it was too late: she had taken her position in the middle of the gallery.

All eyes fell on her. How can you ignore a six-foot Icelandic manic-depressive with a boot-camp hairdo, her mouth sealed with duct tape, wearing a—

'Is that a straitjacket?' Ruby whispered.

It was. A red patent-leather one.

'Asylum, by Jean Paul Gaultier,' Nat whispered.

We were whispering because we knew that we had all been co-opted into a piece of performance art.

It didn't last long. She held her arms up to the sky, arched her back gracefully, and slowly – very, very slowly – began to peel the tape from her face. The sizzle of glue was audible throughout the entire gallery. It hurt to watch. With a flick of her wrist she sent the tape fluttering to the ground. Then she whipped her torso forward and expelled a shockingly large quantity of mucus smack in the middle of my gallery floor, where it sat, glistening, like a frog.

She turned on her heel and marched out.

The first person to react was Ruby's friend Lance. Everyone else was still too stunned to move, but he got up from where he'd been sitting in the corner and ambled toward the loogie, which had begun to send out little drippy green tendrils. From somewhere inside his track jacket he produced a handheld video camera. He switched it on, twisted off the lens cap, and knelt to get a close-up of Kristjana's latest work.

FIVE

The show was a hit. I got good notices in the trades, including one in *Art-Box* by an old friend who loved nothing more than to swim against the stream, and who I had expected to eviscerate me. The Musée de l'Art Brut, the modern-day outgrowth of Jean Dubuffet's personal collection, expressed interest in bringing the work over to Lausanne. And somebody must have tipped off the *Times*, because they sent over a reporter – not from Arts but from the metro section.

I waffled over whether to talk to him. Everyone knows that when it comes to the avant-garde, the *Times* is all but irrelevant; their report on a trend marks the surest sign that said trend has declined and fallen. Furthermore, I worried about how they would spin me. With very little stretching of the truth I could come off as a vulture, feasting off the remains of the poor and disenfranchised.

In the end, though, I had to agree. Otherwise I had no control over the situation whatsoever; I couldn't stop them from running the article, magnifying my lack of comment into a self-indictment.

The same traits that make me a good salesman make me a good interviewee, and when the article came out, I was pleased to see that I had convinced the journalist we were friends. He called the show 'hypnotic' and 'unsettling' and printed a large close-up of one of Victor's Cherubs on the front page of the section. My picture didn't look too bad, either.

Irrelevant or not to me, the *Times* carries a certain prestige, particularly in the minds of Culture Climbers. Within days I had gotten several offers far above the ones I'd gotten on opening night. On Marilyn's advice, I put everyone off until I'd spoken to Kevin Hollister, who she promised would call as soon as he got back from Cap Juluca.

She didn't disappoint. Two days later he asked me to lunch at a place on the ground floor of a midtown skyscraper that he owned. The restaurant staff hovered and swirled around him, whisking away his coat as he shucked it, pulling his chair out, draping his lap with a napkin, pressing his cocktail of choice into his hand before he had uttered a word. Throughout this frenzy he appeared not to notice anyone but me, asking how I'd gotten into art, how I'd met Marilyn, and so on. We were seated in a private room, where the chef personally presented us with an assortment of gemlike sushi. It was excellent. Hollister called for another round and, midway through it, offered me a hundred and seventy thousand dollars for the Cherubs. I told him that sounded low, especially considering that in giving him a single canvas I'd be breaking up the integrity of the piece as a whole – which really ought to stay together. Without batting an eye he doubled the figure.

We settled at three eighty-five. That kind of money wasn't going to make any headlines, but bear in mind that not too long ago the drawings had been bound for the landfill. The pleasure I took in watching Hollister sign the check was secondary to the godlike thrill of making something from nothing, cash from trash, creation ex nihilo.

After the deal was done I detected a change in Hollister's attitude, a surge of confidence. Now that he owned, he knew how to act. Men like him believe that nothing is beyond their grasp – be that thing a piece of land, a piece of art, a brand of savvy, a person. Once they've paid and order is restored, they can go back to being masters of the universe. It's a metamorphosis I recognized from years of dealing with my father.

I RETURNED TO THE GALLERY that afternoon elated by the deal but depressed about the prospect of losing my art. Mine, and I didn't feel ashamed to say so.

When a show goes well, or I make an unusually handsome sale, I will send my assistants home, close the gallery, and invite the artist over to commune with the object we have created together. I'll be the first to admit that it's a sentimental ritual. But no one has ever told me he didn't want to do it. Anyone so jaded that he fails to experience a sense of loss – that person, to me, can neither see art nor experience its transcendency. I don't want to represent him.

Without Victor Cracke, I stood alone in the vast white space, watching the pages of the drawings billow gently. I took off my shirt, bundled it behind my head, and lay down on the floor in front of the nearest canvas, feeling like a child confronting the ocean for the first time, overcome by its vastness and its melancholy.

I LIKE TO ORGANIZE MY LIFE in five-year fragments, give or take. My mother died when I was five. When I turned eleven my father, tired of listening to me, sent me off to boarding school. Then came about five years of getting kicked out of various educational institutions across the globe. Let me see if I can remember the correct order: Connecticut, Massachusetts, Brussels, Florida, Connecticut again, Berlin, Vermont and Oregon. By the time I got back to New York I knew how to say *dime bag* and *blowjob* in several dialects of American English, as well as Turkish, German, French and Russian.

When I turned sixteen, a despairing Tony Wexler – he, rather than my father, had been the one managing my woes – phoned my half-sister, Amelia, and begged her to put me up for a while.

Amelia and I had never been close. She lives in London, where she has been since her mother and my father divorced in 1957; that also gives you an idea of the generation gap separating us. I saw her once in a very rare while – at my own mother's funeral, for instance. Certainly I had done little to endear myself to her. I regarded all three of my half-siblings not as peers but shadowy semiparental figures not to be trusted. My half-brothers, who I saw at least a few times a month, are brown-nosers extraordinaire, and at the time I had no reason to believe that Amelia would be any different. I set out for London with a hard, hard heart.

To everyone's astonishment – not least my own – I thrived. The wetness of English weather aligned with my adolescent sense of impending doom, and the dryness of English humor made more sense to me than the rampant goofiness of American pop culture. At school I managed not to get expelled, and with private tutoring I managed to graduate. I made some of my best friends during those years, friends I still keep in touch with and see whenever I travel abroad for work – which I do more often than I need to, just to catch up. In certain ways I feel like my real life is still over there.

It was Amelia who first stoked my interest in art. Her husband is a lord, and while he spends his time drafting legislation in defense of fox hunting, she spends his money in support of radical aesthetics. During my time abroad she took me to openings and parties at the Tate; I was the charming younger brother, the tousle-haired, devil-may-care Yank. I loved the pageantry, the snobbery, the love and loathing that infused every conversation. People cared – or seemed to, anyway, which is what mattered to me at that age. After living with my father, legendary for his stoniness, my time in London felt like a beautiful, melodramatic dream.

Amelia taught me how to see not through my eyes but through the eyes of the artist, how to accept a piece on its own terms, a skill that enabled me both to understand contemporary art and to explain it to others. With her guidance I used my own savings – money that accrued to me from my mother's bequest when I turned eighteen – to buy my first piece, a Cy Twombly drawing that I took with me when I returned to the United States to attend Harvard, where I lived in a dormitory that had been occupied by my half-brothers and my father and my grandfather and great-uncles before me, and that made people laugh when they learned my name. *You live in Muller Hall?*

Without Amelia standing guard, I slipped back into my old ways. My next five-year period consisted of me drinking vodka, breathing cocaine, having sex, taking enforced 'time off' and flunking out.

You have no idea how difficult it is to flunk out of Harvard. They will do anything to rid themselves of the stink of failure. I finally succeeded by getting into a brawl with one of my professors in the middle of a seminar room, whom I drunkenly – but correctly, mind you – declared a 'know-nothing yeast infection'. Even then, I had to throw the first punch.

After retrieving me from Cambridge, Tony Wexler sat me down and told me that unless I got a job I would be cut off.

It obviously hurt him to have to threaten me, and though we both knew that he wasn't giving the orders, I despised him for carrying them out. I used my last thousand dollars to get on the next flight to London, where I showed up at Amelia's door, virtually flammable from the countless Tanqueray-and-tonics I'd ingested on the way over.

She took me right in. She never asked how long I planned on staying, never asked what had happened. She fed me and let me sleep and never judged me, perhaps knowing that I would come to judge myself harshest of all.

With nothing to do except sit in the garden and read, I began to understand what a mess I'd made of my life, a realization that left me sad and lonely but most of all angry. I remember sitting on a bench at the end of the arbor, listening to the birds and feeling jittery after two days without a drink or drugs. I got up and went to the cabinet where Amelia's husband kept his single malts, fully expecting it to be locked. Tony had probably called ahead and told her to clear out the cupboards. I resented her in advance for pretending to like me, for being no better than the rest of them, just another one of my father's minions.

The cabinet was open. Burning with shame, I closed it and slunk from the room.

The breaking point came a few days later, when Amelia asked in passing what had become of my Twombly, the one we'd bought together and that I'd loved.

Only then did I realize that I'd left it at Harvard. My departure had been so abrupt, so hazy, so filled with lawyers and ultimatums, that I'd forgotten to take it. As far as I knew it was still there.

I called up a friend from the Fly and asked him to go over my room. The Twombly hung above my bed, where it attracted the immediate attention of everyone who entered. Those in the know – art history concentrators, always, and mostly girls – tended to assume, until corrected, that I had picked it up at the Fogg's semesterly Print Rental, where even the hardest-up scholarship cases can plunk down thirty bucks to own a Jasper Johns for two semesters. When I told them that no, in fact, the drawing was mine and all mine, they tended, these art-history-concentrating girls, to sleep with me. I loved my chosen major for many reasons.

At any rate, my friend called back to say that as far as he could tell, the Twombly, like everything else I had abandoned, had been carted away with the trash.

That killed me. For the first time since losing my mother, I cried. Amelia's husband, unequipped to deal with such a wanton display of self-pity, avoided me for days. Amelia brought me tea and held my hand, and gradually it dawned on me that the real tragedy was not the loss of my drawing but the fact that I couldn't muster tears for anything save a piece of paper.

To this day I have no desire to drink. All the black thoughts and bitterness that fueled my self-destruction have been channeled into two new areas of expertise: art and hatred of my father. Fair or not, we all have our outlets.

With Amelia's help I got a job at a gallery in London, and when I decided to go back to the States, she called her friend Leonora Waite, who ran a gallery on the fourth floor of 567 West Twenty-fifth Street.

Leonora and I hit it off famously. A lusty, chain-smoking lesbian from the Bronx, she leaned toward feminist art, pulp novels and slasher flicks. She laughed big, threw incredible parties, and hated Marilyn Wooten with a passion, threatening to fire me when Marilyn and I started dating.

She didn't. Instead, she sold me her space at a shamefully low price when she retired after September 11. Six months later she died, and I had the sign out front changed to MULLER GALLERY. In her honor, my first show consisted of new works by the Lilit Collective, a self-sustaining artistic community in rural Connecticut whose cofounder, Kristjana Hallbjörnsdottir, would soon become my artist.

AS I LAY ON THE GALLERY FLOOR, contemplating the long, strange road I had taken, I felt at peace. Victor Cracke represented my first big-boy step as a dealer. With the exception of Kristjana, I inherited my entire client list from Leonora, and in the minds of many, the Muller Gallery had failed to distinguish itself from its predecessor. As much as I appreciated Leonora's taste, I had long wanted to make my mark felt, to find an artist I loved and make him a star. Victor gave me that chance, and I had not let him down.

'Thank you,' I said to the drawings.

They waved like seaweed.

If I'd known what was about to happen, I would have got up and pre-emptively disconnected the phone. Or perhaps I would have leapt up to answer. That depends on whether you consider what followed good or bad.

Either way: the next part of the story begins with a ringing phone. This is a detective novel, remember?

THE MACHINE PICKED UP. A soft, tired voice, said,

'Mr Muller, my name is Lee McGrath. I read the article and I'm interested in learning some more about the artist Victor Cracke. Would you mind please giving me a buzz?' He left a number with a 718 area code.

That night I went home without returning his call, and when I came in the next morning there was another message.

'Hi Mr Muller, Lee McGrath. Sorry to bother you again. Please, if you don't mind, I'd appreciate hearing from you.'

I dialed his number and introduced myself.

'Hi,' he said. 'Thanks for calling me back.'

'Of course. What can I do for you?'

'I was reading the paper and I came across the article about this person, Victor Cracke, the artist. Sounds like some story.'

'It is.'

'Yes, a really interesting story. Do you mind if I ask how you came across him and the drawings? Because I'd like to learn some more about him.'

Obviously, McGrath hadn't read the article too carefully; the reporter had clearly stated that I'd never met Cracke. At the end of the piece they'd printed my phone number and a request for any further information.

I said as much to McGrath, who said, 'Hm.'

At that point, a lot of people would have made an excuse to get off the phone. Many dealers decide within seconds of meeting you whether you're worth a conversation. In my experience, though, restraint pays. I once had a dowdy-looking couple (Mervyns print pants, Hush Puppies) walk in, stroll around for ten minutes, ask a couple of benign questions, and walk out. Two weeks later they called me from Lincoln, Nebraska, and bought seven paintings at a hundred twenty thousand dollars apiece, followed by another half million dollars' worth of sculpture.

So I try to be patient, even if it means answering redundant questions and waiting for an old man – I'd decided, for no particular reason, that McGrath was old – to formulate his thoughts. If he cared enough to call me about a photo in the paper, he might be the kind of person I could sell to in the future.

He said, 'I understand that there were a lot of those drawings, not just the one they reprinted in the paper.'

Again, a detail the reporter had noted. 'There are lots more.'

'How did they choose which one to reprint?'

I explained about the numbering system.

'Really,' he said. 'That's panel number one?'

'Yes.'

'You don't say . . . I'd really like to see that one for myself. Is that possible?'

'You're welcome to come down anytime you like. We're open Tuesday through Saturday, ten to six. Where are you coming from?'

He chuckled, which turned into a cough. 'I can't drive anymore. I don't leave the house too much. I was hoping I might be able to convince you to make a house call.'

'I'm very sorry, but I don't think that's possible. I can e-mail you pictures of the work. Although I should let you know that the piece you saw in the paper has been sold.'

'Well, geez. Too bad for me. If you don't mind, though, I'd still like to find out about Mr Cracke. Any chance you would like to come by for a bit, just to chat?'

I began to tap my fingers against the desk. 'I wish I had more to tell you, but—'

'What about these, eh' – I heard the sound of a newspaper being lifted – 'journals. The journals he kept. Are those sold, too?'

'Not yet. I've had several offers.' Not completely true. Some collectors had admired the journals, but nobody had put a price on them yet. People wanted objects readily displayed on a wall, not a dense, tedious text.

'Do you think I could see them?'

'If you come to the gallery, I'd be happy to show you,' I said. 'Right now I'm afraid I can't transport them anywhere. They're falling apart as it is.'

'This isn't my lucky day, huh.'

'I'm truly sorry,' I said. 'Please let me know if there's another way I can accommodate you.' Something about McGrath's folksiness made me want to be as formal as possible. 'Was there something else I could help you with?'

'Probably not, Mr Muller. But I have to take a chance and ask you one more time if you'd consider taking a trip out to see me. It'd mean a lot to me. I'm close by.'

Without realizing what I was doing, I said, 'Where.'

'Breezy Point. You know where that is?'

I didn't.

'Rockaways. You take the Belt. You know how to get to the Belt?'

'Mr McGrath. I didn't agree to come.'

'Oh. I thought you had.'

'No, sir.'

'Oh. Well, okay then.'

There was a pause. I started to say, 'Thanks for calling' but he said, 'Don't you want to know what this is about?'

I sighed. 'Okay.'

'It's about the picture in the paper. The one of the boy.'

I realized he meant the Cherub in the *Times*. 'What about him.'

'I know him,' said McGrath. 'I know who he is. I recognized him straightaway. His name was Eddie Cardinale. Forty years ago someone strangled him to death, but we never found out who.' He coughed. 'Can I give you directions or do you know how to get to the Belt?'

SIX

Although technically part of Queens, the long, flat Rockaway peninsula juts beneath Brooklyn's potbelly, like the concealed feet of a perching waterfowl. To get there you drive through Jacob Riis Park, a marshy preserve more Chesapeake Bay than New York City. Turning northeast takes you to JFK and some of the most ghettoized areas in the Five Boroughs, neighborhoods you'd never think of as dangerous, simply because they abut the beach. How can the beach be dangerous? Go to the Rockaways and you'll get your answer.

Breezy Point Cooperative sits at the other end of the peninsula, in every sense of the phrase. Nonwhite faces become less common as you head southwest, as does traffic, which thins out as you approach the parking lot. I pulled up in a cab around three. Just outside the entrance to the community was a pub that had drawn a decent crowd. The driver bobbed his head noncommittally when I asked him to wait, or to come back in an hour. As soon as I paid him, he sped away.

I entered a warren of low-slung bungalows and Cape Codders and right away felt the eponymous breeze: cool and briny, whipping up grit from the beach a hundred yards away. My loafers filled with sand as I walked the alleyways, past houses done up with nautical themes: lifesavers and signs carved from weather-beaten teak: *JIM'S CLIPPER* or *THE GOOD SHIP HALLO-RAN*. Irish tricolors abounded.

Later I learned that most of the homeowners are summerfolk who flee after Labor Day. But in mid-August they were still out in droves: out on their cramped porches or down by the boardwalk, sweating and crushing cans of Budweiser and watching towheaded skateboarders dive-bomb the pavement. Charcoal smoke turned the air heavy. Everyone seemed to know everyone else, and nobody knew me. Kids playing basketball on a low hoop with a water-filled base stopped their game and gathered to stare at me, like I had a big scarlet letter on my chest. *N*, perhaps, for *Not Local*.

I got lost looking for McGrath's house, ending up on the beach beside a memorial to local firefighters killed at the World Trade Center. I shook out my shoes.

'Lost?'

I turned and saw a girl of about nine in denim shorts over a bathing suit.

'I'm looking for Lee McGrath.'

'You mean the professor.'

I said, 'If you say so.'

She hooked a finger and went back into the maze. I tried to keep track of her turns but gave up and let myself be led to a shack with a well-kept front yard, peonies and pansies and a lawn cut golf-course close, good enough to make the cover of *Martha Stewart Living*. A hammock with a lumpy pillow hung at the far end of the porch, and behind it an old Coca-Cola sign leaned against the wooden siding. The mailbox out front read MCGRATH; underneath, an NYPD decal. In the front window was a sun-bleached poster of the Twin Towers, an eagle and an American flag.

I knocked, drawing slow footsteps.

'Thanks for coming.' Though Lee McGrath was not as old as he sounded over the phone, time had not been kind to him. Hairless calves gave him a feminine quality, and slack skin hinted that he had once been a much larger man. He wore a blue terrycloth bathrobe and disintegrating slippers that made a ghostly sound as he turned and shuffled back inside. 'Take a load off.'

The interior of the house smelled of ointments, and its clutter didn't square with the neatly kept yard. Before seating me at the dining-room table, McGrath spent a good five minutes clearing out a workspace, shuttling piles of unopened mail, half-empty paper cups, and pill bottles to the passthrough, one item at a time, a process maddening to watch. I tried to help him but he waved me off, breathing hard and making small talk.

'You find your way okay?' he asked.

'I got help.'

McGrath cackled weakly. 'I told you to take directions. Everyone gets lost the first time. It's an interesting neighborhood but a bitch to walk around. I've been here twenty-two years and I still get confused.' He surveyed the exposed stretch of tablecloth and deemed it sufficient. 'Coffee?'

'No, thanks.'

'There's juice and water, too. Maybe some beer, if you want.'

'I'm okay.' I wanted to leave. Sickness makes me anxious. Watching your mother waste away will do that to you.

'Speak up if you do. Before we get started, mind giving me a hand?'

The back room had a threadbare area rug, a rickety-looking desk, a computer, a small television atop a rolling stand and two large bookcases, one filled with paperbacks and the other with numbered three-ring binders. A yellow La-Z-Boy looked recently vacated, a John le Carré novel splayed on one arm. Along the far wall hung a dozen or so photographs: a younger, more robust McGrath in a police uniform; McGrath holding two squirming girls; McGrath shaking hands with Mickey Mantle. Several framed service commendations had been crowded in at the side of the display, afterthoughts. The adjacent wall was bare, save a laser-printed wanted poster for Osama bin Laden.

On the floor was a box, cardboard with a woodgrain print. McGrath pointed to it. I hefted it – it weighed a ton – and carried it back to the dining-room table.

'This is a copy of the file on the man who murdered Eddie Cardinale,' he said, sitting. He began taking out clipboards, manila envelopes tied with string, two-inch-thick police reports held together with alligator clips. He took out a stack of black-and-white crime scene photos and turned them over rapidly – but not so rapidly that I failed to notice the carnage.

'Here.' He slid a picture across the table. 'Look familiar?'

It did. Every pore on my body opened at once. There was no doubt that the smiling boy in the snapshot was one of the Cherubs from Victor Cracke's drawing.

My shock must have been obvious, because McGrath sat back, rubbing his unshaven chin.

'Thought so,' he said. 'At first I figured I was going crazy. Then I said, "Hey, Lee, you ain't that old yet. You got some brains left. Give the man a call."'

I said nothing.

He said, 'Sure you don't want some juice?'

I shook my head.

'Suit yourself.' He picked up the picture of Eddie Cardinale. 'Poor kid. Some things you don't forget.' He put the photo down, crossed his arms, and smiled at me with an intelligence that belied the Clueless Geezer persona he'd fed me over the phone.

I said, stupidly, 'You're a professor?'

His laughter ended in a coughing fit. 'Oh, no. They just call me that.'

'Why?'

'Hell if I know. I think because of my glasses. I have reading glasses.' He pointed to his head, where said glasses resided. 'I used to read on the porch, and the neighborhood kids would see me and call me that. BA from City College, that's me.'

'BA in what?' I preferred asking the questions.

'American history. You?'

'Art history.' I neglected to mention my lack of degree.

'Look at us, buncha historians.'

'Yup.'

'You all right? You look perturbed.'

'I'm *not* perturbed,' I said. 'I *am* a little surprised.'

He shrugged. 'Look, I don't know what it means. It might mean nothing.'

'Then why did you call me up?'

He smiled. 'Retirement bores the shit out of me.'

'I honestly don't know how much I can help you,' I said. 'Other than what I told you over the phone, I know nothing about the man.'

I don't know why I felt so defensive. McGrath hadn't accused anybody of anything, least of all me. A murder forty years old would have been a bit beyond my reach, unless you believe in karma and reincarnation, and I didn't have McGrath pegged as the mystic type. (There. I hardboiled a sentence. Aren't you proud?)

'You must know a little more,' he said. 'You wouldn't pick up some drawings out of a Dumpster and put them up in your gallery.'

'That's essentially what happened.'

'Did you hope that he'd read the article and show up?'

I shrugged. 'It occurred to me that he might.'

'But you haven't put an ad in the paper or anything.'

'No.'

'Aha.' I got the sense that he thought I had manufactured the 'missing artist' story for publicity. On some level he was right. I wasn't lying when I told people that Victor was missing. I had stopped looking, though.

'If that really is the case,' McGrath said, 'then I might be wasting your time.'

'As I told you this morning.'

'Well, my sincere apologies.' He did not appear sorry at all; he appeared to be sizing me up. 'Since you're here already, let me tell you a little about Eddie Cardinale.'

EDWARD HOSEA CARDINALE, b. January 17, 1956. Residing 34–17 Seventy-fourth Street, Jackson Heights, Borough of Queens, Queens County, New York City, New York. P.S. 069; good kid; well liked. In his class photo he's a prepubescent Ricky Ricardo; big, pointy collar and slicked-back hair, smile revealing a slender gap between his two front teeth.

On the evening of August 2, 1966, a Tuesday night in the middle of a crushing heat wave, Eddie's mother, Isabel, sits on the stoop of their apart-ment, her shirt dusty and creased from bending constantly to pick up litter or toys. She is worried. The twins have just learned to walk, and keeping track of them is a full-time job. To give herself room to think, she sent Eddie to the park with his baseball glove, telling him to be back by six.

Now it is eight thirty and he is nowhere in sight. She asks her next-door neighbor to keep an eye on the twins and goes out looking for her eldest son.

An hour later Eddie's father, Dennis, a shift manager at a Brooklyn sugar factory, comes home from work and, upon being told of Eddie's dis-appearance, goes out to have a look of his own. Isabel stays back to phone the parents of Eddie's friends. According to boys who'd been at the park, the game lasted roughly from one until five, when everyone broke up to walk home. Nobody saw Eddie all day.

At ten P.M. the Cardinales phone the police. Two officers are dispatched to the residence, where they take statements and a description. Patrolmen are notified to be on the lookout for a boy of ten, black hair, wearing a blue shirt and blue jeans and carrying a baseball glove.

Initially, police speculate that Eddie, unhappy with the amount of time his mother has been spending with his younger brothers, has run away to get attention and will likely turn up within a half-mile radius. The Cardinales adamantly maintain that their son is too mature to pull such a stunt – a belief confirmed in the most gruesome way imaginable three days later, when a caretaker at Saint Michael's finds a body just outside the cemetery grounds, near the Grand Central Parkway. An autopsy reveals semen on the buttocks and thighs, as well as traces of semen and blood on the victim's jeans and underwear. A broken hyoid bone and severe bruising around the neck indicate manual strangulation as the cause of death.

However sensational and titillating the case might be, it does not spread beyond the local papers. Another, far more sensational crime is already hogging the national news: Charles Whitman's sniper massacre at the University of Texas, Austin. Only so much dark territory exists in the modern American consciousness, and for a few weeks in the summer of 1966, Whitman has staked out the entire plot. The murder of Eddie Cardinale goes cold.

MCGRATH SAID, 'He wasn't the first.'

I did not look up from the stack of crime scene photos, which McGrath had handed to me as he talked. I saw Eddie; Eddie's mother and father, both of them hollowed out; I saw the body, so ungraceful in death, like a broken violin. According to McGrath, the heat had accelerated decomposition, turning a slender, good-looking boy into a bloated sack, his face inhuman. I decided that the photos were half Weegee and half Diane Arbus, and then I remembered that I was looking at a dead child, a real dead child, not a piece of art. And then I remembered that Weegee and

Diane Arbus had been looking at real people, too. Only my lack of famil-iarity with the subjects made their pictures suitable for looking at. Now that I knew Eddie Cardinale, I found him hard to look at.

I saw, too, pages of transcripts: interviews with neighbors, with local business owners, with the Cardinales, with Eddie's friends who had been at the park. I saw the coroner's report and the accompanying photographs. I saw a map of Queens marked with the location of the body and the loca-tion of the Cardinales' home in Jackson Heights – a distance of less than a mile. Less than a mile from either was another spot, one not marked on the map but whose proximity to Eddie Cardinale's walk of death was all too clear to me: Muller Courts.

Finally, I registered McGrath's words. I looked at him. 'Pardon?'

'There was another before him,' he said. 'Nobody connected the two until they assigned a new detective to the case.'

He didn't need to tell me that he was the detective in question; I knew it from his proprietary mien. I sound the same way when I talk about my artists.

'Back then we didn't have computers. You kept everything on paper, and that made it easy to miss connections, even with a lot of overlap.' He began digging through the file box, removed another large trove of evi-dence marked STRONG, H. 'This kid, Henry Strong, disappeared about a month before Eddie Cardinale, on the Fourth of July. His family was hav-ing a party, and he wanders off. Witnesses were all drunk, and nobody can tell us a damn thing, except an uncle, who reports seeing a colored guy in a leather jacket. They never found a body.'

'Victor Cracke wasn't colo— black.'

'You said in the article that you didn't know what he looked like.'

'I know he was white,' I said. 'That much I know.'

McGrath shrugged. 'All right. Frankly I think the guy who told us that was just trying to make himself feel useful. We never considered it a fruit-ful line of inquiry.'

I said nothing.

'Do you want to see the rest?' he asked.

I asked how many more he meant by *the rest*.

'Three.'

I took a deep breath and shook my head.

'You don't?'

'No,' I said. 'I don't.'

He seemed surprised. 'If you say so.' He closed Henry Strong's file and set it back in the box. 'Did you have a chance to bring that drawing?'

At McGrath's behest, I had brought a color photocopy of the central panel, the one with the five-pointed star and the dancing Cherubs. The original I'd left behind; no reason to overhandle an already delicate piece of art.

'I forgot it,' I lied.

If I imagined myself protecting Victor, I thought wrong; lying could only make him – and me – seem more suspect. Immediately I saw the futility of what I'd done, but what could I do at that point? Take it back? Before he could express disappointment I asked for a glass of water.

'In the fridge,' he said.

I went to the kitchen and stood in front of the open refrigerator. The house had no air-conditioning and I let the cool roll over me as I absent-mindedly touched packages of sliced ham, a half-eaten block of white cheddar, a jar of kosher dills. On the door, adjacent to a carton of OJ and a plastic pitcher full of water, I saw more medications, amber bottles labeled KEEP REFRIGERATED. What did he have? I vowed to be brave enough to ask him.

But McGrath got the jump on me, and when I returned I almost coughed out my water at the sight of him spreading out photos of the other three victims, lining them up like a team portrait: Victor's Victims. The phrase flashed through my head and I let out a startled laugh.

'I . . .' I began but found I had nothing to say. There *was* nothing to say.

What was there to say? Every one of the murdered boys was a Cherub, a perfect five for five.

'All strangled, all within seven miles of one another. If you include Henry Strong, that's starting on July 4, 1966. The last one happens in the fall of 67. Well,' he said, 'so far as I know. I'd be willing to bet there's others that match the MO, later on or in other places. What do you think?'

'Pardon?' I said.

'Do you think I should cast a wider net?'

'I don't have a clue.'

'Fair enough. Doesn't hurt to solicit an opinion, right?' He laughed, again dissolving in coughs.

'Right.' I felt uneasy, as though McGrath was softening me up before springing some trap: the damning revelation that I had Victor Cracke hidden in my walk-in closet.

Which, of course, I did not. I had nothing to feel guilty about.

'I wish I could be more helpful,' I said.

'There's nothing you know about. The places he liked to hang out, maybe?'

'I have his address,' I said, before correcting, 'where he *used* to live. He left long before I came on the scene.'

'Where was that, anyhow? The article said in Queens but didn't specify where.'

'It did. Muller Courts.'

'Did it?' McGrath picked up the *Times* and slid his reading glasses on. 'I must be going senile.' He read. 'Indeed. I stand corrected. Weeell' – he tossed the paper aside and picked up the map of Queens – 'we can probably guess the punchline.' With a pen he dotted the locations of the other three bodies. They fanned out neatly from Cracke's neighborhood, as close as a half-mile and as distant as Forest Hills.

'The last one,' he said. 'Abie Kahn.' He picked up a photo of a boy in a yarmulke. Without referring to the file, he told me the date of the disappearance: September 29, 1967. 'A Friday afternoon. His father's a handyman, runs ahead to the synagogue to fix a leak in the rabbi's office before the Sabbath services. Abie is messing around in the house, his mother finally yells at him to get moving, he's going to be late. Nobody's on the street at that time – they're either already in the synagogue or at home getting dinner ready. Abie sets out on foot and never gets there. He was ten.'

At that point I began to wonder if McGrath knew I was lying about the drawing – if he meant for the macabre lineup to plumb my conscience.

'That's my daughter,' he said, following my gaze, which had until that moment been out of focus. The daughter in question, her picture adjacent to the kitchen, a waify brunette with a studious expression, did not resemble McGrath so much as echo his intensity. On the other side of the doorway hung another photo, also of a woman, similarly shaped but more severe, older than the first by five or six years.

'My other daughter.'

I nodded.

'You have kids?' he asked me.

I shook my head.

'There's time,' he said.

'I don't want children,' I said.

'Well, all right.'

The crash of the ocean; Springsteen on the radio; gleeful shrieks.

'My car is waiting for me,' I said.

McGrath stood. Rising from his chair left him out of breath, rheumy and sallow and smiling like Bela Lugosi.

'I'll walk you out,' he said.

He stopped at the edge of the porch, explaining that if he went down the stairs I'd have to carry him back up, and that didn't make much sense, now did it?

I agreed it didn't.

'You'll let me know,' he said, shaking my hand, 'if you turn up anything.'

'Sure thing.'

'You have my number.'

I touched my breast pocket, where I'd placed the Post-it he'd given me.

'All right, then,' he said. 'Drive safe.'

More time had passed than I realized, and if the driver had in fact decided to come back for me, he was gone by the time I found my way out of the maze and into the cooperative's parking lot. The pub had swelled with happy-hour patrons, and I encountered a host of curious stares as I entered and asked the bartender for the number of a local car service.

'You can try,' she said, 'but they don't like to work too much.'

Thirty minutes later I called the dispatch again, wondering where the fuck my car was. The man at the other end did not seem inclined to help me, so I went back into the bar and got the number for a second service, who told me they had no cars available.

By that time I had been waiting for over an hour, and my options had dwindled to two: get to the subway – itself a good five miles away – or call a friend. I tried Marilyn, who did not pick up. Nor did any of my other friends who owned cars, friends I could count on one hand. I called Ruby, who offered to get in a cab, drive out and bring me back; but rush hour meant the outbound portion of the trip alone would take more than an hour. I told her not to go anywhere yet and walked back to McGrath's house.

This time I found it myself, although I did make several wrong turns. I knocked and footsteps came swiftly, making me wonder if he had been malingering to draw sympathy.

'Yes?' The woman who answered wore a gray pantsuit, a black cotton blouse, simple silver earrings in the shape of fleurs-de-lis. I recognized her as the younger daughter, much better looking in real life than in her photo, which made her seem like the Captain of the Debate Team. Had she been there the entire time?

'Can I help you?'

'I'm Ethan,' I said.

'Can I help you, Ethan?'

'I was just here,' I said. 'With your father. My car didn't pick me up. Would you mind if I came in for a moment to ask him for – I need a number, so I can – I can get back home.' I paused to appreciate the inanity of the preceding paragraph. Not lost on her, I noticed.

'I live in Manhattan,' I added.

From inside, McGrath called, 'Sammy?'

'Is that him? Tell him I'm here. Ethan Muller.'

The woman gave me another quick up-and-down. 'Hold on,' she said, and closed the door in my face. A short while later she returned, smiling apologetically. 'Sorry. He hates solicitors.'

(Did I really look like a Jehovah's Witness?)

'I don't know what it is about Breezy Point,' she said, allowing me inside, 'but we have a hard time getting taxis out here. They think it's in Jersey or something. I'm Samantha, by the way.'

'Ethan.'

'There's a neighborhood guy who drives a cab.' She dialed for me and handed me the phone.

'Thank you.' I let it ring ten times. 'I don't think he's picking up.'

'Sammy.' McGrath's voice crawled down the stairs. He sounded half dead.

'Coming.' To me: 'If you can wait a few minutes I'll drive you to the subway.'

I told her that would be fine and sat down at the dining-room table. Samantha went into the kitchen. I heard her draining a pot into the sink. She emerged with her hands in a dishtowel and set a glass of water in front of me before proceeding upstairs.

Alone, I went into the kitchen. Samantha didn't seem to be much of a cook. A mop of spaghetti dripped from a colander in the sink. Nearby sat an unopened jar of marinara sauce. Saddened by the sorry state of her dinner – or was it his, or both of theirs? – I poured the sauce into the empty pan and put it over heat.

Upstairs, I heard Samantha arguing with her father, the words indistinct but the tone clear enough: pleading, and failing. Amazing how much you can tell about a song without understanding the lyrics; the frustration she sang broke my heart a bit, and mine is a heart not easily broken, not when it comes to fathers.

As I listened to her, the same thought kept occurring to me: if I were her, I would've left a long time ago – had I bothered to go upstairs at all. I thought about my own father, sending me imperious messages via Tony Wexler. *Your father wants. Your father would like. Your father would prefer.* What a nightmare my life would be if my family couldn't afford intermediaries.

Upstairs, I heard Samantha say, '*Dammit*, Dad.'

The sauce began to bubble. I stirred it and lowered the flame.

She came downstairs half an hour later, apologizing. 'He's in a mood.' Then, noticing the saucepan, 'You didn't have to do that.'

'It's better warm.'

'He says he's not hungry.' She rubbed her forehead. 'He's very stubborn.'

I nodded.

She stayed in that position for a moment longer: heel of hand ironing her brow, her fingers curled like a shell. She had a lovely pouting mouth, and her cheeks were brushed with freckles subdued by office work. Did she run a shipping center? Was she in publishing? Administrative assistant at an investment bank? I decided I wasn't giving her enough credit. She was, I decided, the kind of girl who had made good on her parents' hard work. Probably she was a social worker . . .

As I watched her calm herself down, the similarity between her and her father sharpened. What I had earlier interpreted as intensity I now understood as stoicism. Upstairs, her father began to cough and there was almost nothing on her face – just the slightest strengthening of resolve, the slightest narrowing of the eyes and tightened jaw. She was hardly the most glamorous woman I knew, but standing there, unconcerned with what I thought of her predicament, she had an unvarnished quality that I found oddly attractive. I didn't meet many girls-next-door.

She said, 'I'll take you to the train.'

We walked to the parking lot. Her Toyota had a police placard in the windshield.

'You're a cop,' I said.

She shook her head. 'DA.'

During the short ride we fell into conversation. She laughed – a big, snorty laugh – when I told her about her father's first phone call.

'Oh boy,' she said. 'That thing again, huh. Well, good luck with it.'

'With what.'

'He said you were helping him out.'

'That's what he told you?'

'I take it you don't agree.'

'I'd like to help him,' I said. 'I can't. I spent a fair amount of time explaining that to him.'

'He seemed to think you were very helpful.'

'If he says so.'

She smiled. 'Sometimes,' she said, 'he gets *ideas*.'

At the subway I thanked her for the ride.

'Thank you for coming out,' she said.

'You're welcome, although I really don't know that I've done anything.'

'You've given him something to do,' she said. 'You don't know how much that's worth.'

SEVEN

It had been a long time since I'd ridden the subway. Growing up, public transport was off-limits; I took cabs or cars or, when accompanied by Tony, a 1957 Rolls-Royce Silver Wraith chauffeured by a silent Belgian named Thom. I can't call Tony's fear of the MTA entirely illegitimate. Think about what New York City was like back in the 1980s, and then put me – an underweight white preppie with anger issues – on one of those filthy, ungoverned trains, and you have real reason for concern. Of course, blanket restrictions on my freedom made me all the more likely to buy a token or, if I felt particularly rebellious, jump a turnstile. *Viva la revolución.*

The ride home took ninety minutes, plenty of time for me to think about my conversation with McGrath and its implications for me, thoughts I shared with Marilyn the next night over dinner at Tabla.

Her initial reaction was to giggle.

'You took the subway?'

'That wasn't the point of the story.'

'Poor baby.' She stroked my cheek. 'Is your tender flesh sore? Can I order you up a poultice?'

'I've taken the subway before.'

'You're so easy. You might as well have a big button on your chest. "Push me."'

'Did you listen to anything I just told you?'

'I listened.'

'And?'

'And I'm not surprised. You will recall, darlin, that I warned you. I said it on opening night: your artist is a baddie, you can tell by his relish in depicting pain.'

'The fact that he drew pictures of the victims means nothing,' I said. 'He could have seen them in the paper and copied them.'

'Did they print them in the papers?'

'I don't know,' I admitted. 'But whatever the case may be, the piece as a whole is enormous. It contains all sorts of things, all sorts of crazy scenes, and plenty of them are recognizable. We're not ascribing Yankee Stadium to him, but it's in the drawing.'

'Is it?'

'Either it or something that looks a lot like it.'

'So, there you go,' she said. 'There's your defense.'

'It's not a *defense*—'

'You know, I love that you're solving a murder mystery. That's what we need around here, a good murder mystery.'

'I'm not solving anything.'

'Personally, I can think of a few people I'd like to kill.'

'I don't doubt it.'

'Or have killed.' She took a huge swig of wine. 'I'm sure I wouldn't want to do it myself. I'm more of a big-picture kind of a gal, wouldn't you agree?'

I said nothing, swabbing my bread in olive oil until it disintegrated.

'Stop brooding, please,' Marilyn said.

'Do you really think he killed them?'

'Who cares?'

'I do.'

'Why in the world would you care about that?'

'Put yourself in my position,' I said.

'All right,' she said. She got up and made me switch chairs with her, put a finger to her temple. 'Mm. No. I *still* don't care.'

'I'm representing a murderer.'

'Did you know that when you took him on?'

'No, but—'

'Would knowing that have stopped you?' she asked.

I had to think about that one. Even if Victor Cracke was a child-killer, he would hardly be the first artist to misbehave. The greatest outsider artist of all time, Adolf Wölfli, spent most of his life in a psychiatric hospital after being arrested for molesting girls, one as young as three. Taken as a group, nonoutsider artists don't fare much better on the Model Citizen Scale. They do wretched things to themselves and to others: drink themselves to death, shoot themselves, stab themselves, destroy their work, destroy their families. Caravaggio killed a man.

How surprised could I be that Cracke – by most descriptions completely asocial – had a worm-eaten soul? Wasn't that the point? Part of what attracts us to artists is their otherness, their refusal to conform, their big middle finger stuck up in the face of Society, such that their very a- or immorality is what makes their art artistic rather than academic. Gauguin famously called civilization a sickness. He also said that art is either plagiarism or revolution. And nobody wants to be remembered as a plagiarist. Starving painters console themselves by thinking of a day in the distant future when their crazy behavior is admired for being ahead of its time.

But more important, I had divorced Victor Cracke the person from the work. It therefore didn't matter how many people he'd killed. In appropriating the art, I made it my own, transforming it into something larger and more significant and more valuable than he had ever intended, just like Warhol did when he elevated soup cans to iconic status. That Cracke had physically created the drawings seemed to me a rather minor quibble. I owned his sins no more than Andy owned the sins of the Campbell's corporation. That I even paused to consider the question of morality made me feel incredibly stodgy and retrograde. I could hear Jean Dubuffet rolling around in his grave, flabbergasted and scorning me in French for swallowing bourgeois norms.

'Look at it this way,' Marilyn said. 'Whether he did or did not kill anyone, the very suggestion ups his mystique. Spin it right and you have a new selling angle.'

'Bars on the gallery door?'

'Too kitschy.'

'I was joking.'

'I'm not. You have to regain your sense of playfulness, Ethan. This whole experience is making you very *serious*, and it's bad for you.'

'What's playful about rape and murder?'

'Oh, God, please. That's just another way of saying sex and violence, which is just another way of saying mass-market entertainment. Besides, let's remember that you don't know the truth yet. He could have seen the pictures in the newspaper, like you said. Go *investigate* or something.' She smiled. 'Ooh, I just *love* that word. Don't worry, this'll be fun.'

I WENT TO THE NEW YORK PUBLIC LIBRARY and spent four hours with microfiche. Not knowing what kind of news Victor Cracke preferred, I checked the *Times* and all the tabloids for the weeks surrounding the murders, whose dates I obtained from McGrath.

'Any word on that drawing?' he asked when I called.

'Which drawing.'

'You said you'd send me a copy.'

'Right.'

But before I sent him anything, I wanted to see what I turned up on my own.

And what I turned up confirmed my gut instinct: all five of the victims' pictures had ended up in one paper or another. The similarity between the newspaper portraits and the Cherubs struck me as awfully close. Not just faces but positions and expressions. I made copies and took them back to the gallery for comparison. Lo and behold, they matched. Not perfectly – perhaps a little artistic license? – but well enough that I felt confident reporting to Marilyn that I'd found the originals.

'Aren't we resourceful?'

I was grateful to her for sparing me the obvious follow-up question; I knew she was thinking it, because I was, too: why them?

Plenty of people get killed in New York. Plenty of photos make the pages of its public records. In the first two weeks of August 1966 alone I counted three other murders – and those were just the ones gooey enough to make the news. But those boys had become the literal center of Victor's universe, the impetus for a life's work. Why?

And another question poked at me: how had he connected the crimes? Not all of the articles referred to one another. Henry Strong wasn't described as a murder, because at the time of his disappearance, no body had been found. To know that both he and Eddie Cardinale had been the work of one person, and that the same person had gone on to kill three more boys, a reader would have to be able to match up the victim profiles as well as similarities in the cases: the fact that all the boys had been strangled, for example. A person casually leafing through the paper would be unlikely to take notice unless he was particularly astute – or already aware of the common thread.

Either of those conditions potentially applied to Victor, whom I imagined sitting alone in his cell of a room, afraid of going outside, brimming with conspiracy theories, tracing connections between the boys and himself, the boys and the federal government . . . Maybe, by putting the boys around his central star, he hoped to insulate himself from whatever had taken them: a kind of burnt offering to a faceless killer . . . rocking himself to sleep, clutching his talismans, haunted by the notion that he could be the next victim . . . no matter that he was not ten years old, that he never left the building . . . no matter . . . he is frightened, so frightened . . .

Far-fetched? Absolutely. But I badly wanted to believe he was innocent.

Now I have another confession to make: while it's true I wanted to protect Victor, this had more to do with me than with him. I felt for him, yes; wanted to shield his good name, yes. But my most pressing concern was that he become too real. When he had been nothing but a name, I could exert my creative power over the art, control how people read it. The more he made his presence felt, however – the realer he became – the more he excluded me. And I didn't especially like the Victor who had begun to emerge: a frantic scribbling pervert, a cloistered maniac. Pure evil isn't very interesting; it has no depth. Frankly, it conflicted with my vision.

Not to mention that I was worried about the impact on sales. Who'd want to buy a drawing by a serial killer?

AS IT TURNS OUT, a lot of people. My phone began ringing off the hook. Collectors I knew, others I knew of but had never met, and an assortment of unsavory types began leaving me messages or showing up to talk to me about Victor Cracke. At first I was pleased at the spike in interest, but after the first few calls I understood that they were less interested in the art than the sordid tale behind it. Apparently, having 'sociopathic sex offender/ murderer' on your résumé was worth more than an MFA from RISD.

Is it true he raped them, one man wanted to know. Because he had just opened up the perfect wall space in his dining room.

95

I knew things had gotten out of hand when I started hearing from Hollywood. A well-known director of independent films called to ask if I would loan some of the pieces out for use as a backdrop in a music video.

I called Marilyn.

'Oh, relax,' she said, 'I'm just having a little fun.'

'Please stop spreading rumors.'

'It's called creating buzz.'

'What did you *tell* people?'

'As much as you told me. If folks get overexcited, that says much more about them than about you, me, or the art.'

'You're letting the story get away from me,' I said.

'I didn't realize you had a copyright.'

'You know as well as I do the importance of managing the discourse, and—'

'That's precisely what I'm trying to demonstrate, darlin: you need to stop trying to manage the discourse. Loosen up.'

'Even if,' I said, '*even* if that's true, I don't need you spreading rumors.'

'I told you, I—'

'Marilyn. Marilyn. Shh*hhh*. Stop. Just stop doing it, okay? Whatever you want to call it, knock it off.' And I hung up on her, much angrier than I'd realized.

From across the room, Nat gave me a look.

'She told everyone that he was a pedophile.'

He snickered.

'That's not funny.'

'Well,' said Ruby, 'it kind of is.'

I threw up my hands and walked to my computer.

ABOUT A WEEK AFTER MY MEETING with McGrath, I still hadn't sent him a copy of the drawing. When he called, I had Ruby and Nat stonewall

96

him. 'I'm sorry, Mr Muller isn't available right now. Can I take a message? Right. We have your number here already. I'm sure he'll call you when he has a free moment. Thank you.' I felt nervous putting him off; I didn't want to give the impression that I was scared. I wasn't. Let me make that plain: McGrath didn't scare me at all. He was old, he was retired, and he wanted to get Victor, not me; to him I was nothing more than a source of information. And since I had nothing to be ashamed of, not really, I might have decided to play along.

Just because he hadn't threatened me, though, that didn't mean I had to go out of my way to help him. I decided that if he wanted to look at the drawing he could come to the gallery, like everyone else.

All that changed when I opened the mail that afternoon. Tucked in with the bills and postcards was a plain white envelope bearing a New York postmark, addressed to E. Muller, the Muller Gallery, fourth floor, 567 West Twenty-fifth Street, NY, NY 10001.

I opened it up. Inside was a letter. It said, five hundred times,

STOP

The handwriting – cramped, uniform, shaky – I recognized as I might my own. Although it didn't take Sherlock Holmes to notice that the very same handwriting hung all around the gallery, calling out the names of rivers, roads, nations, landmarks – thousands of examples by which to confirm that Victor Cracke had written to me.

And Solomon Mueller rebegat himself, Solomon Muller.

And Solomon Muller begat daughters, who married into other firms.

And his brother Bernard, lazy as always, wed late and had no children. His chief interests – horses, parties, tobacco – kept him occupied until he died at the ripe old age of ninety-one, having outlived all three of his industrious brothers.

And the third brother, Adolph, begat two boys, Morris and Arthur, neither of whom proved financially adept. At first Solomon extended them a long leash. 'People must make mistakes to learn,' he told Adolph. But soon enough the elders came to understand that the only lesson the boys had taken from their mistakes was that they could make mistakes without consequence. Adolph turned his hair white trying to find them jobs worthy of their surnames yet that did not imperil the family fortune.

And the youngest brother, Simon, begat Walter, who became like a son to Solomon, and who inherited the crown when his cousins proved worthless. Walter had an old-world quality to him, a refinement and sly-ness that spoke of the noble European roots the Mullers now boasted.

That Solomon had come penniless, that he had begged seed money, that he had pushed a cart for ten thousand miles – all effaced from the family history. Everyone came together to decide that no, contrary to pop-ular opinion, the Mullers came from regal stock. They hired a genealogist, in whose hands Jewish paupers (Hayyim, Avrohom, Yonason) became German aristocracy (Heinrich, Alfred, Johann). A coat of arms appeared on the company letterhead. Churches were joined, clubs established. Loans to the Union cause, extended by Solomon, came due, leading to dinners eaten at the White House, the signing of lucrative government contracts, the passing of motions on the Senate floor, declaring the Mullers First Citizens of the United States of America.

Isaac Singer spoke the truth. You became your claim.

And Walter, fashioned in his uncle's form, begat Louis.

And Louis begat consternation when he was discovered receiving fella-tio from a kitchen boy. What was wrong with the scullery maids? They had suited Bernard just fine. What was wrong with women, with the debutantes falling all over themselves for the handsome young million-aire, swooning at their cotillions, competing to see who could stand longest in his presence, by silent consensus electing him the most eligible bachelor in Manhattan – if not the entire Eastern Seaboard – what was wrong with them? What was wrong with women? Daughters of partners to strengthen bonds, daughters of competitors to forge new ones, daugh-ters of foreign dignitaries and of city politicians and of state senators, daughters from the old country; what was wrong with any of them? What was wrong with a woman, a polite and pretty and proper and sturdy-hipped heir-bearing woman, what was wrong? What? *What in the world could be wrong with women?*

Louis got married.

*

99

EARLY EVENING, APRIL 23, 1918. Louis walks the halls of the house on Fifth, a gift from his parents on the occasion of his wedding two years ago. On the day he and Bertha moved in, his mother said to him, 'Fill every room,' and since then all he has heard are complaints. One would think they are on death's door, so crazed are they for grandchildren.

Fill every room. A preposterous idea, that. He'd have to have a harem. He'd have to be Genghis Khan. Five towering stories of wood, marble, glass, gold and gemstones, done in the French Gothic style, groined and soaring and drafty – the house on Fifth will never be full. Every year they burn thousands of pounds of coal just trying to keep the place warm enough for human habitation.

All that stone makes the screaming echo like the very depths of hell.

Bertha despises the house. She has told Louis that she'd rather live in a mausoleum. He doubts that this is literally true, although the family resting place *is* in fine taste, and he assumes that fewer things break there. Homeownership holds not the slightest appeal to him, what with its tendency to disappoint: a ruptured pipe, a buckling floor. Such petty disasters would not concern the dead. Let *them* live on Fifth; he and Bertha will move to Salem Hills!

At least he goes to work during the day. Bertha, left alone, has had to hire staff in order to prevent herself from going mad. An average day at the Louis Muller household finds twenty-seven full-time employees, every one of them screened personally by the mistress of the house. To those unfamiliar with Louis's proclivities, Bertha's requirements must seem entirely backward: they must be women or men old enough to have lost their looks.

She got what she wanted. She always does.

On April 23, 1918, the day staff have all been sent home early, and those who reside permanently at the house ordered to take the evening off – leaving a silence unlike anything Louis has heard since their first, terrible night alone together, a silence that turns a ticking clock into a falling axe; magnifies, too, his anticipation, as it is only between screams that the silence prevails. A spring shower has kicked up, smudging the view from the third floor, where he stands and waits for another.

There she goes.

What sounds! Louis admires his wife's energy. He supposes that she has proven as appropriate a companion as he could have hoped for. She does not waste time, money or words. When she became pregnant she stopped demanding that he come to her room at night; she even threw him a bone, in the form of a new sous chef. She had achieved her goal. 'One child,' she told him. 'We will be happy with whatever we get.'

Already he understands that even a single child will work many changes. Every year since he was a boy Louis has gone – first with his parents, and then with his wife – to take the waters at Bad Pappelheim. When he told his mother that Bertha had canceled their upcoming summer tour, that she demanded he stay and instead accompany her and the child-to-be to the house in Bar Harbor, he expected a show of maternal support.

Instead, she defected to Bertha's side. 'Naturally she won't be ready to sail. We'll all stay. We'll all go together; your father will love the idea.'

Big changes coming, seismic changes.

Again she screams, causing him to tear the delicate antimacassar he has been kneading between his fingers. He lets it flutter to the floor and paces the room, massaging his earlobes, which is what he does in moments of crisis.

He should be grateful, he knows. His shame could have been much worse. Nobody raised a finger to him, nobody shouted. They merely took him into a room and introduced him to a girl with wavy brown hair and a beauty mark underneath her left eye. Pretty, he knew, the way girls are meant to be. She had a sleepy smile, as though forever sinking into a warm bath, and appeared unaware of the proceedings. All an act, he later discovered; nobody noticed more, took more precise social notes, than Bertha.

They have that in common, the fight to maintain an outward appearance. He must look the Muller man, and she must look a normal woman – when in fact she could run the company with one arm.

The company. At least he has not let his father down in that regard. They have different styles, he and his father, but they work well together. In his middle age, Walter has become something of a fat cat, his obsession with destroying unionism bordering on the pathological. On several occasions, he and Roosevelt have exchanged words. 'I have never liked the man. He reminds me of a child in need of a spanking.'

Louis, on the other hand, prefers to conciliate. You most often get your way by allowing others to believe that they are getting theirs.

The screams grow more frequent. A good sign? Or a bad one? Is she near the end? Childbirth mystifies him. Pregnancy, too. He hardly saw her the entire time; he would leave for work in the morning before she had risen, come home and find that she had already gone to bed. Each time he saw her she seemed to have doubled in size, so enormous by the end that she seemed not a person but an egg with legs.

Dear God, listen to her.

Should she sound like that? He paces. He might not love her in the way people assume, but nobody could listen to that sort of yowling without feeling a twinge of sympathy. The doctor has sequestered her on the fourth floor, along with a trio of nurses and two of her most trusted maids, two unrelated women who look identical to Louis's eye. He never addresses them directly, because he can never remember their names, Delia and . . . Delilah. As if they were not difficult enough to tell apart! Too many names to keep track of, in general. Why is life so complicated? Many days he does not want to talk to anyone but simply to crawl back into bed and sleep.

The screaming goes on for another hour and then, just as Louis has begun to adjust to the noise – as he begins to wish they had kept at least the chef around, for his hunger is becoming *unbearable* – the house goes dead still.

His heart hiccups. A wild thought: she is dead. Bertha is dead, and he is again a bachelor. The best of times, the worst of times. He will be free, blissfully free – but only until they force him to remarry. And they will do that as quickly as possible. They will find him some pink flower, an innocent ten years younger than he, a girl who knows nothing of his history; who will perceive him as slain by grief; who will want to attend to him, soothe him; who will strive to supplant Bertha's ghost by climbing into his bed every single night . . . Every single night! Oh, God!

His chest aches. He will have to produce another heir. He wishes she would scream again, just to let him know that she's alive. Scream, for God's sake. Scream and I'll know you've gotten your child. He might not love Bertha but he could do worse. More than that – more than that: he has a sort of affection for her. If she died he would be stuck in that house, all alone, incapable of giving orders. Bertha runs the ship. Bertha knows everyone's name and how much they are paid; it is fear of Bertha that prevents them from running off with all the valuables. He holds her in high esteem. She is the Prime Mover. He might even love her a little, as one loves a longtime friend. He does not want her to die, even as visions of liberation whirl through his mind; the stress of clashing emotions speeds up his pacing, the enormous brass coat of arms above the fireplace winking at him malignantly with each circuit. Scream, for God's sake, scream!

Unable to stomach any more, he barges up the stairs and through the door to the designated suite. Beyond the sitting room is a bedroom they have covered in heavy sheets of rubber and canvas. He saw them setting up several weeks ago and wondered what in the world could possibly require such precautions. Did the baby *explode* out?

The bedroom door is locked but inside they are murmuring. Louis pounds.

'Hello! Hello, what's happening!'

The murmuring ceases.

From within, the doctor says, 'Mr Muller?'

'What's happening with my wife.'

The doctor says something Louis cannot make out.

'Bertha?' Louis has had enough. He rattles the knob and the door swings out abruptly, a nurse barreling into him, ushering him away from the threshold. He tries to see past her but a second nurse has already shut the door.

'I demand to know what's happening in there.'

'Please come this way, sir.'

'Did you hear me? Tell me—'

The nurse takes him by the arm and pulls him from the room.

'What are you *doing*.'

'Sir, it's best for the mother and child if you came with me.'

'I – I will not—' He wrests away. 'What was all that screaming about? Answer me or I'll put you out into the street.'

'The birth was normal, sir.'

'Then what was all that screaming?'

'That's normal, sir.'

'Then why did it *stop* like that? Where's Bertha?'

'She's resting, sir. She had a spell.'

'What do you mean a spell?'

'Labor can be trying, sir.' She has no expression but Louis feels distinctly mocked.

'I want to see her,' he says.

'Please, sir, why don't you return downstairs, and when the doctor feels it safe—'

'Nonsense. She's my wife, it's my house, and I intend to go where I please.' He starts to move forward but the nurse blocks his path.

'It's better if you let her rest, sir.'

'You've made your position clear. Now move.'

'I can ask the doctor to come speak with you, if you'd like.'

'Right away.'

She bows her head and turns to go, leaving Louis in the middle of the hall.

Five minutes later, the doctor emerges. He has done his best to tidy up, but Louis is still aghast to see flecks of blood on his collar.

'Congratulations are in order, Mr Muller. You have a new daughter.'

A daughter? Unacceptable. He needs a son. He wants to tell the doctor to try again. 'Where's Bertha.'

'She's resting.'

'I need to speak with her.'

'Your wife has undergone a terrific ordeal,' says the doctor. His hands are trembling. 'It's best if we let her rest.'

'Has something happened to her?'

'Not at all, sir. As I said, she's tired, but otherwise perfectly healthy.'

Louis is no fool. He knows something is wrong. He repeats his question, and the doctor again assures him. But those shaking hands . . . A new thought occurs to him.

'Is something wrong with the baby?'

The doctor opens his mouth but Louis interrupts him.

'I want to see her. Now. Take me to her.'

Again the doctor hesitates. 'Come with me.'

As they pass through the sitting room, Louis thinks about what will happen if the baby dies. They must try again – but wouldn't they have to do that, regardless? A girl will not do. If the baby dies, he will be sad most of all for Bertha, for whom the entire process – conception to delivery – has been a project undertaken virtually single-handedly. Having invested so much hope and desire in one moment, she will be inconsolable until she has a real, live child at her breast. He owes her that much. He promises himself that if the baby dies, he will put up a brave face and get her pregnant again as soon as possible.

The doctor is talking but Louis has not paid attention: '. . . such things happen.'

What is he talking about, such things. Stillbirths aren't rare. Louis knows that. His mother had one before him. Out with it, he wants to tell the doctor. Be a man.

A second bedroom branches from the sitting room. The maid – for the life of him, Louis cannot recall which one – has a bundle on her lap, and her rocking chair creaks soothingly. A flash of red flesh; a brief cry; it's alive.

He did not expect to feel joy. He has not prepared himself. Without having seen the child's face he knows that he will love her, and that this love will be different from any of his previous loves – all of which have revolved around his own gratification. What he feels now is a crushing need to protect.

The doctor takes the bundle from the maid. Louis almost leaps to snatch the baby away. His child. He doesn't want her held by those shaky hands.

The doctor shows Louis how to support the head, resting the bundle in the crook of Louis's arm. Her face is still mostly obscured by a fold of cloth.

'I can't see her,' he says.

Looking queasy, the doctor peels back the cloth. 'You must understand,' he says. 'We have no means of predicting.'

Louis looks at his daughter and is confused. They appear to have given him a Chinese baby. Bertha has been unfaithful? He does not understand. His daughter has a small mouth, and her tongue protrudes in a sloppy way . . . and her eyes. They are narrow and slanted, the irises spotted with white. The doctor speaks of mental defects and therapies of various sorts, words Louis hears but does not understand.

'As I said, we cannot be sure why such things occur, as they are impossible for science to predict, yet, and unfortunately I cannot offer you a definitive course of treatment. Very little success has resulted thus far, although much research remains to . . .'

Louis does not understand any of this babble, does not understand talk of 'mongoloidism', does not understand why the maid has begun to weep quietly. He understands only that he has a new cause for shame, and that some things cannot be hidden, not even in America.

EIGHT

As soon as I saw the letter, I called McGrath.

He said, 'You remember how to get here?'

This time I did some advance planning and hired a car and driver for the following day. It took me the better part of an afternoon to unmount and pack up the journals, which I took along with photocopies of the Cherubs and the newspaper portraits that I'd dug up. I couldn't think of anything else that would help except the letter itself, and that I had in a large Ziploc bag, imagining that McGrath would whip out a fingerprint kit and plug the information into a database yielding Cracke's location and life history.

Instead he just chuckled. He put the bag with the letter on the table and stared at its tight command: STOP. After a few moments he said, 'I don't know why I'm still reading this. I'm pretty sure I know what's going to happen next.'

'What do I do?'

'Do?'

'With that.'

'Well, you could take it to the police.'

'You are the police.'

'Ex,' he said. 'Sure. You can take it to the police if you want. I'll call ahead for you, if you'd like. Let me save you some time: they won't be able to do a thing. You don't know who he is, you don't really know that he wrote it, and even if you had those two nailed, he hasn't broken the law.' He smiled like a death's-head. 'Anybody can send a letter like this, it's in the Constitution.'

'Then why am I here?'

'You tell me.'

'You implied that you had something to offer me,' I said.

'I did?'

'You asked if I remembered how to get here.'

'So I did,' he said.

I waited. 'And?'

'And, well. Now that you're here, I'm just as confused as you are.'

We both looked at the page.

STOP STOP STOP

The same tendency toward repetition that had previously fascinated me now seemed repellent; where before I saw passion I now read malice. Art or threat? Victor Cracke's letter could very well go up on my gallery wall. Were I so inclined, I could probably turn it around to Kevin Hollister for a nice profit.

'I'd hold on to it,' said McGrath. 'In case anything gets more serious, you want to have it on file, to show the cops.'

I said, 'Plus you never know what it might be worth one day.'

McGrath smiled. 'Now, what about that drawing.'

I handed the photocopy of the Cherubs to McGrath. While he studied it I noticed that the number of pill bottles on the dining-room table seemed to have grown in the space of a week. McGrath, as well, had changed: he'd lost weight, and his skin had acquired an unhealthy sheen. I could make out the prescriptions on some of the bottles, but not knowing anything about medicine, I couldn't draw any conclusions except that he seemed to be in a lot of pain.

'That's Henry Strong.' He lightly touched the Cherubs. 'That's Elton LaRae.'

'I know,' I said. I took out the photocopies of the microfiche and showed him the pictures. 'This is where he got them from.' I didn't mention my misgivings about this theory, but McGrath leapt on me right away.

'I have no idea,' I admitted when he asked how Cracke would be able to connect Henry Strong with the others.

'We also have to ask ourselves why he chose to draw these particular people, out of everyone in the paper.'

'I thought about that,' I said. 'You have to bear in mind that he drew literally thousands and thousands of faces. There could be all sorts of real people in his works. The presence of these people only proves that he was thorough.'

'But this is panel number one,' said McGrath. 'They were important.'

'That's subjective,' I said.

'Who said I was objective?'

It felt bizarre arguing with him: me, the art dealer, pressing for a clearer standard of truth; him, the policeman, claiming his critical faculties were sharp enough to draw inferences about the intent of the artist. Strange, too, that he had anticipated my asking certain questions. I felt a weird sort of mental synergy, and I think he did, too, because we stopped talking then and sat looking at the page.

'I'll tell you what,' he said, 'he could really draw.'

I nodded.

He put his finger on another of the Cherubs. 'Alex Jendrzejewski. Ten years old. His mother sends him down to the store before dinnertime to buy some groceries. We find a bottle of milk cracked open on the corner of Forty-fourth and Newtown. It'd snowed that afternoon, so we picked up some tire tracks, as well as a footprint. No witnesses.' He rubbed his head. 'That was end of January 1967, and this time the papers picked up the story and ran with it. "Are Your Children Safe?" and that sort of jazz. He must've got spooked, because he didn't do anything for a long time. Or maybe he wasn't a cold-weather sort of guy.'

'There are fewer children out on the street in the winter.'

'You're right. That could be it, too.' He pointed to another Cherub. 'Abie Kahn, I told you about him, he was the fifth.'

'No witnesses.'

'Well, that's what I thought. I was rereading the case file, and I saw that there was someone we talked to, a neighborhood type, one of these women who sit out on their porch all day long. She remembered seeing a strange car go past.'

'That's it?'

He nodded. 'She told us she knew what everyone drove. Like she made a point of knowing. And this car didn't fit in the neighborhood.'

Had Victor owned a car? I didn't think so, and told McGrath.

'That in itself doesn't mean anything. He could have stolen one.'

'I can't see him being capable of breaking into a car.'

'You can't see him at all. You don't know anything about him. Can you see him being capable of this?' He gestured to the Cherubs.

I said nothing. I knew some of what McGrath was telling me about the victims; I had read the articles in the paper. The critical difference between seeing a story in print and getting it from him directly was the fatherly devotion that came through as he talked.

'That kid, LaRae – him I felt bad for. I felt bad for all of them, but this kid . . . He's a solitary type, likes to take long walks by himself. I don't think he had too many friends. You can tell from the way he's smiling that he doesn't like to have his picture taken. He was the oldest of the bunch, twelve, but small for his age. He had a rough time at school because of his

111

size, and because he's got a single mother, black. You can imagine the kind of ribbing the poor kid took. And the mother, God, it broke my goddamned heart. White husband runs off, leaving her with the kid. And then *he* ends up dead. Oh, brother. She looked like I tore her heart out with my bare hands.'

Silence.

'You want a joint?' he asked.

I looked at him.

'Cause I'm having one.' With difficulty, he rose and shuffled into the kitchen. I heard him open a drawer, and I craned over the table to look. I've seen thousands of joints rolled in my day, but never by a policeman, and never with such diligence. He finished, resealed the bag, and returned to the dining room.

'This works better than anything they give me,' he said, lighting up.

I then asked a supremely silly question. 'Do you have a prescription?'

His laughter sent out little billows of smoke. 'This ain't California, buddy.'

Based on the poster in the front window and the bin Laden wanted sign, I had assumed that McGrath wasn't especially liberal. I asked his political affiliation.

'Libertarian,' he said. 'Drives my daughter crazy.'

'She's . . .'

'Bloodiest heart you'll ever find.' He inhaled, and said in a choked voice, 'Doesn't stop her from putting people away. Her boyfriend used to bust her ass about that.'

I should have been less disappointed than I was to hear that Samantha was already attached. I had spoken to her for a grand total of – what? Perhaps twenty minutes. Nevertheless I couldn't resist reaching over to take the joint from McGrath.

He watched me take a big hit. 'That's an offense punishable by law,' he said.

I made as if to throw the joint away, but he snatched it back.

'I'm dying,' he said. 'What's your excuse?'

NEXT WE CHECKED THE JOURNALS. As I opened them up, I said that unless the weather or Cracke's dietary habits had some bearing on the case, I didn't see the point. McGrath agreed, but all the same he wanted to look at the dates of the murders.

Henry Strong had gone missing on the Fourth of July 1966. The weather journal entry for that day read

sunny.   high of 93.   humidity 90%.

'Sounds about right,' said McGrath. 'Queens in July.'

The next few days proved equally uninteresting.

sunny.   high of 91.   humidity 78%.
sunny.   high of 97.   humidity 82%.
partially cloudy.   high of 85.   humidity 90%.

'Are these numbers accurate?' I asked.

'How the hell would I know?' He paged through the journal. 'I'm not getting very much out of this, are you?'

I shook my head.

'What about the one with the food?'

MONDAY JULY 4 1966
breakfast   scrambled eggs
lunch   apple ham & cheese
dinner   apple ham & cheese

TUESDAY JULY 5 1966

breakfast	scrambled eggs
lunch	apple ham & cheese
dinner	apple ham & cheese

'This is a waste of time,' I said.
'Probably,' he said. 'Let's look at Eddie Cardinale.'

WEDNESDAY AUGUST 3 1966

breakfast	scrambled eggs
lunch	apple ham & cheese
dinner	apple ham & cheese

'You know what I'd like to know,' he said. 'How the guy could eat the same damn thing day in and day out. That's the real mystery.'

SUNDAY JANUARY 22 1967

breakfast	scrambled eggs
lunch	apple ham & cheese
dinner	apple ham & cheese

'Happy now?' I asked.
'Hold the fucking phone.'

MONDAY JANUARY 23 1967

breakfast	oatmeal
lunch	apple ham & cheese
dinner	apple ham & cheese

McGrath looked at me. 'That's the day after Alex Jendrzejewski disappeared.'

I reread the journal entry.

breakfast   oatmeal

'I know,' I said. 'So what.'

'So, it's a difference.'

'Oatmeal? Who gives a shit?' Some part of my brain noted that we'd gotten a lot looser-tongued since our smoking break. 'Who cares about fucking oatmeal?'

'It's a difference, and that's significant.'

'Not the same thing.'

McGrath told me to lift the Jendrzejewski file out of the box. Inside, I found the familiar snapshot: blunt-cut hair, square teeth, beachball face, pug nose. Little Alex, had he grown up, probably would have turned out plug-ugly, had fate not frozen him cute.

'We talked to the mother,' he said, turning over pages of transcript. 'I remember that. She sent the kid to the market. That milk bottle, I remember that.'

'You said you got a footprint.'

'No telling if it was the right guy, though. Lotta people around that area.'

'Then how did he snatch the boy without being seen?'

'Maybe he lured him into a car. He might have offered him a ride home. It was freezing that night. Check the weather book, you'll see.'

I did. The forecast had called for snow throughout the evening.

'Where are you,' he said to the file box.

'What are you looking for?'

'I'm loo – ah. Here. Listen to this, this is the mother talking. "I sent Alex to the store." Detective Gordan: "What time?" Pamela Jendrzejewski: "About five o'clock. I needed some things."'

'Who's Detective Gordan.'

'My old partner,' he said without looking up. His lips moved as he skimmed the transcript. 'Mm, mm, mm, come on. I swear to God I remember her saying something about . . .' He didn't finish.

'About what.'

'It's not here,' he said. He found another transcript and let out a triumphant grunt. 'This is it.'

I scooted my chair over to have a closer look. The transcript was of an interview conducted by Detectives L. McGrath and J. Gordan, New York Police Department, 114th precinct, January 25, 1967. The interviewee was Charles Petronakis, owner and proprietor of the corner market where Alex's mother sent him to fetch groceries.

Det McGrath: You remember seeing the boy?

Charles Petronakis: I saw him, yes.

M: When did you see him?

P: He came in about five fifteen.

M: Was there anybody with him?

P: No.

Det Gordan: Was there anyone in the store at the time aside from you?

P: No.

G: Did you notice anything unusual, either with the boy or anyone outside the store?

P: I don't think so. It was very cold that night, I didn't see too many people. The boy was the first one I seen all afternoon. I was getting ready to close up when he came in. He wanted some milk, some oatmeal, and sugar. I said I could help him carry it home if he waited a few minutes for me to close up. He told me he couldn't wait, he had to go or his mother would get mad at him. So he went

I stopped reading and looked at McGrath, who picked up a pencil and drew a circle around the word oatmeal.

NINE

I have no early memories of my father. This is because he was most often out of the house. He worked (still does, as far as I know) incredibly hard, sometimes eighteen hours a day, and although I wasn't around to witness the demise of his first three marriages, I can guess that his habit of sleeping at the office didn't help. How I even came to be conceived is something of a mystery to me. The age gap between me and my siblings has often led me to believe that I was an accident, and for him, at least, not a happy one.

In his defense – a phrase that rarely crosses my lips, so you can be certain that what I'm about to say is true – it must be said that he singlehandedly restored the Muller name to glory after inheriting a corporate structure swollen with inefficiencies. He downsized before downsizing was downsizing; and he spun off or closed antiquated branches of the company that he had no real business running: a commercial bakery in New Haven, a textile mill in Secaucus. What he understood was real estate, so he focused on that, thereby turning an already healthy sum of old money into a new, towering heap.

It is solely to my mother's credit that I am not spoiled worse than I am. Despite the lavishness of our surroundings, and the dozens of people who waited on me from the moment I entered the world, she did her best to ensure that I never considered wealth a substitute for decency. It's hard to be rich and a true humanist. She was. She believed in the inherent value of every human being, taking that as the premise for her actions. Children have exquisitely sensitive bullshit detectors, and that's why her lessons made an impression on me. If my father had lectured me similarly, I would have seen right through him; he seldom acknowledged the staff, and then only curtly. My mother, on the other hand, did not condescend to the people she employed; at the same time, she didn't pretend that she was their friend, which is in its own way equally insulting. She always said hello and good-bye and please and thank you; if a door was held open for her, she hurried to step inside. She held a few doors of her own. I once saw her stop and help push a stuck taxi out of a snowbank.

I've never fully understood how she tolerated – let alone loved – my father, who could be so indifferent to the distress of others. I can only hope and assume that he was a better man before she died. Either that or she saw in him something invisible to the rest of us. Or maybe she liked a challenge.

My awareness of him thus begins with her death, and the most pungent memory is also the earliest. It was the morning of the funeral and I was getting dressed – or, rather, resisting attempts by the nanny to get me dressed. It's my fault for throwing a tantrum. I probably should have felt the numbness in the air, known that I had a burden to shoulder. Looking back I realize that I was probably more confused than anything else: for days people had been acting skittish around me, making me feel like *I* was the source of everyone's misery. I was in no mood to confront the public; I didn't want anything to do with anybody, and I certainly didn't want to be forced into a suit and tie.

The service was scheduled for nine A.M., and by eight thirty I was still half-dressed. If the nanny managed to tuck in my shirt, I would untuck it while she reached for the necktie. Then when she began again to tuck it back in I would start unbuttoning it from the top. She was on the verge of tears by the time Tony Wexler arrived to escort me downstairs. He found me pulling off my pants and stepped in to take over, and as he reached for my arm I slugged him in the eye.

Normally Tony was a model of patience. (In later years, he would endure much worse.) But that morning he wasn't up to the task. He might have yelled or smacked me across the face; he had that kind of authority over me. He might have told the nanny to hold me down. Instead, he took more decisive action: he went for my father.

It was a Friday. My mother had died on the Tuesday prior, after three days in a coma. During those three days I had not been allowed in to see her – something I've never forgiven my father for. I think in some idiotic way he intended to protect me, but even thinking about it now makes me tense. Since I had been barred from the room, and he had barred himself inside to watch her slip away, we hadn't seen much of each other for a week, my father and I; I had been with the nanny or else Tony. So this would be our first moment together as a family, a downsized unit of two. Though too young for symbolism, I had some idea that the conversation about to take place would be a neat preview of life without a mother.

He came into the room silently. That's his way. My father is tall, like me; like his own father, he has a very slight stoop. He was at the time over fifty, but his hair was still dark and thick, like his mother's. That morning he wore a black suit, white shirt and gray tie; what I saw first, however, were the caps of his shoes. I was lying on the ground, refusing to get up, and these two shiny torpedo heads were coming toward me.

I rolled over and buried my face in the carpet. There was a long silence. For a moment I thought he had left. Then I opened my eyes and saw that he was right there, still looking down at me, although now he was holding the pre-knotted tie, as though it were a leash and I a stubborn puppy.

'If you don't get dressed,' he said, 'then you'll go exactly as you are.'

'Fine,' I said.

The next thing I knew I was being dragged, kicking and screaming, down the hall to the elevator. The nanny had me by one arm, a maid by the other; my father was two steps ahead, never looking back as I howled. You can imagine that the house was especially quiet that morning, so this tantrum sounded even more horrific and piercing than my usual ones. As the four of us stepped into the elevator I saw my father wince. This only encouraged me. Maybe if I shouted loud enough they would let me go. We glided down to the first floor, where the doors parted on a scene that startled me into silence: twenty-some-odd faces – women tearstained, men flushed and grimacing – all staring at me as I thrashed against my captors. The entire house staff had gathered in mourning to see my father and me off.

At that moment I realized what I was doing – what was happening – how I looked – what humiliation I stood to suffer if I didn't get properly dressed. I began to beg my father to allow me to go back upstairs. He said nothing, just stepped out of the elevator and walked stiffly through the parted ranks of the grieving, again two steps ahead of me and the nanny and the maid, who obeyed my father's orders by carrying me, half-naked, through that gauntlet of horrified stares and down the front steps to the idling limousine. Tony had my pants waiting in the car.

THE PROBLEM WITH COLD CASES, McGrath explained, was that they didn't kill anybody. They didn't crash planes into buildings. They didn't release toxic gas on the A train, or detonate themselves in the middle of Central Park, or spray bullets into a crowded open-air market. National and local priorities being what they were, it had gotten harder and harder for cold-case detectives to find the time, money and departmental approval they needed.

McGrath had worked the squad for the last eight years of his career and kept in touch. 'Solid bunch, tip to tail,' he said. 'They're dedicated guys, and they don't like to give up. But it's not up to them. The world's a different place.'

Different meant that old murders got in line and waited. It meant that even as the line grew, the number of detectives working the cases shrank, as the sharpest minds got bounced to counterterrorism or got fed up and left. It meant that literally thousands of boxes of evidence – boxes much like the one McGrath had in his dining room, the box we would spend the next several weeks poring over – had gone unexamined for decades, even though the intervening years had turned the DNA inside to gold.

'Right before I left,' he said, 'we got a Justice Department grant. Five hundred grand to use for pulling old DNA. You know what, I *still* don't think they've used all that money. Crap just sits there, waiting for someone to pick it up. They don't have the manpower. Every time you want something, you have to schlep down to storage, send it to the lab, fill out the paperwork – how the hell are twelve guys supposed to do all that for every unsolved crime in New York? And then we got people breathing down our necks, the Feds whining about port security, the press making noise about stuff that happened last week. You try being the one who gets to approach his commander, "Hey, you know what, I have something thirty years old that I think I might *maybe* be able to put a name on. Sure the perp is probably dead, but wouldn't you like to ease the family's minds?" Never gonna happen.'

Since retiring, he had kept himself amused by paging through old cases that continued to bother him. His former colleagues were all too happy to have an experienced thinker shouldering a small portion of their burden. Most of the time, he said, what solved a cold case was the passage of time, as witnesses who had been afraid to talk now came forward. That had its own set of drawbacks: namely, that people forgot what they'd seen or died before bothering to tell. With the Queens murders, though, there hadn't *been* anyone, willing or unwilling, to talk to. No rumors, no drunken bragging in a bar. It seemed hopeless. But McGrath had long ago prom-ised himself to go down swinging.

'What else am I gonna do?' he asked me. 'Watch *Dr Phil*?'

HAVING GOTTEN USED TO running the gallery while I was working with the drawings, Nat was all too pleased to take the reins back, and so for a few weeks my life went like this: a car would come for me around three o'clock; I would get in and endure the fight to the Brooklyn Battery Tunnel; through the rear window I would watch the Manhattan skyline turn to backdrop, watch the gray highway, listen for gulls circling above Riis Park. We would pull up outside the entrance to Breezy Point just as the bar was setting out the marker board with the evening's drink specials. By four thirty I would be sitting at McGrath's dining-room table, talking about the case. A good por-tion of that time was spent waiting for him to go to the bathroom.

Most nights I stayed until Samantha showed up. Actually, my cue to leave was the sound of her coming up the front steps. There was always a moment when she had to put down the bags of food and her work stuff and look for her keys, which apparently were never where she had last put them. By the time she succeeded in finding them I had opened the front door for her, and while she gathered her bags back up we would have a short and invariably banal conversation. She seemed both puzzled by and grateful for my presence, asking in a detached way if we'd turned anything up. No, I would tell her. She would shrug and tell me not to give up. Really what she meant was: don't leave him alone. If I tried to help her with the bags she waved me away, straggling into the darkened house as McGrath called out to me, 'Same time Wednesday!'

I justified taking off from work by telling myself that I had to protect my artist. I wanted to keep McGrath on a short tether, so that if he turned up anything on Victor Cracke, I'd be the first to know, and could apply the correct spin. As for McGrath, I assumed that his motivations were similar.

By making me a party to the investigation, he could prevent me from interfering, or at least be better positioned if I had done so. Not to mention that – incapacitated, virtually alone – he needed a pair of legs, and I had been the first person to come along.

I had another motive, though, in going to Breezy Point. Being there gave me those few moments with his daughter.

Now that's a detective-novel trope for you: instantaneous romance. But this one requires a little explanation, as I am not generally subject to infatuations. Besides, I had Marilyn. As I mentioned before, she and I expected of each other a certain amount of extracurricular activity. Or at least I did: the size of her sexual appetite put most men's to shame, and we spent too many nights in our own apartments for me to believe that she had never taken home one of the opening-night waitstaff. As for me, I didn't fool around too much. Having gotten a lot out of my system between the ages of fifteen and twenty-four, by the time I hit thirty I realized how lucky I'd been never to catch anything more virulent than a few choice words and a faceful of undergraduate-caliber champagne. There had been only two or three other women in the last five years. You could blame my age, but the fact remained that I still had a full head of hair, I still fit into the same size pants, I still ran four times a week. I hadn't lost my edge; I'd merely learned that the old saw about quantity and quality applied even to sex. Sex without any sort of challenge bored me. To a large extent that explained why I stuck with Marilyn as long as I did: she never failed to keep me on my toes, and she could be ten women in a given day.

Surely, I had less in common with Samantha than with the women I ran into on a daily basis at the gallery, most of whom were trying to be Marilyn. And nothing about our brief encounters on the front steps of McGrath's house suggested anything beyond two people passing a few cordial words, two people seated together on a plane. No prophetic words, no lingering glances, not that I can recall. I wish I'd paid closer attention.

*

MCGRATH AND I BEGAN BY CALLING AROUND. Most of the people mentioned in the files were either untraceable or dead – victims' parents, the
grocer who sold Alex Jendrzejewski his oatmeal, the woman on the porch
in Forest Hills who had seen the strange vehicle – raising the distinct
probability that the killer himself was dead, too.

That reduced the case to paper and physical evidence, the latter in storage at the Queens property clerk. To gain access, McGrath called a friend,
a detective named Richard Soto, who said that if McGrath wanted to go
fishing, God bless.

All the victims had been found outdoors, making analysis of the forensics that much more difficult. The boys had been killed elsewhere and taken
to the dumping grounds or else left outside to be ravaged by weather. Either
way, little remained that could be considered evidence, still less that could
reliably be connected to the killer. There's a lot of junk lying around New
York City, and apparently it was no different in the 1960s. ('It was worse,'
said McGrath. 'We have Giuliani to thank for that.')

Among the items in storage were a cigarette butt, the broken milk
bottle, the cast of the footprint. There was a very slender partial fingerprint, taken from a discarded coffee cup, which itself seemed to have gone
missing in the intervening years. Everything went back to the lab for
reanalysis and reprinting. Of greatest significance was a pair of boy's jeans
crusted with blood and semen. That, too, went to the lab; and when it did,
I had an idea that the case would soon be solved. But McGrath told me to
be patient. The soonest we could expect an answer was December.
'They're still IDing 9/11 remains. Not to mention that whatever they give
us is useless without something to compare it to, something we know was
his. We need to get someone over to that apartment.'

'There's nothing there,' I said. 'I had the place cleaned out.'

McGrath smiled wanly. 'Why did you do that.'

'Because it was a pigsty. Every time I went in I had a coughing fit.'

'Where's all the art?'

'Storage.'

He began to question me: was there anything that might have traces of DNA on it? A toothbrush? A hairbrush?

'A pair of shoes,' I said. 'A sweater. I don't know, maybe I left something behind.'

'Did you?'

'I doubt it. We catalogued everything.'

'Shit. Well, all right. Can't hurt to look. Are you free Monday, around lunch?'

In theory, I had an appointment to show the drawings. The client was an Indian metals tycoon, stopping in New York on his way to the fair in Miami. We'd met at the last Biennale, and since then I had been stoking the embers of a correspondence. This was my first opportunity to make good. If I tried to reschedule I would likely lose him; he was notoriously fickle and impatient.

I very easily could have asked for another day; McGrath didn't seem to be demanding Monday.

'I'm free,' I said and felt the rush of flagrant disregard.

This was, I believe, the first sign that my life had begun to change.

'Good,' said McGrath. 'Someone'll be there. Not me, but I'm sure you already figured that out.'

'Do you ever get out?'

'On a good day, I'm strong enough to piss off the front porch.' He cackled. 'It's not too bad. I have cable. I get all my books off the computer. I got Sammy. So, not too bad.' He passed me the joint. 'Well, you know, that's horseshit. It's like prison.'

I inhaled, said nothing.

He said, 'Every morning the wind comes through here smelling like salt. If memory serves, the beach is nice.'

'It is.'

He nodded and motioned for the joint. 'All right. We got work to do.'

*

ON THE APPOINTED MONDAY, I stood outside the entrance to Muller Courts, right where Tony had stood for me nine months prior. I hadn't been to the building since July, and as I waited for McGrath's team to show up, I felt guilty, as though I was about to throw a party inside a crypt. I had done my best to separate the art on the gallery walls from an actual person who lived in an actual room. I made him a ghost. Now, though, I came in search of the opposite – a literal piece of his body. The better metaphor might be graverobbing.

Who exactly was McGrath's team, anyway? He hadn't said anything more specific, and I kept looking for a big white police van loaded with men in Kevlar.

Instead, I got a small blue Toyota.

'Don't look so surprised,' said Samantha. 'Who else do you think is going to give up their lunch break? I'm a huge sucker or I wouldn't be here.' She seemed to be in a good mood, or at least in a better mood than she was when I saw her in Breezy Point. If going home depressed her, I wasn't in any position to criticize.

She whistled as she tore open a package of peanut butter and crackers and offered me one. 'Nutritious and delicious.'

'I'll pass.'

'I survive on these,' she said.

'Then I certainly don't want to take one.'

'My blood is about two percent peanut butter . . . He didn't tell you I'd be coming?'

'No.'

'That's hilarious. What did you expect, a guy in a lab coat?'

'I was thinking more along the lines of a SWAT team.'

'Do we need a SWAT team?'

'I hope not. I didn't realize that collecting DNA was part of your job.'

'None of this is part of my job. It's a way to keep him occupied.'

'You don't think he's on to anything?'

'Based on what, the oatmeal theory?'

I nodded. 'That, and everything else.'

'As far as I can tell, there isn't much else. It's interesting, but I don't think anyone's going to prison because of what they ate for breakfast. Besides, you don't know where the guy is, do you?'

'No.'

'There you go. I'd rather spend my time going after people I know are guilty, and that I can find.'

'You must know how to track people down. You must have to do it all the time.'

'Not really,' she said. 'That's up to the police. Besides, people who commit crimes are stupid. Most of the time, they're right where we expect them to be: in their mother's basement, getting drunk and touching themselves.'

'Then why are you here?'

'Daughterly love. Anyway, in response to your question, no. I'm not collecting anything. I have a friend coming to do that. Now I owe her three favors.'

Before I could ask what the first two were, she turned to wave at a small dark woman coming up the block. She had curly black hair and purple lips and wore a form-fitting leather jacket. She set down her bag and rose up on tiptoes to kiss Samantha on the cheek. 'Hey doll.' Then she offered her hand to me, revealing a tattoo of a bleeding rose on the inside of her wrist. 'Annie Lundley.'

'Ethan Muller.'

'Pleased to meetcha.' She pointed a finger at Samantha. 'That's three.'

Samantha nodded. 'Let's go.'

'I THOUGHT MY PLACE WAS SMALL.' From the threshold, Annie peered into the apartment. She had on latex gloves and a hairnet. 'You didn't leave much when you cleaned up, huh.'

'Not really,' I said. 'I like things neat.'

'How many people were in here?'

'A lot.'

'We're going to need to rule them out, so make a list.' She checked her watch and sighed. 'You might want to come back in four or five hours.'

Samantha and I stepped outside to give Annie the full run of the roost.

'You don't have to stay,' I said.

'That's funny,' she said. 'I was just going to say the same thing to you.'

'Don't you have to get back to work?'

'Eventually. Civil service isn't as rigorous as you'd think.'

'I don't think it'd be that rigorous at all.'

'Then you'd be right on the money. They're still out to lunch. The guys in my office will do anything to avoid their jobs. You don't know how much porn they send me on an hourly basis.'

'It's a nice thing you're doing,' I said. 'For your father.'

She half smiled. 'Thanks.' Her tone implied that I had no right to grade her behavior. 'It's hard to remember that when he calls up and tells me I have to be somewhere on Monday, noon sharp. He can be pretty over-bearing. Tunnel vision. It's not just this, it's everything.'

'He probably doesn't realize he's putting you out.' I felt hypocritical defending McGrath; who better than I to sympathize with someone suffering under a father's ridiculous demands? But things your own parents do to drive you crazy can seem piteous and understandable when it's someone else's parents doing them.

'Oh, he realizes it. Sure he does. He knows it's a pain in the ass. That's *why* he asks me. I'm the only one who'll do it. If you don't believe me, ask my mother. I'm sure she'll be happy to share her war stories with you.'

I didn't ask about Mrs McGrath. I had a feeling she lived someplace far away.

Samantha leaned against the wall. 'So you're an art dealer. That must be fun.'

'It has its moments.'

'More glamorous than my job.'

'It really isn't. Most of the time I'm sending e-mails and making phone calls.'

'You want to switch for the day? You can interview rape victims.'

'That sounds awful.'

'I hate to say it, but you get used to it pretty fast.' Her phone rang. 'Excuse me.' She walked down the hall to take the call.

Boyfriend calling, I guessed. I tried to listen in but couldn't, not unless I got up and followed her. She talked for a good fifteen minutes. Eventually, I opened the door to the apartment and poked my head in. I saw Annie crouched near the baseboards, slowly playing a flashlight back and forth.

'You really do like things neat,' she said.

Samantha appeared behind me. 'Anything?'

'Hair, but I don't think they belong to your man.'

'Why not?'

'Did your man have a pink dye job?'

'That would be Ruby,' I said. 'My assistant.'

'I have to tell you,' Annie said, 'I'll keep looking, but I don't think I'm going to get much here. What about that other stuff you told me about?'

'The storage locker?'

'Yeah. What's there.'

'A hundred and fifty thousand pieces of paper,' I said. 'And a pair of old shoes.'

'Delicious,' said Annie. 'I can't wait.'

TWO DAYS LATER I had another appointment with McGrath, but when I showed up nobody answered my knocks. I pounded and pounded, and then I tried the door. It was open. I went inside and called his name. From the bathroom came a weak *Hang on.* I sat at the dining-room table and waited. And waited. And finally I went to the bathroom door and knocked. I heard a retch. I tried the knob but it was locked.

'Lee? Are you all right?'

'Yeah.' Another retch.

'Lee?'

'Hold your fucking horses.' He sounded awful; and when he opened the door, and I saw how he looked, and the blood on the rim of the toilet that he had not quite succeeded in mopping up, I said, 'Jesus Christ.'

He shuffled past me. 'Help me with the box.'

'You need to get to the hospital.'

He said nothing, went to the back room. I followed.

'Lee. Did you hear me?'

'You gonna give me a hand or you want me to lift this myself.'

'You need to see a doctor.'

He cackled.

'You look like shit,' I said.

'Thanks, you too.'

'You need to go to the hospital.'

'You want to drive me?'

'Fine.'

'You're not supposed to say *yes*, you're supposed to stop arguing with me.'

'I'm saying yes.'

'My guy, you need an appointment to see him, you can't show up unannounced.'

'Then I'm calling an ambulance.'

'For crissake,' he said. He sounded grief-stricken. 'Pick up the box and—' He erupted in coughs. His hand came away from his mouth bloody.

I picked up the phone on the desk, managing to dial 9-1 before

McGrath hobbled over and wrestled the receiver away from me. He was surprisingly strong for someone in his condition, and he also had the protection of knowing that I wouldn't fight back, for fear of hurting him. He unplugged the receiver and put it in the pocket of his robe. He pointed at the box.

I stood there, trying to decide whether to use my cell phone. He probably would have confiscated that, too, or thrown it out the window. I decided to give him a few minutes to calm down before saying anything. I picked up the box and carried it to the dining-room table. 'Sit,' he said. I sat. Silently, we began spreading out our work. His nose ran and I handed him a tissue, which he used and then tossed on the floor with utter contempt – whether for me or his own condition, I couldn't tell.

He said, 'I called Rich Soto about those cases.'

The cases in question consisted of everything Soto could dig up with a similar MO. McGrath had grown fond of the notion that the Queens murderer had other notches in his belt, and that locating one of them might yield more information – a suspect, perhaps; or someone already doing time.

'And?'

'He's getting the files together. He said two weeks, but don't hold your breath.'

'All right.'

He closed his eyes then, and I could see how badly our struggle had worn him out.

'Lee.' I put my hand on his arm. It was warm and frail. 'Maybe we shouldn't work today.'

He nodded.

'Do you want to lie down?'

He nodded again, and I helped him to the back room, settling him into the La-Z-Boy.

'You want the TV on?'

He shook his head.

'You want some water?'

No.

'Are you going to be all right?'

Yes.

'Are you fixed for food? Is Samantha coming?'

'Tomorrow.'

'What about tonight.' I tapped my foot. 'Lee. What are you going to eat for dinner?'

'Fuck dinner,' he croaked.

'Do you want a joint?'

Yes.

I went to the kitchen, found his stash and his rolling papers. It had been a while since I'd rolled one myself, and I ended up spilling flakes all over the floor. I sponged up the debris, found a lighter, and brought McGrath his medicine.

'Thank you.' He groped around for an ashtray that had gotten moved across the room. I brought it to him and watched him smoke.

'Hungry yet?'

He laughed, a balloon losing air.

'I'm going to call Samantha and have her check in on you.'

'Don't,' he said.

I said nothing. I waited until his eyes closed and his breathing changed, then went into the next room and made the call. I told her what had happened.

'I'm coming,' she said.

When I returned to the back room, I found McGrath feebly smiling.

'You're a real buzzkill, you know that?'

'Well what do you want me to do?'

'Go home,' he said.

'No chance.'

'Go to hell,' he mumbled.

I sat on the floor at his feet and waited.

It would take Samantha a while to get over from Borough Hall, and I considered calling the paramedics in the interim. But I didn't. McGrath looked a little better now; he had stopped coughing, and I knew that waking up in the back of an ambulance would be the ultimate assault on his dignity. He wanted to stay where he was, wanted to make his own decisions. I chose to respect that.

By the time she did show up, McGrath was out cold: snoring and wheezing like a man twenty years older. She gave me a wrung-out smile and mouthed *thanks*. I nodded and started to go. As I turned I heard McGrath say, 'We'll work next week.'

Samantha and I exchanged a look.

'I'm going to Miami next week,' I said. 'You know that, right?'

McGrath nodded loosely. 'Have a good trip.'

'I'll be back soon,' I said. 'We'll finish up then.'

TEN

Victor Cracke's debut show closed the next day. Taking the canvases down put me in a terrible mood, although part of me did note with relief that Victor had nothing to complain about anymore. He wanted me to STOP and I had. I also had much less reason to want to come in in the morning.

Three days before I left for Miami, I arranged to have Kevin Hollister's canvas transferred to his home, an hour and a half outside the city, in an upscale area of Suffolk County that he seemed to own wholesale, as though the bucolic fixtures in the distance – a shingled post office, quaintly decrepit farmhouses, gray-and-blue meadows roamed by purple specks of livestock – had been placed there by his landscaper for that authentic feel. I decided to accompany the piece, to oversee its installation and shake hands with the man himself, who sounded pleased as punch to get his art.

At his request, I hired an armored car. It seemed like overkill to me, but then Marilyn explained that I was not only delivering the Cracke drawing but several dozen items Hollister had bought from her.

'How much stuff are we talking about?'

'Eleven million,' she said. 'Give or take.'

My sale no longer seemed that impressive.

'You haven't seen the house yet, have you.'

'No.'

'Well, darlin, you are in for something rare.'

'You're not coming?'

'No. It'll give you boys a chance to bond.'

Considering where I grew up, it takes quite a bit of house to impress me, and the neoclassical monstrosity that appeared as we cleared security (ID check, bomb sweep) and passed through the imposing over-wrought-iron fence didn't do much to heat my bluish blood. It was large but utterly vulgar, a nouveau-riche temple, no doubt filled with hideous statuary and histrionic window treatments. I was surprised that Marilyn had not warned me.

'Holy shit,' said the driver of the armored car. He gawked at a long structure, evidently the garage; outside, a group of men lovingly detailed a Mayfair and a Ferrari. The garage had eight more doors, like the set of a game show.

At the end of a quarter-mile driveway stood a butler and two men in red jumpsuits. I stepped out of the car and waited while the butler gave instructions to the driver. Then I followed the butler up the steps, which seemed wider and shallower than necessary, causing me to lean forward as I walked. I was reminded of the palaces of Mughal kings, their doorways built purposefully low, so that all entering bent their heads.

'I'm Matthew,' said the butler, in a shockingly Californian voice. 'Kevin is waiting for you.'

Contrary to expectation, there wasn't anything ugly inside. In fact, there wasn't anything at all: the entry hall was empty, its walls gallery-white and bathed in cold light. Soaring ceilings and skylights created a dizzying sense of upward drift, and I felt as though trapped in a Minimal-ist dream: Donald Judd's idea of heaven.

'Would you like a Pellegrino?' asked Matthew.

I was still looking at the ceiling. The place did not seem fit for human habitation.

'You'll have to excuse us. We're in the process of redecorating. Every so often Kevin wants a change of pace.'

'This looks more like a total overhaul.'

'We have a designer on retainer. Kevin likes to make use of her. Did you want that Pellegrino?'

'No, thank you.'

'Right this way, please.'

He steered me down a long, blank corridor.

'Where's the art?' I asked.

'Most of it is in the museum. We haven't really had time to do this wing of the house yet. We'll get there. As Kevin says, it's a work in progress.'

I questioned the decision to leave the front part of the house unfinished. Didn't you want to make a good impression on visitors? I supposed that Hollister didn't have many people to impress.

We stepped into an elevator (blank), walked another hallway (blank), made several more turns down several more hallways (all blank), arriving finally at a heavy-looking door. The butler pressed a buzzer. 'Ethan Muller is here.'

The door clicked, and Matthew held it open for me.

'I'll be right back with your beverage,' he said, disappearing before I could tell him that I didn't want a beverage.

Hollister's office was the first room in the house that didn't feel like the inside of an asylum, although I can't say that it was very cozy. To begin with, there were no windows. Then there was the design scheme, which I can best describe as a hypermodern rendering of the traditional English hunting lodge. Low-slung sofas and Eames-like chaises had been scattered throughout the room. There was a steel globe large enough to incite the envy of James Bond villains; there were five identical jet-black bearskin rugs; there was a moosehead cast in resin. The walls, paneled in black leather and brass nailheads, absorbed much of the ambient light, making an already vast, dark and masculine room seem endless, lightless, and more than a little homoerotic. Hollister's desk – a block of smoked, crackled glass spotlit with halogens – was easily the brightest object there, throwing an unearthly halo around its occupant and making him look like the Wizard of Oz.

On a headset phone, he waved for me to sit down.

I sat. Like in the rest of the house, there was no art up – not unless you counted the room itself, which I think you would have to.

'No,' he said and took off the headset. 'Everything in one piece?'

'I think so.'

'Good. I told them to wait for us before they put anything in place. I'd like to get your opinion, if you don't mind.'

'Not at all.'

A small tone sounded on his computer. He glanced at the screen and touched a spot on the desktop. I didn't see anything like a button, but behind me the door clicked open and the butler appeared with a tray of drinks, which he set on a stand before withdrawing in silence.

We talked about the house, which had taken three years to build. The original design scheme 'was my ex-wife's. All Shabby Chic. When we split up, I decided to give the place a fresh start. I hired a designer, *wonderful* girl, extremely creative and intelligent. So far we've been down several roads. First we put in all Arts and Crafts; then we went the art nouveau route. Nothing quite fit, so on to version three-point-oh.'

I might have suggested he find a designer with less *wonderfulness* – which I took to mean T&A – and more forethought. Instead, I said, 'What are you going for?'

'I'd like it to be a little more intimate.'

I nodded, said nothing.

'You don't think that's possible, do you.'

'Anything's possible.'

Hollister grunted a laugh. 'Marilyn told you to agree with whatever I say.'

'She did. Although with enough money I really do think anything is possible.'

'Did she mention my secret?'

'I don't think so.'

He smiled and touched another spot on the desktop, and a mechanical whirr started up. Slowly, the leather panels in the walls began to rotate, revealing, on the reverse, blank canvases. I counted twenty of them.

'I asked her for a list of the world's greatest paintings,' he said. '*Full Fathom Five* is going there.' He pointed to the next canvas, far smaller. '*The View of Delft.*' Next. '*Starry Night.*' And around the room he went, naming a canonical work and indicating an appropriately sized piece of primed cotton duck.

I wondered how he intended to acquire *The Persistence of Memory*, not to mention *Les Demoiselles D'Avignon*, *The Nightwatch* and the Mona Lisa.

'She recommended an excellent copyist.' He then named an Argentinean, living in Toronto, best known for having been arrested – but never convicted – for forging Rembrandts.

I considered the decision to line up all those competing pictures questionable at best. But Hollister seemed honestly thrilled by the idea. Describing himself as a 'heavily quantitative thinker', he raved to me about Marilyn's ability to cut through the jargon and give a clear picture of what art mattered and what did not. She had given him some sort of numerical guideline for assessing a piece's worth, and it was with this scale that he had decided to make me an offer on the Cracke drawing.

'To be frank,' he said, 'I would have gone as high as four-fifty.' He touched the desk again, causing the panels to slowly rotate back to their original positions.

Except for one – the future resting place of *The Burial of Count Orgaz*, which got stuck after about a quarter turn. Hollister banged at it, found it intractable, and, reddening, touched the desk to summon Matthew. The butler appeared post-haste and, seeing the catastrophe, hurried from the room, cell phone in hand. As Hollister and I stepped from the office and made our way back toward the elevator, I heard a California accent rising to the top of its lungs.

HOLLISTER'S PRIVATE MUSEUM stood at the highest point on his estate. A glass dome, dimpled and latticed with iron pipes, the structure resembled nothing so much as a gigantic, half-buried golf ball. I could only imagine the cost involved: the foundation work alone probably ran toward eight figures, once you took into account that the top of the hill had to be chopped off. Add to that an architect so prominent that Hollister declined to name him ('It was a favor. He doesn't want it getting around that he does residential work') and bulletproof glass for the entire exterior and you began to approach a new universe of money.

The armored car was parked by the loading dock, the jumpsuited men waiting for us. Like the butler, they addressed Hollister by his first name.

A retinal scan later, we stepped inside the dome, and I looked up at a series of concentric balconies culminating in an enormous Calder mobile seven stories overheard. Whoever the architect was, he had ripped off the New York Guggenheim to the extent that I wondered if that had been Hollister's express wish. He wanted copies of the world's most desirable paintings; why not replicate the most famous buildings, too? The glass I saw as a nod to I. M. Pei, and I felt certain that if I looked hard enough I would find other references as well.

A tweedy, greenish man in a well-cut suit met us in the lobby. Hollister introduced him as Brian Offenbach, the museum's manager, who I gathered was basically a glorified picture hanger. In the cadences of a well-rehearsed speech, Offenbach explained the logic behind the museum's layout; the work was displayed not chronologically or thematically but tonally, with the darkest pieces on the ground floor, and every successive floor getting lighter. Light and dark could mean the color of the piece, but more often it meant the emotional response the piece provoked, or the sense of weightiness it gave. Hence the Calder, despite its immensity – five tons of painted steel – occupied the apex, for the feelings of flight it evoked. Hollister had designed the scheme himself, and was proud of it; as one went higher, one transcended the physical realm and found oneself elevated to an understanding of blah blah blah blah blah.

I distrust binary systems – light and dark, good and evil, male and female – and the arrangement seemed to me self-defeating: an attempt to whittle down art's ragged irrationality that ultimately created not order but muddle.

'It's wonderful,' I said.

They had already begun bringing the new art up to the third floor, and when we stepped out of the elevator we confronted a tornado of packing material and exploded crates. Hollister had to keep raising his voice above the whine of drills.

'I've been wondering if the Cracke PIECE BELONGS HERE WITH THE REST OF THE, of the collection. I mean, it's so disturb DISTURBING, AND I WONDER IF I'D BE BETTER OFF PUTTING IT in a separate wing. For outsider art. I could tack on another few rooms. NEAR THE BACK. THAT WOULD HAVE SYMBOLIC RESONANCE, WOULDN'T IT, PUTTING the outsider art segregated in its own sphere. WHAT DO YOU THINK?'

I nodded.

'On second thought. The THE WHOLE POINT OF COLLECTING OUTSIDER ART AS I UNDERSTAND IT – MARILYN HAS BEEN GIVING ME SOME GREAT, great books to read. Have you read' – and he named a bunch of obscure monographs. The only name I recognized was Roger Cardinal, the British critic who gave Dubuffet's term Art Brut its English equivalent.

'The whole point is to REASSESS THE TRADITIONAL STAN-DARDS OF WESTERN CULTURE, AND to bring to light the talent of people untempered by SOCIETY. RIGHT?'

The Cracke drawing had special value to Hollister, as the first piece he had purchased of his own volition rather than Marilyn's; he took a personal stake in its location. Offenbach offered suggestions, each one dismissed: 'It'll get lost.' 'It'll stand out.' 'Too sterile.' 'Not well framed.' It was as though this one piece had revealed all of the scheme's flaws.

As a last resort we moved back to the lobby. It was my idea to have the workers hold the canvas up immediately to the left of the entrance. That would make the Cherubs the first thing you encountered.

'Perfect,' said Hollister.

Perfect meant another thirty minutes of discussion about height and centering and lighting. It couldn't be too perfectly square; that wasn't in keeping with the piece's Otherness. But if you cheated to the left, you had an unpleasant gap; to the right and the edge of the drawing began to jut around the corner . . .

When they were done we all stood back to admire our handiwork.

'What is that?' Offenbach asked. He approached the canvas. 'It's like a star.'

'I believe it is a star,' I said.

'Hm,' he said. 'Is that a reference?'

'What do you think?'

'I think,' Offenbach began, and then said, 'I think it looks marvelous. And that's what's important.'

THE RISE OF THE ART FAIR over the last three decades has drastically changed the contemporary market. A lot of business now takes place over a few frenetic weeks: the Armory Show in New York, the sprawling campuses of Tefaf Maastricht and Art Basel. I made a third of my sales at fairs; less trafficked galleries can do as much as fifty or sixty percent of their yearly totals.

For collectors, fairs provide motivation. If you had to traipse to every last gallery in Chelsea, who could blame you for tiring out and giving up within an hour or two? But when every dealer has his best twenty pieces out, hundreds of them lined up under one neat, climate-controlled tent – and when you can stop at the espresso counter for muffins or duck confit – then you really have no excuse not to get out and see the damned art.

The Miami fair to which I boarded a plane that Tuesday afternoon was an offshoot of a European fair, and over the last few years, as prices went through the roof, it had undergone an incredible transformation, from a regional outpost to a circus entirely its own: red carpets and stretch Hummers; blinged-out hip-hop moguls in floor-length ermine; crusty Brits and unctuous Swedes and Japanese in Day-Glo eyeglasses; fashionistas, heiresses, events and parties and after-parties, hobnobbing and flashbulbing and the electric crackle of a lot of people about to have sex. Hair got dressed.

And then there was the art. So much of it, and so much of it bad. There was a Persian rug woven with images from Abu Ghraib. There were some photos of cups and saucers being shattered by bullets. There were sober paintings of Britney Spears and, courtesy of Damien Hirst, panels of laminated houseflies. In the center of the main tent was an installation by rory z called *Jizz? or Salon Secrets Volumizing Conditioner with Hibiscus Extracts?*, whose title pretty much says it all: a row of hinge-top cases, the lids of which showed a color photo of an object – a pencil, say, or a Tickle Me Elmo – spotted with nacreous liquid from either a bottle of the aforementioned product or rory z's own reproductive glands. Viewers could study the photo and muster a best guess before opening the case to discover the truth inscribed on a little gold placard.

Another piece I took the time to look at was a video installation by Sergio Antonelli, who had filmed himself walking into a midtown Starbucks, ordering a triple-shot espresso, drinking it, getting back in line, ordering another, drinking it, getting back in line, and so forth. (He never seemed to have to pee, although I suppose that could have been edited out.) Eventually, he consumed enough caffeine that he had – or appeared to have – a myocardial infarction. It's hard to overstate the comedy of him thrashing through the mid-morning crowd. One man actually stepped over him en route to the cream-and-sugar station. The final shot showed Antonelli in the emergency room, being revived by a doctor wearing a green apron. The piece was called *Deathbucks*.

But most of the time I wasn't looking at art. For someone like me, part of the fun was that I got to catch up with colleagues I hadn't seen since the last fair. Marilyn had been cranking the rumor mill, and our booth received a steady stream of gawkers who put their noses right up to the drawings, asking was it *true*, had he *really*. Word of the Hollister sale had gotten around – no doubt I had Marilyn to thank for that as well – and by week's end I sold everything. Ruby began referring to our booth as the Cracke House and to us as the Cracke Whores. Guilty or not, Victor was a gold mine.

Nat calculated that were I to turn the whole collection around at the prices I'd been getting, I'd net close to $300 million. That would never happen, of course; I could ask as much as I did because most of the drawing still sat unassembled, in boxes. Since closing the show, I had moved the remaining material to a secure warehouse in the east twenties, and made plans to start assembling some new canvases – just a few, enough to moisten the market without flooding it.

Cracke's success rubbed off on the rest of my artists, too. I sold some Ardath Kaplans, some Alyson Alvarezes, the remaining Jocko Steinberger; I had a request for first pick of the new Oshimas when they came in. I even got rid of an old piece by Kristjana, one that I'd begun to think of as a white elephant. I tried to let her know the good news, but she wouldn't take my call.

*

I ARRIVED BACK IN NEW YORK exhausted and in desperate need of dry cleaning. I left the gallery closed for a day and lay around my apartment, letting my head clear. Then I called McGrath to see if anything had come up since our last meeting.

He didn't answer, not then nor on the subsequent two days. By the time somebody picked up, on Wednesday afternoon, I'd begun to worry.

The voice that answered was a woman's, unfamiliar.

'Who's calling.'

'Ethan Muller.'

A hand muffled the receiver. I heard talking. The woman came back on. 'Hold on.' A moment later another female voice came on, cracked and dry to the point that at first I didn't recognize it as Samantha's.

'He's dead,' she said.

I told her I'd get in a taxi.

'Wait. Wait. Don't come, please. The house – everything is crazy right now.' Someone said her name in the background. 'One second,' she said. Then she said, 'The funeral's on Friday. I can't talk right now, I'm sorry.'

'What happened?' I asked, but she had hung up.

ELEVEN

In retrospect, I'm glad she didn't hear my question, which I asked reflexively and which needed no answer. I didn't need her to tell me what happened; I knew what had happened. I had been watching it happen for the last month and a half.

Since she hadn't told me where the service would take place, I spent the rest of my day making awkward cold calls, inquiring after the McGrath funeral party. I found the right place, a church in Maspeth, and hired a car for Friday.

I'd always heard about police funerals being large, ceremonious affairs, but perhaps that's true only when an officer goes down in the line of duty. At McGrath's service there were a fair number of blue uniforms, but nobody that stood out as top brass, and definitely no representative from the mayor's office.

Mass began. Prayers were offered, hymns sung. Not knowing what to do – the Mullers are not a pious bunch – I stood at the rear of the sanctuary with my hands knotted behind my back, trying to see all the way to the front, where Samantha rested her head on the shoulder of a woman I assumed was her mother.

The Word of the Lord
Thanks be to God

McGrath's brother delivered a eulogy, as did Samantha's older sister, whose name I could not remember. Had McGrath told it to me? I didn't know. Our time together had been spent under strangely intimate circumstances, but almost everything about him remained a mystery to me. I told myself I had an idea of who he was – a wry sense of humor, a lust for justice – but how much could I possibly know? I looked out at the sea of heads, trying to put names on people: his old partner? The famous Richard Soto? I did spot Annie Lundley, and, glad to find a familiar face, I almost waved.

'I doubt that anybody here can think of him as anything other than a police officer. And that's what he was, that's what he always was, and he was great at what he did. I remember when I was a little girl, and he would take me out for a drive. He'd switch on the sirens, just for a couple of seconds, and people would look at us as we passed. And I remember thinking, That's my dad. They're looking at my dad. I was so proud of him. Daddy, I'm so proud of you. We all are, and we know how much you put into your life, how much you cared about the people you helped. You never stopped being the man I was proud of.'

The Eucharist; the wine, the wafer.

Into your hands, Father of mercies, we commend our brother Leland Thomas McGrath.

Six brawny men shouldering the casket.
The processional was brief, five blocks. I walked along alone, keeping

pace with the somber train of SUVs and Town Cars. The day was brisk, the light harsh, as though the sun had turned on its own headlamps in sympathy.

During the burial I kept my eye on Samantha. She stood apart, no longer leaning on her mother, who instead took the arm of a man with a walrus-like moustache. He wore a light blue blazer that stuck out against the predominant black, and I got very clear dislike vibes from Samantha regarding him. Her sister didn't seem to bear him as much animosity, and at one point clasped his hand.

In my mind, I tested out several explanations, rejecting all but the most obvious: the man was the wife's second husband. Evidently, the collapse of McGrath's marriage had fallen harder on Samantha than on her sister. Maybe the sister had been out of the house already, leaving Samantha to watch her parents' relationship in its dying throes.

Lord hear our prayer

The service concluded, and people broke off in twos and threes. I approached Samantha to offer my condolences but turned away when I saw her arguing quietly with her mother, their heads cocked forward and their hands fluttering. Mother and daughter shared the same slightly insolent mouth, the same jutting hips. The former Mrs McGrath had an unhealthy tan, the work of someone who spends too much time on a UV bed; by comparison, Samantha's pallor looked like the work of someone trying desperately not to look like her mother.

'Do you want to split a cab?'

Behind me stood Annie.

'There's a reception at the house,' she said.

I told her I had hired a car. 'No charge.'

'I hope not,' she said.

On the ride out I pumped her for information about the McGrath family dynamics. Many of the conclusions I'd drawn were correct: the tanned woman was in fact McGrath's ex-wife, and the man with the walrus face her second husband. There was another wrinkle, though: walrus face was also McGrath's former partner.

I poked around in my memory for the name on the transcript. 'Gordan?'

'I think his name is Jerry,' she said.

'That's right. J. Gordan. Jerry.'

'If you say so,' she said.

'That must be a little tense.'

'You think?'

'Here I thought *I* was the odd man out.'

'Not by a long shot.'

'What happened?'

'I don't think it's very complicated. McGrath's a workaholic. His wife is lonely. Roll credits. Although she really went for the jugular, didn't she?'

I thought of Samantha's sister's speech. *I doubt that anybody here can think of him as anything other than a police officer.* Originally I'd interpreted that comment as a compliment. Now it sounded more like an indictment. That Samantha had decided to go into law enforcement seemed to me a way of siding with her father. Then why had she not spoken her farewells, made her defense?

I said to Annie, 'You're close.'

'Very.' They met, she told me, at a forensics conference, during a training session for cops and ADAs.

'We hit it off right away,' said Annie. 'Like sisters.'

'Her sister – remind me of her name?'

'Juliette. She lives in North Carolina.'

'Uh-huh. Well, thank you for the inside scoop.'

'You're interested,' said Annie.

'Interested?'

'In her.'

I laughed. 'I have a girlfriend.'

'That's too bad, she could use somebody like you.'

'Like me how.'

'Rich,' she said and started laughing.

'What makes you think I'm rich?'

'Your shoes.'

'My shoes?'

Still laughing, she shrugged.

I said, 'Anyway, I thought she had a boyfriend.'

Annie gave me a strange look.

'They broke up?'

She said, 'He was a firefighter.'

'Oh,' I said.

And like that we ran out of words. Both of us remembered where we had come from and where we were headed. Annie shifted around to stare out the window. I did the same. The ride took longer than I remembered.

TRAYS OF CUT FRUIT and soggy sandwiches had replaced the pill bottles on the dining-room table. Samantha was nowhere to be seen; nor could I find her sister or mother. Most people congregated around the liquor, and after Annie and I drifted off in different directions, I found myself in conversation with a thickset man with a tangle of gray curls. He shook my hand and introduced himself as Richard Soto. 'You're Lee's guy,' he said when I told him my name.

'I guess so,' I said.

'I owe you a drink,' he said, guiding me to a sidetable stocked with bottles.

'What for.'

'For getting that bastard off my back. He used to call me up every five damn minutes until you came along. Jameson,' he said, and handed me a cup, which I held politely. 'You really did him a world of good. You're a good man. Bottoms up.'

As he threw back his shot, I quickly spilled mine into the carpet. Then I raised the cup and pretended to wince.

'The next one'll be easier,' he said, taking my cup and unscrewing the bottle.

'What's going to happen now?' I asked.

'What?'

'With the case. Thank you.' Again he drank and I poured out.

'Good stuff.'

'Are you going to take it over?'

Soto looked at me blankly. 'What.'

'The case.'

'What about it.'

'Are you going to take it over? There's a lot left to do. I told Annie I'd get her a list of people who had been in the apartment, but I'm having trouble getting in touch with the superintendent of the building, who seems to be on vacation. I was planning to go over there myself this week. She and I also have to go over to the storage locker, because once the lab results come back—'

As I talked, I saw Soto's gaze slide away from me and over my shoulder, toward a group of detectives joking loudly and making toasts. He got a mean look in his eye and said, 'Would you excuse me.'

I followed him over and joined the group. Jerry Gordan had the floor. Through his moustache I noticed the impetus for growing a moustache to begin with, a large mole on his upper lip. He was ruddy and sweating and talking about old times with his buddy Lee McGrath. The other cops exchanged smirks.

'Hey Jerry, you and Lee were pretty close, huh?'

'The closest.'

'All for one and one for all, eh Jerry?'

That prompted snickering. Gordan didn't seem to notice.

'He was a good fuckin man,' he slurred.

'Hey Jerry,' said Soto. 'Was he honest?'

'Oh you know it.'

'Let me hear you say it: Lee McGrath was an honest man.'

'The honestest man in Queens County, Lee McGrath.'

'You swear?'

'I sweardagod.'

'Honest enough for the both of you, isn't that right, Jerry.'

'Sure was.'

'You bet he was. And giving, too, huh? A generous man, huh?'

Gordan laughed insensibly.

'That's right, Jerry. He gave his all. Share and share alike, right Jerry?'

More snickering.

I didn't like the tenor of the conversation, so I detached myself and paddled through the crowd. I intended to look at the file, to make sure it was still there and to give myself a reason for being in McGrath's home.

The door to the back room was locked. I didn't knock, but my rattling the knob brought a red-eyed Samantha to answer.

'Oh,' she said, wiping her face. 'I didn't know you were here.' Her body blocked the doorway, but over her I saw her sister in the La-Z-Boy, a wet towel across her forehead.

'I came with Annie,' I said. I meant it by way of explanation; she, however, heard a request for her to come out of hiding.

'That's so sweet. It's very sweet of you both. I'll be out in a little bit.'

'You don't have to come out.'

'I want to. Don't go anywhere. Don't leave until I come out.'

'Okay.'

'Promise.'

'I promise.'

'Okay. I'll be out soon,' she said, and closed the door.

I waited in the corner, gnawing on celery and nodding at strangers. All I intended to do was give Samantha my best and head home, but after forty minutes she still hadn't emerged, and I wandered past the group of cops, all of them by now pink and talkative. They hadn't noticed my absence, addressing me as though I had been standing with them all along, pulling me into their circle and handing me shot glasses that I would discreetly dump into a nearby floor plant. When I had all but guaranteed its death from poisoning, I slipped away and went into the kitchen, where I found an army of women in dish gloves trying to cope with the stampede of dirty glasses.

I gave up. I left the house and walked down to the beach.

Samantha was standing barefoot by the 9/11 memorial. Her pumps lay on their sides where the concrete boardwalk met the sand. I kept my distance, watching the wind turn her hair into streamers, resisting the urge to come up behind her and hold her. Slumping to one side, her hand on her hip, she looked frail, like McGrath had been toward the end, and I had an odd fear that she was dying, too. The wind bit down hard; she shivered.

As I turned to go she noticed me and gave a little wave. I made as though to take off my shoes and she nodded. I stood beside her and together we looked at the memorial.

'I'm sorry I snuck out,' she said. 'I meant to say hello, I really did.'

'It's okay.'

'I can't go back in there right now.'

'You don't have to.'

The wind bit again and she trembled. I gave her my coat.

'Thank you.'

I nodded.

'Did you make any new friends?' she asked.

'We're all going out tonight after the depressing shit gets finished.'

She smiled faintly.

152

A silence.

'I am so *tired*.' She looked at me. 'Do you know what I mean?'

'After my mother's funeral I slept for a week. They thought something was wrong with me. They took me to the hospital.'

'I didn't know your mother died.'

I nodded.

'How old were you?'

'Five.'

'Do you mind if I ask what she died of?'

'Breast cancer.'

'That must have been hard.'

I smiled at her. 'Is this helping you?'

'It is, actually.'

'Okay.'

'Do you mind?'

'Not at all.'

'All right,' she said, but she didn't say anything else.

I said, 'Maybe you have narcolepsy.'

She smiled.

Silence. The sea fired glittering buckshot.

She said, 'They were up all night with him. The cops. They had a party, like it was his birthday. I know they meant well, but they can go back to work tomorrow. I'm the one that has to deal with it after today.'

I nodded.

She pointed to the memorial. 'I knew him.'

'I know.'

She looked at me.

'Annie told me,' I said.

'She did?'

I nodded.

'I wish she hadn't done that.'

'I'm sorry.'

'It's not your fault.'

'I'm still sorry.'

'It is what it is.'

I said nothing.

'That's him.'

'Ian.'

She nodded, wiped her face, laughed once. 'I mean, it's kind of ridiculous. As soon as I've begun to deal with that . . . and now *this*. Come on.' She laughed again. 'You've got to be kidding.'

I put my arm around her shoulder, and she leaned against me. We stood there until the wind turned ferocious and her feet began to go numb.

THE FEW PEOPLE THAT REMAINED were halfway into coats. Jerry Gordan had left, as had Samantha's sister. Samantha told me to go on upstairs and wait for her there, but before I could, her mother emerged from the kitchen, grinding a dishtowel into a mug.

'Where did you go?' she asked Samantha.

'I needed air.'

'I needed *you*. Julie had to take Jerry' – she looked at me, then at Samantha, then back at me. She put on a terrible smile. 'Hello. Who're you.'

'Ethan Muller. I was a friend of Mr McGrath's.'

She snorted. '"Mister"!'

'Mom.'

'I don't think he's ever been called that.'

'Mom.'

'What, sweetheart. What's the problem.'

Samantha was staring at the ground, her fists balled.

'He must have liked when you called him that,' Samantha's mother said to me. 'He must have *loved* that. R-E-S-P-E-C-T.' At first she had seemed merely angry, but now I saw that she was very drunk. Over and over the mug started to slip from her hands, only to be caught at the last moment.

'What happened to Jerry,' said Samantha.

'Your sister had to drive him to the emergency room. Don't look like that, he's fine. He needs some stitches.'

'What happened.'

'One of your father's shithead friends' – she stopped again, looked at me, seeming to appraise whether what she had to say could harm my tender ears – 'what the hey, we're all friends here, aren't we.'

I nodded cautiously.

'Richard hit him,' she said. 'He cold-cocked him in the middle of a toast.'

'Oh my God.'

'I threw them out, the bunch of fucking apes. They split his lip open. I needed you. Where did you go.'

'I told you. I went out for a walk.'

Her mother stared at her, reloading; then she turned abruptly toward me and smiled. 'And what's your story?'

'I'm an art dealer.'

'Well la-dee-dah. I didn't know Lee was into that. Excuse me, *Mr* McGrath.'

'I was helping him look into an old case,' I said.

That set Samantha's mother off; she laughed and laughed. 'Really,' she said. 'Which one would that be.'

'Mom.'

'It's just a *question*, Samantha.'

'Why don't you go upstairs?' Samantha said to me.

'Actually, I think I'm going to go home—'

'Oh, Lee. All the way til the end. Oh, Christ, what a joke.'

'Can I talk to you for a minute, Mom.' Samantha yanked her mother into the kitchen. I vacillated, then went quietly upstairs.

In all my time at McGrath's, I'd never been upstairs, and on the second floor I faced two options, a yellow-and-brown master bedroom still filled with signs of illness: a cane, a bucket for vomit. The other room had woodblocks glued to the door.

JULIE AND

SAMS

OOM

Inside I found a bunk bed with matching comforters, pilled and smelling of dust. Girlish stickers adorned the bedframe. On the floor was a duffel bag emblazoned with the logo of the Queens County District Attorney's office, half open and spilling out hastily crammed clothes, a stick of deodorant, a running shoe.

Downstairs I heard yelling.

I looked through the books on the desk. *A Wrinkle in Time. The Catcher in the Rye. Are You There God? It's Me, Margaret.* Julie had *friendz forever,* according to the picture frame. Samantha's paper number from the 1998 New York City Marathon hung on a corkboard.

The yelling crescendoed. A door slammed.

A few minutes later Samantha entered and closed the door behind her.

'Fucking bitch.' She stood for a moment with her face in her hands. When she looked up again, her expression was sober and purposeful. She stared at a blank spot on the far wall as she unbuttoned her shirt, shook it off, let it fall to the floor. 'Help me with this, please,' she said, turning around.

'DO YOU WANT ME TO GO ON THE TOP BUNK?'

'It's all right.'

'I don't think this was made for someone your size.'

156

'Probably not.'

'How tall are you, anyway?'

'Six-three.'

'You must be uncomfortable. I can go up there.'

'Stay.'

'Are you sure?'

'Yes.'

'Okay. Good, because I don't want to go up there. That one's Julie's.' A silence. I felt her smile. 'How does it feel to take advantage of a vulnerable woman?'

'Fantastic.'

'This isn't really what I do,' she said.

'Grief makes us do strange things.'

'In bed.'

'Yes.'

'No: in bed. You never played that game?'

'What game.'

'The fortune cookie game.'

'I'm not familiar.'

'You read your fortune cookie and then you add "in bed". You've never done that?'

'I think you're saying that I sound like a fortune cookie.'

'You did just then.'

'When.'

'When you said, "Grief makes us do strange things."'

'It does.'

'Okay,' she said, 'but it's still silly to talk like that.'

My first instinct was to be offended, but then I saw how she was smiling and I had to smile, too. For years Marilyn had been telling me that I had to lighten up; how irritated would she be to learn that all it took was a single goofy look?

I said, 'Your lucky numbers are five, nine, fifteen, twenty-two and thirty.'

'In bed.'

'In bed. I don't remember the last time I had a fortune cookie.'

She said, 'At my office we get Chinese twice a week. It's horrible but it's better than peanut-butter crackers.'

'I could buy you lunch sometime.'

'That might be nice.'

'Well all right.'

'All right.'

A silence.

She said, 'But, I mean, really. I'm not used to this.'

'So you said.'

'I don't know what this is.' She turned onto her elbow. 'What is it?'

I said, 'I don't know,' and she burst out laughing.

'What?'

'You should have seen the look on your face.'

'What.'

'You were like, "Oh shit, now she thinks she's my girlfriend."' She fell on her back, laughing. '"What have I done!"'

'I didn't think that.'

'Okay.'

'I didn't.'

'Okay, I believe you. You just had a funny look.'

I smiled. 'If you say so.'

She finished laughing and wiped her eyes. 'I feel better now.'

'I'm glad.'

She nodded, then fixed me with a serious look. 'I don't really want to think about this right now. All I want is to not be crying.'

I nodded.

'Good,' she said. 'I'm glad we've gotten that out of the way.'

I nodded again, still unsure of what'd been gotten out of the way.

'You and my dad seemed to get along.'

'I liked him,' I said. 'He reminded me of my father, except not an ass-hole.'

'He could be an asshole, too.'

'I'm sure he could.'

'What's wrong with your dad?' she asked.

'A lot of things.'

'You're not going to tell me?'

'Nope.'

'All right,' she said. Then she said, 'I know who he is, you know.'

I looked at her.

'I Googled you. You're hanging out with my dad, I wanted to make sure you weren't one of those guys who scams old people.'

'As far as I could tell, Lee McGrath was not the easily scammed type.'

'You can never be too careful.'

'Fine, then, you know who I am.'

'I know a little bit. Enough not to worry about you going after my dad's retirement fund.'

I laughed. 'If you think I'm as rich as my father you're sorely mistaken.'

'Darn.'

'What.'

'I was hoping I'd get, like, a morning-after present in the mail. Like a diamond necklace or something.'

'I can give you a lithograph.'

'That's it. I don't even get a painting.'

'For preferred clients only.'

'Aw,' she said. 'Go fuck yourself.'

'Kiss your mother with that mouth?'

'Please,' she said. 'Where do you think I learned it.' There was a pause. 'I'm sorry about when I called her a bitch. She's not.'

I nodded.

'We're all a little on edge right now.'

'That's understandable.'

'She was angry that I brought you here.'

'I can apologize to her, if you'd like.'

'Are you kidding? Absolutely not.'

'I will if it'll help.'

'She's not angry at you. She's angry at me. And, you know, she's not even angry at me, either. She never drinks. This is the first time I've seen her that way in my entire life. She used to hate my father's drinking.'

'I didn't know he drank.'

'You didn't know him most of his life.' She sniffled. 'He smoked, too. You don't get esophageal cancer at sixty-one unless you're trying pretty hard.'

I said nothing.

'I'll never get them,' she said. 'She loved him. I don't think she ever stopped. You know what she said one time? Julie told me this. My mom was visiting her in Wilmington. They were driving along, and she goes, "Other than the fact that Jerry's a total moron, he's a good husband."' She shifted; I felt her smile against my arm. 'Can you believe that?'

'Easily.'

'I'd get upset except I agree with her.'

'You and Jerry don't get along.'

'We have nothing to say to one another.'

'So I gathered.'

She smiled again. 'Did Annie tell you that, too?'

'I figured it out myself. She did tell me about your mom and Jerry.'

'She really gave you the goods, didn't she?' She turned over and our faces were close. I brushed the hair out of her eyes. She said, 'Anything you don't know?'

'Plenty,' I said and kissed her again.

TWELVE

And then nothing happened.

For a week my life became as quiet as it ever had been, pre-Victor Cracke quiet. At the gallery we began hanging a new show. For the most part, the frantic phone calls had tapered off; after a big fair, everyone needs time to recuperate, to make sure they're still solvent and still care about art. I had lunches and dinners with clients and friends. A totally ordinary, totally empty week, and in trudging through it, McGrath's void loomed unexpectedly large. I kept picking up the phone to call him and then standing there dumbly, holding the receiver and wondering who was in charge of the case now.

The answer, of course, was no one. The mystery of Victor Cracke would remain exactly that.

I had to ask myself if that was such a bad thing. The show had come and gone; the sales had gone through, the checks cleared. I stood very little to gain by asking more questions. It's true that we are, by design or by fluke, a curious species, and ignorance grates inside us like sand in an oyster. But I had long trained myself to accept and love ambiguity. Why should five boys, four decades dead, matter to me when every day I read about murder, war, global injustice – without being moved to act? Any obligation I felt toward McGrath was strictly my own invention. I had not known the man long enough to feel guilty letting his last wishes go unfulfilled. The sense of loss that overtook me, then, was as surprising as it was overwhelming.

As I mentioned, my reasons for helping McGrath were purely selfish. So I had told myself every time I got into a car and went to Breezy Point. With him gone, though, I had to admit that I actually missed the old bastard. Going back to work made me realize the degree to which he represented the polar opposite of everyone I normally dealt with. Without pretension, unafraid to admit ignorance or to show his hand when he wanted something. He had never attempted to keep up appearances, even as he fell apart; and in his physical frailty I discerned a profound honesty, verging at times on beauty. He became in my mind a walking work of art, a human Giacometti: sanded down by illness to within an inch of his bare essence, radiance peeking through the cracks.

And I began to wonder if there hadn't been something else motivating McGrath, as well. Why had he trusted me to begin with? Surely he had believed I had a vested interest in proving Victor innocent. (If he'd known the truth – that Victor's popularity had tripled following the rumors – he might have suspected me of bias toward guilt.) By putting off his requests for a copy of the drawings as long as I did, I had made my caginess clear enough. And then – freaking out over the phone, turning up with that letter – I could hardly have seemed rational and levelheaded enough to be of any use. I was going to either conceal or exaggerate.

Maybe, as Samantha had implied, I was the only person willing to help him.

Or maybe he liked me, too.

In any event, the idea that the case would simply return to some slush pile, never to be resolved, depressed me immensely. I've already mentioned that I hate to fail. You might find that amusing now that you know a little bit more about me and how much my early years consisted of failure. But here's the thing: I always took my self-debasement very seriously. Once I had committed to becoming a fuckup, I strove to be *the best* fuckup around: a prince of debauchery. That drive is part of my character, as much a gift from my forebears as my inflated sense of self-worth – one is probably an outgrowth of the other, although I'm not sure which is which – and having reopened the case, I did not want to believe that it had bested me.

The easiest opening move would have been to call Samantha. But I couldn't very well do that. The fact that she hadn't called me I took as a sign that she regretted our night together. Who was I to argue? But that couldn't stop me from thinking about her. It had been one of the more physically awkward bouts of lovemaking of my life, the bedframe seemingly about to collapse into splinters and the sheets curling off at the corners – and for that, all the more exhilarating.

All of a sudden my life was back to normal, and the drudgery crushed me. The phone was leaden in my hand; a client in the doorway gave me the beginnings of a headache. My mind wandered, and I found myself unable to concentrate for more than a few minutes at a time, let alone hold a sparkling conversation.

'*Ethan.*'

Marilyn put down her cutlery, for her a grave gesture. She had been going on about something someone had done to someone else in Miami, could I believe the au*da*city. 'Can you at least pretend to listen, please.'

'I'm sorry.'

'Where *are* you? Are you sick?'

'No.' I paused. 'I was thinking about McGrath.'

Notice that I hadn't lied. I had merely failed to specify which McGrath. 'Who? Oh. Your policeman?'

Of the three or four – or maybe I'm misremembering, maybe it was five or six – digressions I'd taken since Marilyn and I got together, I had never once bragged to her afterward. But I'd also never lied.

Your policeman.

I lied, then: I lied with a nod.

'Yes,' she said. 'It's very, *very* sad. Are you too sad to eat that?'

It came quickly, then, a stab of hate for her. Many times in the past I had been annoyed with her, but this was different, and I had to excuse myself.

I went to the bathroom, washed my face, and slapped myself a couple of times. Pay attention. Common courtesy. I resolved to put the McGrath family out of my head and to be civil. And then – not tonight, but in a few days – and in a vague way – I would hint to Marilyn that I'd been with someone else. I didn't have to say who. She'd be fine. I'd get it off my chest. I'd get over it, and so would she. I dried my hands and returned to the table. Marilyn had paid the check and left.

THE END OF MY QUIET WEEK came with a phone call – again a phone call – from Tony Wexler.

'Your father would like to see you. Before you say no—'

'No.'

Tony sighed. 'May I speak, please?'

'You can try.'

'He wants to buy some art.'

That was a new one. My father owned plenty of paintings, but his taste ran rather toward seascapes and bowls of fruit. To be fair, I hadn't been to the house in years, and in the meantime he might have assembled a pre-eminent collection of twentieth-century art; he could have hired Julian Schnabel to design his wallpaper and Richard Serra to do the flatware. But I had the distinct feeling that Tony was struggling to sound serious.

'You can laugh,' I said. 'I give you permission. I won't tell.'

'The offer is one hundred percent genuine.'

'I thought you'd run out of pretexts. Well done.'

'It's not a pretext. He wants you to come to the house. Think of him, in this context, as a customer.'

'If he's a customer then he can come by the gallery like everyone else.'

'You know as well as I do that not all your clients come into the gallery.'

'I bring work to clients when I have a prior relationship with them.'

He gave a tired chuckle. 'Touché.'

'If he wants to buy some art I'll gladly set him up with someone who can better suit his needs. What's he in the market for?'

'The Cracke drawings.'

That caught me off guard. It took me a moment to reply: 'Well, in that case, he's out of luck.'

'Look, why don't you come by the house tonight?'

'I already sa—'

'You don't have to see him. You can deal directly with me.'

'I don't believe you.'

'Just come by the house. If you're unhappy you can leave. Or – forget the house. I'll meet you someplace of your choosing. You can send some-one ahead and make sure I'm alone. It'll be like a spy movie. Name your terms, name the circumstances.'

'You come here.'

'I would really rather keep it private.'

'You said name my terms. Those are my terms.'

He stopped and started several times, and his fumbling confirmed my suspicion that the deal hinged on my coming to him, and not vice versa. Either he was trying to get me in the same room as my father, or he had been ordered to make sure that I understood who was working for whom in this transaction.

'This is childish,' he finally said.

'What's childish is calling me up and demanding that I conduct my business according to someone else's rules.'

'He's serious. It's a serious offer. A serious and committed offer.'

'How many.'

'Pardon?'

'How many does he want? I don't make house calls except for my most serious and committed clients, so let's see how serious and committed he is. How many does he want to buy?'

'All of them.'

I sighed. 'I don't know what you're trying to do here, Tony, but I don't have time for it.'

'Wait a minute, wait. I'm being straight with you. He wants them all. He wants the ones you've sold, too. You've sold some already, am I right?'

'Tony, for God's sake.'

'You answer me now. How many have you sold?'

'A few.'

'Ah? Ah? *You* tell *me*.'

'A dozen.'

'Exactly a dozen.'

'Give or take.'

'Well which is it, give or take.'

'They're already sold. They're not coming back.'

'How much did you sell them for?'

I told him.

There was a silence.

'I'll be damned,' he said.

'Yes. Now, you can make offers on them, but I don't think anyone's going to want to part with them that fast, not unless you pay through the nose.'

'We'll worry about that later. How much do you want for the rest of them.'

'You had the pieces. You could have kept them without paying a cent. Now you want to buy them back? Excuse me when I say that this doesn't make a bit of sense.'

'He didn't want them before. He wants them now.'

'It's an impulse buy?'

'Call it that if you want.'

'Bullshit. My father's never done anything impulsive in his life. He's a calculating son of a bitch and I'm sorry that he's put you up to this. Let me ask you something, Tony: how do you work for him? Doesn't it bother you? Doesn't it drive you nuts, having to go work for that son of a bitch every day?'

'There are things about your father that you don't know.'

'I don't doubt it. That's life. Thanks for calling.'

IMMEDIATELY AFTER HANGING UP I regretted the way I'd spoken to him. Tony had been the one to hand me Victor Cracke, after all; and he'd borne my ingratitude for far too long already. I felt the urge to call him back and agree to a meeting – not at the gallery, not at the house, but at a museum or restaurant – an urge that I fought off, fought off repeatedly throughout the rest of the day, so that by the time I went home I had grown downright indignant about the entire matter.

Who the hell did my father think he was? The decision to throw the art to me had obviously come down from him, not from Tony; Tony was acting in his capacity as capo. Typical of my father; so typical. Make a deal, then change the terms. Give a gift that becomes an obligation. I had no reason to feel guilty telling Tony to get lost, no reason at all; no more reason, at least, than all the other times I had shunned my father's warped attempts at intimacy. I owed them nothing. Victor Cracke's art had come to me as though out of the void, like I'd found it in the trash. I had done the work. Alone.

I'd nearly come to convince myself of this, two days later, when I got another letter in the mail. Like its predecessor, it was written in Victor's neat, uniform hand, on white 8^1/$_2$-by-11-inch paper. Like its predecessor, it had a simple message, repeated over and over and over. I AM WARNING YOU.

THIRTEEN

Getting Samantha on the phone took more work than I expected. The home number she'd given me rang indefinitely, and her cell phone went straight to voicemail. I left two messages the afternoon I received Victor's second letter, and two more the next day. Fearing I was becoming a pest, I waited an agonizing twenty-four hours before calling her at work. She seemed surprised to hear from me, and not particularly thrilled. I told her I'd been trying her for days, then waited for her to offer an excuse. When she didn't, I said, 'I need to see you.'

'I don't know if that's the best idea.'

She sounded remote, and I realized she had misunderstood me. 'It's not about that. I got another letter.'

'Letter?'

'From Victor Cracke,' I said. When she said nothing, I added, 'The artist?'

'Oh. I didn't know you'd gotten a first one.'

'Your father didn't mention it?'

'No. So you can contact him, then.'

At first I thought she meant her father, and that she was making a sick joke. 'There's no return address. You're sure your father didn't mention it.'

'Positive.'

'That's strange.'

'Why's it strange.'

'Because I assumed he would've wanted you to know what was happening with the case.'

'It wasn't my thing. It was his and yours.'

'Be that as it may, I need to show you this. Let me pick you up, I can—'

'Wait,' she said.

'What.'

'I don't think you should do that.'

'Why?'

'Because I just – I just don't.'

I said, 'It's got nothing to do with that.'

'I understand. I still don't want to get together.'

'Why.'

'Because I don't *want* to.'

'Samantha—'

'Please. I don't want to talk about it anymore, okay? I think it's better for the both of us if we just forget all about it and go back to doing what we were doing before.'

I said, 'I swear to you, it isn't *about* that.'

And furthermore, what exactly did she mean by *forget all about it*. It might never happen again, but we couldn't undo reality. I had enjoyed that night, and I thought she had, too. My fantasies had been feeding on its memory for two weeks, the film reel turning in my mind. At the time she seemed fine, but now I wondered if there had been something wrong with her that I, in my eagerness, failed to notice, an abstraction in her face that

I had interpreted as ecstasy. And afterward: lying there, feeling fatigue, satisfaction, embarrassment, some small part of loneliness, need – had she felt something else, something unspeakable? She hadn't seemed in any hurry to get me out the door. Did we look each other in the eye as we dressed? No, but that's not uncommon. I had kissed her good-bye, and it had been a nice kiss. A lingering kiss. She hadn't said anything indicating that she intended to blot me out.

She said, 'If you're trying to figure out a way to—'

'To what.'

'To see me, then this—'

'Are you kidding, it's got *nothing* to—'

'This is not the way to—'

'Are you even listening to me?' I could imagine her, hunched over her desk, the hand on the forehead, the pout. The other hand wiggling a pen. Inventing reasons to put me off. Sorry to have bothered with me; I was turning out to be *clingy* . . .

'I'll fax you a copy of the letter,' I said. 'You can decide for yourself.'

'Fine.'

Ten minutes later she called back.

'All right,' she said.

'Thank you.'

'But I still don't think I'm the person you should be calling.'

'Then tell me who to call.'

'The police.'

'Your father said they wouldn't be able to do anything.'

'They can do more than I can,' she said. 'I'm not even in your borough.'

'Then what am I supposed to do?'

'I—'

'You're the only other person aware of what's going on. We still have the DNA to deal with, we still have transcripts left—'

'Whoa whoa whoa. I don't have anything to do with this.'

171

'He must have talked to you about the case.'

'In passing, but—'

'Then you're involved, whether you want to be or not. Don't tell me you don't care whether this gets finished or not.'

'I don't.'

'I don't believe you,' I said.

'Believe whatever you'd like,' she said.

'He would've wanted—'

'Oh please don't start with that.'

'I'm involved. You're involved. It might have been his, but he's gone and it's ours now and I need your help.'

'I *can't*,' she said and burst into sobs.

Right then I realized that I'd been – if not shouting, then at least speaking with great force. I began to apologize, but she would have none of it.

'You don't get it, do you. I want to be *away* from all of this.'

'I really am sorry—'

'*Shut up.* I don't care about the case. Okay? I don't give a fuck about the case, or about your letter, or anything else. I want to be left alone. Do you understand me?'

'I—'

'Just acknowledge that you understand me. I don't want to hear anything else.'

'I understand, but—'

'*I don't want to hear it.* All right? I'm hanging up and that's the end of it.'

'Wait—'

She was gone. I held the phone until it began to croak.

I CALLED THE NYPD. The person who answered seemed not to understand me, so I gathered up the letter and a copy of the first one (the original was still at the crime lab) and headed over to the station on West Twentieth. Construction in the lobby made it impossible for the desk sergeant to hear me; he directed me and a patrolman into another room, away from the clatter.

'Huh,' said the patrolman after I'd explained the story. He seemed thoroughly confused. 'So you already talked to someone in Queens?'

'Not exactly. He was retired. And then he passed away.'

'Huh.' He picked up the letters, one in each hand, as though checking them against each other.

'We've been trying to track down . . . Look, I don't mean to be rude, but is there anyone else I can talk to?'

He glanced at me. Then he looked at the letters. 'Hang on.'

While he was gone I watched through a window of reinforced glass as a female officer asked a snotty-looking kid questions. Behind her hung a banner congratulating the tenth precinct on another quarter of record lows. On a bulletin board hung a sheet of statistics, and adjacent, a poster of the Twin Towers.

The patrolman came back. His name, I saw, was VOZZO. 'I made copies,' he said, giving me back the letters. 'We'll want to have them in case the writer does anything actionable. It's probably just a prank, though. I wouldn't freak yourself out.'

'That's it?'

'Unfortunately, there isn't much more I can do for you.'

'It doesn't look like a prank to me.'

'I'm sure it doesn't, and I wish I could tell you more. From our end, though, I can't do a whole lot, not with this.'

'And there's nobody else—'

'Not at the moment.'

The dropping crime statistics and the 9/11 poster told me a story, a continuation of the one McGrath had begun. September 11 had changed the way crime got handled in New York. A couple of angry letters, an unsolvable murder – who cared.

'Anything else I can help you with?'

'No thanks.'

'Okay. If you need anything, here's my card. You can call me.' He held up the photocopies. 'Meantime I'll hang on to these.'

I doubted that he'd hang on to them much farther than the next trash can, but I thanked him again and went back to the gallery.

ANTSY AT SPINNING MY WHEELS, I decided to return to the only evidence I had at my disposal: the cache of drawings. Ruby and I hadn't nearly finished going through them, and the ones I'd seen had been given a cursory examination at best. Somewhere in that vast map, I hoped to find the road to Victor Cracke.

After closing up, I took a cab across town to the storage warehouse. I signed in and rode the elevator up to the sixth floor, where I made my way through corridors overlit by fluorescent tubing. Mosley's was New York's preeminent art depository; any given locker might hold a Klimt, a Brancusi, a John Singer Sargent. In my temperature-controlled, humidity-controlled, UV-radiation-controlled, vibration-controlled, air-quality-controlled, $5,760-a-month locker, all I had was Victor Cracke, thirty boxes of him – the embodiment of ten months' emotional and professional energy.

There was a viewing room at the end of each floor, but I didn't intend to sit in an airless cell all night long; I'd had enough of that. Instead I chose a box at random, dollied it back to the front desk, signed out, and shlepped down to the street to catch a cab.

I live in TriBeCa. I don't think I've mentioned that. My apartment has a deck in back, with a quaint garden left by the previous owner that has survived my every attempt to kill it through negligence. I'm not much of a caretaker. The rest of the apartment is all me: pieces that I've set aside, either because I thought they would sell better down the line or because I wanted them for myself. I have a good deal of period Deco furniture, and an alcoholic neighbor who leaves a huge shopping bag clinking with empty wine bottles in the trash closet every Sunday night. I like my home and my chosen neighborhood. It's close to the gallery but not so close that I feel like I'm living in The Scene; close enough to Marilyn's town house that I can be there within minutes, not so close that we drop by unannounced. Around the corner from me is a fifteen-seat sushi bar where I eat two nights a week, and that's where I went.

The hostess greeted me by name. Usually I sit at the bar, but that night I asked her for a table. 'For me and my friend,' I said, indicating the box.

'Oooh,' she said and, when I nodded permission, pried open the top. I asked her what she thought. She bit her lip. 'Dizzy,' she said finally.

Indeed.

I ordered dinner for myself and a carafe of sake, which I set in front of the box of drawings. 'Cheers,' I said. 'Drink up, motherfucker.'

Before I left, the hostess asked if I would show the art to the manager. I obliged. Soon the entire staff had gathered round, oohing and aahing their approval, or disapproval – I couldn't tell. Either way, they sounded fascinated. I showed them how the drawings connected, eliciting further admiration. Their reaction delighted me, and seeing the work through their eyes, I remembered why I'd been attracted to it in the first place. It was enormously complex, enormously rich. If I looked hard enough, I would find a clue. Had to be there. Had to.

It was chilly that night, October hardening. There was no moon, and many of the streetlights were burnt out or obscured by the scaffolding that crops up in my neighborhood like kudzu. Once I stumbled and almost lost control of the box. A block and a half can seem pretty far to walk when you're wearing a Savile Row suit and topcoat and carrying fifty pounds of paper. At that point, though, I couldn't possibly indulge in a cab: my building was less than ten yards away.

I set the box down on the sidewalk and arched my back. It was eleven thirty, and I was tired. I wouldn't be able to get to the art tonight. I'd get up early the next morning and work until I found something or until Samantha changed her mind.

In New York you don't notice other people. They're there, always, but you don't see them. Who pays attention to people on the street? My neighborhood is safe at night. That's why I didn't turn around to see who was walking a few feet behind me. In fact, I don't think I was aware of anyone else, not until I got hit on the back of the head with something extremely hard and heavy, and by then I was unconscious.

INTERLUDE: 1931.

On Friday nights Mother reads while Father listens to the radio. David does not make noise. He sits on the rug and plays in his head, he has lots of games he plays. Or he tells himself stories. His favorite stories to make up involve a great exploring pilot named Roger Dollar. Roger Dollar always gets into trouble but then he always gets out because he's clever and he has a suitcase full of tricks. Sometimes David will play with the train but then he forgets to keep still and sooner or later Mother will tell him to be quiet. If you want to make noise you can play in your room.

David does not like to play in his room. He hates his room; his room scares him. His room is tall and damp and dark. The whole house is tall and damp and dark. When he was born his mother painted the room a bright creamy boy's blue. But all colors look the same in the dark, and no paint can prevent the bureau from turning into a hulking beast. David will lie with his blanket jammed up under his chin, shivering because the room is so cold. The bureau will gnash its teeth and open its jaws to swallow him. David will scream. The maid will come running. When she sees that he is fine, only having a nightmare, she will scold David for being such a fraidy-cat. Does he expect to grow up and be strong, or does he want to be a fraidy-cat all his life? No, he wants to grow up. Then why does he act like a fraidy-cat? Why isn't he brave? Why doesn't he shut his eyes and go to sleep? The maid's name is Delia and she looks like a monster, too, with blotchy cheeks and bony fingers and a nightcap sitting high on her head, like brains swelling out of a broken skull. She yells at him all the time. She yells at him if he is late and if he is early. She yells at him if he eats too much and if he does not eat. She bakes cakes but won't give him a slice, she leaves them under crystal domes until they turn stale and crumble. Then she discards them and bakes new ones. David doesn't understand. Why bake a cake if not to eat it? What else are cakes for? Once he tried to take a piece and she whipped him. He now regards the cake stand as a betrayer, giving it a wide berth when he passes.

On nights when he screams, she will scold him and perhaps whip him, if she is in a sour enough mood; then she will leave him there, in bed, among the monsters. He will try to be brave, he will try to go to sleep. Roger Dollar would not scream so there's no reason for him to scream, he ought not to be such a fraidy-cat. But then every time he opens his eyes, he will see more of them: the bureau, yes; also the mirror, the miniature wooden valet, the carved posts at the end of his bed. His hat rack, so cheery in daylight, teems with snakes, hissing and spitting and crawling up the mattress toward the only exposed part of him: his eyes, they are going to bite him, bite his eyes, slither into his face and then he will be unable to scream, they will eat his tongue, he had better scream while he still can . . . Nevertheless he learns not to scream. He learns his lesson. At home you must keep your mouth shut and not say anything. That is the rule.

On Friday nights (Father calls them *Family Nights*), David sits on the rug and plays in his head, because although Mother does not often yell her rules are the same as Delia's, and more swiftly enforced. Sometimes he wonders if they are in fact sisters, Mother and Delia, so similarly do they behave. David has noticed that Delia sometimes talks to Father the way that Mother does: with *sass*. She is the only employee who may do so, and she does it under Mother's protection. Certainly David cannot sass. He has been warned. How it is that Delia can sass to Father and Mother can sass to Father and Father can sass at everyone else but David cannot sass to anyone, he does not understand. When he sasses he gets whipped. Does Delia get whipped when she sasses? Does Mother? Does it happen out of his sight? There are many things he does not understand. David turns six soon. Perhaps then he, too, will be allowed to sass. Perhaps that is what it means to grow up.

The news on the radio is all about the *Depression*. Like Delia's untouched cakes and the rules of sass, the Depression is another thing that David wants to understand. Father talks of tightening his belt and Mother in response says that they must live like human beings. David does not understand the connection. If you tightened your belt, why couldn't you live like a human being, except with tighter pants? Could you live like a human being if your pants were falling down? Of course not. David sides with Father, decisively.

The Depression has always existed. Yet his parents talk about Before. Before, we used to have more help around the house. Before we made adjustments. Delia talks about Before, too; Before, she had a friend, and now there is nobody for her to talk to. David can see that Delia is lonely. Why? There are plenty of other people around her. There's Mother and Father and the cook and the driver and the butler and the man who comes to take the pictures and the doctor with the oily leather bag and all sorts of people, all the time. The house is never empty. So why does Delia seem so lonely? And if she's so lonely, why does she act so nasty? David can easily see that more people would smile at her if she smiled herself. That much he understands. There may be a lot she knows that he doesn't, but at least he can feel smarter about that.

The Depression, as far as David can tell, has something to do with the weather. So says Father. We'll have to weather it. Or horses: we'll have to ride it out. Perhaps – and here David feels on uncertain ground – it has to do with ships, and leaking. He wishes he understood better, because these storms and horses and leaky vessels exert a strong effect on his parents' mood, particularly Father's. Sometimes Father will come home in a terrible state, casting a black spell across the household. Dinners will be silent, no sound but squeaking knives. Father might start to talk about the news but Mother will then say Not at the table or Please, Louis and Father will fall quiet again.

Friday night, Family Night, Father retreats to the corner with the big radio and switches on the lamp with the pretty green glass shade and sits with his legs crossed, tenting his fingers or chewing at the corners of his nails, a habit Delia calls dirty. Or he pulls gently on his earlobes, as though he's trying to stretch them like taffy. He seems to disappear into the cushions, and David will sometimes stop playing the game in his head and look at him, with his hairy lip and his sunken cheeks and eyes like marbles that want to shoot across the floor. He fiddles with his necktie but never removes it. His shoes are a lustrous black, and if David creeps close enough he can see his bulging reflection in their shiny, rounded caps.

Mother reads books. They have names like *The Rose of Killarney* and *The Wife of the Saxon Chieftain*. David tried to look inside one of her books once, but could not understand. This is not because he cannot read. He learned to read, the tutor taught him. To practice he reads the picture books. Sometimes, when Delia has thrown away the newspaper – she reads it out loud to the chef, who is from Italy and whose accent makes him sound like he's singing, all the time, even when he is not – he will fish it out of the trash and sit in the cupboard with it. Like Father, all the newspaper seems to care about is the Depression.

On Friday nights David stands at the window and looks down at the men and women walking in their hats and their scarves. Cars used to honk until the noise drove Mother loony and she couldn't stand it a second longer and she had the men come and put on a second set of windows, glass as thick as David's fingers. Now the picture show in the street makes no sound at all. David doesn't mind. He can supply the voices and the sounds in his head, where he keeps so much.

Come away from there, David.

He goes back to his spot on the rug, lies down, and looks at the ceiling, where there are paintings of angels that Father had put there. They are playing trumpets and flowers are coming out of them. The trumpets, not the angels. It would be funny if flowers came out of the angels. But coming out of the trumpets they just look silly. David never says anything because Father seems quite fond of his angels.

This Friday night in particular, he is in the middle of extracting Roger Dollar from a very difficult situation. Roger has been kidnapped by lawless bandits who want to take his gold. He is using an oar to fight them off, and as the bandits fire their guns, David hears someone coming down the stairs. He is surprised. Nobody may come into the drawing room on Family Night; anybody who does will probably get whipped, worse than if they sassed.

He looks at Mother and Father. Neither of them have noticed anything.

David wonders if he imagined the footsteps. He has a strong imagination, so strong he sometimes gets lost in it. Instead of reviewing his lessons, math or German or music, he will focus on the faint whoop of a cardinal, two slow calls and then a series of sharp ones, or on the way a crack in the plaster traces its way up the wall, like a river flowing upward. He will spin such impressions into elaborate stories, jungle exploration, clashes between savage tribes full of men with pointy teeth and drawings on their bodies, he saw them in *Ripley's Believe It or Not*. David knows that distraction takes him easily. When he returns to the world, it is usually through a tunnel of shouts, at the end of which Delia stands, grinding her jaw and cracking her knuckles.

He did not imagine the footsteps. They are coming closer, in bursts of four or five, as though the person is learning how to walk.

Should he get up? He could pretend to go to the bathroom, and on the way warn the approaching stranger to turn back. It's Family Night, don't go in there!

But what if the stranger is dangerous: a monster, or worse? What if David needs to protect Mother and Father? What if he can save only one of them? Who would he choose? The answer comes quickly: Father. Father is skinnier, and David likes him more. Mother, with her heaving bosom, her huge raft of skirts, could probably defend herself. If she didn't manage that would be okay, too.

Now Mother puts down her book.

'Louis.'

Father has passed out, his eyelids fluttering.

'Louis.'

Father wakes. 'What's that, Mother?'

'There's someone in the hall.'

'Who's that.'

'I heard a noise.'

Father nods sleepily. 'Yes.'

'Well? Go see what it is.'

Father takes a deep breath and unfurls himself from deep within his armchair. His legs looks like a spider's, frail and long and jointed, and though he looks small in his chair, when he rises, it is always to an awesome height.

'Did you hear something?' he asks David.

David nods.

Father tugs at his collar and yawns. 'Let's have a look, shall we?'

Before he can, the door swings open with a shriek. Father jumps back and Mother puts her hand to her chest and David blinks furiously, trying to keep quiet. In comes a girl he has never seen before. She is wearing a

182

white nightgown, so thin that the fabric is see-through; and she is weird-looking, with small bosoms and a rounded stomach and hairy arms. She is short. Her face is squashed, like a frog's. Her tongue sticks out of her mouth like she has tasted something rotten. Her hair is smooth and tied back with a yellow bow. She has slanty eyes that dart around the room, looking at this chair and that wall and then at Mother and Father. Then she looks at David and she seems to start to smile. He does not smile back; he is frightened and he wants to hide.

Mother leaps up, dropping her book on the floor.

Father says, 'Bertha—'

Mother crosses the room in three big steps; she takes the girl by the wrist and pulls her from sight. David hears them going up the stairs.

Father says, 'Are you all right?'

Why wouldn't he be all right? Nothing happened to him. David nods.

Father runs a hand down his shirtfront, smooths down his tie. He touches his moustache, as though the commotion might have ruffled it. He looks for his glasses – they are in his breast pocket, where they always are – but instead of putting them on he repockets them.

'Are you sure you're all right?'

'Yes, Father.'

'Good. Good. Good.' Father smooths his tie again. 'Dear God.'

Dear God what? It sounds to David as though Father wants to write a letter. But he says no more.

Mr Lester Schimming's variety hour is sponsored by Mealtime, Mealtime, the once-a-day nutritional powder that—

Father shuts the radio off. He curls into the armchair, once again becoming small. He is pale, his breathing is loud, and he pulls on his earlobes. David would like to go to him, to put a hand on his forehead the way Mother does when David is sick. He would like to bring him water, or some of the sharp-smelling purple stuff that Father drinks before going to sleep. But David knows to be quiet. He stays in place. He says nothing.

Later, Mother comes back. Her mouth is a wire. She does not look either at David or at Father, but picks up her book and returns to the chaise. She lies down and begins turning pages as though never interrupted, and although Father is staring at her with a fearful expression, she clears her throat loudly and he looks away.

NOW DAVID HAS A MYSTERY.

More than one. So many mysteries that he can barely contain himself, and when he lies awake that night, it isn't from fear but from excitement. He can be an explorer, like Roger Dollar. He will make a plan; he will – as the detective on the radio show says – get to the bottom of this.

He begins by making a list of questions.

Who is the girl?
Why does she look weird?
How did she get in the house?
How old is she?
Where is she now?
Why did Mother react the way she did?
Why did Father react the way *he* did?
Why did Mother grow angry at Father?
Why did they ignore David for the rest of that evening? (Actually, that
    question needs no answer. They always ignore him.)

The questions flap around his head like owls whooping *who who who, how how how, why why why.*

He knows one thing for sure: he cannot ask Mother or Father. He feels certain that to ask is to earn a whipping. The same applies to Delia. He must seek out the answers on his own. And he must be very careful, because he has the feeling that Mother will not tolerate one ounce of mischief.

First he gathers information. The next night at dinner David observes his parents, watching for anything unusual. They eat barley soup and roast beef and the tiny pasta ears that the cook makes. Father has his purple drink early. When he motions for another Mother gives him an evil stare, and he changes his request to a half a glass. Otherwise all goes normally.

At least until the end of the meal. Then – instead of parting, as they usually do, Father to his study and Mother to her sewing room – both of them rise and head out the same door, the one that leads to the east wing of the house. David would like to follow, but Delia arrives to escort him to his bath.

Afterward he climbs into bed. Delia asks if he wants a story and he says no thank you. He cannot wait for her to leave, and when she does he counts to fifty, then slips quietly from underneath the blanket and stands in his socks, shivering, strategizing.

The house has four stories. Like his bedroom, Mother's sewing room is on the third floor. Father's study is on the fourth. David reckons that they are not likely to meet in either of those places; they have changed their pattern, and will probably choose a third place. But where?

The first floor has a foyer where guests take cocktails. There are lots of rooms hung with paintings, one of which has the family portraits: his grandfather and great-grandfather, as well as great-uncles, great-great-uncles, men stretching back almost a hundred years, an inconceivable amount of time. There is Solomon Muller, smiling kindly. Beside him, his brothers: Adolph with the crooked nose and Simon with the warts and Bernard with the bushy balloons of hair at either side of his head. Papa Walter, looking like he has eaten too much peppery food. Father's portrait is halfway done, David knows. Father has shown him where it will go once completed. And yours will go here. And your son's, there. David saw the empty panels as windows into the future.

The second floor does not seem a likely meeting place: aside from the dining room and the kitchen, it is mostly taken up by the ballroom, which stays shuttered and dark all year, except for the night when Mother throws her Autumn Ball. Then the doors swing open and the featherdusters fly. Chairs are unbelted and unstacked, tables erected, linens spread, silver polished and aligned. The orchestra arrives and the room fills with swishing silk of all colors. Last year David was allowed to attend for the first time. Everybody fawned over him in his coat. He waltzed with Mother. They gave him wine; he fell asleep and woke up the next morning in his bed. He feels confident assuming that his parents will not have their meeting there.

The third floor is his bedroom, Mother's sewing room, and lots of guest rooms. That is what his room is: a guest room they have made into a special room for him. You are always a welcome guest, says Father. David's not sure what that means. Also on the third floor are the library, the music room, the Round Room, the radio room (where they spend Family Night), and many rooms full of breakable objects whose purpose he has yet to discern. All of these seem too small and ordinary to contain an event David expects to be momentous.

The fourth floor, the top floor, belongs to his parents' private suites. It is a realm seldom visited and redolent of unanswered questions. He will try there first.

It's not an easy operation. He cannot take the elevator; too much noise. He cannot take the east stairs, because servants use them to go up and down, and if they see him, he will be returned to bed. The south stairwell is near Delia's room – she, too, has a guest room, unlike the rest of the help, whose rooms are in the basement. She leaves her door open at night, so that if David needs something he can call her with the bell. That way, too, she can hear him screaming when he sees monsters. Surely she will hear him if he walks past. He wraps his blanket around his shoulders and thinks.

Sometimes Delia has visitors in her room. David can hear them laughing, can taste the smoke drifting down the hall. He could wait until they arrived and hope to slip by unnoticed . . .

No. Tonight she might not have any visitors, and even if she does, who knows when they will come. He has already wasted too much time. He needs a different plan.

Down the hall is a bathroom adjacent to Delia's room. The toilet there has a big chain you pull on, and it makes a lot of noise, enough to cover a quick dash from there to the stairs. A problem: he has his own bathroom. Using a different one will arouse Delia's suspicions. What would Roger Dollar do?

As usual, Delia's door is halfway open. He knocks. She says to come in, sounding friendly; when she sees that it is him, she frowns and asks what's wrong.

'I need to use the bathroom.'

Her frown deepens. 'Then use it, then.'

'There's no paper,' he says.

She crushes out her cigarette and turns over her book and sighs, flicking a finger at the hallway behind him. 'Use mine, then.'

He thanks her and says goodnight. She does not answer.

He closes her door on his way out. Not all the way; that would arouse her suspicion.

He goes to the bathroom. It's not hard to pee when you want to. He wads up some paper and throws it in the bowl. Then he takes a deep breath and pulls the chain, bringing a roar of water and eight seconds of freedom. He goes.

He does not stop moving until he has reached the fourth-floor landing. He tiptoes down the hall until he comes to two pairs of large wooden doors, each carved with the family crest, separated by twenty-five feet of satiny wallpaper: the entrances to his parents' private suites.

Behind one door, his father is talking.

David presses his ear to the door but cannot understand the conversation. The door is too heavy and thick. He must get inside. But how? He remembers that the two suites are connected by an internal passageway. If he enters one suite, he could hide in that passageway and listen. Success depends on whether he chooses the right suite to begin with. Otherwise he will walk straight into them, and he will be in hot water. He listens at the other set of carved doors. The voices sound stronger – still incomprehensible, though – leading him to conclude that his best bet is to go through Mother's room.

His heart speeds up as he reaches for the doorknob, turns, and pushes. It is bolted from the inside.

Now what? He scans the hallway for another option, and right away he finds one: a closet. He checks to make sure that he can fit inside. Then he goes to the door of his mother's suite and presses the buzzer.

The voices inside cease. Footsteps approach. David scampers into the closet and closes the door. He waits in the darkness.

'Damn you,' he hears his father say, 'I gave' – the snap of a deadbolt – 'instructions' – the squeal of a door – 'not to be—'

Silence.

The door closes.

David lets out his breath. He counts to fifty, exits the closet, and goes to the doors, which he prays his father has forgotten to lock.

He has.

In David goes, moving stealthily across the large Persian carpet. From the passageway drifts the sound of his father's voice. His parents' suites are enormous, consisting of many rooms – a bedchamber and a bathroom and a sitting room; drawing rooms and Father's study . . . and each of those rooms is ten times as big as David's. In Mother's suite she keeps her own gramophone and radio, a matched set inlaid with mother-of-pearl. David knows what mother-of-pearl is because he has a toy box with mother-of-pearl on the top. When he asked Delia what it was and she told him, he thought she meant a person. He asked where she lived, Pearl's mother who made boxes, and Delia laughed at him. Also in Mother's suite are a grand piano and a small painted harpsichord, neither of which she plays. Atop a carved table sit three dozen glass eggs. He knows the name for them: hand coolers. He picks up a brightly colored one and indeed it helps soothe his sweaty palms. He goes barefoot into the passageway and follows the voices until he reaches the entrance to Father's sitting room. He gets down on the ground and crawls forward, peeks out through the crack in the door. He cannot see Mother's face, as it is obscured by a tall vase. All he can see of her is a motionless arm. Father is pacing the room and flinging his hands in every direction. David has never heard voices quite like these: angry whispering, whispers that would be shouts if they were only a bit louder.

Father is saying, '– forever.'

'I'm aware of that.'

'Then what do you propose. Give me a better idea and I will do it.'

'You know what I think.'

'No. *No. Aside* from that. I told you already, I will never – *never*, never – consent to that, never. Can I possibly make myself clearer?'

'I have no other suggestions. I'm already at wits' end.'

'And I'm not? Do you imagine that this is easier for me than it is for you?'

'Not at all. Frankly, I would think that it has been a great deal *more* difficult for you. You are vastly more sentimental.'

Father says a word David has never heard before.

'Louis. Please.'

'You aren't helping me.'

'What would you like me to do?'

'*Help me.*' Father stops pacing and stares where Mother's face should be. He looks like he's on fire. He points up at the ceiling. 'Don't you feel *anything.*'

'Stop shouting.'

'Don't tell me you don't feel it too.'

'I will not have a conversation with you when you're like this.'

'Answer me.'

'Not if you insist on sh—'

'Look, Bertha. Look up. *Look.* You can't feel that? Tell me you cannot, I don't believe that anyone has so little heart, not even you, to pretend as though you can walk around without being crushed by that weight.' Silence. 'Answer me.' Silence. 'You have no right to sit there and say nothing.' Silence. 'Damn it, answer me.' Silence. 'You do not behave like this. Not after everything I've given you. I've given you everything you've asked for, been exactly what you demanded—'

'Not everything, Louis. Not exactly.'

Silence of a different kind: infused with terror.

Father upends a table. Ceramic dishes and a wooden cigar box and crystal figurines sail across the room, producing a mighty crash. The glass table-top shatters. Mother screams. In the passageway, David cringes, ready to bolt. From another place in the room comes a second, smaller shattering, and when the noise finally subsides, he hears weeping, two different rhythms in two different registers.

HE WORKS OUT THE CLUES. It takes a few days, because he has to wait until he goes to the Park with Delia in order to confirm his hunch. As they return from their walk, David counts windows and discovers that he has been wrong. The house does not have four stories. It has five.

How this could have escaped him until now, he does not know. The house is big, though, and he has often been scolded for wandering into forbidden territory. A whole wing remains off-limits, and David, generally lost in his own head, prone to long bouts of stationary dreaming, has never been one to overstep, not under threat of a whipping.

But to get to the bottom of this, he must break the rules.

The entrance to the rear wing lies through the kitchen, a place thick with steam and hazards. He has never ventured beyond the sink. Four days later, when he is supposed to be in his room, reviewing his German lesson, he sneaks downstairs. The cook is rolling dough. David straightens his backbone, puts on a bold face, and walks past him. The cook never looks up.

Through a swinging door he comes to a second room, where a pile of raw meat lies on a huge, scarred table. With its reek of fat and flesh, its spattered walls, its lakes of blood pooling round the table legs, the room exerts a queer, morbid pull, and David has to remind himself to keep moving, not to stop and examine the heavy, menacing instruments hung on the wall, the bloodstained grout . . .

He comes to a hallway checked black-and-white. He tries a number of doors before finding the one he wants: an alcove for the service elevator.

He gets in. Unlike the main elevator, this one has a button for a fifth floor.

As the car rises, it occurs to him to worry about who he might run into up there. If the girl is indeed there, what will he do? What if there are other people – a guard, say. Or a guard dog! His heart skips. Too late for worrying. The car bounces to a stop and the doors open.

Another hallway. Here the carpeting is loose and worn, pulling away from the walls. At the end of the hall are three doors, all closed.

The wind sings, and he looks up at a skylight. The sky is cloudy. It might rain.

He walks to the end of the hall and listens. Nothing.

He knocks softly on each of the doors. Nothing.

He tries one. It is a closet full of sheets and towels.

The next door swings open and the smell of camphor rolls over him. He stifles a cough and steps inside.

The room is unoccupied. There is a small bed, neatly made, and opposite it an armoire, painted white with horses and other animals, a peaceful little scene. He throws it open and jumps back, ready to fight off a snarling beast.

Bare hangers stir.

Disappointed, he tries the third door and finds a bathroom, also empty.

He returns to the bedroom and walks to the window. From it he has a wonderful view of Central Park, perhaps the best in the house. The trees are soft and green and shivering beneath the slaty sky. Birds turn circles over the Reservoir. He wants to stick his head out and see more but the window is nailed shut.

He tries to put together what he has learned, to set out all the clues in front of him, but they do not add up. Perhaps he will learn when he gets older. Or perhaps he was wrong: there was no girl, and he imagined the entire episode. It wouldn't be the first time he accidentally grafted one of his fantasies onto a real memory. He might have misunderstood his parents' argument. He doesn't understand, and he knows he doesn't understand, awareness making ignorance twice as painful.

Spirits sinking, he turns to go. For a moment he hopes something will have changed. But the room is still empty, the bed still mute, the floor still dusty and plain.

Then he sees something he missed. Under the bed, against the wall, almost invisible; he kneels down and reaches for it and grasps it and pulls it out and holds it up. It's a girl's shoe.

FOURTEEN

I woke up in a bed at St Vincent's, and the first thing I said was, 'Where's the art?'

Marilyn looked up from her magazine. 'Oh good,' she said. 'You're up.' She went into the hallway and returned with a nurse, who began subjecting me to a battery of tests, hands and instruments shoved up my nose and down my throat.

'Marilyn.' It rather came out as *Mayawa*.

'Yes, darlin.'

'Where's the art?'

'What did he say?'

'Where's the art. The art. Where's the art.'

'I can't understand him, can you?'

'Art. Art.'

'Can you give him something so he won't bark?'

Some time later I woke up again.

'Marilyn. Marilyn.'

She appeared through the curtain, her smile fatigued. 'Hello again. Did you have a nice nap?'

'Where's the art?'

'Art?'

'The drawings.' My eyes hurt. My head hurt. 'The Crackes.'

'You know, the doctor said you might be a little disoriented.'

'The drawings, Marilyn.'

'Do you want some more pain stuff?'

I grunted.

'I'll take that as a yes.'

I'll spare you further details of my reemergence. Suffice it to say that I had a wretched headache, that the busyness of the emergency room made my headache worse, and I was glad when they determined me well enough to leave. Marilyn didn't want me going home, though, and through money or influence she secured me a private room on the inpatient floor, which she told me I'd have as long as I felt unwell.

They wheeled me upstairs.

'You look like Étienne,' Marilyn said.

'How long have I been here?' I asked.

'About sixteen hours. You know, you're very boring when you're unconscious.' Underneath her sarcasm was genuine terror.

I was not too confused and miserable to wonder how she had gotten there.

'Your neighbor came back from walking his dog and found you on the front step. He called the ambulance and the gallery. Ruby called me this morning. Here I am. Incidentally, she's going to try to come by again this evening.'

'Again?'

'She was here. You don't remember?'

'No.'

'She and Nat both. They brought a box of éclairs, which the nurses took away, I believe for themselves.'

'Thank you,' I said to her. Then I thanked the intern pushing me. Then I fell asleep.

THE NEXT VISIT I REMEMBER CLEARLY was from the police. I told them as much as I could remember, starting from the moment I left the gallery and up until I set the box down on the sidewalk. They seemed disappointed that I couldn't given them even the thinnest description of my assailant, although my account of dinner at Sushi Gaki seemed to interest them particularly. Even in my semi-addled state, the idea that someone from the restaurant had assaulted me for a box of drawings struck me as outlandish. I tried to convince them of this, but they kept harping on my 'showing the stuff around'.

'I wasn't advertising anything,' I said. 'The hostess asked to see it.'

'Does she know what you do?'

'I don't know. I don't think so. I might have mentioned it at one time or another. She's ninety-five pounds, for God's sake.'

'It didn't have to be her, necessarily.'

They continued to pursue this line of questioning until my headache forced me to close my eyes. When I opened them next, the police were gone and Marilyn was back. She'd brought éclairs to replace the ones the nursing staff had filched.

'You don't deserve me,' she said.

'You're right,' I said. 'Marilyn?'

'Yes, darlin boy.'

'I'm feeling something on my face.'

She took out her compact and pointed the mirror at me.

I was aghast.

'It's not that bad,' she said.

'It looks bad.'

'It's just a big bandage. It won't even scar.'

'Am I missing a tooth?'

'Two.'

'How did I not notice that?' I poked my tongue around in the gaps.

'You're on a lot of drugs.' She patted her purse. 'I've got some myself.'

Ruby came. 'Sorry I couldn't make it earlier, things've been crazy. We'll be ready, don't worry.'

'Ready for what?' I asked.

'You have an opening tonight,' said Marilyn.

'We do? Whose?'

'Alyson.'

I sighed. 'Shit.'

Ruby said, 'She sends her best. She's going to visit tomorrow.'

'Tell her not to come,' I said. 'I don't want to see anyone. Shit.'

'It'll be fine. We have everything under control.'

'I'm giving you a raise,' I told her. 'Nat, too.'

Marilyn said, 'Ask for a health plan.'

'They already have a health plan.'

'Then ask for a company jet.'

'Actually,' Ruby said, 'we could do with a new mini-fridge. The old one's been making noise.'

'Since when?'

'A few weeks.'

'I hadn't noticed.'

Ruby shrugged, the meaning of which was clear enough. Of course I hadn't noticed; I hadn't been around the gallery.

'Go ahead,' I told her. 'Get whatever you need. And call me after the opening.'

'Thank you.'

She left, and I said to Marilyn, 'I hope they're okay.'

'They'll be fine. In fact, as far as I can tell, your absence is serving only to prove how irrelevant you are.'

*

THE COMBINATION OF A SEVERE CONCUSSION and all-you-can-eat painkillers doesn't do wonders for your ability to gauge the passage of time. I think it was on my third morning when I woke up and saw that Marilyn, sitting in the purple vinyl chair, reading *Us Weekly*, was no longer Marilyn but Samantha.

I considered this a fairly nasty joke on the part of my subconscious. I said, 'Give me a break.'

Samantha/Marilyn looked up. She put down the magazine and stood by my bedside. 'Hi,' she said. Her warm hand made the rest of me feel cold. I began to shiver.

'Are you okay?' she said.

'Give me a break . . .'

'I'm going to get the nurse.'

'That's right, Marilyn! Get the nurse!'

I expected the nurse to have Samantha's face, as well. But she was black.

'Very funny,' I said.

'What's he talking about?' Samantha/Marilyn asked.

'I don't know.'

Then Marilyn herself came in, carrying two cups of vending-machine coffee. She saw the nurse checking my blood pressure and said, 'What's going on.'

'He called me your name.'

'Well,' said Marilyn/Marilyn, 'that's better than if he called me your name.'

I fell asleep.

AN HOUR LATER I woke up feeling clearheaded. Both Marilyn and Samantha were still there, engaged in a lively conversation that, thankfully, had nothing to do with me, Marilyn in the middle of one of her Horatio Alger stories about when she was penniless and used to steal fruit from the lobby of the Plaza Hotel. I groaned, and they both turned to look. They came and stood by the bed, one on each side of me.

'Did you have a good nap?' Marilyn asked.

'I feel much more awake now,' I said.

'There's a reason for that. I was noticing that you looked a little glazed over. Then you started to call everyone Marilyn, so we brought the doctor in and he scaled back your drip a tiny bit. Better?'

'Yes. Thank you.'

'I have to admit: I found it rather flattering that it was *me* you saw everywhere.'

I smiled weakly.

'Samantha was telling me about your case,' said Marilyn. 'There's so much more to it than you shared with me, so many lovely little details. Oatmeal?'

I said, 'It's just a theory.'

'Well, I'll let you two do your *sleuthing*. I'm going home. I need a shower. Nice to meet you. Take care of him.'

Samantha pulled the chair up to the bedside. 'You didn't say anything about having a girlfriend.'

'Our relationship doesn't work that way,' I said.

'What way would that be? Honestly?'

'It wouldn't bother her if she knew,' I said. 'I'll tell her right now, if you'd like. Catch her before she gets in the elevator and bring her back.'

Samantha rolled her eyes.

'What did you two talk about?' I asked.

'Clothes, mostly.'

'She's got plenty to talk about.'

'So I gathered.'

'That's it?' I asked. 'Clothes.'

'I didn't tell her, if that's what you're getting at.' She shifted around, straightened up. 'Are you surprised to see me?'

'A little.'

'You should be. I'm a little surprised to be here myself. When do you get out?'

'Soon, I hope. Maybe tomorrow or Friday.'

'Okay. In the meantime I'm going to finish up collecting DNA from people who were in the apartment. I found the list you made. I also spoke to the lab. We'll have results on the semen and bloodstains within three weeks. Anything else I'm missing?'

'The other cases.'

'What other cases.'

'Your father wanted to look through old cases to see if any of them fit the profile. Detective Soto was working on it for him.'

'All right. I'll call him. You rest up and get out of here and we'll talk then.' She stood up. 'You know, you really made me feel like shit about my dad.'

'I'm sorry.'

She shrugged. 'Too late now.'

'I'm still sorry.'

'So am I,' she said.

FIFTEEN

I checked out the next day. Marilyn sent a limousine to pick me up, instructing the driver to take me to her town house. Certainly I had no intention of going back to my place. The person who had assaulted me had to be familiar with my comings and goings; either he had followed me from the warehouse or he'd been waiting around the corner from my building. Either way, I thought a few days under the radar would be prudent.

My prudence was nothing compared to Marilyn's. In the back of the limo was a bodyguard, a mammoth Samoan in a Rocawear tracksuit. He introduced himself as Isaac; his hand swallowed mine; he was at my service until further notice. To me, this was going overboard, but I wasn't about to start arguing with a man his size.

As one would expect, Marilyn's house is done in the best taste; it's also surprisingly livable, albeit tailored to her quirks. She has two kitchens, a full one on the bottom floor and a smaller one near her bedroom, so she can cook herself waffles or eggs or a steak or whatever strikes her fancy at three in the morning. You've seen her block before; it has appeared as the backdrop for many a television show, the downtown real-estate equivalent of Murderer's Row – tall, skinny, picturesque West Village brownstones, each with a patio out back and a throng of camera-happy Midwesterners out front. The *Sex and the City* bus tour stops two doors down to allow its patrons the opportunity to memorialize the spot where, I'm told, Carrie and Aidan had an argument during season four.

Isaac, used to battling paparazzi, had no trouble getting me through the crowd.

The maid let us in. Marilyn had ordered a room made up on the first floor so that I wouldn't have to walk up the stairs. On the bed were three new sets of clothing, Barneys tags still attached. She had set out a tray of spice cookies and a little plastic jack-o'-lantern with a note tucked inside. I opened it up. It said *Boo*.

I went into the bathroom and got my first good look at myself in days. They had changed the dressing on my face several times, each time putting on a slightly lighter one, until all I had were Band-Aids covering my left cheek from dimple to hairline. I peeled one of the bandages back and saw a thin patch of scab, like someone had gone after me with a potato peeler. The missing teeth were also on the left side. The shock of seeing them gone started me laughing; I looked like I'd just wandered down out of the Appalachians.

I found a bottle of ibuprofen and shook out four. In my jacket I had a prescription for OxyContin, which I intended to fill and then give away, either to Marilyn or as party favors. I went to grab a bite from the lower kitchen and found Isaac on a folding chair outside my room, blocking the hallway with his girth.

'I really think I'll be okay,' I said.

'That's what they want you to think.'

We went to the kitchen. I swallowed my pills. My appetite dwindled as soon as I took a bite of my turkey sandwich, so I offered Isaac the other, bigger half. He accepted gratefully, discarding the bread before eating the meat, lettuce and tomato.

'No carbs,' he explained.

'Right.'

All I wanted to do was sleep. Three days of sleeping will do that to you. I made myself a cup of coffee and called Marilyn at work.

'Did you find everything all right?'

'Yes. Thank you.'

'How's the man I sent you?'

Across the kitchen, Isaac was pouring himself a bowl of cereal. So much for his diet. 'Superb.'

'Greta recommended him. He used to work for Whitney Houston. Don't tell me you don't need it, I can tell you're about to say that.'

'I wasn't, in fact. I was just going to thank you.'

'You're welcome.'

'Really – I'm so grateful for—'

'Hush,' she said and hung up.

Next I called the gallery. Nat picked up. I asked how the opening had gone.

'Beautifully. Alyson was ecstatic.' Like me, Nat went to Harvard, but he graduated summa cum laude, writing his thesis on ambisexual iconography in Renaissance tapestry. His Boston accent is clipped and wry and fabulous, making him sound sort of like a gay Kennedy.

He told me about the show, concluding, 'And the fridge is on order. Oh, and something came in the mail for you from the Queens District Attorney. Do you want me to open it?'

'Please.'

'Hold on.' He put the phone down and came back a moment later. 'There's a little cotton swab thingy and a vial. It's some sort of – what is this?'

I heard Ruby say, 'A paternity kit.'

'It's a paternity kit,' Nat said. 'Did you impregnate the Queens District Attorney?'

'Not yet. Messenger it over here, would you.'

'Sí, señor.' Then, to Ruby: 'You know, you sound awfully well acquainted with this paternity thing. Are you in a family way *again*?'

'Bite me,' she called.

I smiled. 'Listen, I'm worried about the two of you. Whoever did this to me is out there and I don't want anything happening to you.'

'We're fiiine.'

'It would make me more comfortable if you didn't hang around the gallery. Close down for a couple of weeks and take a vacation. Paid.'

'But we just opened. Alyson will go ballistic. And I wouldn't blame her.'

'Keep your eyes open, then. Please. Do that for me.'

'We're fine, Ethan. Ruby knows kung fu. Tell him.'

'*Ki-yai!*'

I LEFT A MESSAGE FOR SAMANTHA and she called back within the hour, her tone all business.

'Did you get the kit?'

'Yes. Thank you. I'll do it today.'

'Good. I need you to think, Ethan: was there anything else that might possibly have a trace of Cracke's DNA on it?'

'There might be,' I said. While watching the nurse change my dressing in the hospital, I'd noticed that the color of the bloodied gauze looked eerily like that of the five-pointed star at the center of the Cherubs, a theory that appeared to me more and more brilliant as they continued to feed me drugs. In the sober light of day, it seemed not quite as brilliant, but given our shortage of viable leads, I didn't see how it hurt to consider the possibility.

'Even if it's blood,' she said, 'it might not be his blood.'

'That's true.'

'But it can't hurt. Let's give it a whirl.'

'Well, hang on. Here's the tough part. I don't have the drawing any-more.'

'Why not?'

'I sold it.'

'You're joking.'

I told her about Hollister.

'Are there any other drawings like that one?'

'I don't know. I don't think so. We can go through all of them but it'll take a while. First let me see what I can do about that one.'

I had no doubt that Hollister liked me enough to invite me back to his house. But he'd have to like me a lot more than that to allow me to start cutting samples out of his artwork. Which left me one option: if I really wanted that piece, I'd have to buy it back.

I hate to buy back art. Some dealers guarantee that if an item's market drops, they will repurchase it at sale price, allowing the buyer to walk away even. I won't. I think it infantilizes the client; part of the point of collecting is to hone one's own aesthetic sensibilities, and that happens only when one takes a personal stake in the matter.

And, understandably, I balked at forking over a large amount of money only to discover that the bloodstain was not a bloodstain, or not one that could give us any information. My hesitation turned out to be moot; when I called Hollister the next morning, his secretary told me he was unavailable.

Monday and Tuesday I lounged around Marilyn's house, Isaac tailing me, like I'd swapped shadows with a sumo wrestler. When I went to get my missing incisors replaced, he lobbied for gold rather than porcelain: 'All the big dogs got gold.'

On Wednesday the NYPD sent two men over to the house. These were not the same two I'd met in the hospital – at least as far as I could remember, which wasn't very far – but detectives from the major case squad who specialized in art theft. Immediately, I flagged them as rather an odd couple. Phil Trueg was all belly; his garish Jerry Garcia print tie stood out like an abdominal Mohawk. He had a strong Brooklyn accent and a tendency to laugh at his own jokes, which came fast and furious. His partner, on the other hand, was ten years younger, taut and tan and reserved, his outfit likewise muted, khaki bleeding into itself. His name was Andrade, although Trueg told me to call him Benny, an instruction that I decided to disregard.

Andrade and Trueg believed that the attacker's primary motivation had been to get the drawings rather than to injure me, and in support of this theory, they pointed to the fact that my wallet hadn't been taken. Nor, said Trueg, had I been beaten up 'any more than necessary'. (I replied that I didn't think any beating was necessary at all.) The thief was almost certainly an insider, connected to the art world or working for someone who was; otherwise, it was hard to understand how he would know of me or how he could hope to resell the drawings. The detectives asked me a long series of questions. I evaded the ones about my clientele; I didn't want the police pestering people who were obviously innocent and who would take strong umbrage at having their privacy invaded. I showed them the threatening letters I'd received from Victor Cracke and described at length my attempts to find him, my meetings with McGrath, my visit to the precinct.

Andrade squinted at the letters. 'Are you sure these came from him?'

'They look like his handwriting.'

'What does he want you to stop?' Trueg asked.

'I have no idea. I assume he was unhappy about the show. But in that case I can't understand why he would still be angry; the show came down almost a month ago.'

'He might want his drawings back,' said Andrade.

I didn't know what to say to that.

'Anybody else you can think of might have a grievance with you?'

The best name I could come up with – and I gave it to them reluctantly – was Kristjana Hallbjörnsdottir.

'Spell that, please.'

The plan was to wait and see where the art popped up. Since I was presumed to have in my possession all but a few of the drawings, any that came onto the market would by definition be stolen. This strategy was far from foolproof. There might have been other Crackes out there that I didn't know about, or the thief might never sell. But without eyewitnesses, we had few other options. And since I could not confirm my attacker's identity, a conviction would be difficult, if not impossible, without a tangible link – to wit, the drawings – between the crime and the perpetrator.

They left me in a state of utter exhaustion.

For the first few days of my convalescence, Marilyn played the role of overbearing mother. She called to check on me every half-hour, often cutting short my naps. She sent her assistants over with books that I couldn't concentrate on. At night she brought in dinner or else made me something, chicken, hamburgers – anything with protein – and forced me to eat, saying that I had lost too much weight and that I was beginning to look like Iggy Pop. I think she was trying to buoy my spirits, but the relentless stream of mockery began to grate on me. Her fear of losing me came in just shy of her fear of appearing corny, and so whenever she considered herself verging on sentimentality, she would pull back and make some unreasonable demand of me, resulting in conditions that were both doting and ruthless, as when she brought me in a sushi platter but ordered me out of bed to eat it.

'You have to move,' she said.

'I'm not an invalid, Marilyn.'

'Your legs are going to atrophy.'

'I'm tired.'

'That's the first sign. You need to get up and walk around.'

I told her that she would have made a terrible doctor.

'Thank God I'm a bitchy art dealer.'

Improbably, she also tried to insist on having sex. I told her I had a headache.

'You don't expect me to fall for that, do you?'

'I have a head injury.'

'All you have to do is lie there,' she said. 'Like you usually do.'

'Marilyn.' I had to physically pry her from my neck. 'Stop.'

She stood up, red-faced, and left the room.

The more she did things like that, the more I thought of Samantha. I know that it's cliché to run from those who love you most, and equally cliché to want what you cannot have, but for me these were new emotions. I'd never wanted to run from Marilyn; why would I? She gave me all the latitude a man could ask for. Only the most recent display of affection had caused me to feel stifled. And I'd never desired someone out of reach — mainly because nobody has ever been out of reach for me, not really.

KEVIN HOLLISTER CALLED ME BACK from Vail, where he was enjoying an unseasonably early snowfall.

'Eighteen inches of fresh powder. As close as it gets to perfect. God's country.' He sounded out of breath. 'I'll send a plane, you'll be on the slopes by noon.'

As much as I liked to ski, I couldn't stand up quickly without feeling like I'd been shot in the face. I told him I was under the weather.

'Next year, then. I'm having a birthday party at the house. My ex-wife put in a kitchen that can cook for two hundred. There are twelve ovens and I can't even make toast. I'm having' — here he named a celebrity chef — 'cater the whole thing. You'll be there.' He was huffing and puffing now, and I heard a faint noise, like Velcro.

'Are you skiing?' I asked.

'We are,' he said.

'I hope you're on a headset.'

'My jacket has an integrated microphone.'

I wondered who else he had with him. His interior designer, probably, or some other special lady friend two decades his junior. That's who my father would have had.

I told him our conversation could wait until he got back to New York.

'I'm traveling until after New Year's. Better now.'

'It's about the drawing.'

'Drawing.'

'The Cracke?'

'Aha, right.' He sniffled. 'You know, you're the second person this week to ask about that piece.'

'Really.'

'Yes. I had a long conversation about it, just a few days ago, in fact.'

'Who with?' I asked. He didn't hear me.

'Hello? Ethan?'

'Hi.'

'Ethan. Are you there.'

'I'm here. Can you—'

'Ethan? Hello? Shit. Hello? Fuck. Piece of shit.'

He hung up.

'I need to get a new system,' he said when he called back. 'This thing's always breaking. What was it you were saying?'

'I wanted to know about the drawing.'

'What about it.'

'I'm wondering if you might be interested in selling it back to me.'

'Why.' Instantly his voice went cold. 'Someone made you a better offer?'

'No. No. Not at all. I just feel a little regretful, is all, breaking up the piece the way I did. That section you have is the center, after all, and I think the integrity of the work should be preserved.'

'You had no problem breaking it up before.'

'Fair enough. But having had some time to think it over, I've changed my mind.'

'Out of curiosity, how much are you offering me?'

I quoted purchase price plus ten percent. 'That's not a bad return for one month.'

'I've had plenty of better months than that,' he said.

'Fifteen, then.'

'You seem like you're on a mission,' he said. 'And while I'd love to see where this goes, unfortunately for you, I'm a man of my word. The piece is spoken for.'

'Pardon me?'

'I sold it.'

I was dumbstruck.

'Hello?' he said. 'Are you there?'

'I'm here.'

'Did you hear me?'

'I heard you . . . Who's the buyer?'

'I'm not at liberty to say.'

'Kevin.'

'I'm sorry about that, I truly am. You know me, I'd love to tell you. But the buyer was very specific in wanting to remain anonymous.'

He sounded more like an art dealer than I'd thought possible. Marilyn had created a monster.

'What did you get for it,' I asked, expecting the same answer. Instead he replied with an absolutely staggering number.

'The nuttiest part? That was the first offer they made. I might have asked for more but I thought, "No sense in being greedy." Still, I made out like a fucking bandit.'

You'd think that, to a man like Hollister, selling a piece of art – even for a big profit – would provide little thrill, especially if you looked at the numbers in comparison to his net worth. What he made on the drawing, while mind-boggling to me, would at most take a decent bite out of his electricity bill. Yet he sounded like a gleeful child; I could almost see him rubbing his hands together. Rich men get rich in the first place because they never lose that lust for the kill.

I asked if he'd delivered the piece yet.

'Monday.'

I thought about asking if I could take one last look at it. But what would I do? Grab it and sprint away? How far could I get: running, with a head injury, carrying a sixty-square-foot canvas made of one hundred individual sheets of disintegrating paper? Besides, I had a clear notion of who the buyer was. Very few people had that kind of money to drop on an essentially unknown artist, and fewer still had the motivation.

Still a little shellshocked, I congratulated him on his sale.

'Thank you,' he said. 'Invitation stands if you want to join me.'

I wished him happy skiing and dialed Tony Wexler.

SIXTEEN

'What can I say? He's in love with it.'

We had agreed to meet up at a steakhouse in the east thirties. The first part of our conversation consisted of Tony oy-veying about my injuries (*Why didn't you call me? What did the police say? I don't like this, Ethan. Your father would want to know about this kind of thing. What if something worse happened? What would it take for you to give us a call? Would you have to lose a limb? Would you have to be run over? Because by that time, you won't be able to call anymore*) and me putting him off (*Fine, Tony. I'll call next time, Tony. No, I hope there won't be another next time, either*).

Then, glancing at Isaac, sitting three tables down, he had said, 'Where on God's green earth did you get *that*?'

I went on the offensive, accusing him of going behind my back.

He scoffed. 'The last time I checked, we live in a free-market society. We wanted something, we had the right price, everyone was in agreement, we bought it. I'm not sure you should be complaining. We significantly raised the profile on your artist.'

'That's not the point.'

'What's the point, then.'

'That drawing is part of the piece as a whole, and it should be restored.'

'Then why'd you sell it in the first place?'

'It was my mistake.' I turned my clenched teeth into a smile. 'Let me buy it from you. I'll give you – don't shake your head, you haven't heard my offer yet.'

'I seem to recall having this same conversation with you, in reverse.'

'I'll give you what you paid Hollister, plus an extra hundred grand.'

He looked offended. 'Do me a favor. Anyhow it won't matter: he's not selling.'

'You haven't even asked him.'

'I don't need to. If you're truly worried about leaving the piece incomplete – is that your concern? It's a matter of principle?'

'. . . yes.'

'Then I have a very elegant solution.'

I looked at him.

'Sell us the rest.'

'Tony.'

'Sell us the rest. Then it'll be complete.' He took a sip of water. 'That's the principle at stake, isn't it? You want to reunite the drawings. Fine. Sell us the rest of the piece and you can sleep easier at night.'

'I don't believe this.'

'What's not to believe?'

'Why are you doing this?'

'What am I doing?'

'You know what you're doing.'

'Tell me.'

'You're fucking me.'

'There's no need for that kind of language.'

'I mean, seriously, Tony, what do you expect me to say? "Thank you, what a great offer"?'

'Actually, I do. It *is* a great offer.'

'It's a shitty offer. I don't want to sell the pieces to you, I want one piece *back*. That's a lot more reasonable than me selling you the rest of the art.'

'As far as I can tell, the result is the same.'

'No, it isn't.'

'What's the difference?'

'You'll have it, and I won't.'

'You're an art dealer, aren't you? Isn't that what you do? Sell art to other people?'

'This isn't about the sale,' I said. 'You've already tried to buy the pieces from me, and I've already said no.'

'Then I believe we're at what they call an impasse.'

The clatter of forks and knives grew as the tables filled up, and my head began to pound. I turned from Tony and watched Isaac tuck into his porterhouse. I must have looked distressed, because he caught my eye and asked: thumbs-up or thumbs-down. I gave him a thumbs-up and he went back to eating. Under Tony's watchful, judgmental eye, I swallowed four ibuprofen, these in addition to the four I had taken before lunch.

'Are you feeling all right?' he asked.

'Yes.' I rubbed my eyes. 'Listen, it's not just for the sake of getting the piece back together that I want to buy it from you. There's something else going on.'

He waited.

'It's too complicated for me to explain.'

He raised an eyebrow.

'It is.'

He waited again.

I sighed. 'All right, listen.' I explained to him about the murders. As I talked he nodded sagely, taking it all in, and when I got through he said:

'I know.'

'What?'

'I heard all about that already.'

To tell you the truth, I wasn't that surprised. As I've mentioned, Tony knows more about the art world than he lets on. He keeps his ear to the ground, and I had no doubt that he'd done his homework before approaching Hollister. He'd know exactly how much to offer in order to avoid the inconvenience of haggling.

'Then what'd you make me repeat it for?'

'I knew about the rumors. I didn't know what you needed the drawing for.' He sat back, pursing his lips. 'Let me get this straight. You want to cut a hole in it.'

'A small one, I hope.'

He half-smiled. 'What happened to restoring the piece's integrity.'

'I'll have it repaired.'

'And you think – what. This is going to slam the coffin on him?'

'I have no clue. It might. It might not.'

'As far as I can see,' he said, 'even if you sample the piece, *and* it turns out to be blood, *and* that turns out to match, you're still facing the same problem.'

'Which is?'

'Which is you don't know where it came from. It could be Victor's, it could be someone else's.' The same point Samantha had made. 'If he did all that stuff you're accusing him of, I don't see why it's that big a stretch for him to keep an inkpot with blood in it. So getting the drawing won't help you very much.'

'Well, let me be the judge of that.'

'I don't think so,' he said. 'In case you've forgotten, the piece belongs to us.'

'Can we not make this an issue of territory?'

'Listen to you. You're the one making the demands here. You're the one crying *droit moral*. And you're telling me not to be territorial? That's some chutzpah you're putting out on display there.'

'Why shouldn't I have the *droit moral*? I discovered him.'

He smiled. 'Is that so. Because the way I remember it, I had to beg you to—'

'Once I saw them—'

'That's right. *Once* you saw them. If anybody's got a claim, it's your father. The land belongs to him, the contents of the apartment were his. We did you a favor.'

I said, 'I'm not going to argue about this with you.'

'What is there to argue?'

'You're right. Okay, Tony? You're right. I don't care about that. I want to make a deal. Let's make one. I'll pay you double what you paid Hollister.'

He shook his head. 'You're missing the—'

'Triple.' That was far too much money for me, but I didn't care.

'Forget it,' Tony said. Perhaps he knew I couldn't afford to pay him.

'How much do you want, then? Name it.'

'It's not the money. You have your principles. We have ours. We're not going to sell you art so you can destroy it.'

'Will you give me a fucking break.'

'If you keep talking like that, I'm not going to pay for dessert.'

'I'm not *destroying* the art, Tony.'

'Really. What do you call it.'

'They sample canvases all the time,' I said. 'For research.'

'Not from the dead center. Not on a piece of contemporary art. It's not the Shroud of Turin, for crying out loud. And why the hell do you care, anyway?'

'Because this is important, Tony. It's more important than a drawing.'

'Listen to you,' he said. He took out his wallet and put two hundred dollars down on the table. 'You sound like a different person, you know that?'

'Wait a second.'

'That's for lunch.'

'That's it?' I asked. 'You're not even going to ask him?'

'I don't need to,' he said, standing up. 'I know his priorities.'

I CALLED SAMANTHA.

'It's a delicate situation,' I said. 'I'm sorry.'

'There must be another panel with blood on it.'

'Can't you, I don't know. Subpoena him.'

'I'm not sure that anybody's going to believe we have compelling reason to seize the drawing from your father. What he said to you is essentially correct: the blood might not be blood, it might not be the right blood, it might not tell us anything. If we start asking for permission to slice up a multimillion-dollar piece of artwork—'

'It's not worth that much.'

'In your opinion.'

'I'm telling you, he overpaid. He'd never get that much on the open market.'

'Well, I'm reasonably sure your father can find another expert who'll testify it's worth more. And I'm sure he has some pretty good lawyers with a lot of free time. All I'm saying, if you can find me another drawing, that'd make both our lives easier.'

'The last time I got a box out of the warehouse I got assaulted.'

'I hope you're more careful, then.' She paused. 'Sorry. That was a little harsh.'

'It's all right.'

'Look, we'll go through the drawings together. How does that sound.'

'Fine.'

A silence. When she spoke again, she sounded much milder: 'How's your head?'

'Better every day. It'd be a lot better if I had some idea who did this to me.'

'I hate to break it to you, but you'd be better off forgetting about that.'

I lightly fingered the bandages on my face. 'Is it really that bleak?'

'Without a witness or a description? It really is.'

I found this enormously depressing.

'Let's meet up in a few days,' she said. 'We'll start by reviewing the evidence that you and my dad had.'

I suggested dinner.

'I was thinking more like you come to my office. Did you send back that swab?'

'Yes.'

'I'll call and find out what's going on with the rest of the samples.'

'All right.'

'And Ethan?'

'Yes?'

'Don't ask me to dinner anymore.'

SEVENTEEN

The Queens District Attorney's office comprises several bureaus, scattered throughout various buildings in and around the criminal courthouse in Kew Gardens. The Investigations Division occupies several stories of a shiny sublet across Queens Boulevard, set toward the street at a rakish angle. Young men and women in suits bustled up the sidewalk, carrying salads, congealing pizza, take-away noodles. Traffic roared along the Union Turnpike and the Van Wyck, both of them edged with black frost. Stepping out of the car, Isaac and I were nearly bowled over by a blast of wind.

That's not exactly true. I was almost bowled over. Isaac seemed to feel nothing. He was wearing a Hawaiian shirt underneath a denim jacket that could have yielded enough pairs of jeans to outfit a dude ranch. He attracted the attention of the cops sitting in front of the building, who halted their shit-shooting to jab gloved thumbs at the giant coming up the steps.

We made our way into the lobby, where Samantha was waiting. She saw Isaac and blinked in wonderment. 'Uh, hi.'

'Hi,' Isaac said. Then he chucked me on the arm, more like a good hard punch by most people's standards. 'Zit okay if I wait in the car? Police make me nervous.'

I told him I'd call when I was ready. Samantha watched him lumber out.

'Wow,' she said.

The elevator required a keycard and a code. On the fifth floor we walked into the midst of a raucous lunch break, three young men and two young women whose conversational leitmotifs appeared to be *fuck, fuck you*, and *fuck you you fucking fuckface*. Samantha introduced me as a friend, which I thought was generous.

'Hey,' they said, variously.

'What's going on?' Samantha asked one of the girls.

'Mantell's car got broken into.'

'Right in front of the fucking building,' said one of the men. He had black hair and wore a heavy gold watch.

'They took his GPS.'

'You bet they did. It's ten o'clock in the fucking morning. There's fucking cops everywhere. There's fucking Mr Wong's across the street, with a *picture fucking window*. And nobody saw anything?' He shook his head in disgust. 'What the *fuck*. The cop I talked to goes, "Do you know anyone who might have anything against you?" And I'm like, "Well, only about three hundred people I've put in prison. How's that narrow it down for you."'

Everyone laughed.

'The apocalypse is nigh.'

'The apocalypse, my friend, is old news.'

'Did they take your badge?'

'Why would they take my badge? If I were them, I wouldn't want to impersonate us. We can't stop a break-in – in broad daylight – in the fucking *epicenter of borough law enforcement*. So, no. They did not take my fucking badge. You know what Shana said, though. I couldn't fucking believe this. You know what she said?'

'What.'

'I told her what happened, and she was like, "Who did it?"'

There was a pause. Then everyone broke up laughing.

'*No* . . .'

'She said that?'

'Sweardagod.'

'Who *says* that?'

'She does.'

'She's a fucking moron.'

'Hey Shana.'

'Yeah,' came a voice from a distant cubicle.

'You're a fucking moron.'

'Fuck you.'

Samantha escorted me across the floor. For the most part, it looked like any other office, with fuzzy gray partitions, desks crammed into corners, a copy machine loose at the hinges, bulletin boards, file cabinets shingled with magnets, family photos pinned up wherever room could be found. Any other office, except for the anti-domestic violence campaign posters; or the state trooper with the shaved head and large gun, chickenpecking on an old-fashioned word processor; or the significant chunk of a compact car – hood, two doors and a tire – lying in the hallway ('Evidence,' Samantha explained). She greeted and was greeted by all.

'Why is everyone so young?' I asked.

'Dick Wolf does the hiring,' she said.

Her office had a glass door that she shut to drown out the curses and laughter.

'Did he really get his car broken into outside the building?'

'Wouldn't be the first time.'

'That's crazy.'

'That's Queens.' She rummaged around on her desk, shuffling forms and e-mail printouts and files and unopened envelopes. Atop the windowsill were three mugs: a DA seal, Fordham, NYU law. A matted teddy bear dressed as a fireman. A photo of her father, and another of her and her sister in bathing suits on the beach. A brass Gordian knot, dangling on a string tacked to a shelf holding legal books. The screen saver on her computer faded in and out hypnotically, rotating images of a green countryside.

'Ireland,' she said, noticing my stare.

'Is that where your family's from?'

'County Kerry. My dad's side. My mom's Italian. I've never been to either place, but if I start saving up what's left of my salary at the end of every month I should be able to afford a trip when I'm seventy-five.'

She found what she was looking for, a set of keys for her file cabinet. She opened up a drawer full of compact discs and transcripts. I glanced inside but she closed it.

'Not ours.'

'Love letters?' I asked.

'Wiretaps.'

From the next drawer down she produced our box of evidence. It looked bigger than when I'd last seen it, and as she started taking out files and laying them on the desk I realized that she had contributed to its growth.

'This is what Richard Soto came up with.' She handed me a list of old cases, fifteen pages of names, dates, locations, brief descriptions, and the names of the arrested party, if any. I glanced through it and was about to ask her a question when I looked up and saw her staring at the photo of her father, a tissue loosely crumpled in her hand.

She said, 'I miss him so much.'

I almost said 'I do too.' But I didn't. I laid a hand on the files and said, 'Let's talk about something else.'

*

OVER THE NEXT SIX WEEKS we met frequently, either in person or on the phone. During her lunch break we would meet at the Chinese place near the DA's office; Isaac would take his place three tables away and commence to consume mind-boggling amounts of pork fried rice. We gave him our fortune cookies.

We decided to start from scratch, laying out a fresh timeline of the killings, examining it for patterns. We had the footprint cast reexamined, and were told that the person who'd made it was probably taller than six feet. Samantha asked how big Victor was, and I had to confess that, although one person had told me he was short, in truth I didn't know. Now that I think about it, that was how we spent the bulk of our time, at least at first: outlining what we did *not* know.

'Did he go to school?'

'I don't know.'

'Did he have family?'

'I don't know.'

'What do you know, exactly?'

'I don't know.'

'How hard were you looking for him?'

'Not very,' I admitted.

'Well,' she said, 'now's your chance to redeem yourself.'

We picked up where I'd left off: calling churches, but this time with greater success. Through dumb luck or diligence, we found a Father Verlaine, at Good Shepherd in Astoria, who gave us our first sign that Victor had been a real person and not a figment of someone's imagination. We drove to the rectory and found the priest; he was doing a crossword puzzle, and he greeted us cheerfully.

'Of course I knew Victor,' he said. 'He had a better attendance record than I do. But I haven't seen him in a year or two. Is everything all right?'

'We want to make sure he's safe. Nobody's heard from him in a while.'

'I can't believe he would ever do anything wrong,' said the priest. 'His conscience was cleaner than anyone's, with the possible exception of the Holy Father.'

I asked what he meant.

'Every time I opened the confessional window I'd find him on the other side.'

'What did he confess?'

The priest clucked his tongue. 'Those are matters between a man and God. I will tell you that he had far less reason to be there than most people, including the ones who don't come to confess at all. I told him once or twice not to be so hard on himself, and that if he didn't, he'd be in violation of the sin of scrupulosity.' He smiled. 'All that meant was that I found him in there the next day, confessing to me about that.'

'You wouldn't happen to have a photograph of him, would you?'

'No.'

Samantha said, 'Could you describe him?'

'Oh, let's see. He was small, about five-foot-four and on the thin side. He sometimes grew a little moustache. Always he wore the same coat, no matter how hot or cold it was. That coat had seen better days. You're probably not old enough to remember – how old are you?'

'Twenty-eight,' she said.

'Well, then you're definitely not old enough, but I'll tell you that he looked a bit like Howard Hughes.'

'Was he unwell?'

'He didn't seem especially healthy. He often had a cough. I could always tell he was there, because I'd hear it coming from the back pews.'

I said, 'Did he have any obvious psychological problems?'

He hesitated. 'I'm afraid I can't tell you much more than I have. My office forbids it.'

In the car, Samantha said, 'That's a start.'

'He said he was small. Doesn't that rule him out?'

'Not really. Footprinting isn't an exact science. A photo would be more helpful, so we could ask around the neighborhood. What about that cough? He might have gotten treated for it.'

'It sounds more like he wasn't treated at all.'

'But if he was, then there's a record of him somewhere. Based on what you've told me, the picture I'm getting, people like him, they fall through the cracks. They don't have a regular doctor. They show up at the emergency room.'

'Then let's call the local emergency rooms.'

'I'll work on it. You'd be surprised how hard it is in this state to get medical records. Did he have a job?'

'Not as far as I can tell.'

'He had to pay for things. He paid his rent.'

'The building manager told me he paid in cash. His apartment was rent-controlled from back in the sixties. He was paying a hundred dollars a month.'

She whistled in admiration, and for a moment she wasn't the arm of the law but just another New Yorker envying someone else's lease. 'Still, that's a hundred dollars he had to come up with every thirty days. Maybe he panhandled.'

'It's possible,' I said. 'But how does that help us? There isn't a panhandlers' union we can call.'

'You know what else,' she said, her gaze wandering toward the sky – and away from me. I sometimes got the impression that when we were talking she paid attention to me only long enough to start thinking on her own. In this she differed from her father, who had taken – or seemed to take – a real interest in my opinion. I have to give her credit for her honesty. From the outset, she never pretended she was doing this for anyone other than him. Certainly not for me.

'The paper,' she said. 'He had to buy lots of it; you'd think he'd be on good terms with whoever sold it to him. And food. Why don't you tackle that. I'm going to keep chasing down the witnesses in the old cases and see what I can come up with. Here. I pulled some of the old mug shots from those cases and made copies for you so you can show them around. Don't worry. We'll get something.'

'You think so?'

'Not a chance.'

I WENT BACK TO MULLER COURTS, starting at one of the two bodegas. Once the countermen got through staring at Isaac, they confirmed my description of Victor. They knew who he was – 'Weird dude' – but, other than a preference for a certain brand of wheat bread and Oscar Mayer ham, could provide no information. I asked about paper, and they handed me a notepad with greenish, lined pages.

'What about white,' I said. 'Plain white.'

'We don't got that.'

Thinking of the food journal, I asked what kind of apples he bought.

'He didn't buy apples.'

'He must've bought apples,' I said.

'Did you see him buy apples?'

'I didn't see him buy no apples.'

'No, he didn't buy no apples.'

In an effort to be helpful, one of them suggested that he had bought, rather, pears.

I said, 'What about cheese?'

'No cheese.'

'He didn't buy no cheese.'

'No cheese.'

I went to the other bodega. This time I had Isaac wait outside, which he did happily, on condition that he could run across the street and get a meatball hero. I gave him ten bucks and he bounded off like a little kid.

The girl behind the register, a pretty Latina with red plastic glasses, put down her poetry magazine when I approached. She, too, recognized Victor by my description.

'I called him "sir",' she told me.

'Why's that.'

'He looked like the kind of person who you call sir.'

'How often did he come in here?'

'Twice a week when I was here. I don't work on Friday or Saturday, though.'

I asked what he would usually buy.

She went to the rattling dairy case and handed me a package of inexpensive presliced Swiss cheese. 'Same thing every time. Once I think I asked, "Sir, maybe you want to try something else?"'

'What did he say?'

'He didn't say anything. He never said anything to me.'

'Can you remember if he ever talked about—'

'He never said *anything*.'

She was equally firm in her conviction that he had purchased neither apples nor paper.

'We don't sell paper,' she said. 'There's a Staples on Queens Boulevard.'

Ten months prior I would have resisted the idea that Victor's life extended beyond the confines of Muller Courts – that he'd gone anywhere without my imagination giving him permission to do so. Now I found myself obeying him. I spent several chilly November afternoons walking in and out of local markets, canvassing the neighborhood in widening concentric circles: a one-block radius, two blocks, three . . . until I reached the triangular plaza at Junction Boulevard and a fruit stand run by a middle-aged Sikh.

'Oh, yes,' he said. 'My friend.'

He held up a small mesh bag of Granny Smiths.

The vendor, whose name was Jogindar, said that he and Victor would talk for at least a few minutes every day.

'The weather,' he said. 'Always the weather.'

'When was the last time you saw him?'

'Oh, a long time. Perhaps a year and a half. Is he okay?'

'I don't know. That's why I'm looking for him. Did he sound okay to you?'

'He had a terrible cough,' said Jogindar. 'I told him he must go to the hospital.'

'Did he?'

He shrugged. 'I hope so.'

'Was he ever with anyone else?'

'No, never.'

'Let me ask you this: was there anything strange about the way he behaved?'

Jogindar smiled. Wordlessly he gestured all around us, at the steam-breathing pensioners slouched on park benches; at Queens Boulevard, its lumbering parade, its tangle of wind-whipped powerlines. The whole honking throb of the metropolis, ethnic markets and 99-cent stores and CHECKS CASHED and pawnshops and nail salons and dialysis centers and a wigmaker that sold hair by the pound. He gestured to Isaac, standing ten feet off; to an ancient-looking lady making her way through the intersection, heedless of the red light and the horns exploding at her. She kept shuffling, shuffling, until she made it to the other side. Then everyone drove on.

I understood what he was saying. He was saying *It's all crazy.*

He breathed into his hands. 'When he stopped coming I thought it was a sign.'

'Of what.'

'I don't know. But after so many years he became very comforting to me. I am thinking of finding a different job.'

'How long have you known him?'

'Since I came here. Eighteen years.' He smiled. 'That is a kind of friend-ship.'

For the heck of it, I bought a bag of Victor's favorite apples. On my way back to Manhattan, I bit into one. It was unusually sour.

*

THE BRANCH MANAGER of the local Staples had no idea what I was talking about; nor did any of the cashiers, although most of them seemed to have started on the job that very morning. They did offer to sell me paper, though.

When Samantha and I next conferred, she pointed out Victor's tendency to routinize. 'Think about the picture of him that we're getting so far. He gets his bread from one place. He gets his cheese someplace else, his apples. He does this every day for God knows how long. How long has that Staples been there, five years? That's not our man. That's not where he's going to go for something as important as his paper.'

I called around until I found the oldest place in the neighborhood, a stationer's a half-mile due west of the Courts, open Tuesday through Thursday, from eleven to three thirty. I had to leave work especially early – earlier than I'd been leaving, which was already beyond self-indulgent – to get out there on time.

My first impression of Zatuchny's was that it could have been managed by Victor himself, so clogged was it with junk. I walked into a cloud of that same woody smell I'd first encountered in Victor's apartment, only several orders of magnitude more powerful. It made me wonder how customers could shop without keeling over.

More to the point, I had a hard time believing that the store had customers at all. From the outside the place looked closed, windows plastered over with curling fliers, neon sign extinguished. I stood at the counter and dinged the bell a couple times.

'Shaddap shaddap shaddap. Shaaaddap.'

An old man appeared, his cheeks flecked with tomato sauce. He paused briefly to stare at me, paused longer to stare at Isaac, and then, frowning, he snatched the bell off the counter and tossed it in a drawer. 'It ain't a toy,' he said.

If I hadn't known any better, I might have taken him for Victor Cracke. Moustachioed, disheveled, he fit with my preconceived notion quite nicely. So did the disorder of the surroundings . . . and the smell . . .

A crazy thought occurred to me: he *was* Victor.

I must have been staring a bit too intensely, because he sneered and said, 'I didn't interrupt my afternoon repast so you could ogle my titties. Whaddaya want.'

I said, 'I'm looking for someone.'

'Yeah, whossat.'

I showed him the mug shots.

'Ugly bastards,' he commented as he leafed through them.

I said, 'Do you mind if I ask your name?'

'Do I mind, sure I do.'

'Well, can you tell me anyway?'

'Leonard,' he said.

'I'm Ethan.'

'You a cop, Ethan?'

'I work for the District Attorney,' I said, which wasn't totally untrue.

'What about you, fatso,' he said to Isaac, who remained unmoved behind his sunglasses. 'Whassis problem. Can't he speak?'

'He's more of the strong silent type,' I said.

'He looks more like the big fucking fatso type. What do you feed him, whole sheep?' He handed me back the photos. 'I don't know these sons of bitches.'

I couldn't bring myself to come out and ask about Victor, scared as I was that he would turn out to *be* Victor, and that my questions would send him scurrying out the back door. In trying to dance around the central point, I allowed my questioning to get more and more convoluted, until, eyeing the Band-Aids on my face, he said to Isaac, 'You must be the brains of the operation.'

'I'm looking for a man named Victor Cracke,' I blurted, half expecting him to press a button and drop through a trapdoor. But he only nodded.

'Oh yeah?' he said.

'You know him.'

'Sure I know him. You mean with the—' He wiggled his index finger atop his upper lip, meaning *moustache*, which was bizarre, because he had an actual moustache.

'He was a customer?'

'Sure.'

'How often did he come in here?'

'I'd say a couple times a month or so. All he ever bought was paper. He ain't been by in a while, though.'

'Can you show me what kind of paper he bought?'

He looked at me like I was insane. Then he shrugged and led me to a tiny stockroom, metal shelves sagging with unopened boxes of pens, stencils, photo albums. Atop a card table sat a microwave, and in front of it, a plastic bowl with fusilli floating in watery marinara sauce. A fork rested atop a stack of comic books.

Leonard grabbed a box on the lowest shelf and dragged it to the middle of the room, huffing and puffing as he bent, revealing a preexisting split in the seat of his pants. He took a utility knife off his belt and sliced open the packing tape. Inside was a box of plain white paper, less yellowed than the drawings but – insofar as plain white paper can be positively identified – correct enough.

'How long has he been shopping here?' I asked.

'My father opened up after the War, passed in '63, the same day Kennedy got his head blown off. I think Victor started showing up around then. He came in maybe twice a month.'

'What kind of relationship did you have with him?'

'I sold him paper.'

'Did he ever talk about his personal life?'

Leonard stared at me. 'I . . . sold . . . him . . . *paper*.' Satisfied that he had impressed my own stupidity upon me, he went back to his lunch.

'Excuse me—'

'You're still here?'

'I just wondered if you ever noticed anything unusual about Victor.'

He sighed, scooted around in his chair. 'All right, you want a story, I'll tell you a story. I once played him checkers.'

I said, 'Pardon?'

'Checkers. You know what checkers is, dontcha?'

'Yes.'

'Well, I played him. He came in here with a little checkers set and put it down and we played checkers. He beat my pants off. He wanted to play again but I didn't want to get beat so bad twice in one day. I offered to box him but he just left. The end.'

Something about the story broke my heart, as I pictured Victor – how I saw him in my mind's eye, I can't say; I suppose I saw his spirit, translucent and fuzzy – wandering the neighborhood, a board tucked under his arm, desperate for a competitor.

'Happy now?' Leonard asked.

'Did he use a credit card?'

'I don't take credit cards. Cash or check.'

'All right, then, did he use a check?'

'Cash.'

'Did he ever buy anything else?'

'Yeah. Pens and markers. Pencils. What are you, the goddamned paper gestapo?'

'I'm concerned about his safety.'

'How the hell is knowing about a bunch of pens going to help him stay safe?'

Despairingly, I thanked him for his time and handed him a card, asking him to call if Victor came in.

'Sure,' he said. As I left, I glanced back and saw him tearing the card into confetti.

EIGHTEEN

Because Samantha worked during the day, I did most of the footwork on my own. This, of course, implies that I did not work during the day, which was increasingly true. I felt restless and trapped at the gallery and kept inventing excuses to leave. Even when I didn't need to go to Queens, I didn't want to stay in Chelsea. I would take long walks and ruminate about Victor Cracke and art and myself and Marilyn, fancying myself a private investigator, narrating to myself. *He stumbled into the coffee shop and ordered a cuppa joe. Cue saxophone.* These self-indulgent fantasies, these stirrings of dissatisfaction, were all too familiar to me. I had them on average every five years.

Samantha's job was to go down Richard Soto's list of old cases. Right off the bat she concluded that the majority of them were irrelevant to us – the victim was either female or older or had been murdered without any sign of sexual assault – but she followed them up, just in case. Listening to her, I began to understand that the most outstanding feature of policework is its tedium; throughout November and December there were plenty of idle days, plenty of blind alleys, plenty of conversations that went nowhere. We groped blindly, crushing together hunches to form theories that we then discarded, trial-and-error but mostly error.

The week of Thanksgiving we began meeting at night at the storage warehouse. Samantha would take the train in after work, and we'd select a box at random, have Isaac lug it to the viewing room, and spend three or four hours flipping pages in search of bloodstains. The task went faster this time around than it had before, as I was looking now with a single criterion, rather than to evaluate the work. Nevertheless, I still had trouble focusing for more than thirty or forty minutes at a stretch. My headaches, though diminishing, still made squinting painful. At those moments, I would surreptitiously watch Samantha as she worked; her delicate fingers hovering over the surface of the page, her lips extruded in that beautiful pout, concentration coming off her in waves.

'I can't tell whether he was sick or a genius,' she said.

'They're not mutually exclusive.' I told her about the phone calls I'd received after Marilyn began spreading rumors.

'That doesn't surprise me at all, actually,' she said. 'It's like those women who write love letters to serial killers.' She set aside the drawing she'd been looking at. 'Would it bother you if he was guilty?'

'I don't know. I've thought about it.' I gave her my mini-lecture on artists misbehaving, concluding, 'Caravaggio killed a man.'

'In bed,' she said and laughed.

Eight weeks might not sound like very long, but when you're spending much of that talking to or sitting alone with the same person – we essentially learned to forget about Isaac – often engaged in an extraordinarily monotonous activity, your sense of time begins to distort, much as I imagine it does in prison. No matter how hard we tried to stay on point, we couldn't talk only about the case. I can't tell you exactly when the thaw began to accelerate. But it did, and we dared to make jokes; we chatted about nonsense and about important things, or things I'd forgotten were important.

'Jesus,' she said when I told her I'd been expelled from Harvard. 'I'd never guess.'

'Why.'

'Cause you look so . . .'

'Boring.'

'I was going to say normal,' she said, 'but that'll work.'

'It's a façade.'

'Evidently. I had a rebellious phase, too, you know.'

'Did you, now.'

'Oh yes. I was into grunge. I wore flannel and played the guitar.'

I laughed.

'Don't laugh,' she said gravely. 'I wrote my own material.'

'What was the name of your band?'

'Oh, no. I was strictly a solo artist.'

'I didn't know one could play grunge on one's own.'

'I wouldn't describe my own *personal* music as grunge. I would say that I was more inspired by the grunge lifestyle. Everything *I* sang sounded like the Indigo Girls. One time this friend of mine—' She started giggling. 'This is actually really sad.'

'I can tell.'

'It is, but I' – giggling – 'I'm sorry. Ahem. This friend of mine junior year had to have an abortion—'

'Oh, that's hilarious.'

'Stop. It *was* sad, it was *really* sad. That's not what's funny. What's funny is that I wrote a song about it, and it was called—' She broke up completely. 'I can't.'

'Too late,' I said.

'No. Sorry. I can't.'

'"The Procedure".'

'Worse.'

'"The Decision".'

'I'm not going to tell you. But I will tell you that there was a lyric comparing a woman's body to a field of flowers.'

'I think that's very poetic.'

'I thought so, too.'

'Although,' I said, 'Dalí said that the first man to compare the cheeks of a woman to a rose was obviously a poet; the first to repeat it may well have been an idiot.'

'In bed.'

'In bed. Well,' I said, 'I think your parents got off easy.'

'By the time I was old enough to rebel they were too busy imploding to notice. It really pissed me off.'

'Did you write a song about it?'

'About their divorce? No. I wanted to write a poem, though.'

'"The Separation".'

'I'd call it "A Pair of Assholes".'

I smiled.

'I took photographs, too,' she said. 'God, what happened to me. I used to be so creative.'

'It's never too late.'

She got very quiet.

'What,' I said.

'What you said. Ian used to tell me that.'

I said nothing.

'When I complained about my job he would tell me that.' She paused. 'It's not like that's a very unusual thing to say, but I remember him saying it a lot. Maybe because I complained about my job a lot.'

I said, 'I'm sorry.'

'It's all right. I can think about him now without getting hysterical. That's a positive step.'

I nodded.

'I think about him now and it's warm, rather than hot. You know?

Like he was a really good friend. He was. You don't want to hear about this.'

'I do if you want to talk about it.'

She smiled, shook her head. 'We have work to do . . .'

'What was he like?'

She hesitated, then said, 'He and my dad were good friends. I think my dad took it harder than I did. I sort of expected that something would happen to him eventually. That's the nature of the job. I didn't expect that, though. Who expects that?'

I said nothing.

'Anyway, that's that,' she said, wiping her eyes. 'Now I'm on the rebound.' She grinned at me. 'You were just a temporary stop on my road to recovery.'

'Whatever I can do to help.'

She smiled, started turning pages again. I watched her for a little while. Eventually she saw me staring and looked up. 'What.'

'I don't know why you're unhappy with your job,' I said. 'To me it's way more interesting than what I do.'

'I can't believe that.'

'It is.'

'If you say so.'

'What would you do, if not this.'

'I don't know,' she said. 'I've never had a good answer to that part of the question. I wanted to do this and now I'm here. I had an idea that this was going to distinguish me from my dad. His father was a cop. My uncle is a cop. My mother's father was in the Secret Service. Naturally, I didn't want to become a cop, so I thought, oh, yeah, well, but a DA – now *that's* different.' She laughed. 'That was my final attempt at rebellion. I've accepted my fate.'

I said, 'I think I felt the same way about my father.'

She rolled her eyes.

'I mean it,' I said. 'Growing up I saw him as basically soulless and profit-driven – which he is. Unfortunately I chose the one line of work possibly more soulless and more profit-driven.'

'If you really feel that way, then why don't you get out?'

'Lately I've been wondering. I don't know what else I would do.'

'You could become a prosecutor.'

'I don't think so.'

'Why not?'

'I'm a little old to start over.'

'I thought it was never too late.'

'For me it is,' I said.

'Can I ask you something?' she asked. 'Why do you resent him so much?'

'My father.'

She nodded.

I shrugged. 'I can't give you one single reason.'

'Then give me a few.'

I thought. 'After my mother died, I felt like a pet that belonged to her, and that he got stuck with. He barely spoke to me, and when he did it was to give me an order or to tell me I was doing something wrong. She was the only wife that he didn't divorce, and whether or not they would have lasted – I have my doubts – when she got sick, they were still getting along. That's why he's hasn't gotten married since: he idealizes her. I feel bad for him. I do. But I'm not going on Oprah or anything to make up with him.'

'Your siblings get along with him?'

'Well, my brothers work for him, so whether they like him or not, they kiss his ass. Amelia lives in London. I don't think they have much of a relationship, but it isn't overtly hostile.'

'That's your specialty.'

'Correct.'

'You know anger shortens your life expectancy.'

'Then enjoy me while I last.'

She smiled wryly. 'No comment.'

AFTER FOUR WEEKS IN MARILYN'S HOUSE the situation had become intolerable. Taking me in was incredibly kind of her, considering that things had already been tense between us before the attack. Although, looking back, I have to wonder if she didn't extend the invitation primarily to keep an eye on me. If there were clues I missed them. When I returned home late at night, having spent the evening with Samantha, nothing Marilyn said or did indicated that she was silently building a case against me. And really, she had nothing to build on; even if she had somehow been able to eavesdrop at the warehouse, she would've come up with nothing concrete to hold against me. Everybody flirts, don't they? If I flirted with Samantha while we worked, I did so under the assumption that it wouldn't produce results. She had made that plain. So then what was Marilyn thinking, those nights when she greeted me in a kimono, pulled me up to the 'boudoir' (her word), and threw herself on top of me? Did she think she would catch a glimpse of me with my eyes closed and learn the truth? She may have a keen nose for betrayal, but she's not a mind-reader.

Maybe I'm being uncharitable. But I can't help thinking that she set up the whole cycle of guilt and expectation in order to trap me, to make me ruin us, so that she could stand back from the wreckage and accuse me. The longer I stayed with her, the more indebted I felt; the more indebted I felt, the more resentful I felt; the more resentful I felt, the harder it was for me to pretend I was excited when we made love, and the more obvious my detachment became, the more petulant and biting she acted – which in turn fueled my guilt, resentment, detachment, etc.

It's amazing how fast things can collapse. For the longest time, I had been unable to imagine anybody better suited to me than Marilyn. Now, though, I had basis for comparison. When Samantha and I talked I felt better – about myself, about the world. She was no Pollyanna; perhaps more than anyone, she was familiar with the awful things people did to one another. But she believed that not giving up the fight was what kept us from devolving; she believed that right and wrong had no expiration date and that five dead boys were worth giving up her lunch breaks and evenings and spending them with a man who made her uncomfortable. She was her father's daughter, and you know how I felt about him.

With Marilyn I found myself repelled by the effect we had on each other, the way we feasted on scorn. Irony has its place. But it can't be everywhere. And it disturbed me greatly that I could not recall a single unironic conversation between me and Marilyn. Everything that had transacted between us – seven years of dinners and sex and arm-in-arm appearances and talk, reams of gossip – started to feel artificial. I never wanted to look stupid in front of Marilyn. How well could she really know me? How well did *I* really know me? I never wanted to feel stupid, either. And that's simply not realistic, not unless you turn everything into a joke.

Thanksgiving dinner was atrocious, the two of us sniping at each other across the table while the rest of her guests – all art people – kept trying to steer the conversation back on track. Marilyn got very drunk and began to tell ugly stories about her ex-husband. I mean truly savage; she mocked his inability to sustain an erection; she imitated his pillow-talk; she railed about his three daughters and how stone-dumb they were, how none of them had scored higher than eight hundred on their SATs and how he'd had to bribe their way both into and through Spence, piling detail upon humiliating detail, all the while staring at me, so that if you'd walked into the room midway through her speech you would've likely figured me for the buffoon in question. Finally I couldn't stand any more. 'Enough,' I said.

Her head swiveled loosely toward me. 'I'm boring you?'

I said nothing.

'Am I?'

I said – I couldn't help myself – 'Not just me.'

And she smiled. 'All right, then, *you* pick a topic.'

I excused myself and left the table.

Knowing she'd be hungover, I got up early the next morning and told Isaac that I wouldn't be needing his services anymore. I packed my things and went downstairs to catch a cab back to TriBeCa. The clothes from Barneys I kept.

AS I MENTIONED, work wasn't going so well, either. I shouldn't say that; I actually have no idea what the gallery was like during those months, because I was seldom there. While it was true that I had been gone a lot longer dealing with the Cracke drawings, at least then I'd been working *for* the gallery. Now what could I say? Mornings when I should have been able to step into a suit, I couldn't bring myself to leave my apartment. At the time I told myself that the cause of my lethargy was physical. I was tired; I needed to rest; I had just gotten out of the hospital. But by December I was feeling mostly fine, and I still didn't want to get back on the floor. Having missed Alyson's opening, I had a hard time getting invested in her show; and at moments, I couldn't even remember what was hanging, let alone muster the energy to sell it.

This surprised me, most of all because I had so recently felt better than ever about my job. Victor Cracke's work had reawakened my love of art and made the exercise of buying and selling seem worth more than the dollars involved. But I suppose that that was the very essence of the problem. Without the kind of charge that Cracke provided, I was back to pushing work that I didn't fully believe in, lots of cleverness and allusiveness that now rang hollow. And since I couldn't count on a Victor Cracke coming along very often, I looked at my future and saw one big blank.

So there you have it, a neat dichotomy: Marilyn and my gallery and my day job on the one side; and on the other side Samantha and Victor and five dead boys. I've wrapped it up neatly in a story and served it to you on a bed of symbolism. You'll never really understand how profoundly that winter changed me, though, because to this day I don't understand it myself.

With time I have come to see that these changes were lying in wait longer than I realized. When people we know do something radically out of character, we force ourselves to revise our impressions; we look back and the insignificant becomes illuminating. It's hard to look at yourself critically, objectively; but as a narcissist, I've spent a lot of time examining my own life, and I know now that I had been dissatisfied longer than I realized. When I entered the business I thought I had found the place for me. Until that point I was half a personality, unformed and uninformed by anything except my desire to distance myself from my father. He was cold and art was hot. Art was – so I told myself – as different from real estate as possible. I'm a little embarrassed to admit that I thought that. You might be laughing at me; I know Marilyn would. But the fact that I tell you what I thought and don't worry whether you're laughing is, I think, a pretty good indication of how far I've come.

IT WAS THE THIRD WEEK OF DECEMBER before the DNA results started coming back in, and we met with Annie Lundley to review the forensics reports. It was a frustrating afternoon: none of the evidence allowed us to draw firm conclusions. All of the hair recovered from the room, for example, matched samples taken from the excluded group – including me.

Samantha looked at me. 'You know what this means.'

'What.'

'It means your hair is falling out.'

The old pair of jeans yielded two DNA profiles, one from the bloodstain and the other from the semen, the latter presumably belonging to the perpetrator. Although the state crime lab still hadn't gotten back to Samantha about her request to check the profile against CODIS (see how fast I was learning?), Annie had been able to scrounge up dead skin cells from the sweater found in Victor's apartment. That profile did not match the profile taken from the jeans. Although we had been assuming that the sweater belonged to Victor, we had no proof; and we furthermore could not rule out the possibility that the wearer of the sweater (if it was in fact Victor) had been present at the crime scene but failed to leave DNA.

The most promising lead was the partial fingerprint taken from the inside of the weather journal. At my request, Annie had tried to be as non-invasive as possible when handling the art; and, going slowly, she had page by page examined the journals for usable evidence. The print had also been sent to the FBI, request still pending. As Samantha and Annie talked it once again became clear to me how much of what they did was paper-work, how much time got wasted in leaving messages and sending follow-up e-mails. In that sense, our jobs had a lot in common.

When Annie left, Samantha and I turned our attention to the group of comparison cases. She had whittled it down to three, one of which left a surviving victim. The two other murders were cold, their evidence in stor-age, and we planned to get those boxes out of storage once the holiday had passed. The survivor was a boy – a man now, assuming he was still alive – named James Jarvis. At age eleven he had been sexually assaulted, beaten and choked, and left for dead in a park four miles from Muller Courts; this happened in 1973, six years after the presumed final murder. So far, Samantha had been unable to locate Jarvis, but she was determined to keep trying. When she told me that, she got the little familiar bulge in her jaw.

It was December 21. We were in a booth at the Chinese restaurant, tired of talking about homicide, content to watch the traffic. It was dark out, the sidewalk slush painted red and green by the stringlights in the window. I never found Queens beautiful, but at that moment it seemed realer than any place I had ever been.

'"You will endure a great trial",' she read.

'In bed.'

'In bed.' She chewed loudly. 'Your turn.'

'"You have many friends."'

'In bed.'

'In bed. Please,' I said, holding up a hand, 'don't even bother.'

She grinned and reached for her wallet.

'On me,' I said.

She studied me. 'Is this a ruse?'

'Consider it a gift to the working class.'

She gave me the finger. But she let me pay.

Outside we stood shivering and talking about the upcoming holiday. Samantha was headed to Wilmington with her mother and sister and their respective spouses. 'I'll be back on the second,' she said. 'Try not to miss me.'

'I will.'

'Miss me, or try not to.'

I shrugged. 'You decide.'

She smiled. 'And what are your big plans?'

'Marilyn's having a party this Thursday. Yearly thing she does.'

'That's the twenty-third,' she said. 'I meant Christmas itself.'

'What about it.'

'Are you going to be somewhere?'

'Yes,' I said. 'At home.'

'Oh,' she said.

'You can hang on to your condescension just a little longer, if you don't mind.'

'Why don't you call your father?' she asked.

'And do what, exactly.'

'You could start by saying hello.'

'That's it? Say hi?'

'Well, if that goes okay, you could ask how he's doing.'

'I don't see this scenario playing out in a way that leaves anyone happy.'

She shrugged.

'We never celebrated Christmas,' I said. 'We never even had a tree. My mother used to give me presents but that was the extent of it.'

She nodded, although I sensed something vaguely accusatory. I said, 'If I called him up and said hi, he'd expect more. He'd start asking why I hadn't called before. Trust me, you don't know him.'

'You're right, I don't.'

'No thank you,' I said.

'Whatever you say.'

'Why are you doing that.'

'Doing what.'

'You're making me feel guilty for something I haven't done.'

'I'm agreeing with you.'

'You're disagreeing with me by agreeing.'

'Will you listen to yourself?' she said.

I walked her to the subway.

'Enjoy the canapés,' she said. 'I'll see you next year.'

Then she leaned over and kissed me on the cheek. I remained standing there long after she'd gone.

TO CALL MARILYN'S ANNUAL WINTER BASH a 'holiday party' verges on sacrilege, insofar as that term implies drunken co-workers standing round the punchbowl, fondling one another to the strains of Bing Crosby. The event that takes place at the Wooten Gallery the week before Christmas is more like an opening par excellence. Everyone comes out for it, even when weather makes getting there a misery. Whatever the theme – 'Underwater Cowboys' or 'Warhol's Shopping List' or 'Yuppies Strike Back' – Marilyn always hires the same band, a thirteen-piece ensemble made up entirely of

244

transvestites whose songbook never deviates from note-perfect Billie Holiday and Ella Fitzgerald covers. They're called Big and Swingin'.

Busy as I'd been with the case, I'd forgotten to get my costume. For the life of me I couldn't find my invitation, which meant that I didn't know the theme. (I couldn't very well ask anyone without making it scandalously clear that Marilyn and I weren't talking, which at that point I still believed was a matter between the two of us.)

When I arrived at the gallery in a suit, however, I found myself improbably appropriate, wading through a sea of revelers all dressed like members of the newly reelected Bush cabinet. Without a mask, I attracted a lot of attention, as people tried to guess my identity. It's a real test of one's patience to listen to someone insist that you look exactly like Donald Rumsfeld.

'I'm sure he meant that in the nicest way possible,' said Ruby.

'What way would that be?'

'He has nice cheekbones,' Nat offered.

I mingled. Some people asked if I was feeling well; I touched the one remaining Band-Aid on my temple and said, 'Minor brain damage.' Other people tried to involve me in conversations about artists and shows that I hadn't heard of. The pace of the contemporary market is such that you can be away for a little more than a month and find yourself completely out of the loop. I didn't know what people were talking about and I didn't care. After two or three minutes of group banter I would find myself drifting, my attention drawn by the surreal spectacle of a kickline consisting of Dick Cheney, Dick Cheney, Condoleezza Rice and Dick Cheney. When I did try to follow along, I could not help but get annoyed. Regardless of who or what was under discussion, the true subject was money.

'I hear your murderer's developed a strong following.'

'How much of that stuff do you have in a vault, Ethan?'

'More than he's telling.'

'Have you sold any more?'

'Have you sold any more to Hollister?'

'I heard he unloaded his.'

'Is that true? Ethan?'

'You went to the house, didn't you? I know someone who's been there, he said the place is *too* tacky. He hired Jaime Acosta-Blanca to paint all these tacky copies but he gave him seventy percent up front and Jaime ran off with the money to Moscow where he's defrauding neo-oligarchs.'

'Who'd he sell to, Ethan?'

'Nobody knows.'

'Ethan, who did Hollister sell to?'

'Rita said it was Richard Branson.'

'Does that mean you're going to get shot into space, Ethan?'

After two hours Marilyn was still nowhere to be seen. I made my way through white rooms covered in red canvases, white rooms covered with pink canvases, white rooms ready to be filled. As the Wooten Gallery has grown, it has gobbled up its neighbors, left and right and upstairs and downstairs. It takes up nearly a fifth of 567 West Twenty-fifth Street, not to mention the overflow space on Twenty-eighth or the Upper East Side prints gallery. As I fought through a clutch of John Ashcrofts, it struck me that I'd never be as big as Marilyn; even had I the ambition, I lacked the vision.

I buttonholed one of her many assistants, who, after consulting a series of people on walkie-talkies, returned with the verdict that Marilyn had retired to the fourth floor.

In the elevator I prepared an apology. My heart wasn't in it, but it was Christmas.

Marilyn has two offices, much in the way she has two kitchens: one for the world and one for herself. The big office with the high ceilings and the immaculate desk and the Rothko is downstairs, and she uses it to make deals and to impress her grandeur upon the uninitiated. The real one, with the Post-its and the coffee rings and the corner table mosaicked with slides, is off-limits to all but a few. I didn't learn of its existence until we'd been dating for a year.

I found her slumped in her rocking chair, a quaintly mismatched piece of furniture and the only thing she kept when she sold the house in Ironton. Her fingertips dangled near a tumbler of scotch sweating into the rug. The room vibrated with the noise of the band four stories below.

'Where've you been?' I asked. 'Everyone's wondering what happened to you.'

'That's funny. Lately people have been asking me the same thing about you.'

I waited. 'Are you going to come downstairs?'

'I don't really feel like it.'

'Is something wrong?'

'No.'

I wanted to deliver my apology, but I didn't feel ready. Instead I knelt by her and put my hand on her arm, as hard as a crowbar. It occurred to me, not for the first time, that Marilyn's beauty had a sharp, almost masculine edge to it, all strong features and sharp angles. She smiled, her breath scalding me.

'I hate these parties,' she said.

'Then why do you give them?'

'Because I have to.' She closed her eyes and leaned back in the chair. 'And because I like them. I just hate them, too.'

'Are you sick?'

'No.'

'Do you want some water?'

She said nothing.

I went across the room to the mini-fridge and got a bottle of Evian, which I set on the floor near the scotch. She didn't move.

'You're not having fun, are you,' she said. 'You wouldn't be here if you were.'

I leaned against the edge of the desk. 'I'd have more if you came down-stairs.'

'I bet you're seeing a lot of people.'

'I am.'

'People have been asking about you,' she said.

'You said.'

'Like you went off to war or something.'

'I haven't.'

'Mm.' She sighed, her eyes still closed. 'I tell them I don't know a thing.'

I said nothing.

'What else am I supposed to tell them,' she said.

'You can tell them whatever you want.'

'They ask me like I should know. They assume I have a direct line to you.'

'You do.'

'Do I?'

'Of course you do.'

She nodded. 'That's good.'

'Of course you do,' I said again, although I don't know why.

'Did you have a pleasant stay, living in my house?'

'You were wonderful,' I said. 'You know I can't thank you enough.'

'I don't remember you trying.'

'If I didn't say it before, then I'm sorry, and I'll say it now: thank you.'

'I shouldn't need any thanks, but I do.'

'Of course you do.'

'No,' she said. 'I shouldn't need anything from you. That's not the way it's supposed to be.'

I said, 'It's manners, Marilyn. You're a hundred percent right.'

She said nothing.

She said, 'Is it.'

'Is it what.'

'Manners.'

I said, 'I don't understand.'

'Is that how we're supposed to behave toward one another? Decorously?'

'I thought so.'

'I see,' she said. 'News to me.'

'Why wouldn't we be polite to each other?'

'Because,' she said, looking at me, 'I love you, you fucking idiot.'

She had never told me that before.

She said, 'When people ask me how you are and I can't say, I am humiliated. But they ask and I'm supposed to know. I have to tell them something. Right?'

I nodded.

A silence.

She said, 'You'll never guess who called me.'

'Who.'

'Guess.'

'Marilyn—'

'Play along, will you.' The drawl crept into her voice. 'Have a little holiday spirit.' *Holidee spurrut.*

'Kevin Hollister,' I said.

'No.'

'Who.'

'*Guess.*'

'George Bush.'

She snickered. 'Wrong.'

'Then I give up.'

'Jocko Steinberger.'

'He did?'

She nodded.

'What for.'

'He wants me to represent him. He said he doesn't feel like he's getting enough personal attention from you.'

I was stunned. I'd known Jocko since he burst onto the scene as part of a group show organized by the late Leonora Waite. First her artist, then mine, he had always been a stalwart member of the gallery roster. I considered him moody but by no means treacherous, and the fact that he had gone to Marilyn, without speaking to me first, cut deeply. Losing Kristjana had been my doing, and no tragedy, but now I was down two artists in six months, an alarming rate of attrition.

Marilyn said, 'He has new stuff and he wants me to show it.'

'I hope you told him no,' I said.

'I did.'

'Good.'

'I did,' she said, 'but now I think I'm going to tell him yes.'

A silence.

'And why's that.'

'Because I don't think you're doing a very good job of representing him.'

'Really.'

'Nope.'

'Don't you think you should give me the chance to talk it over with him before you make that decision for me?'

'I didn't make the decision,' she said. 'He did. He approached me, remember.'

'Tell him to talk it over with me,' I said. 'That's what you're supposed to do.'

'Well I'm not doing that.'

'What's the matter with you, Marilyn.'

'What's the matter with *you*.'

'Nothing's the m—'

'*Bullshit.*'

A silence. My head throbbed.

'Marilyn—'

'I haven't seen you for weeks.'

I said nothing.

'Where have you been.'

'Busy.'

'With what.'

'The case.'

'"The case"?'

'Yes.'

'How's that coming.'

'We're making progress.'

'Are you? That's good. That's wonderful news. Hooray. Are you going to shoot any guns?'

'What?'

'You know,' she said. 'Bang bang bang.'

'I don't know what you're talking about.'

'Yes you do.'

'I honestly don't,' I said, 'and if it's all right with you, I'm not done talking about Jocko yet. Just where do you get off thinking you can—'

'Oh please,' she said.

'Answer me, how do you think you—'

'Stop talking,' she said.

A silence. I stood up to leave. 'Drink some water,' I said. 'You'll have a headache if you don't.'

'I know you're fucking that girl.'

'Excuse me?'

'"*Excuse me*",' she mocked. 'You heard what I said.'

'I heard it, but I don't know what you're talking about.'

'Blah blah *blah* blah, blah blah *blah* blah, blah blah *blah*.'

'Goodnight, Marilyn.'

'Don't you walk out.'

'I'm not going to stand here and listen to you make a fool of yourself.'

'You walk out of here and you do not know what I will do.'

'Please calm down.'

'Tell me you fucked her.'

'Who?'

'*Stop that*,' she screamed.

A silence.

'*Tell me.*'

'I fucked her.'

'Excellent,' she said. 'Now we're getting somewhere.'

I said nothing.

'You can't lie to me. I know. I get reports from the field.'

'What are you talking about?' Then I said, '*Isaac?*'

'So don't bother.'

'Jesus Christ, Marilyn.'

'Don't act so goddamned entitled,' she said. 'That's your problem. You're spoiled.'

'Yes, well, I hate to break it to you, but you're not getting your money's worth with him. I slept with her once, and that was before any of this got started.'

'I don't believe you.'

'Believe what you want, that's the truth.'

'You weren't fucking me,' she said. 'You have to be fucking someone.'

'For God's sake I was in the *hospital.*'

'So what.'

'So I wasn't – I'm not going to indulge this.'

'Tell me you fucked her.'

'I already – do you have to keep saying that?'

'What.'

'"Fuck".'

She started laughing. 'What would you call it?'

'I call it none of your business.'

In a single motion she was up out of the chair, tumbler in hand. I ducked and it shattered against the wall, bits of glass and water and scotch spraying across the top of her copy machine.

'Say that again,' she said. 'Tell me it's none of my business.'

I stood up slowly, my hands raised. In the carpet was a wet spot where the tumbler had been.

'When did you fuck her.'

'What's the purpose of this.'

'When.'

A silence.

'About two months ago.'

'*When.*'

'I just tol—'

'*Be more specific.*'

'You want the time and date?'

'Was it during the day? Was it at night? Was it on a bed or a couch or the kitchen counter? Do tell, Ethan, inquiring minds want to know.'

'I don't remember the exact date.' I paused. 'It was the night of the funeral.'

'Oh,' she said. 'Oh, well, that's extremely classy.'

I quashed the impulse to snap at her. Instead I said, 'You can't be this upset. It's not as though you haven't slept with anyone else in the last six years.'

'Have you?'

'Of course I have. You know that.'

She said, 'I haven't.'

I didn't know what to say. Under normal circumstances I doubt I would have believed her, but just then I knew she was telling the truth.

She said, 'I want you to leave.'

'Marilyn—'

'Now.'

I stepped into the hallway, into the elevator, my head racing with esprit d'escalier. Obviously, there had been some sort of miscommunication, a root misunderstanding of the terms of our relationship. Someone had not spoken up. Mistakes were made. I reached the first floor. The doors parted and music flooded in. The party was in full swing. I got my coat and went into the street. The snow was like cream, and I could see we were in for a blizzard.

INTERLUDE: 1939.

Like most people, doctors tend to fear him, and in that fear, they never come right out and say what they want. It drives him mad. The one on the telephone, the superintendent, keeps talking in circles, such that Louis cannot fathom the reason for the call. More money? Is that it? He can give them more money. Already he pays fees that Bertha deems extortionate, a peculiar position for her to take, considering that the arrangement was entirely her idea, and that those fees come out of bank accounts to which she has never contributed a penny.

Louis would not mind paying more. He would, in fact, be happy to pay much more, give and give and give until he has left himself bloody and shattered. But here is the punch line: he has too much money to ever be broken. Writing checks will never be an effective method of expiation, and unfortunately for him, he knows no other way.

As Louis listens to the superintendent, he tries to convey the message to Bertha, who stands nearby, grinding her teeth impatiently.

'He says – one moment. He says that she – what was that?'

Fed up, Bertha seizes the receiver. 'In plain English, please,' she says. Over the next minute and a half, her face shifts from exasperation to incredulity to fury to determination and finally to the blank, chill mask she puts on during difficult times. She says a few short words and puts down the phone.

'The girl is pregnant.'

'That's impossible.'

'Well,' she says, pushing the button for the maid, 'obviously, it isn't.'

'What are you going to do?'

'I don't see what choice we have. She can't stay there.'

'Then what do you inte—'

'I don't know,' says Bertha. 'You haven't given me much time to think.'

The maid appears in the doorway.

'Call for the car.'

'Yessum.'

Louis looks at his wife. 'Now?'

'Yes.'

'But it's Sunday,' he says.

'What's that got to do with anything?'

He has no answer.

She says, 'Do *you* have a better idea?'

He does not.

'Then run along. You're not dressed for an outing.'

AS HE PERFORMS HIS TOILET, he wonders how he has gotten here. The events of his life do not seem connected in any way. First he was there, then somewhere else; now he is here. But how did he arrive? He does not know.

He reaches for his comb; his valet steps forward and hands it to him.

'That's all right,' Louis says. 'I'll be alone now, thank you.'

The valet nods and withdraws.

Once he has gone, Louis removes his shirt and stands bare-chested. The last eight years have aged him. Once he had ringlets so dense that the teeth of the comb would get stuck. He had smooth skin, not the elephantine wattles that appear at his waist as he bends. His is not the dense, cannon-ball belly men of wealth and power should have but a soft paunch, a loosening around the ribs. His hips are wide and feminine, and his trousers must be let out at the seat. He repulses himself. He did not always look this way.

He puts on his shirt and his shoes and descends to the foyer.

The Home is near Tarrytown, a few miles off the Hudson. Once they leave the city, the roads become lined with deep ruts that the car is ill equipped to handle. The drive takes several hours; his suit is stuffy and his back stiffens; by the time they arrive, he can hardly move. It's hard to say what would be worse, getting out of the car or turning right around and going back to Fifth.

The superintendent stands outside the gate, indicating where they may park, a gesture that annoys Louis, insofar as it implies that this visit is the Mullers' first. Bertha might not come, but he does, at least once a year.

The grounds are lush and colorful, thick with wildflowers and weeds that make Louis's sinuses buzz. He blows his nose and glances at his wife, staring impassively out the window at a building that did not exist the last time she was here. He knows this to be true because he paid for a portion of its construction. Anonymously. Bertha would not allow him to disgrace the family name. Another irony, that little bout of possessiveness, for it is he who turned her from a Steinholtz into a Muller.

She has changed, too, although he has a hard time putting his finger on how. Everything that made her a beautiful girl has lingered, more or less, into middle age, without the need for heavy investments in cosmetics. Other women spend half their day staving off wrongs done by time and childbearing. Not so Bertha.

What, then? Louis watches her gazing out the window and notices that all of those lovely features are still there – but more so. The beauty mark a touch larger; the nose a trifle rounder. It is as though the real Bertha, for years tightly wrapped in youth, has pushed her way through to the surface, causing tiny ruptures all over, individually imperceptible but together enough to render the whole grotesque. Perhaps these changes are real, or perhaps familiarity has bred contempt. Whatever the case may be, what scant desire he could conjure up for her, back when he was supple and highly motivated, has long since dried out and blown away. His appetites in general have waned, leaving in their stead regret, a multipartite regret made up of all his poor decisions. Because although he has a hard time understanding how he came to the present, if he is honest with himself he will say that the path has been of his making. What seemed like inevitabilities he now understands as choices. When, so many years ago, they brought him into the room to meet her and they told him she was to be his bride, and he agreed, and the whole machine swung into motion – that was his choice, wasn't it? His father said to him: marry or go to London. Well, why not London? At the time he told himself that marriage would follow eventually, so he might as well accept his fate and be allowed to stay on. But perhaps his father had been giving him an out. Perhaps he could have spent his life in bachelorhood, like great-uncle Bernard. What might have happened in London? Louis wonders. And when Bertha sent the girl away – hadn't he had a choice? He argued and argued and finally gave in, but he could have stood his ground. He could have done something. What, he does not know. But something.

In business he never second-guesses himself; in life he has no peace.

The car rolls across the gravel, slows, comes to a halt. Bertha gets out but he is impaled on regret.

'Get out of the car, Louis.'

He gets out of the car.

The superintendent's name is Dr Christmas. Though normally full of good humor, today he has a bilious look about him.

'Mr Muller. Mrs Muller. Did you have a pleasant drive?'

'Where's my daughter,' Bertha says.

They pass through the lobby. Louis allows his wife to take the lead, and she does, pushing out in front of everyone else, as though she knows where to go. *Her* daughter. Preposterous. An insult to the effort he has expended over the last twenty years. The girl has never been hers, not since the moment they parted company on the delivery table. But does he really want to claim that the girl is his? If so, then that makes her his responsibility; it makes everything that has happened his fault.

Dr Christmas has decided to turn their walk into a tour, pointing out the Home's prouder features, such as the hydrotherapy rooms, with their hippopotamus-sized tubs and stacks of linens. They perform more than a thousand cold wet sheet packs every year.

'Recently we've had some success with insulin treatments,' he says, 'and you'll be pleased to know that thanks to your—'

'What I will be pleased to know,' says Bertha, 'is where my daughter is. Until then I am not pleased to know anything.'

They walk the rest of the way in silence.

Or – not silence. From other rooms, other floors – from far away on the grounds – muffled by concrete and plaster, oozing through ducts – come the most ungodly sounds. Screams and weeping and a jagged laughter that stands Louis's hair on end, and a variety of noises that no human being should be able to produce. He has heard these noises before but they never fail to unnerve him. They do not have a daughter, they have a son; Bertha has repeated this mantra enough, forcing him to recite it with her, and he has come to believe. Thus every visit to the Home brings fresh horror.

Their child, their real child, David – he is growing up handsome and articulate, a model young man. At thirteen he has already read Schiller and Mann and Goethe in German, Molière and Racine and Stendhal in

259

French. He plays the violin and has a knack for mathematics, especially as applied to business. While it is true that education at home has left him shy around other children, he is nonetheless charming toward adults, fully capable of engaging in conversation with men thirty years his senior.

By comparison, what hope does the girl stand? Bertha made the pragmatic choice, and she made it without hesitation, excommunicating her from her heart, something Louis has never quite managed to do. And yet what has he done except wallow in self-pity? Where has all his suffering gotten him? Surely it hasn't improved the girl's lot.

Thank God David is away, visiting his mother's relatives in Europe. Louis shudders to imagine inventing excuses for this afternoon jaunt. Mother and I are going for a ride in the countryside. Mother and I need to take the air. More than anything, Louis hates to lie to his son.

As far as he can tell, David remains unaware of the girl's existence. There was that one awful night, eight years ago, when Delia left the door unlocked and the girl wandered downstairs, attracted by the sound of the radio. For a time Louis had wanted to put a radio in the girl's room, but Bertha had exercised her veto. A radio would serve no purpose, she argued. The girl wouldn't understand anything, and the noise might draw attention. Instead they gave her picture books and dolls, which seemed to occupy her. But Louis knew that books and dolls weren't enough, a suspicion borne out when she appeared. If Bertha had only listened to him and bought a damned radio, the girl might never have come calling, none of this ever would have been necessary . . .

That awful night; the arguments that followed. He lost them all, with one exception: he managed to get rid of Delia, whom he had always considered indolent, sensuous and untrustworthy. Even Bertha had to admit that leaving the door unlocked constituted grounds for dismissal. Although no longer employed, Delia remains on the payroll. Her continued silence costs Louis seventy-five dollars a week.

David has never said anything about that night, never asked about the girl. If he somehow discerned her identity – and Louis cannot imagine how he would have – then he seems to have forgotten all about her. They are safe. Hundreds of lies, each one thin, but layered until their accumulated strength allows passage across the chasm.

Dr Christmas holds a door. Bertha and Louis sit on one side of the desk. On the other side is a seedy-looking fellow with an ostentatious pocketwatch. Christmas locks the door and takes the remaining chair.

'Allow me to introduce Winston Coombs, the Home's resident legal counsel. I hope you won't mind if he sits in on our little meeting. As a matter of course, I—'

'I don't see my daughter anywhere.'

'Yes, Mrs Muller. I have every intention of—'

'I came here with one purpose, and that is to see my daughter and what you idiots have managed to do to her.'

'Yes, Mrs Muller. I would however like to inform you that—'

'I don't care what you would like. This is not the time for you to express preferences.'

Says Coombs, 'If I may—'

'You may not.'

'Mrs Muller,' says the superintendent, 'all I'd like to do is reassure you and your husband of our intention to take the appropriate punitive measures toward the young man responsible, and—'

Then Bertha says something that surprises Louis. 'I don't care one bit about him. As far as I'm concerned, he doesn't exist. I want to see my daughter. I demand to see her, this instant, and if you continue to do anything other than take me to her I will call my own attorneys, who I can assure you will make Mr Coombs very sorry that he ever entered the profession.' She stands. 'I take it you don't have her in that closet.'

'No, ma'am.'

'Then walk.'

They exit the building and step onto the back lawn, neatly mown and hemmed in on three sides by trees. Golden light pools in the grass. They follow a stone path into the woods. Fifty feet hence they come to a small house enclosed by a whitewashed fence, a place new to Louis and certainly to Bertha.

Dr Christmas finds the correct key from a clanging set and holds the gate open for Bertha, who pushes past without a word. The house requires another key, which requires another minute or so of noisy fiddling. Bertha taps her foot. Louis stuffs his hands in his pockets and gazes up through the leaves at the bloody sky.

'And here we are,' says the doctor.

In the foyer they are met by a nurse, who stands as Bertha enters.

'This suite is reserved for patients during their most sensitive or stressful episodes,' says Christmas. 'And our finest staff—'

Bertha does not wait for him to finish but goes on to the next room. Louis is close behind, bumping into her when she stops short on the threshold.

'Oh,' she says. 'Oh, God.'

Louis looks over his wife's shoulder and sees his daughter. She is lying on a cot, wearing a blue gown through which her belly bulges visibly. Her entire trunk, already short and squarish, looks ominously distended. She blinks at them woozily.

Louis would like to step into the room, but Bertha is gripping the doorposts. Gently, he pries her hands free and enters. The girl sits up, watching him curiously as he drags a chair to her bedside and sits.

'Hello, Ruth.' She gives a bashful smile when he touches her cheek. 'I'm very glad to see you. I'm sorry I've been away so long. I don't know what's kept me.'

The girl says nothing. She glances over Louis's shoulder, at Bertha, who has begun to make a series of low, mournful chuffing noises.

'Ruth,' Louis says. The girl looks at him. 'Ruth, I see that – that something has happened here.'

The girl says nothing.

'Ruth,' he says again.

Bertha turns and leaves. From the next room, Louis hears her threatening the superintendent but he tries to focus on his daughter. 'Ruth,' he says. He had wanted to call her Teresa, after a great-aunt of his; Bertha had a Harriet to name for, as well as a Sarah. But Bertha insisted on a name with no connection to either of their families, which was precisely the point.

Still, love adjusts, and he has come to hold the name dear. Ruth, he says. He picks up her hand and begins to rock back and forth. Ruth. She watches him guilelessly, confusion spreading over her face as he sways and says her name.

THEIR OPTIONS ARE LIMITED. Dr Christmas hints that he has the capacity to end the pregnancy right away, but when he does so Bertha spits at him. She of the expedient solution; apparently, she clings to some taboos.

The next day their family physician – the one who delivered the girl, the one who recommended the Home – arrives on the afternoon train. He takes a taxi to the hotel and is shown to Mr and Mrs Muller's suite, into which he steps with no small amount of trepidation. Hat literally in hand, he begins to offer an apology-cum-defense.

'Never mind that,' says Bertha. 'You're going to need clothes. We have moved the girl to a nearby cottage for the duration of her pregnancy. There is a nurse with her. The adjacent cottage isn't for sale yet but we'll have it soon enough. You will live there until this is finished. Once the baby has arrived we'll decide what to do with the girl. In the meantime, you will have whatever supplies you require, and we will cover your expenses, as well as whatever losses you incur being away from your practice. Until you can further determine your needs this ought to suffice. Give it to him, Louis.'

As the doctor takes the check, his hands begin to shake, the way they did that night twenty-one years ago. Louis is dismayed. There must be someone better – someone younger, with more energy and greater expertise. But Bertha will not budge. No specialist, no matter how good his training, has as much experience as Dr Fetchett in one area: discretion. He has kept the family secrets well, and now he will be punished for his loyalty.

'I understand your urgency,' says the doctor, 'but I can't possibly leave New York for—'

'You can and you will. She's already quite far along. Why they waited until now to telephone us is another matter, for discussion at another time. Right now I'm concerned only about her well-being and the well-being of the child. Your room key is there, if you'd like to refresh yourself. We leave for the cottage in thirty minutes.'

SHE HAS SO MUCH TO LOSE. The woman the world sees is the product of many years of hard work. In becoming that person, erasion has played as great a role as creation, a lesson she has never forgotten.

On their honeymoon, Louis took her to Europe for six months. They visited his ancestral homeland, over the Rhine from where she still had relatives. They rented châteaux; they were received by heads of state, escorted in grand fashion from one magnificent edifice to another, shown the world's greatest art in private sessions, allowed to press their noses right up against the canvas, to run their fingers along the gold and silver surfaces. What she remembers most of all are the Michelangelos. Not the muscular *David* or the languid *Pietà* but the rough, unfinished Florentine sculptures, human form struggling to wrest itself from a solid block of marble. That has always been her great battle, a lifelong battle, won by divestiture. We shed; we lighten and rise.

She came over at the age of five, and in the beginning she was friendless.

The other girls teased her about the way she said the letter *s*. It came out as a *z*. Or when she said *shpelling* instead of *spelling*. They would tease her about that, too. *Shhhh* they would say, laughing their little heads off. *Shhhhh*. A clever joke, at once playing on her shortcomings and telling her that what she had to say was of no interest to anyone.

Her accent, then – that had to go. Day in and day out she sat with the tutor. She sells seashells by the seashore, the shells she sells are surely seashells. The exercises made her jaw ache. They numbed her with boredom. She worked. She chipped away at herself – the *z*'s and *sh*'s falling off, bits of stone and clouds of dust – until she sounded like any other American girl. It was a painful process but a worthwhile one, certainly after the War broke out.

Off came her baby fat. She kept herself away from certain foods, and gradually she emerged as a woman who could turn heads in the street. Boys wanted to be by her side, and girls wanted to be by the sides of the boys. She shed her timorousness, shed her resentment, generously extending friendship to those who had maligned her in childhood. She shed her inhibitions, becoming known as a girl not only of exceptional beauty but of great wit. She tamped down an unbecoming tendency toward sarcasm and built up a tolerance for the inanity of social niceties. She entertained drawing rooms with lightning-fast passages from the Goldberg Variations. Everyone applauded. She learned to enjoy parties, to laugh on cue, to reflect in others what they most wanted to see.

By her eighteenth birthday, several men had asked for her hand. She turned them down. She had bigger plans, and so did her mother.

Her father thought them both ridiculous, and said so.

'I don't see why you say that,' said Mama. 'They like German girls. And I know that they will want to marry that one off as soon as possible.'

Mama was right. Bertha marveled. One moment she was a debutante; the next she was a bride, dancing with her husband in a ballroom as big as her imagination.

The first years of her marriage were her happiest. She barely noticed her husband's lack of interest in her; she was too busy making the most of her newfound omnipotence. Papa was rich, but nobody was rich like the Mullers. It became a challenge for her to dream up new ways to spend. And still she continued to rise, cultivating important relationships and pruning dead ones. She invited and was invited by others. Her wardrobe was the envy of all, her clothing cut closely in homage to her figure. She became a regular in the society pages, noted for her grace but also for her charitable work. In her name grew a concert hall and a collection at the Met. She endowed functions and sponsored schoolchildren. She was only twenty-one but already she had done so much good. Her parents were proud; her life was full; and if her husband did not desire her, so much the better. It freed her up to work on refining herself, a new person, reborn as a Muller. It was she who had to ensure the bloodline. Louis could not be trusted. He had done everything in his power to sabotage his family's future. She came to stitch up the damage, and in doing so, she took possession of her new name in a way that he – a Muller by dint of Fate – never could. Unlike Louis, she had to work, to position herself, to choose; she became more of a Muller than he ever was; and thus her obligation ran much deeper than his, her mandate divine. How else to explain the rapidity of her ascent? Someone wanted her to succeed.

And she made sure Louis did his duty when the time came around.

During the early part of Bertha's first pregnancy, Mama died. Before she went, she said, 'I only hope your children take such good care of you.'

The disappointment, then, was twofold. Bertha felt as though she had denied her mother's deathbed wish. After all, no defective child could ever take care of her. And the shame she stood to reap: oh the shame. Her whole life would fly apart, springs and gears and hinges scattering. All the good she did would come to naught. Who would give the kind of charity that she did if not her? Who would throw the Autumn Ball? Who would be the focal point? She had obligations to the people of New York City.

An accent, an inch of waistline, a recalcitrant husband – the problems she fought always had clear and concrete solutions. She likewise approached the problem of the girl with a level head and a steady hand. This, too, was merely another problem to solve; the real question was how. The Home gave her her answer. Dr Fetchett told them that such a decision was not uncommon, and she took comfort in knowing that she was following a well-beaten path. For every hurdle rising higher.

What she finds so troubling about the latest turn of events, this abomination, is the sense that she has stalled. Or worse – begun to sink. She sees now that the problem of the girl will never be solved, not as long as people have the capacity to reproduce themselves. Family is the problem that recurs.

IN AUGUST, DAVID RETURNS FROM BERLIN. He entertains his parents with stories of his travels, and shares his firsthand account of the rising political turmoil. Louis, who has been following the news closely, speculates about their economic effects. Several high-ranking officers in his Frankfurt branch have been forced out of their jobs, a trend that Louis disapproves of. Jewish or not, they were fine businessmen, and nobody with half a brain can believe that stripping a nation of its most qualified and experienced workers will lead to greater prosperity.

Having left at so young an age, Bertha has no strong feelings about the annexation of Austria or the breaking of synagogue windows, events that she does not regard as having any direct impact on her. She is happy to have her son back, to have the tableau of her life reestablished. Lately, she and Louis have spoken even less than usual, and his willfulness angers her. He has never fought back as hard as he is fighting now.

His chief complaint is that she has not gone to visit the girl. He goes every two weeks. Would it kill her, he wants to know, to show her face?

But she can't. There are so many reasons why. Somebody needs to stay at home. What if a guest drops by unannounced. They couldn't *both* be out of the house, now could they? People would want to know where the Mullers had gone in the thick of summer. The Mullers live fashionably, and what they do influences the whole crowd of Good People. Inquiries would be made; a rumor would ignite. One of them, at least, has to stay behind, and she is the more reasonable choice.

Besides, how could she help? Having been pregnant herself, Bertha knows that it is a highly individualized form of suffering. She knows how to soothe only one pregnant woman: herself. Whereas the doctor has soothed hundreds. Let him do his job.

And most of all she is afraid, afraid of feeling the way she felt for those few short minutes at the Home, afraid of feeling the way she felt during the drive back to New York, afraid of having her heart once again turned upside down.

Would it kill her to show her face?

It might.

One night they are eating when a maid appears with a folded note, which she places on the table. Madam. Bertha is about to scold her for interrupting dinner when she notices that the note has opened slightly, revealing at the bottom the name E. F. Fetchett, MD. She slides it under the base of her wineglass.

After dinner she sequesters herself in her sewing room.

Dear Mr and Mrs Muller—
Kindly request your immediate attention by telephone.
Sincerely,
E. F. Fetchett, MD

She picks up the line and asks for Tarrytown four-eight-oh-five-eight. The doctor answers. In the background there are sounds.

'This is Mrs Louis Muller,' she says.

'Labor has begun. I thought you might want to know.'

Bertha fingers the phone cord.

'Mrs Muller?'

'I'm here.'

'Will you be present for the birth?'

She looks at the clock. It is eight thirty. 'Will she last til tomorrow morning?'

'I don't think so, no.'

'Then I won't be present,' she says, and hangs up.

THE NEXT MORNING, she orders a picnic packed. She and David spend the day in Central Park.

WHEN LOUIS RETURNS FROM TARRYTOWN late that night, he looks as though he has run the entire distance on foot. His tie is gone, his shirt sweat-stained and missing studs. He goes directly to his suite and shuts the door.

'What's wrong with Father?'

'He's ill. Did you have a good time today?'

'Yeah.'

'Excuse me? I didn't understand that.'

'Yes.'

'Yes what.'

'Yes, Mother.'

'You're welcome. Who loves you more than anyone else in the world?'

'You do, Mother.'

'That's right. What are you doing after supper?'

'Practicing my violin.'

'And?'

'Reading.'

'And?'

'Listening to the Yankee game.'

'I don't remember that being on the agenda.'

'Can we put it on the agenda? Please?'

'Practice first.'

'Yes, Mother. May I be excused?'

'Certainly.'

He lays down his napkin. Good boy.

'Mother?'

'Yes, David.'

'Can I visit Father?'

'Not tonight.'

'Will you please tell him that I hope he feels better?'

'I certainly will.'

When he is gone, Bertha lingers at the table, rubbing her temples. The maid asks if she would like anything else.

'I am going to see my husband. I don't want to be disturbed under any circumstances. Is that clear?'

'Yessum.'

She steps in the elevator and girds herself for battle.

HE ARRIVED IN THE VILLAGE as the heat peaked. The air blurry with gnats, the sweet rot of manure, half-naked children throwing water at one another. The chauffeur steered along the rutted road and forked onto the rural byway leading to the cottage they chose – *Bertha* chose – their advance halted by a cattleguard and a swing-arm gate that necessitates stopping the car, getting out, opening the gate, driving through, and stopping again to close the gate behind. Louis ordered the chauffeur to leave it open. He didn't care who might wander in. Let them.

As he stepped inside the cottage, he felt nauseated and dizzy, and his instinct was to reach for his wife's arm. Since his last visit, the place had been converted into an operating theater. A pile of bedsheets, rank with antiseptic and bodily fluids. The quiet disturbed him: shouldn't there be crying? Ruth herself barely made any noise as a newborn, and he had always understood that to be symptomatic of her condition. What if her child is the same way? What untold miseries will he endure?

Dr Fetchett looked cadaverous, although he had only good things to say. The baby was a boy, his heartbeat strong and regular. The mother's health was excellent; better, in fact, than many normal mothers after a similar ordeal. In the interest of cleaning up, they had moved both mother and child to the neighboring cottage, where nurses were attending to her.

'How is she, is she happy?'

The doctor rubbed his cheek thoughtfully. 'Who can say, really.'

They went first to see the baby. Red and squashed and swaddled; black, spiky hair on the top of his head. Utterly ordinary.

Actually, he looked a little like Bertha.

Dr Fetchett explains that it is indeed possible for a mongoloid mother to have a normal child. 'Of course, we can't say for sure that other problems won't arise down the line. I say that not to disturb you but because I'm trying to prepare you for any eventuality.'

Louis asked to hold him. In his arms the baby felt like paper.

'Should he be that red?'

'It's normal.'

At first he is relieved. Normal, normal, everything normal. But the longer he holds the sleeping boy in his arms, the more clearly he comes to see that normalcy is the worst curse of all. If the child is normal, he represents a claim on the estate and a threat to David's sovereignty. Louis can only imagine what Bertha might do.

The doctor asks if Mrs Muller will be coming to visit.

Louis said, 'I don't believe she will.'

Now, lying on the floor of his drawing room to quiet his screaming back, looking up at Bertha – she towers over him, standing behind two armchairs she has pulled together like an embrasure – he says, 'The child is dead. The girl is dead, too. They both died in childbirth.'

A MONTH LATER, under the pretext of business travel, Louis goes back to the Home.

'I want to know the name of the father.'

Dr Christmas's eyes dart around the room, in search of his missing legal counsel.

Louis says, 'My wife doesn't know I'm here. The least you can do is help me give the boy a proper name.'

After a moment, the doctor goes to a cabinet and takes out a file. He hands Louis a photo of a young man with wild, dark hair; wild, dark eyes.

'His name is Cracke,' says the doctor.

Louis compares features. 'A patient.'

'Yes.'

'He doesn't look defective.'

'He had other problems. Many of them. A troublesome boy.'

Louis puts the photo down. He should be feeling something. Anger, perhaps, or disgust. But he feels nothing, only mild curiosity.

'How did he know my daughter?'

The doctor shifts uncomfortably. 'I can't say. As you're aware, we segregate the sexes. Sometimes for a concert we bring everyone into the main hall. Presumably, they slipped out together unnoticed.'

Louis frowns. 'Do you mean that she went consensually?'

'I would have to think so,' says the doctor. 'She asked for him repeatedly.'

Louis says nothing.

'He's no longer with us.'

Louis is confused. 'He's dead?'

'I ordered him moved.'

'And where is he now?'

'At another home, some miles outside Rochester.'

'Does he know?'

'I don't imagine so.'

'Are you going to tell him?'

'I hadn't planned on it.'

'Please don't.'

As he opens the car door for Louis, the doctor smiles unctuously and says, 'I hope you don't find it rude of me to ask how Ruth is. We were all quite fond of her.'

'She's right as rain,' Louis says.

The doctor offers his hand. Louis declines.

HE HIRES A STAFF OF THREE, overseen by an anvil-jawed Scotswoman named Nancy Greene, a former employee at the Home. She is kind to Ruth, kinder still to the baby; she understands – or seems to understand – when Louis presses upon her the importance of keeping secrets. No good could come of anyone knowing, he tells her, and she seems to agree. He pays her very well.

IN 1940, THE WORLD IS AT WAR. David has entered his first year of formal schooling at the N. M. Priestly Academy, and Bertha has been reelected president of her women's club, a position to which she devotes increasingly large amounts of time once her son leaves the house on Fifth. The Frankfurt office has been closed since the invasion of Poland, and the Muller Corporation has begun to shift its priorities from international banking to domestic property management, which Louis regards as a more stable arena for investment. His instincts will prove prescient when American GIs begin coming home and the demand for housing skyrockets. But that will not happen for years. At the moment, he is operating on a hunch.

November is wet and cold. The worst storm in a decade comes and goes, leaving Manhattan smelling of earthworms. Louis sits in his office on the fiftieth floor of the Muller Building.

Few people know the number for the phone that rings directly at his desk.

He answers. It is Nancy Greene.

'Sir, she's very sick.'

He cancels his afternoon meetings. When he arrives at the cottage, he spots a dire sign: Dr Fetchett's mud-spattered car.

'I can't control her fever. She needs to be moved to a hospital.'

Despite their best efforts, the infection rages out of control, and within a week Ruth is dead of pneumonia. Dr Fetchett attempts to console Louis by telling him that in general, people with her condition have a short life expectancy. That she lived as long as she did – and went as fast – is a kind of blessing.

Louis buries her on the grounds. No clergy are present. The nurses sing a hymn. Mrs Greene stays inside to mind baby Victor.

NINETEEN

I didn't talk to Marilyn for several weeks. When I did call, a few days after the new year, I was told by her assistant that she had gone to Paris.

'For how long?'

'I'm not supposed to tell you. I'm not actually supposed to tell you she's in Paris, either, so you didn't hear it from me.'

I suppose I didn't have the right to be angry at her, but I was. I felt as though I was the aggrieved, that she had no right to be hurt; as far as I knew, I had been acting with her permission. I reacted the way I did after my mother's death, the way I always have whenever I've felt, or been made to feel, rightfully ashamed. Narcissism can't stomach too much guilt. It vomits back up rage. I thought of all the times Marilyn had wronged me – all the gibes I'd taken, the condescension I'd swallowed with a smile. I thought of how she often treated me like arm candy and how she interfered in the running of my business. I thought of her forcing me to kiss her when my head felt like a rock tumbler. To this list of crimes I added others that had nothing to do with me; I labeled her a homewrecker, a vengeful divorcée, a liar, a bully. I erased her kindnesses and inflated her cruelties until she seemed so bad to me, so thoroughly corrupt, that her unwillingness to overlook my tiny indiscretion became the height of hypocrisy. And just as I got through holding her responsible for global warming and the burst of the dot-com bubble, I reached into my jacket to take out my phone and leave her a voicemail telling her *exactly* what I thought, and instead of the phone I found a stray price tag that someone at Barneys had forgotten to remove. The upper portion of my outfit had cost Marilyn $895.00, plus 8.375 percent sales tax.

To my surprise, my lengthy apology e-mail brought an equally lengthy reply – in French. Since Marilyn knows I don't speak French, she had to have sent it knowing I'd need a translation; who knew what kind of mortification she intended to subject me to. I hesitated before calling Nat over.

"'Following the death of King Louis XIV, the court returned to Paris from Versailles. Residences were constructed on the Faubourg, displacing the horticultural marshes . . .'" He scanned down. 'There's something in here about a restaurant . . . You know what this is, it's the history of her hotel. It sounds like she cut-and-pasted it off the website.' He looked at me. 'Does that have any meaning to it that I'm missing?'

'It just means fuck off.'

THE SNOWSTORM DELAYED SAMANTHA'S RETURN, and when I talked to her, she urged me to continue without her. I decided to use the time to follow up on the information I'd gotten at the stationery store. For weeks I'd been calling local game rooms and chess and checkers clubs, thinking that Victor might have gone in search of a challenge. The places nearest the Courts were actually in Brooklyn, and without exception they turned out to be full of two-bit academics; anxious teenagers with bad haircuts; dead-eyed prodigies salivating over their victories, or else sitting in chairs too high for them, swinging their feet and clutching electronic clocks as they waited for a worthy opponent. I would tiptoe around, trying to ask if anyone knew a Victor Cracke, small man with a moustache, looked a little like—

'Shhhhh.'

The second-to-last place on my list was the High Street Chess and Checkers Club, located on Jamaica Avenue. Thursday, the answering machine said, was checkers night, round-robin at seven thirty, five-dollar entry fee, winner take all, soda and chips provided.

Calling the place 'High Street' could not mask the fact that it was a shithole: a grimy room four floors above a bail bondsman, up a vertiginous stairwell, to which you gained admittance by hammering on a metal door until someone came to fetch you. I arrived fifteen minutes early. A painfully thin man in a flannel shirt and hideous corduroys came down and demanded to know if I had a reservation.

'I didn't know I needed one.'

'Aahhh, I'm just messing, har har har. I'm Joe. Come the fuck on up.'

As we mounted the stairs, he apologized for the lack of access.

'Our intercom's broken,' he said, wheezing. He had a slight limp that caused his hips to swing aggressively behind him, like he was trying to shake free of himself. 'The rest of'm work, just ours is screwed. Landlord's not interested. We have to keep it locked cause there's been some break-ins. Somebody got aholda the fire extinguisher and sprayed down the carpet. I don't know what the problem that is, piecea wet carpet never hurt a man, har har har.' He took out a hankie and blew his nose.

I said, 'I was actually hoping to ask you about one of your players.'

He halted, one foot on the top stair. His whole demeanor shifted; I saw him withdraw. 'Oh yeah? Who'd that be?'

'Victor Cracke.'

Joe scrunched up his face, scratched his neck. 'Don't know him.'

'Do you think someone else might?'

He shrugged.

'Is it all right if I come up and ask around?'

'We're about to play,' he said.

'I can hang around until after you're done.'

'It's not a spectator sport.'

'Then I can come back,' I said. 'What time do you finish?'

'Depends.' He drummed his fingers on the banister. 'Could be an hour, could be four.'

'Then I'll play,' I said.

'You know how?'

Who doesn't know how to play checkers? 'Yes.'

'Are you sure?'

'Reasonably.'

He shrugged again. 'Okeydoke.'

Taken as a whole, the checkers constituency of the High Street Chess and Checkers Club made the Brooklynites look positively trendy. Queens, I gathered, drew a more diverse crowd: a jittery man with an immense Afro and Coke-bottle glasses; an obese man wearing Velcro sneakers and purple sweatpants; twins who stood against the far wall, steadily consuming Coca-Cola and mumbling to each other in Spanglish.

Joe was clearly in charge. He made announcements, reminded them about the Staten Island tournament, and then went around the room pairing people up. I was shown to a rickety card table where my opponent sat in a fully buttoned parka, moonface luminous from within his hood. 'This is Sal. Sal, meet new guy.'

Sal nodded once.

'You might as well play,' Joe said to me. 'Without you there's an odd number. Five dollars.'

We took out our wallets.

'Thaaaank *you*,' he said, plucking the bills from our hands and moving on.

Despite the room's mounting heat, Sal continued to wear his parka. He also wore mittens, making it hard for him to pick up my pieces when he captured them, which he did with dismaying frequency. As a courtesy I began handing them over.

I said, 'What happens—'

'*Shhhh.*'

'What happens when you have an odd number?' I whispered.

'Joe plays two at once. King me.'

The game took about nine minutes. It was the checkers equivalent of an ethnic cleansing. When we were done, Sal sat back, grinning. He tried to put his hands behind his head in a pose of casual triumph, but, as he was unable to lace his fingers together, he had to content himself with cupping his chin and staring at the board, now free of any pesky black pieces. The rest of the room played on in silence, save the click of a plastic disk or the occasional *King me.*

I whispered, 'Did you ever meet someone na—'

'Shhhh.'

I took out a pen and a business card and wrote my question on the back. I handed it to Sal, who shook his head. Then he motioned for the pen, and with his paw loopily wrote out a response.

No but I only started

He motioned for another card. I handed it to him. He waved impatiently and I gave him three more. As he wrote he numbered each card in the corner.

1 *coming here a few months ago so I don't know*

2 *everyone's name, Joe knows everyone though did you*

3 *know he used to be a national champion*

I took out another business card. I was down to three.

Is that a fact I wrote.

4 *Yes he was the nat champ in 93, he is also a master*

5 *in chess and backgammon*

On my final card I wrote *Impressive.*

Then we endured an awkward silence, both of us nodding at each other, having established just enough of a connection to make our lack of ability to communicate excruciating.

'Next match,' Joe called.

I played and lost eight more games. The closest I came to victory was making it past the fifteen-minute mark, a feat I achieved largely because my opponent, a veteran with hearing aids in both ears, fell asleep midway through. By the end of the night only Joe had gone undefeated. When it came time to play him, players groaned as though they'd been kicked in the crotch. My own game against Joe was my eighth and final. I pushed a piece into the center of the board.

'Twelve to sixteen,' he said. 'My favorite opening.'

He then proceeded to wipe me out in calm, steady strokes. It was as if we were playing different games. In a sense, we were. I was playing a game from childhood, when the goal is to entertain oneself, and my decisions must have seemed to him random or nonsensical, achieving no more than short-term gain, if that. He, on the other hand, was engaged in self-analysis, which is what any activity becomes at the highest level.

Watching him, I felt a kind of thrill similar to what I felt the first time I saw Victor's drawings. That might sound strange, so let me explain. Genius takes many forms, and in our century we have (slowly) come to appreciate that the transcendence given by a Picasso is potentially found in other, less obvious places. It was that old reliable provocateur, Marcel Duchamp, who showed this when he abandoned object-making, moved to Buenos Aires, and took up chess full-time. The game, he remarked, 'has all the beauty of art, and much more. It cannot be commercialized. Chess is much purer.' At first glance Duchamp seems to be lamenting the corrupting power of money. Really, though, he's being much more subversive than that. He is in fact destroying the conventional boundaries of art, arguing that all forms of expression – *all of them* – are potentially equal. Painting is the same as chess, which is the same as rollerskating, which is the same as standing at your kitchen stove, making soup. In fact, any one of those plain old everyday activities is *better* than conventional art, better than painting, because it is done without the sanctimony of anointing oneself 'an artist'. There is no surer route to mediocrity; as Borges wrote, the desire to be a genius is the 'basest of art's temptations'. According to this understanding, then, true genius has no self-awareness. A genius must by definition be someone who does not stop to consider what he is doing, how it will be received, or how it will affect him and his future; he simply *acts*. He pursues his activity with a single-mindedness that is inherently unhealthy and frequently self-destructive. A person much like, say, Joe; or a person like Victor Cracke.

I will be the first to admit that I swoon in the presence of genius, the burning pyre onto which it throws itself in sacrifice. I hoped that, standing beside the fire, I would feel it reflected in me. And as I watched Joe capture my last piece and set it down among the pile of victims, the little plastic corpses that used to be my men, I remembered why I needed Victor Cracke and why, now that I'd lost my ability to create him, I had to keep looking for him: because he was still my best chance, perhaps my only chance, to feel that distant heat, to smell the smoke and bask in the glow.

THE DISTRIBUTION OF PRIZES – by which I mean the lump sum of $50, awarded to Joe by Joe – took place with little fanfare. One of the players, long knocked out of contention, left after losing his sixth game in a row, a streak that made me feel a tad less alone in my wretchedness, although as he stormed out I felt a twinge of concern at not being able to question him.

It turned out not to matter, though: everyone else knew Victor. They told me he had been a regular at the club up until a year ago. If I really wanted to know about him, they said, I should ask Joe, who was around more than anyone else. I found this puzzling, to say the least, as he had already disavowed knowledge. When I turned around to ask him what was going on, I discovered that he had disappeared.

The man with the Afro counseled me to wait around. 'He'll be back.'

'How do you know?'

'He has to lock up.'

I waited. One by one the rest of the players drifted out. From the window I watched them humping up the sidewalk through the snow or scrambling after the Q36. Two stuck around, playing additional games until eleven thirty, at which point I was left alone among the tables and chairs, listening to the fluorescent lights buzz and staring at a torn, crumby package of Lorna Doone shortbreads.

It was after midnight before Joe returned. He had to come back. I knew this not only because the man with the Afro had told me but because no true genius would ever leave the object of his obsession in disarray. I heard the key rattle in the gate below, heard him huffing and puffing to the top of the stairs. He walked into the room as though I wasn't there and began stacking chairs. I got up to help him. We worked in silence. He handed me a roll of paper towels and a spray bottle and we wiped down the tabletops.

'I saw you in the paper,' he said finally. 'You're the one put up the show.' He tied off a trash bag with an elaborate knot. 'Am I right?'

'That's partly why I want to talk to Victor. I have money that belongs to him.'

'Partly why else.'

'What?'

'What's the other reason you want to talk to him.'

'I want to make sure he's okay.'

'That's very nice of you,' he said.

I said nothing.

'How much money?' he asked.

'A fair amount.'

'How much is a fair amount?'

'Enough.'

'Any reason you're not answering me?'

'At least I'm not lying to you.'

He smiled. He transferred the garbage bag from his right to his left hand; his body likewise slumped. He had terrible posture, and a tendency to lapse into a grimace when not speaking, the look of someone whose basal state is discomfort.

Outside, snow had again begun to fall. Joe tossed the bag into the alley and walked toward the bus stop. His limp seemed worse, his gait almost spastic. He also looked larger than before, as if he'd grown a layer of blubber. A breeze opened his coat, revealing a second coat, and protruding from its collar, the collar of a third.

'Do you want a ride?' I asked.

He looked at me.

'I'm going to call myself a car,' I said. 'I can have it drop you wherever you need to go.'

In the distance the bus turned the corner. He looked back at it, then at me, and he said, 'What I really am is hungry. You hungry?'

WE WENT TO AN ALL-NIGHT DINER. All I wanted was a cup of decaf, but when I said I was paying, he ordered fried eggs, bacon, hash browns and a milkshake. Listening to him gave me heartburn. The waitress started to walk away, and he called her back to add onion rings and a green salad.

'Gotta get all the food groups,' he said.

He ate slowly, giving everything about fifty chews, until I couldn't imagine he was tasting much more than mush and his own saliva. Long gulps of milkshake followed, his face stuck so far forward into the glass that his nose reemerged tipped with froth. He would then wipe his face on a napkin, crumple it, and drop it on the floor. All the while his eyes kept up a nervous hopscotch, to the door, to the counter, to me, the table, the waitress, the jukebox; his fingertips red and feathery with hangnails.

He asked when I had last played checkers.

'Probably twenty-five years ago.'

'I could tell.'

'I never claimed to be any good.'

'Victor's a good checkers player. He'd be better if he slowed down a bit.'

This tidbit intrigued me, as for some reason I'd always pictured Victor as contemplative, at least when not drawing. I mentioned to Joe that the art had a strong gridlike feel to it, especially when assembled as a whole. He shrugged, either in disagreement or out of apathy, and went back to eating.

'You live around here?' I asked.

'Sure. Sometimes.'

I didn't understand, and then I did, and when he saw that I'd caught on, he started to laugh.

'I could have you over sometime. We'll have a sleepover. You like the great outdoors? Har har har.'

I smiled politely, which made him laugh even harder.

'You know what you look like,' he said, 'you look like I just took a dump on your living-room rug and you're trying to ignore it. Hell, I'm just messing. I don't really live outside . . . Feel better now?'

'No.'

'Why not? Don't believe me?'

'I—'

'Yes I do, then. I sleep in the park. Har har har. No I don't. Yes I do. No I don't. What do you think?'

'I don't know.'

He smiled, kicked back the last of his milkshake, and waved the empty glass at the waitress. 'Chocolate, please.'

There were still a couple of onion rings left, as well as the entire untouched salad. With his new drink he resumed the process – chew chew chew chew swallow gulp gulp wipe – and I got the impression that he was obeying some weird ritual, that he needed to finish his food and drink at the same time. I had a vision of us sitting there until sunrise, ordering and reordering until a happy coincidence gave him permission to stop.

Either that or he was just really, really hungry.

He said, 'You see that?'

His chocolate-tipped nose pointed across the street to an unlit church.

'They got a shelter,' he said. 'Doors close at nine, though, so on game nights we finish too late.'

I didn't need to ask why he chose checkers over a bed. It would have been insulting for me to ask. Instead I said, 'Where did you learn to play?'

He wiped his face with a revoltingly soiled napkin. I handed him another and he wiped, crumpled, dropped. 'The nuthouse.'

Again, I smiled politely, or tried to.

'Har har har, dump on the rug, har har har.' He forked his salad and held the dripping leaves up to the light before popping them in his mouth. 'I love me some greens,' he said, chewing.

'When were you there?'

'Seventy-two to seventy-six. You can learn to do anything in there. Lots of time, you know? It's like the best college in the world. I got my four-year degree, har har har. If you weren't nuts before they put you in there, you'd go nuts from boredom.' He laughed and drank and coughed out some milkshake and wiped his chin.

'Sal told me you used to be world champion.'

'Coulda beena contendah. Har har har. Yeah, I won some fucking money. Not much money in checkers. They got a computer now that can't be beat. The human being is obsolete.' He sat back, patted his stomach. It was hard to tell where all the food had gone. All that remained on the table was three fingers of milkshake, which he eyed spitefully. 'You want to know something about Victor, buy me dessert.'

I flagged the waitress. Joe asked for coconut cream pie.

'We don't have it.'

He looked at me. 'I want some coconut cream pie.'

'What about strawberry,' I offered.

'Does that sound like an adequate substitute?' he asked.

'Well—'

'How bout some hair pie,' he asked the waitress. She looked at him, looked at me, shook her head, and walked away.

'Whatever happened to *service*,' Joe shouted at her. He looked at me. 'I'll have a brownie sundae.'

I got up and went after the waitress.

Joe stared sullenly at the tabletop until his dessert came. When it did, he didn't touch it. He said, 'Victor was in the nuthouse, too.'

'With you?'

'No.' He snickered. 'You never met him, huh?'

'No.'

'He's a lot older than me. We didn't meet until he started coming to the club.'

'And when was that.'

'Right after I started advertising the tourney. So, 83. I used to make fliers and stick em up on telephone poles. He shows up, one of the fliers in his hand, like it was his ticket. I remember that night, there were only three of us, me, Victor and Raul, who kicked it in a couple of years back. He and I played all the time cause nobody else showed on a regular basis. I knew Victor was decent cause he clobbered Raul.'

'Did he beat you?' I asked.

He began shoveling in the ice cream. 'I said he was *good*.'

I apologized.

'*I* don't care. But if you're trying to get the facts, then that's the fucking facts.'

'Did he ever mention where he was institutionalized?'

'Someplace upstate.'

'Did he mention the name?'

'That's privileged information,' he said.

He didn't say anything more until he'd finished his sundae, scraping his spoon along the inside of the bowl to gather the last threads of chocolate sauce. Then he grunted and took a deep breath and said, 'The New York School for Training and Rehabilitation. That's what it's called.'

I wrote it down.

'It's near Albany,' he added.

'Thank you.'

He nodded, wiped his mouth, dropped the napkin on the floor as the waitress passed. She hissed at him and he blew her a kiss. Then he sighed and said, 'Pardon me while I drain the main vein.'

I paid the check and sat waiting for him to return. He never did. He went out the back door, and by the time I figured it out, his footprints were already filling up.

INTERLUDE: 1962.

Bertha lies on the top floor of a private hospital on the east side of Manhattan. Well-wishers have filled her room with bouquets, but as she prefers the dark, the nurses have left the shades drawn and the flowers have all begun to die, producing a cloying stench that gets into one's clothes. Nevertheless she will not consent to have the vases removed. She is impervious; she has tubes up her nose; and the comfort that the flowers provide means more to her than the momentary comfort of her visitors. Visitors come and go, but she is stuck; and if the room smells like a compost pile, that's nobody's business but hers. Who are these visitors, that they should have an opinion? Not her friends. Not the committees and boards of directors who have sent the flowers. Those people are not allowed in. She does not want to be seen in a state of decay. Only with the greatest of reluctance did she agree to come to the hospital in the first place. She wanted to stay at the house on Fifth. David prevailed upon her: she could not remain at home; she would die if she did not get proper care, in a proper setting. And what, exactly, was wrong with that? Louis had died at home. But David argued that if she went to the hospital she might live *longer*, and wasn't that the idea? To stay alive – to clutch at life – to dig fingernails into its greasy surface?

Lying here, she isn't so sure.

Hospital or no hospital, she's dying all the same. Her body is a city and the tumors that riddle it little insulting middle-class suburban outposts of disease, springing up overnight in her liver, her lungs, her stomach, her spleen, her spine. They have tried one treatment; they have tried another. Nothing helps. Better to go in a favorite bed, with a favorite view, surrounded by people she has known and trusted. Not these men with clipboards. Not these women with needles and white hats. Not lost in an artificial jungle of sympathy. Where is her son? He brought her here. Where is he, that son of hers? She calls his name.

'Yes, Mother.'

'I want to go home.'

She cannot see his reaction – he sits slightly behind her, where he knows she cannot turn to see him – but she knows what he's doing: tugging on his earlobes. His father did the same thing.

'You can't go home, Mother.'

'I can and I will.'

He says nothing.

'David.'

'Yes, Mother.'

'If the child is a girl I don't want you to name her for me. That's morbid.'

'It's a boy, Mother. We're going to name him Lawrence. You already know that.'

'I know nothing of the sort. What kind of a name is Lawrence?'

He sighs. 'We've talked about this already.'

'When.'

'Several times.'

'When.'

'Weeks ago. Several times. In fact, you asked me the day before yesterday.'

'I asked no such thing.'

He says nothing.

'When are the children coming to visit.'

'They were here, Mother.'

'When.'

He says nothing.

'When were they here,' she says, afraid to hear the answer.

'Yesterday,' he says.

'That's a lie.' She grips the bedsheets, terrified. Why is it that she can remember events and faces and stories and whole conversations from thirty years ago – and yet she cannot remember her grandchildren, yesterday? That shouldn't be possible. Her memory is impressionistic; the closer she gets, the less she can resolve. Her nose to the canvas and all she gets are dots and smudges. And her mind has worse tricks than that up its sleeve, much worse. Old memories keep springing up where they do not belong; at times she calls David by his father's name. She overhears David and the doctor discussing the president, and she expresses her opinion about Roosevelt and the two men look at her and David says, 'It's Kennedy, Mother.' The doctor is a young Jew named Waldenberg or Waldenstein or Steinbergwald or Bergswaldstein. He is bald and joyless and she doesn't trust him. She asks David for Dr Fetchett and is informed that he has been dead since 1957. That is nonsense; Fetchett has been in the room. He comes in daily to take her temperature. He stands at the foot of her bed, commiserating. Dear Bertha, you look so pale. Would you like a glass of whiskey? A kind of second sight has taken hold of her; before her illness, she never would have been able to see him so clearly. The forehead filigreed with blue veins and the enormous pores and moist nostrils, like a cow's. Not a handsome man, Dr Fetchett . . . And yet she sees the wilting flowers and cannot remember who sent them; demands over and over to know why she cannot go home.

Worse than the loosening of her mind still is her awareness of that loosening. She had expected that one of senility's few comforts would be its self-negation; she might be confused, but she wouldn't know she was confused. But she sees how people talk to her. They use soothing tones meant for animals and children. They push food upon her. They ask her to sign documents relinquishing her authority. They coax and wheedle and she sends them away. They don't have her best interests in mind. She won't deal with them, not as long as they continue to patronize her. Still they come, these lawyers with their pens and notaries and contracts and wills and lawsuits and mortgages. She refers them to David and still they come. They are crafty. They wait for him to leave and then they sneak in. It's enough to drive a lesser woman up the wall.

Bertha has never been one to succumb to anger; hers has been a life of self-control. She did not become a Muller – remain a Muller – save the Muller name from extinction – by losing her head. She may be sick, but she's not dead yet, and as long as she can draw breath, she will believe that all problems have solutions; that no turn of events, no matter how bleak, cannot be turned further, bent into an advantage, the barrel twisted back toward the shooter. Her memory has decided to run riot. Fine. Let it. She might not be able to remember the day of the week, but she can bring back her childhood with a thrilling vividness. She will enjoy herself. She opens the album and remembers.

She remembers: walks in the forest and wonderfully sour *Kirschkuchen* and the yeastiness of her father and the soapiness of her mother. Baths in a small wooden tub, the stump of a barrel. A wooden soldier that clapped its hands when you pulled a string in its back, a painted top that cut bright orange circles in the air. The housekeeper taught her to sew until she was reprimanded for doing so and thus Bertha never learned more than a simple running stitch. The day her parents told her they were moving to

America she ran crying to her best friend Elisabeth's house, but nobody answered and in her time of greatest misery she felt lonelier than ever. At home she cried in her mother's arms and her mother promised We will always be together, I will always take care of you. The journey will be long but you will see so many things girls your age never get to see. Bertha was unconsoled.

The port at Hamburg, the ship's huge fluted mouth belching loud enough to shake her in her shoes. The waiters in long black coats who called her *Mademoiselle*. In the big dining room she ate snails; they tasted like rubber and butter. She did not get seasick; her mother did. They sunbathed on their private veranda. Her mother read to her from a book of fairy tales, using different voices for each character. The princes were noble and the princesses gentle and the witches sounded like grinding chains, everyone exactly as they should be. As they sailed into the sunset she thought of her home and she wrote lots of letters to Elisabeth that she intended to deposit in the mailbox as soon as they landed but forgot about when she saw the green lady in the sea.

She remembers her first sight of Central Park, from their hotel window. She was disappointed. She'd hoped it would be bigger. It didn't compare to the parks and woodlands she knew. It was full of wheelbarrows, trenches, overturned earth. It wasn't a park; it was a pit. She cried, and to quiet her down, her father gave her a package of peppermints that she ate, one by one, until she was sick.

She remembers school. She remembers being teased. She remembers the tutor. She sells seashells. Who sold those seashells? She never found out.

At Bloomingdale's, tailors stuck her with pins. She didn't enjoy the process but then the dress came. Everyone fussed over her, but she didn't need their confirmation, she could see for herself: she had talent. In yards of green silk, she outshone Lady Liberty herself. Standing before her mother's three-sided mirror, she decided that it would be terribly ungrateful if she did not use her gifts to become someone important.

She remembers her debut. The eyes all on her, not just the men but the women, too, whether jealous or shamed or in unabashed worship. She remembers descending the stairs on a cloud, her tiara held in place with so many hairpins that she thought her head would break off and roll away. Dancing and champagne and young men's sweaty hands slipped into hers over and over. Her mother pointing out a certain young man in a narrowly cut jacket. That is Louis Muller, of the Mullers.

And her wedding.

She remembers early summers in Bar Harbor, the gleaming sailboats white, so white, her smocks flawless and dry even in the woolly heat. She changed her outfit four times a day: after breakfast, after lunch, in the afternoon before tea, and then for dinner. So many meals, piled high with those coarse American dishes she would never quite get used to, the Southern-style cornbread that her father-in-law liked but that tasted to Bertha like a block of animal feed. She ate sparingly. While other women talked about the need to reduce, she wore a bathing costume that emphasized her bust. She was the most divine creature on the Eastern Seaboard. So said her father-in-law. Dear Walter. He called her his little Bavarian rose; never mind that her family came from Heidelberg. He was always a little in love with her, openly scornful of his son's indifference. What a catch Louis had landed, what radiance, what wit, what charm, what skill. She could play the piano. How many girls had a figure like hers? She could count them on one hand. And could any of those girls play the piano? She could count them on one hand, too . . . if you cut off all her fingers . . . but then she wouldn't be able to play the piano. Ha ha ha ha. Walter always implied that, had the vagaries of time not torn them asunder . . . But she ended up with Louis. Oh Louis. Dear Louis. She wants to be charitable to him. She will choose to think of him fondly.

Think of the delight he took in buying her things, how he loved to adorn her. In the cushions of her house, she has lost diamonds worth a king's ransom. Think of how he took her everywhere. After David was born she felt sad. It came from nowhere and gummed up her mind. Nights she could not sleep; dragging herself from bed in the morning became torture. To cheer her, Louis bought a villa in Portofino. Every summer after that they would spend a month, the baby tucked away with a nurse and Louis promising not to work at all. They would eat rich meals and drink luscious wines and travel the coast, down to Rome or round the bend to Monaco, where the Prince himself would escort them through the casino. They played with chips made of real gold. Servants brought deep saucers sloshing with champagne and wet towels to cool their necks. And then during the War, when travel became impossible, Louis bought another house for her, a thirty-five-thousand-acre ranch in the middle of Montana. She tired of it quickly. He sold it at a loss. He bought her a home in Deal. He did whatever she wanted. He was a good husband. She cannot think of him now without tearing up; oh, how maudlin. He was a decent man, after all. She was glad that he went without suffering. His heart stopped a few months before the birth of David's first child. What is the girl's name. Amelia. For a moment she almost forgot, but she triumphed through sheer willpower. Amelia, yes. And her baby brother, Edgar. The year after Edgar was born, her old friend Elisabeth died. Elisabeth's husband had been an officer in the SS and after the War they got to him; the stress killed him and then her. What luck. What timing. Every time David has a baby someone dies. A lesser woman might have ordered him to stop having children. He had a son and a daughter; enough already, stop killing off the rest of us. If anyone is to go next it will be her. But she was glad when Yvette got pregnant, regardless of the outcome. Bertha will sacrifice herself for the cause, because Yvette will be a good mother, far better than David's first wife, who Bertha never liked and never approved of, even though she and Louis played along for appearance's sake. They even footed more than their share of the bill at the wedding. David argued that they should foot the entire bill; it wasn't as though they had a shortage of funds. Everyone argued. David was twenty-five then and his bachelorhood had begun to worry her;

he might turn out to have his father's tendencies. Where she had never doubted her own ability to manage Louis, how could she ensure that a prospective daughter-in-law would have the same strength and conviction? Women could not be relied on. Nobody could be relied on. You had to do everything yourself these days. Thankfully, David did get married. A relief to her, on the one hand; and on the other hand, she did not trust the girl he chose, the daughter of a man who owned clothing stores in the Middle West. She called New York ugly. Who was she to be so stuck-up, she came from Cleveland. Whatever Bertha's opinions of the changes that have taken place in the city since her arrival so many years ago, she firmly believes that nobody has the right to make comments when they've been in residence for less than a month. That wicked girl. Bertha can remember her name all right but chooses not to. Picking fights with David over everything, making scenes everywhere, icy dinners where nobody spoke: Bertha thinks about them and suddenly two sets of memories collide: silence and silver on china and crystal on linen . . . and silences, and – and – and notes delivered by hand, notes from Dr Fetchett. No, that is not right. That did not happen then. She is mixing up the chronology and she does not want to think about certain things. With tremendous strain she turns the page and finds another one, a page full of good memories, another night, a happy occasion . . . back to her wedding. Think about her wedding. Think about the liveried footmen and the mighty brass instruments and the dancing legions spinning in her honor; think about her wedding cake, that magnificent tower of buttercream in the shape of a pyramid, the biggest cake anyone had ever seen; they printed a picture of it in the newspaper, and her picture, too. The wedding of Mr L. I. Muller and Miss Bertha Steinholtz proved undoubtedly the most spectacular event of the season. The bride wore a taffeta gown of surpassing elegance, and the groom his traditional black. The ceremony was performed at the Trinity Church by the Most Reverend J. A. Moffett, and festivities continued . . . They called it a fairy tale, and for once they got it right. Her life has been magical.

And now she is old and in a bed and it is 1962. There are things that remain hidden. They should not bother her now, not after so much time. Water under the bridge. But memory, nasty beast, returns again and again.

Not the girl. She can think about the girl without flinching. She has never doubted her decisions and she does not doubt them now. There was too much at stake. Louis could never see that. He told her once that she had no heart but that just showed how deeply he misunderstood the world, how deeply he misunderstood her. She did what she did not because she lacked a heart but because she knew, all too well, how merciless people could be. She remembered being mocked, nightly sobbing, pillows soaked, years of struggle before she came into her own and they could not deny her any longer. Because she was beautiful, and beauty cannot be denied.

But for the girl? An eternity of faux pas. She stood to suffer. What Louis failed to grasp was that Bertha had been acting with mercy.

For David's tenth birthday she threw a luncheon, hired entertainment, and opened the ballroom. After dessert David played his violin for the guests, most of whom were adults, friends of hers; in those days, he did not have many friends. All told a pleasant afternoon, at least until Louis bolted from the room. She found him on the edge of his bed, face in his handkerchief. It disgusted her: this soft cruelty he had the gall to call mercy. He did not know what true mercy meant. He had never suffered. He had been coddled, fawned over, given a pass on the most vile transgressions. So naturally he assumed that the world would do the same for the girl. Bertha knew better. She knew disgrace. All she wanted was to spare the girl the same.

She wanted to think fondly of him but bitterness seeps through. The girl's fate began as an argument but grew, over the years, into a towering obstruction between them, a wall of thorns, curling in on itself until they lost sight of each other completely.

It would be easy for a novelist to write And though they continued to live in the same house, they never spoke again. It would be easy but untrue. For the truth is, she still felt kindly toward Louis at moments, and she sensed that he, too, had a kind of lukewarm desire to be in her good graces. In forty years of marriage they laughed many times, shared much mutual pleasure – though not often sexual – and raised a son.

When Louis died, everything came out. By that time the boy was eleven. Eleven years old! Living like a hermit. One old woman to care for him; God knows what sort of perversions took place between them. He barely spoke. The woman, whose name was Greene, said he'd never been one to babble. Bertha told her to be quiet until spoken to.

She wanted to ship the boy as far off as possible, to Europe or Australia, but Dr Fetchett advised against it, and in a rare moment of equivocation, she had consented to send him to the farthest point in New York state. The problem went away again. This time permanently.

But as she lies high above the earth, full of drugs, wired to electronics, she worries that her efforts have been in vain. The bills come directly to her; she pays them from a personal account. What will happen when she stops? They will come looking for her; they will contact David. With horror, she realizes that they might have done so already.

'David.'

'Mother?'

'How long have I been here.'

'In the hospital, you mean? Six weeks.'

Six weeks sounds like ample time for a bill to come past due. The crisis is upon her, then. David will find out. The story will emerge and everyone will know. She needs to make him understand the need for secrecy. But he comes from a different generation; smugly they call themselves enlightened, without the faintest notion of how quick life is to knock out your teeth. Louis's softness has found its way into him. She must find a solution. She thinks. Her mind stumbles back and forth between the present and the past. She talks to her husband and her maid. She talks to the television. The room David got her looks less like a hospital and more like a hotel. The walls are wood-paneled; a leaded window in the shape of a star glows gently. She squeezes down on her mind and the answer comes: she will pay the fees now, in advance. She will establish an endowment. She has done that before. At Harvard and Columbia and Barnard people work and learn because of her generosity. She has given money to charities of all stripes, been feted by politicians from every side of the aisle . . . *she squeezes down.* A problem at hand, she will solve it. She will call the man at the school in Albany and give him an enormous sum of money. Where is her checkbook. Where is the telephone.

'Mother.'

They hold her arms.

'Mother.'

'Call the doctor.'

No, don't call the doctor. The doctor is dead. He died in 1857. He died in 1935. He died in 1391, he is nothing but bones. Memories are his flesh and she can burn him up with the blink of her eye. Memories are fickle. Memories taste smoky. They taste like *Kirschkuchen.* Everything withers and turns to bones. Walter is bones. Louis is bones. Soon she too will be bones. Give enough money and problems turn to bones. She will grind them up and cast them upon the water; she will be remembered forever in the minds of people who have never met her; she will live in their minds the way memories live in hers, the way she so starkly recalls the flood that destroyed their basement; lightning seen from the bow of a ship; the pain of childbirth; the pain of childbirth; the dullness of intercourse; the men who attempted to woo her when Louis died, imagine that, she a wrinkled old woman and men thirty years younger offering her roses; she remembers and remembers and remembers and it is not a flashing of her life so much as a cascade, events superimposed and time seesawing, people who never met shaking hands, conversations a moment ago crystalline now fizzy and roaring like the surf, the frame of her mind creaking and buckling inward, a mineshaft, rivers of dirt snaking down the incline toward blackness.

'Mrs Muller.'

'Mother.'

Mrs Muller.

Mother.

Yes, she is Mrs Muller. She had a husband. Yes, she is a mother. She has a son.

TWENTY

It took an afternoon of phone calls, but I managed to track down the New York School for Training and Rehabilitation, right where Joe said it would be: ten miles outside Albany, operating under the name Green Gardens Rehabilitation Center. An assistant director named Driscoll told me that in its previous incarnation, the place had been an honest-to-goodness asylum, of the padded walls and shock treatment ilk. Like many such institutions, it had fallen victim to the civil rights movement, its programs disbanded and its charter revised to reflect a kinder, gentler approach: Green Gardens specialized in spinal injuries. Driscoll took evident relish in recounting all this to me; he seemed to consider himself the unofficial historian.

I asked about the old patient records, and he said, 'A couple years ago we had a problem with the boiler, so I go down to the basement with a flashlight. I'm crawling around, sneezing my head off, and I stumble right through a big pile of letters, medical records, all the physicians' notes. Nobody had touched any of it for twenty years. The paper was disintegrating.'

'So you still have them,' I said.

'No. When I told Dr Ulrich she had them shredded.'

My heart sank. 'There's nothing left?'

'There's probably one or two down there that we missed, but even so, I couldn't give you access to them. They're confidential.'

'That's really a shame.'

'I'm sorry I can't be more helpful.'

I thanked him and started to get off the phone when he said,

'You know what, though.'

'Yes?'

'Well, I'll have to look into this. But we have some photos.'

'What kind of photos.'

'Well – and this gives you an idea of what ideas about privacy laws *used* to be like – they're up on the walls in one of the old wings. They're black-and-whites, sort of like class photos. Groups of patients in ties and jackets. I even think there's one where they're wearing baseball uniforms. Some of them have names and some don't. I don't know if the person you want is there, but I might be able to show them to you. I don't see what kind of rules we'd be breaking, considering that they're already on display.'

'That would be fantastic. Thank you.'

'I'll talk to Dr Ulrich and let you know.'

I called Samantha, finally back from South Carolina.

'Strong work,' she said.

'Thank you.'

'I mean, really, you're turning into Columbo.'

'Thank you.'

'Like, a metrosexual Columbo.'

'Tell me you have good news, too.'

'I do,' she said.

'And?'

'It's a surprise.'

'Oh come on.'

'I'll tell you when I see you.'

We agreed to meet up the following week. In the interim I went back to the doctor for a checkup. He looked into all the orifices in my head, pronounced me well, and offered to give me more painkillers. I filled the prescription and set it aside to give to Marilyn when she got back from France.

That Sunday, the second in January, I received a second e-mail from her. This one was in German. I turned to an Internet translator for assistance.

On 24 October 1907 the Vossi newspaper reported: 'During the daily of yesterday emperors had, Empress, princesses and prince the magnificent Building of hotels visits and Mr Adlon their acknowledgment here in glorious capital the work in most honoring way expressed.'

Taking this to mean she had gone to Berlin, I swallowed my pride and responded with a second long, pleading e-mail. As soon as I pressed SEND, I regretted it. I had already put myself out there in my first letter, already degraded myself. Now I didn't know what I was trying to achieve. Reconciliation? I wasn't sure I wanted it. For the past two weeks I had been entirely Marilyn-free, and while on some level I missed her, I also felt for the first time in years like I could fully relax. That's the way you're supposed to feel about your parents, not your lover. Not that I was an authority on either.

Mostly I wanted her to forgive me so I could feel less guilty breaking things off, assuming it came to that – which I assumed it would. Or else I wanted her to be so livid, so beyond reason, that I could walk away without any fanfare. I wanted a starting point: she was either totally okay or not okay at all. I could work with either. What I couldn't deal with was limbo, and so that's where she kept me. She knew me well enough to have predicted the effects of her silence. She was drawing out my discomfort on purpose. It made me mad, although looking back, I suppose I deserved it.

THE NEXT AFTERNOON I got a call from Detective Trueg of the major case squad, who asked if I had time to come over to the station. Eager to be out of the gallery, I hopped in a taxi, and upon arrival was escorted to a cubicle, where he sat ensconced in a ring of discarded Burger King wrappers. Andrade, too, had his lunch out: a half-finished Tupperware container of tofu and brown rice.

'You want a Coke?' Trueg asked me.

'No, thanks.'

'That's good,' he said. 'Cause we don't got none.'

The investigation, the detectives informed me, had taken an odd turn around the time they decided to question Kristjana Hallbjörnsdottir.

Trueg said, 'We go over to her studio, we're talking to her. She's not saying anything too suspicious or not suspicious, one way or the other. I excuse myself and ask if I can use the restroom. Down the hall I go and what do you know, up on the wall are some drawings that look a hell of a lot like yours.'

I sat up straight.

Trueg nodded. 'Yup. Right out there for everyone in the world to see. Naturally, this is very interesting to us, but we don't say anything about it. We finish asking her about her relationship with you, we say thank you very much, and then we go and get a warrant.' He smiled crookedly. 'That lady is one live wire when she's mad.'

'You have no idea.'

'We had to have someone take her outside to calm her down.'

'You're not the first.'

'What did you do to her, anyway? I never was clear on that.'

'I canceled a show of hers,' I said, trying to contain my impatience. 'She has the drawings?'

Andrade reached into his desk and took out a handful of pages sealed in evidence bags: a dozen Crackes, easily identifiable by their wild sense of scale, their surreal imagery, the oddball names and recurrent faces. The backs were numbered in the mid-thirty-nine thousands. As Andrade spread them out in front of me, I felt a rush of relief that Kristjana had not destroyed the pieces out of spite. But then it occurred to me that these might be all that remained from the several thousand she had stolen.

'The box I had was full,' I said. 'It had probably two thousand drawings.'

'Well, that's all she wrote,' said Trueg.

'Please tell me you're kidding.'

Andrade shook his head.

'Oh, no.' I put my head in my hands. 'Oh, shit.'

'Before you get too upset—' said Trueg.

'Did you search her apartment? Shit. I don't believe this. Shit.'

'Hang on,' said Trueg, 'that isn't the half of it. I'm just gettin warmed up here.'

'Shit.'

'I think you want to listen to this,' said Andrade.

'Shit . . .'

Trueg said, 'So we take her in and question her, and as soon as we bring up the drawings she gets this very offended look on her face and says—' He looked at his partner. 'Go on, you do it. You do it good.'

Andrade said, in a stilted Scandinavian accent, '"But I made them my*selv.*"'

Absorbed by the thought of my destroyed art, I barely heard him. When what he said finally did register, I said, 'Excuse me?'

'Go on,' said Trueg. 'Do it again.'

'She claims she made the drawings herself,' said Andrade.

'Aw, come on, Benny, one more time.'

'Wait,' I said. 'Wait a second. She made what herself.'

'The drawings,' said Andrade.

'*Which* drawings.'

'These,' said Trueg, indicating the Crackes.

I stared at him. 'That's ridiculous.'

'Well, that's what she said.' He seemed disconcertingly calm, as did Andrade.

'Well,' I said. 'But that's ridiculous. Why would she do that?'

'She says someone hired her to make copies,' said Trueg. 'You know, in the style of.'

'What?'

'I'm just tellin you what she said.'

'Who hired her?'

'She wouldn't say,' said Andrade.

'Nope,' said Trueg. 'On that she got real stubborn.'

I sat back and crossed my arms. 'Well. That's – I mean – that's ludicrous.'

'We thought so, too,' said Andrade. 'So we asked her to produce one for us. I sat in the room and watched while she did it. See for yourself.'

He opened his desk again and pulled out a second batch of evidence bags containing drawings virtually indistinguishable from the first. I take that back. They *were* indistinguishable. I kept blinking and staring and blinking, certain that I was hallucinating. Most disorienting of all was that the drawings connected, seamlessly, just as the Crackes did – and not only that, but they connected to the first set of drawings, the ones confiscated from the studio, as though Kristjana had taken a smoking break and then carried on working. I asked if she had been looking at the first drawings at the time and Andrade shook his head and said no, she'd done them from memory. Suddenly I began to sweat, and what I'd once said to Marilyn popped into my head: 'She used to be a good painter.' Kristjana was classically trained, after all, and it would be just like her to get a kick out of copying the work of the very artist who had displaced her. It probably tickled her sense of martyrdom, that preachiness that made her worst work intolerable. It fit, all right; but at the same time I could not accept that the work was so easily parodied. *I* was the expert on Victor Cracke's iconography; *I* knew what was and what wasn't; *I* had the goddamned *droit moral* goddammit, and the work I was looking at was as authentic as anything I'd dragged out of that shitty stuffy little apartment. Had to be. Look at it, for crissake. Both sets of drawings on the desk had to have been done by the same person; even the tones of the inks – which in the Cracke drawings varied from one section to another, depending on age – were a perfect match. And then the room began to spin: what if the drawings I had in storage didn't belong to Victor Cracke. What if the whole thing was part of an elaborate prank orchestrated by Kristjana herself? Victor Cracke *was* Kristjana. In my agitation, this idea seemed absurd enough to be plausible. She loved that sort of self-referential swill, and I could imagine the masochistic frisson she would get from getting me to cancel a show of her work *in order to put up another show of her work.* Who was Victor Cracke, anyhow? Nobody. Nobody that I knew, or that anybody else knew. It was all Kristjana. Everything was by Kristjana. The Mona Lisa? That was her. The Venus de Milo? Also her. Everything that Kevin Hollister wanted to hang in his office, from *Allegory of Spring* to *Olympia – all her!* I began to wonder how she had gotten Tony Wexler in on the joke, not to mention Superintendent Shaughnessy, the neighbors, the fruit vendor, Joe the checkers champion . . . double agents, all. But – but – but I had talked to people who'd *seen* Victor Cracke, passed him in the hallway . . . and but none of them could give me a complete physical description . . . but wasn't that more realistic, wouldn't people retain differing impressions? . . . but wouldn't Kristjana know that, and account for it, couldn't she script something *just so* . . . ?

My headache returned, with gravy.

Mixed in with my confusion was a strong sense of annoyance that she'd been wasting her time planning destructive installations involving one-ton sea mammals when she could so easily produce shit that people would buy.

I don't know whether Andrade and Trueg thought I was having a breakdown or what, but when I said, 'It sure looks like the real McCoy,' they nodded sympathetically, the kind of nod you give a crazy person to keep him calm while the men in white coats get their nets out of the van.

Trueg said, 'Hang on, show's not over yet. We also found this in her apartment.'

Andrade opened his desk again – what was he going to pull out now? A picture of Kristjana and Victor having tea? – and handed me another bagged piece of evidence, this one containing a half-completed letter, written in the same tiny, threatening hand as the two letters I had supposedly gotten from Victor himself. It said, many times, LIAR.

'Why does she think you're a liar?' Andrade asked.

'How the hell do I know?' I said. 'She's insane.'

LIAR LIAR LIAR LIAR LIAR

'If you ask me,' said Andrade, 'this would seem to lend some credence to her claim about having done the drawings.'

LIAR

'You said those first two letters came from the artist, right?' Trueg asked.

'I thought so.'

'Well, this looks like the same person to me,' he said. He looked at Andrade. 'Benny? What do you think?'

'I think so.'

Trueg smiled at me. 'That's our professional opinion. Same person. So she fooled you once, I don't see why she couldn't do it again.'

'But.' I picked up the letter. LIAR LIAR LIAR. 'Don't you think – I mean, she's threatening me, why don't you arrest her for assaulting me?'

307

'Well,' said Trueg, 'that's not so straightforward, either. She admits to sending you the first two letters—'

'All right,' I said. 'There you go.'

'—and she says she was going to send another. But then she tells us that the first two were intended as some kind of practical joke.'

'You have got to be—'

'And when you got jumped, she started to worry about implicating herself, so she stopped sending them. She'd written half of the next one but she didn't finish it, and that's the one we found. This one.'

'And you believe her?'

Trueg and Andrade looked at each other. Then they look at me.

'Yeah,' said Trueg. 'I do, actually.'

Andrade said, 'That was my instinct, as well.'

'She offered to take a polygraph.'

'Oh come on,' I said. 'This. This is . . . So what are you saying – that she's the one or not.'

'We don't know,' said Trueg. 'She might have arranged for you to get beat up, but it wasn't her who did it. At eleven forty-five she was at a party across town. All the other guests we talked to swear she was there from ten until at least one in the morning.'

'She could get them to say that,' I said. Even to my ears I sounded paranoid.

'That's true,' Andrade said kindly.

'She could get someone to do it for her,' I said.

'That's true, too.'

I said, 'I don't know what else to think.'

'Right now we don't have anything we can charge her with that's going to stick. Maybe, like, harassment for those first couple of letters. But I gotta be honest with you, I don't think they're going to bother. She says it was just a joke.'

'Do you find this funny?' I demanded, holding up the letter.

Trueg and Andrade exchanged another look.

'Well,' said Andrade, 'not a hundred percent funny.'

'But like sixty percent,' said Trueg.

I stared at them. Why did everyone keep finding my distress so amusing?

'Maybe more like thirty,' Trueg said.

Andrade said, 'Essentially, we're where we were before. We'll keep looking for the art to pop up. In the meantime you can relax about those letters. I don't think you'll get any more of them.'

I nodded dumbly.

Said Trueg, 'Wheels within wheels.'

I LEFT THE STATION IN A FOG and stayed that way until my meeting with Samantha. She saw me and immediately asked if I was feeling all right. I explained to her what the detectives had told me and she said, 'Wow.'

'Indeed.'

'That's messed up.'

'Indeed.'

She grinned. 'Well, allow me to add a little clarity to your life.'

She told me that she had found James Jarvis, the man who, thirty years prior, had survived an assault reminiscent of the Queens murders. He now lived in Boston, where he taught marketing at a community college. Samantha had spoken with him, and although he claimed not to remember much, her gut told her that he was holding back. Having dealt with many victims of sexual assault, she believed we would get more from him face-to-face; the telephone made it easier for people to detach themselves and to repress frightening memories. And when, the next day, the assistant director at Green Gardens called to let me know that while he couldn't send out copies of the photographs, we could come have a look for ourselves, Samantha and I decided to make a trip of it.

Wednesday morning two weeks later, we boarded a puddle-jumper from LaGuardia to Albany International Airport. The previous evening's weather report warned of an incoming nor'easter, and I expected a long delay, if not a cancellation. But that day dawned bright and clear; the terminal's picture windows threw long rectangles of sunlight, a big blank filmstrip through which Samantha moved, illuminated, toward me. She wore lavender corduroys and a black sweater and no makeup; she swung a battered duffel bag, and when she stood at the ticket kiosk, she hooked her thumbs into her back pockets. I stood off a ways, looking at her, reluctant to break the spell she had cast around herself, and when I finally did come over to say hello and she smiled at me, it was hard not to tell her how lovely she looked.

We got our tickets and boarded a bus that took us across the tarmac to a rickety-looking prop plane, its wings glistening with deicer. There were only thirty seats, and as we took our places across the aisle from each other, Samantha turned her attention out the window, to the maintenance worker spraying down the blades.

'I hate flying,' she said.

I took her at face value. Who doesn't hate flying? Especially these days.

But I underestimated her. At every bump – and in a tiny plane, you feel them – she clutched at the armrests, sweat beading at her hairline.

'Are you okay?'

She was pale. 'I just really hate this.'

'Do you want some water?'

'No, thank you.' The plane dipped and her whole body tensed. 'I'm not like this,' she said. 'It started after Ian died.'

I nodded. I did a quick risk assessment and, hoping I was making the right decision, reached across the aisle and took her hand. She held on to me for the remainder of the flight, letting go only to allow the beverage cart past.

*

I DIDN'T KNOW MUCH ABOUT ALBANY except that Ed Koch had once referred to it as a town without a decent Chinese restaurant, and as we pulled out of the airport I saw the wisdom of his words. A limp sense of obligation compelled us to take a spin past the Capitol, which proved an ostentatious red-and-white mess, an attempt at dignity in a place obviously discredited by time. In hindsight, it might've been prudent of the first New Yorkers to reserve judgment a bit before choosing their capital. What seemed important three hundred years ago – an abundance of locally procurable beaver pelt – might eventually matter less than, say, being the worldwide center of culture and finance. But we'll not Monday-morning quarterback.

Green Gardens was over the Hudson, off Route 151. We drove through low neighborhoods still festooned with tinsel; we came to a highway junction where, in a wet asphalt lot adjacent to a gas station, two men stood watching a third as he walked backward atop a truck tire. Before letting Samantha get behind the wheel, I'd made her promise she was calm enough, and by now she had returned to her dry, rational self, spending the bulk of the drive flatly relaying holiday horror stories.

'My mom called Jerry my dad's name.'

'You're joking.'

'Wish I was.'

'Was she drunk?'

'No. But he was. That's why she did it, I think. I think she was having one of those flashbacks to when she used to yell at my dad. Jerry was being an ass about something she cooked and she goes, "Goddammit Lee!" Right away she put her hands over her mouth, like in a cartoon.'

'Did he notice?'

'Yup.'

'Oh boy.'

'Yup.'

'That's appalling.'

'It is what it is.' She looked at me. 'Did you call your father?'

I hesitated. 'No.'

She nodded, said nothing.

Feeling defensive, I said, 'I was going to. I actually did pick up the phone.'

'But?'

'I had no idea what to say.'

'You could have asked why he wanted to buy your drawings.'

'That's true.'

'It's up to you.' She signaled left. 'We're here.'

The stone columns flanking the entrance to Green Gardens had once supported a gate; similar columns ran all along the frontage, stained with rust runoff near the empty bracket holes in their tops and sides. Thickets of pine and alder blocked the view from the road; as we cleared them, I felt a rising sense of anticipation. A towering white house came into view, gabled and turreted and encircled by a porch. We parked and mounted the steps and were greeted by a man with a little red goatee.

'Dennis Driscoll,' he said.

'Ethan Muller. This is ADA Samantha McGrath.'

'Howdy.' One corner of his mouth turned up. 'We don't get a lot of visitors.'

The interior of the house was creaky and musty and berugged, its original Victorian trimmings intact: god-awful wallpaper, push-button lightswitches, an off-kilter chandelier. Steam pipes hissed. In the foyer hung a severe oil portrait of a jowly, baldpated man: THOMAS WESTFIELD WORTHE, according to the nameplate.

'He was in charge until the mid-sixties,' Driscoll said. 'In its time, it was considered a fairly progressive place.' He led us upstairs, pausing on the landing to point out the window. Across a wide, snowy meadow stood a second building, this one squarely modern. 'That's where the dormitory used to be. They knocked it down in the 70s to make room for the main rehab facility. The house is from 1897.' He started up toward the third floor. 'I was surprised to hear from you so soon. Frankly, I don't think Dr Ulrich expected you to show up, which is probably why she agreed.'

'Here we are.'

'Yessirree.' We walked along a cramped, dark hallway, went up another flight of stairs. 'This part of the house isn't used very much, because the heat doesn't work that well. And in the summer it's like a kiln. Mostly we use these rooms for storage. Long-term patients can leave their bags. We get a lot of out-of-staters, a few Canadians tired of being on a waiting list. In theory family members could sleep here, but I always recommend they use the Days Inn. Voilà.' We turned the corner.

He said, 'You can see why I didn't want to go through them all myself.'

All along the hallway hung hundreds of photographs, their frames cracking from decades of seasonal fluctuation in humidity. Virtually every inch of wallpaper was covered, evoking one of those claustrophobic seventeenth-century 'paintings of paintings', some Flemish archduke's personal gallery smothered floor to ceiling in art. A few of the photos were of individuals, but most were as Driscoll had described, in the style of a class portrait, the subjects arranged in rows, tallest in the back, shortest sitting cross-legged, all of them dead-eyed, their hair slicked down and their collars buttoned up; all of them rigid and sullen, as befits the subjects of an old photo. But I detected, too, an extra dose of insolence; sneers lingering and chins jutting out farther than strictly necessary. Was I overreading? I did know, after all, that they'd been sent here for bad behavior. Either way, I felt a profound sympathy for them, these castoffs. Had I been born in a less indulgent era, to a less indulgent family, I might have ended up among them.

Knowing that somewhere in this array of faces we might find Victor Cracke gave rise to the temptation to rush, but we proceeded methodically, squinting to read the legends. Some were unlabeled. I lifted one frame off the wall and found nothing on the reverse but *June 2, 1954*. All these faces and names; all these forgotten souls. Where were their families? What kinds of lives did they lead before coming here? Did they ever leave? Ghosts tugged at my sleeves: spirits looking for a living body to carry them away.

I think I expected fireworks when we found him. All that happened, though, was Samantha saying,

'Ethan.'

Seven men in a single row. She put her finger near the bottom of the frame.

STANLEY YOUNG   FREDERICK GUDRAIS   VICTOR CRACKE   MELVIN LATHAM

Shorter than the men to either side of him by at least four inches, wearing an uneven moustache, his eyes wide and terrified as he waits for the flash. A high forehead and a rounded chin give his face the shape of an inverted tombstone, its width out of proportion with his torso, which is sunken and slight. He might be hunchbacked. Based on the other men in the photo, seemingly from the same cohort, I put him at about twenty-five, although he looked prematurely wizened.

Driscoll said, 'I'll be darned.'

My hands shook as I took the picture from Samantha. I felt a lot of things – sadness, relief, excitement – but most of all I felt betrayed. Once, he had not existed. Once, I had been the one to create him; I had been the prime mover. Then, as we hunted him down, I had been forced to forfeit those beliefs, piecemeal and painfully. I talked to people who knew him. I ate his apples. I walked in his footsteps. He became realer and realer, and afraid of losing him entirely, I had grabbed at him. Instead of minimizing him, I inflated him. I had expected that when I finally did lay eyes on him, he would be more: more than a typed name; more than a bunch of muddled grays and chalky whites, a piece of institutional arcana; more than a sad-looking golemlike little man. I wanted someone monumental; I wanted a totem, a superman; I wanted a sign that he was of the Elect; I wanted a halo hovering above him, or devil's horns sprouting from his forehead, or anything, anything at all to justify the sweeping changes he had wrought in my life. He was my god, and his plainness shamed me.

INTERLUDE: 1944.

In the little house he has everything he needs. Mrs Greene cooks for him
and does his laundry. She teaches him how to read and how to do simple
math. She teaches him the names of birds and animals, she gives him a big
book, she puts him on her lap and reads to him from the Bible. The story
he likes best is Moses in the bulrushes. He imagines the basket on the Nile,
surrounded by crocodiles and storks. Mrs Greene uses her hands to make
their snapping jaws, scaring him with loud claps. Chomp! But Victor
knows that the story has a happy ending. Moses's sister watches from the
banks. She will not let anything happen to him.

Most of all he likes to draw, and when Mrs Greene goes to town she
brings back boxes of colored pencils and paper so thin he has to be careful
not to tear through. She does not go often enough to satisfy his hunger for
blank space and so he draws on the walls. When she sees she is angry. You
must not do that, Victor. There is never enough room to draw, so he learns
to hoard paper of all kinds: envelopes he fishes out of the trash, the insides
of books Mrs Greene reads and puts away on the shelf. One time she pulls

down a book and sees what he has done and then she is angry again. He doesn't understand. She has already read them, what does it matter? But she says You must never and then she beats him.

But she does not beat him too often. Most of the time she is tender and he loves her like a mother although he does not have a mother and Mrs Greene will not let him call her that. He doesn't understand where he came from, but he doesn't worry, he has everything he needs, food and Mrs Greene and paper.

They walk all around the property. Mrs Greene teaches him the names of the flowers and he studies their petals up close. There are bees but he never gets stung. He stares at a flower until he sees it in his mind perfect, then he goes back to the cottage and draws. Mrs Greene calls him an odd duck but she smiles when she says it. Victor, you're an odd duck. Look at that daffodil. Look at that dandelion. Foxglove, chicory and clover, they all have different shapes. You're an odd duck, you are, but you are quick with a pencil.

He is six. He sees other children moving along the road on funny things and she says Those are bicycles. They move so fast! He wants one. Mrs Greene says No, you cannot leave the property. He replies that he will not leave the property, but please oh please give me a bicycle.

No.

Victor hates her. To get back at her he waits until she has fallen asleep in the afternoon, which she often does, and then he pulls a stool over to the wall where the key hangs on a ribbon. He unlocks the front door and the front gate and walks all the way into town. He has been to town before but always hanging tightly to her hand. Before the town seemed exciting but now it is loud. A car honks at him. A dog barks at him. He feels dizzy and to escape he goes into a store. The storekeeper looks at him like he is a big bug. It starts to rain and he cannot leave. He stays in the store for hours. He gets hungry. He wants something to eat but he has no money so he takes the first thing he sees, some rock sugar. He puts it in his pocket and runs out. The storekeeper chases him. Victor runs as fast as he can. The storekeeper slips in a puddle and falls and when Victor looks back the man is blotched with mud brown-and-white like a cow. But he is no longer chasing. He yells still and still Victor runs. By the time he gets to the front gate his feet hurt and fire burns in his chest.

Mrs Greene is not in her room. Victor climbs on the stool and puts the key back and goes to his room and lies on his bed, wheezing and touching the sugar rock in his pocket. He is not hungry anymore. He doesn't like sweets, he should have taken something he liked more. He doesn't like to eat very much at all, and so he is very skinny and not too tall, he knows this because when the man with the mirror and the tongue stick came to visit he told Mrs Greene that the boy needed to eat more, his growth was already stunted. And she replied that didn't he think she had tried. The man was a doctor. He left. Mrs Greene said he would return.

Victor takes the sugar rock out of his pocket. He likes the way it feels, sharp and hard and delicate. He plays with it until it begins to melt in his hands. He puts it on the table and observes the way it bends the sunlight. He takes a piece of paper and traces the jagged shape. He starts to shade its different faces and then Mrs Greene bursts in with her face red like a chicken's. She says she knows what he has been up to, she has been half mad looking for him. Where did he think he was going, what did he think he was doing? Never again oh you wicked boy, you must learn, you are a fool. She smashes the sugar rock on the floor. Then she puts him over her knee and paddles him until he wails. You wicked boy. She takes his half-completed sketch and tears it to pieces.

But most of the time she is kind. She takes him to church. Victor likes the windows. They show the Annunciation and the Sermon and the Resurrection. They shine with blue and purple fire. Victor likes to imagine them when he lies in bed at night. He likes their colors but more so their shapes. Mrs Greene teaches him to pray and he often lies awake at night and whispers the rosary.

Another man comes to visit. He comes in a long black car. He wears a big felt hat like Victor has never seen. Hello, Victor. The man knows his name. He has a moustache. Victor wants a moustache. He thinks of what it would be like to have a friendly pet on his face all the time. He would never be alone the way he is. He is often alone but does not often feel lonely. Sometimes he feels very lonely, though. Why is that?

The man with the moustache comes often. Sometimes they are walking the property and when they come home the man is waiting for them, reading the newspaper. When Victor is lucky the man forgets to take the newspaper when he leaves. Victor tears it into strips and saves them for future use.

He likes the man's visits. They are brief and they always end with a gift. The man brings Victor a model ship and a big glove and a ball and a spinning top. Victor puts on the glove and it is like his hand has gotten bigger. He doesn't know what to do with it until Mrs Greene tells him that you use it to catch the ball. But who will throw the ball to him? Mrs Greene says she will but she never does. The glove goes unused. The ship he likes to draw. The top he can make spin for a long time.

When the man with the moustache comes he spends a great deal of time looking at different parts of the house, poking his head into rooms. He opens and closes doors. When they squeak he makes a sour face. He wipes his finger along the tops of the tables and rubs his fingertips together. Then he asks Victor questions. What is three multiplied by five? Write your name for me, Victor. If Victor gets an answer right the man gives him a nickel. If he gets it wrong, or if he does not know, the man frowns, the fuzzy creature on his upper lip standing up in disgust. Victor aims to get as many right as possible, but as he gets older the questions become more complicated. He begins to dread the man's visits. He feels ashamed. He turns seven and the man says We must get him some lessons.

A few days later another man comes to the house. His name is Mr

Thornton and he is the tutor. He carries a stack of books, which to Victor's amazement and joy he leaves behind. Victor has never seen so much paper in his life, and that night he sets to it like a fiend, scribbling in the margins, making patterns, stars, faces. When the tutor comes back the next morning and discovers that not only has Victor failed to do the assignment but that he has ruined three brand-new textbooks, he paddles Victor much harder than Mrs Greene ever would. Victor cries out but Mrs Greene is in town buying groceries. The man beats Victor's bottom hard enough to make him bleed.

Lessons are not all bad. The man teaches him how to weigh things on a scale; how to look at plants under a microscope. The shapes are beautiful snowflakes. They are called cells. Victor hopes the man will leave the microscope for him to use, but alas he packs it back into its leather case and takes it away when he leaves. Victor draws the cells from memory. He does not dare show the results to the tutor, who has already shown his distaste for Victor's drawings.

One time while Mrs Greene is in town the tutor tells Victor to stand up and take off his trousers. Victor screams because he does not want to be paddled again. He has done nothing wrong! He screams and the tutor grabs him and puts his hand across Victor's mouth until Victor cannot breathe. Victor tries to bite the tutor's fingers but the tutor slaps him flat. The tutor unbuckles Victor's belt and pulls his trousers down. Victor prepares himself for pain but the tutor touches his legs and Victor's bottom and then he puts his hand on Victor's privates. Then the tutor tells him to get dressed and they study some grammar. Sometimes this happens.

The next time the doctor comes he tells Victor to take off his trousers and Victor screams. He bites the doctor on the elbow and runs around the room until Mrs Greene grabs his arms and the doctor grabs his legs and they tie him to the chair with a garden hose.

What in the world has gotten into him.

I don't know.

Dear Lord look at him.

The doctor points a light in Victor's eyes. Does he do this a great deal?

No.

Hmm. Hmm. Off goes the light. Well, it's very strange.

They go into the next room. Victor can still hear them.

Does he have fits?

No.

Anything else?

He speaks to himself. He has imaginary friends.

That's perfectly natural for children.

A boy his age? He speaks more to them than to me. Something is out of joint.

Hardly surprising.

He isn't like his mother.

No. But feeblemindedness takes many forms.

It's not natural to keep him here.

It isn't our decision.

It can't go on like this. How long?

I don't know.

I won't stay here forever.

Victor wriggles his hands against the hose.

Mercy says Mrs Greene. Mercy.

I'll talk to Mr Muller.

Please do.

I'll tell him that something needs to be done.

Where has he been? I've heard nothing in months.

He's abroad. He went to London. They're building a wharf.

Dear Lord. Is there nobody in the world besides you and I?

At the moment, no.

It isn't right.

No.

Oh.

Mrs Greene.

Oh. Oh.

I am at your disposal.

Oh.

The hose starts to loosen. Victor pulls his arms free. Then he unties his feet. He creeps to the door and sees Mrs Greene and the doctor standing close together. The doctor's hands are inside her blouse. She stands away and together they go into another room. They are gone a long time. When Mrs Greene comes back for Victor she does not seem surprised to find him at his desk, drawing. She gives him a mug of hot chocolate and kisses him on the head. She smells like bathwater.

Soon after that he sees Mrs Greene's body. He crouches at the keyhole while she takes a bath. The steam makes it hard to see but when she steps from the bathtub her bosoms shake, they are large and white. He makes a noise and she hears him and she puts on her towel. She opens the door as he is running away. You're a dirty boy. He runs to his room and hides under the bed. She comes in wearing a dress that she put on inside out. Her hair drips, it sprays as she pulls him from under the bed. He scrapes at the floor but she is stronger. Dirty dirty boy. She does not paddle him, though. She sets him on the edge of the bed and scolds him in a loud voice. You must never. That is not what a good boy does. You must be a good boy not a bad boy.

He wants to be a good boy.

Time passes. The man with the moustache comes to visit. He looks unhappy.

It's simply intolerable sir says Mrs Greene.

The man paces the room, pulling on his ears. I understand.

Victor is amazed. He likes to pull on his ears, too. Mrs Greene does not like him to do that, she slaps his hands and tells him to stop being such an odd duck. Yet here is the man with the moustache, so tall and majestic in his big hat, pulling on his ears just like Victor does. It makes Victor feel proud.

He needs to be in school sir.

I'm aware of that. I've asked Dr Fetchett to find a more suitable place for him. It's not as simple as sending him to Priestly. The man with the moustache stops to look at one of Victor's drawings, which Mrs Greene has stuck on the wall. This is quite good.

I can't take credit for that sir.

You mean – really.

Yes sir.

All of them? My goodness. I had no idea. I always assumed they were yours.

No sir.

He's quite talented. He should have paints.

Yes sir.

Let's get him some, then.

Yes sir.

I'll be back soon. I'll talk to Fetchett, we'll figure out a way.

Yes sir.

And the lessons? Any progress?

No sir. He still will not do his work. He tears it up.

The man sighs. You must discipline him.

Don't you think I've tried.

Mind your tone.

I am sorry sir. I'm at the end of my tether.

I understand. Here is something for you.

Thank you sir.

And buy the boy some paints, please.

Yes sir.

Be a good boy, Victor.

He never sees the man again.

Time passes. He is eleven. Mrs Greene makes a birthday cake for him and when she brings it to the table she starts to cry. I cannot. I simply cannot.

Victor wants to help her. He offers her some of his cake.

Thank you dear. That's very kind of you.

A new car comes. Victor stands at the window and watches as it rolls up. It is gray. A man in a blue jacket jumps out and runs to the back door and opens it for a woman with a big swirl of hair and a hat high and brown like a toadstool. Mrs Greene runs to answer the door and the woman in the hat walks past her. She stands in the middle of the room and looks down her nose at everything. Then she looks at Victor.

He is filthy.

He has been playing in the yard mam.

Don't answer me back. The boy's filthy and that is all there is to say. Well do you have anything to say for yourself?

The woman is talking to him. He says nothing.

He isn't the talkative sort mam.

You shut up. The woman in the hat moves around the room, picking up plates and tossing them down roughly. And this place is a pigsty, too.

I'm sorry mam. Usually I do the washing in the afternoon, after—

I don't care. Clean him up. He's leaving.

Mam?

You are not to be faulted for my husband's poor decisions, but you must recognize that he is gone and the decisions are now mine and mine alone. Do you understand me?

Yes mam.

Now clean him up, I can't bear to look at him.

Mrs Greene draws him a bath. He does not want to take a bath; he already took a bath the day before. He struggles and she begs him. Please Victor. She sounds like she might cry and he allows her to take off his clothes and put him in the tub.

The woman in the hat says The car will be here in an hour.

Where are you sending him mam.

That's no concern of yours.

With all due respect . . . I'm sorry mam.

You may stay here as long as you'd like.

I wouldn't like to at all mam.

I don't blame you. My husband was a damned fool. Well don't you think that this is an idiotic plan?

I couldn't say mam.

Yes you can, you have an opinion, don't you.

No mam.

You're very well trained. How much did he pay you.

Mam.

I'll see to it you're taken care of. You call this number. Do we have an understanding?

Yes mam.

Idiot. How long did he intend to keep this up?

I couldn't say mam. He talked about finding the boy a school.

The woman in the hat looks at Victor and shudders. Well it's done now.

They put him in a car and drive him through the snow. He has never been so far from home. Mrs Greene sits with him, holding his hand. He does not know where he is going and many times he feels frightened. He screams and Mrs Greene says to him Please Victor. Look at the trees. What do they look like? Here, take the paper. The bumping car makes drawing difficult. He tries to steady his hand but then when he starts to get something on paper he feels sick and has to close his eyes. He wants to go home. When will they turn back? He wants his bed and his cocoa, he wants his spinning top. He cries and Mrs Greene says Look at the trees, Victor.

The trees are pointy and tall and white. They look like sugar rock.

At dusk they come to a house. It is bigger than any house he has ever seen, much bigger than his house. The house has a sooty face with yellow eyes. The car stops and Mrs Greene gets out. Victor sits in the car.

Come on dear.

Victor gets out of the car. Mrs Greene holds a small suitcase in her hand. She is standing very stiffly. Then she kneels down in the snow in her stockinged knees. Her eyes are small and red. You must be a good boy. Do you understand me?

He nods.

Good. Promise me you'll be a good boy.

Ah here he is, our young gentleman. A man with stuck-down hair stands at the top of the stairs. He smiles. Hello there, young sir. My name is Dr Worthe. You must be Victor. He holds out his hand. Victor puts his hands behind his back.

He's very tired sir.

I can see that. The rest of the boys have just sat down to dinner. Would you like something to eat, Victor?

He's quiet sir.

Dr Worthe, who does not resemble the other doctor at all, crouches so that his face is near Victor's. Are you hungry, young man? He smiles. Well, cat's got his tongue. Victor doesn't know anything about a cat.

They go inside. There is a big wooden staircase and a sparkly light. Mrs Greene puts the suitcase down. We didn't have time to pack all his things. I'll send them along.

We'll make sure he has everything he needs. Won't we, Victor?

Then Mrs Greene says I'm going to go now, Victor. You must listen to the man and do as he says. Be a good boy, be on your best behavior. I know you'll do me proud.

She walks toward the front door. Victor follows.

No, you must stay.

Come, young man, let's put something in your stomach, hey?

You must stay Victor.

Come on young man. Let's be grown-up about this.

Victor. No. No Victor no. No.

They hold him.

Then he is alone.

Dr Worthe puts his hand on Victor's shoulder and leads him out a different door. They walk along a stone path to a brick building with a puffing chimney. Victor hears a car start and he wants to see if it is Mrs Greene but Dr Worthe squeezes his shoulder and says Now, now.

In the brick building they go first to the dining room. It is bigger than any room Victor has ever seen, running the length of the building and filled with tables and benches, boys and men of all ages wearing white shirts and brown sweaters and ties. Some of them look over when the door opens. They stare at Victor. Everyone is talking, the noise hurts Victor's ears. He covers his ears but Dr Worthe pries off his hands.

Let's introduce you to some people who can be your friends.

Dr Worthe shows him where to get food. There is a window and you go with a metal tray. The man in the apron gives you a plateful of stew. You take the tray and you sit at the third table.

Boys I'd like you to meet your new classmate. This is Victor. Say hello boys.

Hello.

Say hello Victor.

Victor says nothing.

Be friendly now. It is not clear who Dr Worthe is speaking to.

Victor sits at the end of the bench. It is crowded and uncomfortable. He sees that there is another table with more room and he goes there.

No they say. You must go back. A man with a long neck takes him by the arm. Victor screams and bites him. The man lets out a shout and then everyone begins to shout. The noise makes Victor's ears crackle. He has hot liquid on his arms, it burns him. The shouting grows louder and louder until Dr Worthe stands on a chair. That's enough. Victor is on the floor. Dr Worthe comes near him and he screams. Dr Worthe picks him up, another man also picks him up and they carry him away. He screams. They put him on a bed. You must stop screaming, nobody will hurt you. Dr Worthe tells them to turn him and they turn Victor over and then he feels a jab and he falls asleep.

DURING THE DAY HE HAS LESSONS. Victor takes the pencil and paper they gave him and he draws the other boys. He draws the backs of heads, the sides of heads, the teacher's face. Sometimes he imagines what it would look like to see the room from another place and he draws that. Outside the classroom window there is a big tree that reaches with its arms, he draws it. He draws pages of snowflakes. He puts the papers inside his desk.

He does not do his lessons well. Dr Worthe says You must study.

The only lessons he likes are geography. He likes the shapes. Some of the maps have countries and some have continents. Africa and South America dragons' heads nodding. He draws Italy a boot. He draws Spain a man with a big nose coughing out islands. He draws Finland. He draws Ceylon a teardrop. He draws Australia. The teacher says that there are kangaroos in Australia. He does not know what a kangaroo is. The teacher shows them a picture. A kangaroo is a big rat. He draws the teacher with whiskers and a tail. He draws the other boys in the class in the shapes of countries they resemble. George is Chile and Irving is Germany. Victor draws them and puts them in his desk. His desk is bottomless. He will never fill it up.

The older boys play football. Victor does not understand. Instead of watching the players he watches the patterns their boots make in the snow. At first the snow is smooth, then they begin and the dimples spread like bubbles in a pot. They are beautiful but then the snow gets too mushy. Victor wishes they would stop in the middle so they don't ruin the beautiful patterns. But the next day it snows again and the surface is clean.

The other boys do not talk to him. They call him Twitter. Victor thinks about Mrs Greene. He asks for her often and the teacher does not understand. Dr Worthe brings him into his office.

I understand you miss your old friend. Do you know how to write a letter?

He does not.

I'm going to show you what to do. Then you may write to her anytime you want. We encourage you to write, and to be friendly. How are you liking your friends? Do you know everyone's name? Do you enjoy your classes?

Victor says nothing.

Naturally it has been difficult for you. You must try harder. It will get easier the more you practice. I see that you have not done your homework. That is not acceptable. You must do your homework. If you have trouble then ask for help. I will help you personally. That isn't something I say to everyone. I say it to you because I think you're a special child. I know that you're capable of more than we've seen from you. I would like you to succeed. Would you like to succeed? Well would you?

He nods.

Good. Very good. Now let's write that letter.

Dr Worthe shows him the salutation. Now you write whatever you'd like.

Victor chews his pencil. He does not know what to do. He draws a picture of Belgium.

Dr Worthe looks at the paper. This is what you want to write to her?
Victor nods.

I don't think she'll understand this. Wouldn't you like to tell her how you are? Do you want to tell her about your friends? Let me have that for a moment if you please. Dr Worthe erases Belgium, leaving a faint outline that he writes over. Dear Mrs Greene. Hello. How are you? I am fine. I am trying very hard to do my best in school. I am enjoying my schoolwork. I have many friends. What else can we tell her? Yesterday we had potato soup. It was – Victor? Did you like the potato soup?

He did not eat the soup. He shakes his head.

Dr Worthe says All right. Yesterday we had potato soup. It was not my favorite although still very tasty. My favorite foods to eat are—

Dr Worthe is staring at him. Victor?

Victor is frightened. He feels stupid. Oatmeal he says.

Oatmeal. Excellent. I enjoy eating oatmeal, which – Dr Worthe smiles – is very fortunate because we receive it for breakfast almost every morning.

This is true. Victor has never eaten so much oatmeal in his entire life. He does not mind it, but he has a feeling that he will not like it soon.

I hope that you are very well and that you will come to visit. You may visit whenever you'd like. Perhaps when it is not so cold you will come to visit. Dr Worthe stops writing. Is there anything else you'd like to tell her?

Victor shakes his head.

Now you need to sign the letter. How would you like to close? You may say sincerely or cordially or your friend. Here, take it. You choose.

Victor thinks. He writes Your friend. ·

Now sign your name.

He signs his name.

Good. Dr Worthe turns the letter around. This is not correct. Let me – may I? He takes the pencil from Victor. Friend is spelled like this. Do you see?

Victor nods.

Very good. Now we need to address the envelope.

Then Dr Worthe licks a stamp. He puts it on the envelope. You see, Victor? Now it goes in the mailbox. And now you've written a letter. Let's see if she writes back to you.

She does. Many months later he receives a letter from Mrs Greene. It is very short. Dr Worthe gives it to him in his office.

Dear Victor Victor reads.

Read it aloud please. Speak up.

Dear Victor Victor says. I am so happy to hear about you. I think of you often. I have left the house, so I did not get your letter until they sent it along to me. I have a new home. The address is at the top of the page. I have a new job, too. I work for Dr Fetchett. Do you remember him? He sends his regards. He thinks of you often, too. Love, Nancy. Inside curvy lines she has written Mrs Greene.

Dr Worthe looks pleased. That is a very nice letter. And now that we have her correct address we may write to her as much as we'd like. What shall we write?

This time he lets Victor lick the stamp. It tastes funny.

TWENTY-ONE

Our flight to Boston was delayed several hours; we didn't make it to Cambridge until almost eleven P.M. We took a cab to the hotel where Tony Wexler would stay whenever he came to Harvard to fix my mistakes, and I gave my credit card for both rooms. In my attaché I had a plain-paper copy of Victor's picture, as well as a CD-ROM with the scanned image. I hadn't spoken much since that afternoon, and I must have looked morose, because when we got in the elevator, Samantha put her hand on my back.

'I think my blood sugar's low,' I said.

'We can get dinner.'

I looked at her.

She shrugged. 'I'll make an exception.'

I smiled feebly. 'I think I'm going to get room service.'

'Call me if you change your mind.'

In my room I stripped down to my underwear and ordered a tuna sandwich that I couldn't bring myself to eat. I set the tray outside my door and lay down on the bed, staring at the darkened TV set, waiting for it to spring to life and fill up with Victor's face. I'm no spiritualist, but I honestly expected at least an *attempt* at communication. If not through the TV then taps on the wall in Morse code or the lights flashing on and off. I waited and waited for him but he never came. My eyes started to close, and I was almost under when a soft knock woke me.

I put on my trousers and my shirt and opened the door a crack. It was Samantha. She apologized for disturbing me.

'It's fine, I just passed out. Come in.' I stood back to let her in. She stayed outside, looking first at me, then at the uneaten sandwich on the floor.

'I wasn't hungry,' I said.

She nodded, staring at the ground. I realized that my shirt was unbuttoned and hanging open. I drew it closed. 'Please. Come on.'

She balked, then crossed the room to the armchair, where she sat looking out on the green Eliot House cupola. I stood next to her, and for a few minutes we said nothing, watching the moon flirt with us from behind the shifting clouds.

I said, 'Did you see the size of his hands?'

She said nothing.

'They were like paws. Did you see them?'

'I saw.'

'I have a hard time picturing him strangling someone with those hands.'

'They were children.'

I said nothing.

'It must be jarring,' she said.

I nodded.

We watched the sky.

'Thank you,' she said.

I looked at her.

'For what you did on the plane,' she said.

'Of course.'

'You probably expected me to smack you.'

'I can take it.'

A silence.

She said, 'I'm sorry I've been so cold to you.'

'You haven't.'

She raised an eyebrow.

'A little, maybe.'

She smiled.

'It's all right,' I said.

She said, 'I can't stand acting like this. I used to be such a stable person.' She paused. 'I missed you when I was away.'

'Me too.'

A silence.

She said, 'I want you to wait. Is that terrible for me to say?'

'No.'

'Yes, it is, it's terrible to put you on notice like that.'

'It's not terrible, Samantha.'

'Please call me Sam.'

'All right.'

'My dad used to call me Sammy.'

'I can call you that, if you'd prefer.'

She said, 'Just Sam's fine.'

SHE LEFT MY ROOM, and I got back into bed. I turned on the news. A clip of Bush, Cheney and Rice in conference gave me an unpleasant flashback to the night of Marilyn's party, and I switched to paid programming.

My hotel phone rang. I muted the TV. 'I thought you went to sleep.'

'I didn't wake you up, did I? I'll feel awful if I woke you up.'

'I was awake.'

A silence.

She said, 'Can I come back over?'

SHE WAS DIFFERENT NOW. She looked me in the eye, something I only then realized she had not done the first time. She moved more, too. It might have been the freedom afforded by a king-sized bed; or because we knew each other a little bit, had the advantage of a mental map; or maybe, probably, she was different this time because this time she wanted to feel not nothing but something.

BEFORE SHE DRIFTED OFF, she said, 'I'm sorry I made you pay for two rooms.'

AT FOUR IN THE MORNING I awoke bullhorn-alert. Sam had one arm hanging off the edge of the bed and the blanket bunched between her thighs. I slipped from the bed and sat watching her change shape. Then I showered and dressed and went out for a walk along the Charles.

The river in winter becomes a patchwork of crackling ice and dark, poisonous water. Memorial Drive crackled beneath a speeding taxi. I stopped near the boathouse to zip up my jacket and to stare at the blinking Citgo sign. I've always had a soft spot for Boston. Its snootiness appeals to me, as does its anarchistic streak. It's that odd combination of Puritanism and decadence that makes Harvard such a perfect breeding ground for the American elite.

I walked up Plympton, toward the trainlike hump of the Lampoon, turning west to head past the Fly. Inside, music was playing. I hadn't kept in touch with anybody I knew back then, much less paid my alumni dues, but on a whim I went around to the front door and knocked. I was about to leave when the door swung open. A tall, handsome young man with shaggy blond hair stood there. He looked like a kid. He was a kid. He looked me up and down.

'Can I help you?'

'I used to be a member,' I said.

He seemed skeptical.

'Can I come in?'

'Uhm.' He looked at his watch.

From inside, a girl called *Danny.*

'One minute,' he yelled.

'It's okay,' I said. 'I understand.'

'Sorry, man.'

I turned and the door shut behind me. To my left was the backyard, fenced off, where in spring we held the Garden Party. I suppose they still do. Life keeps going.

I walked to the front gate of Lowell House, where I spent my latter two years. I wondered how short I was of a BA. I wondered if they would take me back. I pictured myself waiting in line for registration; carrying a futon up three flights of stairs; spooning myself green beans in the dining hall; whooping it up at the Game. The blond kid would be my friend. He would punch me for the Fly. We would hang out together and get stoned. I laughed and arched my thirty-two-year-old back.

Down the road was a Dumpster. I had a crazy urge to go rooting through it for my abandoned Cy Twombly. Maybe they hadn't picked up the trash in twelve years.

I stood back and counted windows, picking out what I thought was my sophomore year room. The light was off. From its sill I had been able to see over the tops of the buildings, northward to the Yard and the Gothic spires of Muller Hall, a clear view of my past.

*

BY THE TIME I GOT BACK to the hotel, Sam was gone. She wasn't in her room, either. I found her in the gym, pumping away at an elliptical machine. An MP3 player was strapped to her arm. One earplug in; its partner dangled at waist-level, freeing up the side of her head to pin a cell phone to her shoulder. A copy of *Fitness* lay upside down and unopened on the machine's magazine thingie. With her right hand she swigged a bottle of water, and with her left she tattooed a Palm Pilot. Every part of her seemed to be moving in a different direction, like some marvelous sweaty cubist paroxysm.

'I appreciate it,' I heard her saying as I approached. 'Thank you.'

'Good morning,' I said.

'*Oh* my gosh. You startled me.'

'I'm sorry.'

'What happened to you. I thought you were gone.'

'I couldn't sleep. I took a walk.'

'Leave a note next time, will you . . . I just got off the phone with James Jarvis.'

I looked at the gym clock. It was seven fifteen.

'*He* called *me*,' she said. Something new in her voice, a new timbre. Happiness. And it made her speak a little faster, despite her huffing and puffing. 'He's teaching today but he said we could come by after four. Do you know where Somerville is?'

'Five-minute drive.'

'Then we have a day to spend together.' She slowed down and stopped, her feet still on the pedals. 'I'm gross right now, but I'm going to kiss you anyway, and you're going to have to deal with it.'

'That's fine with me.' And it was.

SOMERVILLE, CAMBRIDGE'S POORER COUSIN, is home to many a grad student. I remembered it primarily as the location of the Basket, a lowbrow

337

supermarket favored by Harvard students as a place to buy liquor in plastic bottles with handles. I think they do more sales in food stamps than in cash; the employees walk around with the pall of death on them; we used to call the place the Casket.

A stone's throw away (assuming you had a very energetic throwing arm) is Knapp Street and its short run of town houses. Our buzz summoned a young man in surgical scrubs, who introduced himself as Elliot and who, upon showing us to the living room, immediately began berating us for upsetting James.

'He was crying,' said Elliot. 'He didn't even cry when our dog died and he was sobbing. I really hope you realize what you're doing here. You just sent years of therapy down the drain. I begged him not to talk to you but he's his own person. If it were up to me I wouldn't have let you in the front door.'

Sam said, 'He might be able to help us catch the person who did it.'

Elliot snorted. 'Like *that* matters. Whatever. He should be home in a few minutes.' He left the room; a door slammed.

I looked at Sam. She seemed unruffled. Quietly she said, 'It's never what you expect. It's always the father who's freaking out, or the older brother. The women are calm when you talk to them. They can describe the most horrific stuff and it's like they're reading the phone book. In a way that's worse, you know? Like I remember this girl, nine years old, raped by her grandfather. I was asking her these very specific questions and she doesn't flinch. The only time she gets upset is at the end. All of a sudden she gets this *look*. She goes, "Don't send him to jail, I'll go instead."'

'That's sick.'

'People are weird.' She picked up a copy of *Architectural Digest* and began to leaf through it. I was too tense to do anything but tap my fingers against my knees.

Jarvis had promised to be home by four thirty. At four forty-five Elliot reemerged, wearing running tights and a fleece, his bangs held back with a sweatband.

'He's still not back?'

'No.'

He frowned and stooped to double-knot his shoes. It was obvious that he wanted to leave, wanted us to leave, as well; and everyone breathed a little easier when we heard a car pull up. Elliot ran out the front door and clomped down the steps. I heard the sound of an argument. I went to the window and pulled back the curtain. In the street he was yelling at a thin, balding man in an overcoat and bright blue galoshes. This, I presumed, was James Jarvis. He was older than his partner by at least fifteen years, with a fatherly aura, the look of someone resigned to constant ingratitude. He said nothing as Elliot ranted and gesticulated and finally turned on his heel and sprinted off. I hurried back to the couch.

'Sorry I'm late.' Jarvis set his bag down. 'There was an accident on the pike.'

'Thanks for taking the time,' Sam said.

'It's – well, I was about to say it's my pleasure, but I think that might be overstating it a bit. Can I get a cup of coffee before we begin?'

'Of course.'

In the kitchen he loaded up an espresso maker and set out three small porcelain cups. 'I'm sorry if he was nasty.'

'There's no need to apologize.'

'He's very protective.' Jarvis set the machine running, then crossed his arms and leaned against the counter. 'He has the zeal of youth.'

Sam smiled.

'I probably shouldn't say that,' he said. 'Look at both of you. You know what my first reaction was when you called? "I'm so *old.*" That's what really stung.' The machine clicked, and he fiddled with it. 'Here I am living my Dorian Gray fantasy, and then you come along to remind me that in 1973 I was *eleven*. Elliot wasn't even born then.' He made a face like *The Scream*. Then he laughed gloomily and turned to pour our drinks, which he set out for us at the breakfast nook. He also pried open a tin of biscotti. 'Enjoy.'

Sam thanked him. 'We don't want to inconvenience you any more than we already have, so—'

'Oh, it's no inconvenience to me. I might get the silent treatment for a couple of days but he'll come around.'

'Well, all the same, thank you. If it's okay with you we'll just get started?'

He gestured *Go ahead*. I took the photocopy out of my attaché and put it on the table. Jarvis stared for a long time, his expression inscrutable. I looked at Sam and she looked at me and nobody said anything and I started to believe that we'd gotten it all wrong and I felt something like elation and something else like exasperation and I wanted to tell him that he didn't *have* to pick Victor out; he shouldn't rush to point a finger.

'That's him.'

Sam said, 'Are you sure?'

'I think so.' He scratched his cheek. 'It's hard to tell because it's so grainy.'

I started to speak but Sam said, 'We have a scan that's higher-resolution. Do you have a computer we could use?'

We went to an office at the back of the house. Jarvis's armpits were dark; his good-natured slouch gone. Violently he jerked the mouse to revive the screen. He put in the CD and clicked on the icon and the photo exploded onto the screen: much larger, shockingly crisp. Victor had a small mole on his neck that I hadn't noticed.

'It's him,' said Jarvis.

'You're sure.'

'I'm sure.'

'All right,' she said. 'All right.'

Was that it? Wasn't there going to be something more catastrophic? Where was Victor's spirit now? When did he come swirling out of the heating ducts, all undead vengeance? That could not be the end, not that whimper. Totem crumbling, I began to panic. I wanted to argue. Jarvis was mistaken. How much could he possibly remember? Not remember: *know*. We weren't in a court of law. I had a higher standard than reasonable doubt. I wanted zero doubt. Now I saw Jarvis as the culprit, Jarvis as the antagonist, Jarvis as the liar. He had to prove to me that he wasn't just a lonely boy vying for attention. He had to provide corroborating evidence. He had to describe the size and shape of Victor's penis; he had to supply choice snippets of dialogue; he had to tell me the weather that day and what he'd had for lunch and what color socks he'd had on, something concrete and verifiable that would allow us to determine if his memory was as perfectly one hundred percent grade-A pristine as he claimed.

'When you're ready,' said Sam, 'I'd like to ask you a couple of questions.'

He nodded distantly. He scrolled down to the bottom of the image, to the legend. Magnified, the type looked ragged. 'Do you know where he is?'

'We're looking.'

He nodded again. 'It's strange to have a name,' he said. 'For years all I had was a face. It was like he wasn't a real person.' He looked at Sam. Then he looked back at the screen and said, 'Frederick Gudrais. He's probably not even alive anymore. Is he?'

There was a silence. I looked at Sam, who said, 'Pardon me?'

'He'd be – what – in his seventies by now. I guess he could be alive.'

Sam looked at me.

'That's not his name,' I said. Those were the first words I'd spoken since introductions, and Jarvis gave me a strange look, one not without resentment. I reached for the mouse, scrolled up, tapped the screen. 'That's Victor Cracke.'

'So what.'

'So.' I looked at Sam. 'So that's him. Victor Cracke.'

'Fine,' said Jarvis, 'but that isn't the man who attacked me. This is.' He pointed to the man on Victor's left.

INTERLUDE: 1953.

At mealtimes he sits where he is supposed to. He never makes the same mistake as the first night. The other boys say Look, it's Twitter. Victor hates them but he says nothing. Some of the boys try to take his dessert. He fights them and everyone ends up scolded. Instead of taking his dessert they stick their fingers in it or blow their noses in his milk. Victor fights them. Everyone gets scolded.

Dr Worthe says I can't understand why it's always you sitting in this chair. You must stop fighting. I don't want to punish you anymore. I'm tired of punishing you.

Simon is the worst. Simon pinches him under the table. He ties Victor's shoelaces together so that Victor falls and cuts his lip. Everyone laughs. Victor fights him but Simon is much bigger and it is no use. Simon laughs, his breath smells like garbage. He says Twitter you're a piece of shit. Victor knows that you don't want to be a piece of shit. Twitter why don't you stop staring at the ground? What's the matter with you Twitter? There are other boys who do not talk and Simon beats them up, too. But he has a special liking for Victor. Twitter I am going to cut your balls off when you're sleeping. Victor does not understand why anyone would do such a thing, but he is frightened. At night he sleeps with his hands over his balls. Sometimes Simon tries to punch Victor and Victor curls up on the floor and screams until a teacher comes. The teacher tries to lift Victor up but Victor snaps at him, he cannot help himself. They take him to Dr Worthe's office where he gets a scolding or else they put him to sleep.

Twitter who you talking to? There ain't nobody there.

Victor ignores him. He is trying to do his assignment.

Gimme that. Simon tears up his assignment.

Victor leaps on him and they roll around. Everyone begins to cheer. Simon says into Victor's ear I'm going to rip your balls off you piece of shit. Victor bites Simon on the chin and Simon howls. He turns Victor over and pins down his arms with his knees and begins hitting Victor in the chest and stomach. Victor throws up. Stop that says the teacher. Stop it right now.

They take him to the hospital. He likes the hospital. There is no oatmeal. All he does is lie in bed and draw. He draws chairs and faces. He draws countries. Some are real and some are pretend. He plays with the bandage on his nose and the nurses say No.

When he comes back Simon is mad. Simon got punished and now he wants to kill Victor. You wait. One night you're going to wake up and your balls will be gone.

Time passes. Victor is fourteen. He and Simon fight often, but they learn to fight in private so that nobody scolds them. Victor grows weary. He does not like to fight but he does not like the scolding even more. Dr Worthe takes away his library privileges. The library is where he sits and copies pictures from books. There is an atlas that he reads many times. The library gives him all his happiness, and rather than lose that he fights quietly. Simon doesn't care if he gets his privileges revoked, he only likes to beat up Victor.

They move to another table because now they are older. Some boys have left. Some boys stay behind at the old table. People come and go. In the spring a new boy comes to the school. His name is Frederick. He is tall, taller than Simon, although skinnier. He has black hair and a long pointy face and a very big mouth. At first he is quiet but sometimes he winks. He has no trouble finding a place at the table. He sits near Simon and Simon says Gimme your cake.

Frederick does not answer him. He eats his cake. Simon reaches for the cake and Frederick moves the plate out of his reach.

Gimme your cake.

Frederick stops eating. He looks at Simon. He says All right. He gives Simon his cake. Simon eats it with his fingers.

That night Victor is lying in bed when he hears someone moving across the room. He covers his balls and prepares for a fight, bunching up in the corner. He waits. It is Frederick. He is smiling. He whispers.

Victor.

Victor stares at him.

My name's Freddy.

Victor says nothing.

I'll tell you something, Victor. That son of a bitch is going to leave you alone.

Cautiously, Victor uncurls.

You know what I'm talking about?

Victor shakes his head.

Freddy smiles. You'll find out.

At dinner Simon says to Freddy Gimme your pudding.

All right.

That night Simon is sick. They all hear him running to the bathroom. They hear wet noises. The teacher comes to investigate and Simon is spitting blood. That's what the other boys say.

Freddy says to Victor Too bad about him huh.

Victor smiles.

Freddy and Victor become friends. Freddy gets in trouble a lot but he always seems to get away without punishment. He is much cleverer than Simon. Simon says he is going to kill Freddy but Victor can see how scared Simon really is. He stops beating people up as much and he leaves Victor alone.

Freddy says I told him he'd better lay off.

Victor is grateful. He draws Freddy a picture of a heliocanthus.

You did this for me huh Vic? Freddy calls him Vic. Nobody else calls him that; Victor likes it. Well bow-wow. It's pretty good.

Victor shows him the rest of his drawings. By now there are too many to fit in the desk, so he hides them atop a shelf in the library. He stands on a chair to reach them. The box is very heavy. Inside are pictures of flowers and snowflakes, pictures of people and animals, maps with names he made by combining other names together.

Lookee that says Freddy. Not bad Vic.

It rains often and he and Freddy sneak to the attic. It is locked but Freddy has the key. They sit under the eaves and watch the swirling tree-tops. Victor takes note of the weather. He never wants to forget being with Freddy so he writes everything down in a little book he got for Christmas, Mrs Greene sends him one every year. While they lie in the attic Freddy talks about himself. Victor likes the sound of Freddy's voice.

I don't know Vic. I might stay here awhile. They say I gotta leave when I'm seventeen but I don't know about that. I might find my way back in. There's fellas here older than that so I don't see why I shouldn't be. They think I'm stupid. They gave me some tests but I flunked them all, I knew that they had to send me here. I know what's good for me. I like it better here than some of the other places I been. The food's all right. You know? I don't mind it. I'll stretch it out as long as I can.

Nobody knows about their place in the attic. They go there alone. Freddy talks about everything and Victor listens. Time passes. Victor is fifteen. They go to the attic and Freddy says Look. He shows Victor his privates. They look different from Victor's. Freddy's privates have hair. He says Your turn. Victor opens his pants. Freddy laughs and Victor is embarrassed. He tries to put his pants back on but Freddy says Aw naw I wasn't laughing at you. He moves Victor's hands away from his groin. I think it's just great. Bow-wow. You know how to make it grow? Freddy puts his mouth on Victor's privates. They get swollen and then Freddy says You ain't never seen it leak did you? Maybe you ain't big enough yet. I can. Here. Victor puts his mouth on Freddy's privates. Now move around. Victor moves around. Freddy touches the back of Victor's neck. It tickles. Victor loves his friend. He loves Freddy. Freddy says Watch. Victor watches and Freddy's privates cough up stuff. Milky drops roll down his wrist. Some fly through the air and land on Victor's foot. He touches them. They feel like oil.

Victor loves Freddy. He doesn't mind going to the attic. He remembers the tutor but he doesn't mind. They take off all their clothes and hold each other. When it is cold they hug together to stay warm. They get dirty on the floor.

One time Victor gets a nail stuck in his leg. Freddy says Shhh you want them to find out? Stop crying. Victor cannot stop crying. He loves Freddy and he wants to listen but it hurts. Stop it you damn crybaby. Stop it. Freddy slaps Victor. Victor stops crying. Freddy says Christ amighty. By the next morning it stops bleeding and Victor knows Freddy was right to slap him. He will not disappoint him again.

You ever been on a horse?

Victor shakes his head.

I was when I was a kid. My grandpop had a horse. I liked it good enough. One time it kicked my grandpop and broke his arm. Freddy smiles. You shoulda seen it. The bone was sticking out. You ever seen that Vic? It's got stuff on the inside, bones. You ain't never gonna believe it. They had to cut off his whole arm cause it didn't heal right. He was a son of a bitch anyhow. I'm sorry the horse didn't take off his whole head. But I like horses plenty. They got more nobility than us. You know what nobility is?

Victor shakes his head.

It's what they got. Freddy scratches his bare bottom. He yawns. We ought to get downstairs fore the lesson's over. Hey look at that. I'm a rude son of a bitch. I bet you know what to do with that don't you Vic.

Victor knows what to do.

People come and go. Simon leaves. Other boys come. Victor takes no notice of them. He sees only Freddy, thinks only of him. He stops writing to Mrs Greene. Still she sends him books and letters. One year for Christmas all the boys get chessboards. They come with checkers pieces too. Freddy doesn't like chess. He likes checkers. He and Victor play checkers together in the attic. They kiss and hug and touch each other and play checkers. Victor draws pictures for Freddy. He is happy.

Victor is seventeen. Freddy says They're kicking me out.

Victor begins to cry.

Don't worry, I'll be back.

But he does not come back. Victor thinks about him every day. He writes letters but Freddy does not write back. Before Freddy left he gave Victor the key to the attic but going there makes him too sad. So he prays. He bargains with God. He makes deals and waits for them to be paid off. He hurts himself and says Now he will come. They find him bleeding and send him to a quiet room. He hurts himself again and they give him pills that make him sick. They give him electric shocks that make him forget things. Before he felt lonely sometimes but this is new. He wants to die. He starts to draw a map, hoping to find Freddy in it. He will draw until he finds him.

Dr Worthe takes off his spectacles and rubs his eyes. We've known each other a long time haven't we.

Victor says nothing.

I understand that you haven't been eating. Is that true Victor? You look like you've lost weight. What do you have to say for yourself?

Victor says nothing. He doesn't care. He feels half-asleep. He hardly speaks to anyone, not even to say please and thank you, which he always tried to do because Mrs Greene taught him it was good manners to look someone in the eye and say those words. He dreams of Freddy, wakes up with the taste of salt in his mouth. Underneath the blankets he pretends his hand is Freddy's mouth. It isn't the same.

HE RUNS AWAY. He goes at night when everyone else is sleeping. Now that he is older he sleeps in a room with four other boys, instead of the big room where all the younger boys sleep. He waits until everyone is asleep, then he puts on his shoes and goes quietly down the stairs. It is summertime. Outside insects cottonball around the orange lights. He walks across the rear lawn. In the House some lights are still on. He sees in the window the shape of a man lifting dumbbells. It's the recreational teacher, Mr Chamberlain. He is not looking in Victor's direction but Victor sinks into the shadows along the fence. He comes to the front gate. He rarely goes beyond. Sometimes they take them on outings. Once they went to watch a baseball game, and another time they went to see a circus. They went on buses.

The front gate is locked. He climbs over the fence and falls into the bushes, cutting his arm. He leaves a trail of drops as he walks along the road. He takes off one sock and ties it around his arm. Then he puts his shoe back on and continues walking.

Freddy lives in a town called Yonkers. Victor found it in the atlas. But he doesn't know what direction to go in. He walks for hours, until the foot missing the sock begins to blister. He unties the bloody sock. It is crusty. The cut hurts but it isn't bleeding anymore. He puts the sock back on his foot and keeps walking until he crosses over a bridge. It is pitch-black and muggy. He takes note of the stars. He sees many strange and attractive things but he has no time to waste, he has someplace to go.

As the sky brightens some trucks drive past. He sees houses, shops and parked cars. He smells bread baking and his stomach hurts. A boy rides a bicycle with a basket full of newspapers. Victor sees a man sleeping in a car. Victor knocks on the window and the man twitches. He wipes the fog off the windows and squints out at Victor. Then he cranks the window down.

Victor says Bus station.

The man points. That way. Then he sees Victor's arm. Whoa there pal.

Victor says Thank you and walks away.

The bus to Yonkers does not depart until eight fifteen, so after he buys his ticket he sits in the station and waits. The clock says six forty-five. Victor counts his money. He has twenty-two dollars and nineteen cents left. Some of the money he saved up over the years, gifts from the man with the moustache. Some of it is money that Mrs Greene sent on his birthday. He is glad he spent it on a ticket to see Freddy. For the first time in months he feels alive. Hunger rushes into him like a wild dog. Across the street is a store where people are eating. The sign says Pip's. Victor leaves the station and crosses the street and goes inside and sits down. People read from a piece of paper to a woman and she brings them food. She comes to see him. She stares at his arm.

Golly. What happened to you?

He says nothing.

She gives him a funny look. What'll it be.

He does not know what to say.

Listen kid, I don't have all morning.

He picks up the piece of paper and points.

You want steak for breakfast?

He senses that he has made a mistake. He points again.

Coming right up.

The woman brings him a bowl of oatmeal. He stares at it, poking it with his spoon. He does not eat a bite. Nearby two men sit down and say to the woman Bacon and eggs. When Victor smells their food he regrets.

What's the matter?

He looks at the woman.

No good?

He points to the other booth.

The woman shrugs. You want me to leave that?

He pushes the bowl away. She takes it and comes back with bacon and eggs.

He has never tasted anything like it. He savors every bite. The bacon is too greasy but the eggs remind him of Freddy's mouth. He eats them and asks for another plate of just eggs. She brings it to him. He asks for a third.

Golly we're hungry.

Midway through his fourth plate of eggs he remembers the bus. He hurries out without paying and runs across the street. The woman shouts at him.

In the station he asks the man for the bus to Yonkers.

The one left. There's another this afternoon.

Victor sits on the bench and puts his head in his hands. He has made a terrible mistake. He is as stupid as they said. When lunchtime comes he is too afraid to go back across the street. He wishes Freddy was there to help him. He counts his money, he still has twenty-two dollars and nineteen cents.

That's him.

A policeman and Dr Worthe are there along with some people from the home. They take him. He fights. They put him in the van and he falls asleep.

He wakes up in the quiet room. He tries to get out of bed but he is tied. He shouts and they come in and he falls asleep again.

The next time he wakes up Dr Worthe is sitting at his bedside.

What are we going to do with you my boy.

He spends a long time in that room and then they let him go back to his regular room. His roommates say Welcome back Twitter.

He runs away again. They took his money so he cannot take a bus. He will hitchhike. Freddy told him about hitchhiking and one of his class-mates said once he hitchhiked to Miami and back. Victor walks to the highway and sticks out his thumb. The first car that pulls up is a police car. Victor runs. He jumps off the side of the road and hides in a barn. They find him and bring him back. They give him shots and pills and shocks. They put him in the room. He does not try to run away any-more.

TIME PASSES.

Victor is nineteen and Freddy comes back. Victor cries with happiness. His prayers have been answered.

See says Freddy. Told you.

Victor discontinues his map, which he has been drawing whenever he isn't too sleepy from drugs. Life is fine again. He and Freddy go to the attic, they go for walks on the grounds and find quiet places where they can hide themselves and cling to each other in the leaves. Freddy is always very gentle except sometimes he scratches Victor's thighs with his nails. It hurts and he bleeds but he doesn't mind.

Freddy says Next time they ain't sending me here no more. Next time they want to put me in the pen.

The days fly by. Victor is twenty. He is twenty-one and twenty-two and twenty-three. They take a picture and in that picture Freddy stands next to him. The photographer says Say cheese. Then he is twenty-five and things change.

Dr Worthe says You have a visitor Victor.

Victor has never seen this man before. His name is Mr Wexler. He does not look much older than Victor but he has a tie and a suit and dark eyes and a sagging face and he sees Victor and says Oh brother.

Mr Wexler asks Victor questions about the home. He seems unhappy with how Victor is being treated. Dr Worthe keeps apologizing. Mr Wexler keeps saying It's over now.

Victor doesn't like the sound of that. He has heard that before and he does not want anything to be over.

Dr Worthe tells Victor that he will miss him. You've been here a long time my boy. I wish you the best.

Victor does not want to go. He tells Dr Worthe but Dr Worthe says Mr Wexler will take care of you.

Victor does not want to be taken care of. He is already taken care of. He has his room and the eaves and his drawings and the library and Freddy, he has Freddy, who was taken away from him but given back. Much worse than losing someone you love is losing them twice. God is playing tricks. Victor hates Him. Still he prays to Him. He says the rosary. He bargains. If You will let me stay. Then I will. If You will bring him with me. Then I will. If You change Your mind. Then I will.

They take him on a fall morning. All through the ride Victor stares out the window at piles of burning leaves. Sometimes he cries. When the car slows he wants to jump out. The only thing that stops him is what Freddy said to him before he left. Don't worry Vic. I'll get out of here and I'll come stay with you. You'll see. Don't act up and give yourself more problems.

Victor cannot imagine how things will ever get better, they feel so awful. But he believes in Freddy and Freddy said to do as the man told.

Mr Wexler's name is Tony. He rides in the car with Victor. He says that they are going to New York City. They drive and drive. Outside the trees are orange and gold but Victor sees only their shapes, their forked ends and their delicate spindles. He wishes he could show them to Freddy. He will draw them so he can show Freddy later. He will have to get some paper. He hopes they have paper in New York City.

New York City roars. Victor has never seen anything like it in his whole life. He sees buildings the size of mountains and streets filled with cars filled with people. He sees bright neon signs. He sees Negroes. He sees boys hitting a ball with a broomstick. He sees men with hard hats. A train disappears into the earth. Tony says Have you ever been on a train? Victor has suspicions about Tony; Tony talks to him like he is a child. But he is not a child. He understands. He understands that he is stupid and he always has. That is what makes him different from a child. He wants to tell Tony but he cannot find the words.

Over a bridge they go. Tony says This is Queens. There are men in blue coats. There are yellow and black cars that look like beetles. They drive down a busy street full of people walking, pulling carts behind them filled with paper bags. Men stand on the sidewalk smoking. The streets ooze steam. Victor is overwhelmed. He remembers the town from when he was a boy; he remembers Albany from the time he ran away; but neither of those places is as impressive as New York City.

They turn from the busy street and up a little hill past a park with children on swings. They come to some tall brick buildings. There are many of them, splitting the bright blue sky. Tony says Here's your new place.

Victor cannot imagine a house so big. It is bigger than the dormitory, a hundred times bigger. He worries. He does not want a house so big. But then he sees other people going in and out. Maybe it is actually a dormitory. He can't figure things out. Too many things are happening at once. He wants to lie down and put his head in Freddy's lap. Freddy understands. Freddy could explain.

Tony leads him through a maze. The buildings are so high they bend inward, like they want to kiss. Victor feels lost. He wants a map. He wants his drawings. He asks for them but Tony doesn't understand. He tells Victor that they'll bring up his suitcases later. But what about the box in the library. He tries to explain. Tony says If you left something we'll call Dr Worthe and get it back. But Victor is not comforted.

354

Tony shows Victor a sign that says CARNELIAN. This is where you will live. Victor knows what carnelian is, he read about it in the almanac. Tony opens the door for Victor. Inside Tony pushes a button on the wall and a door slides open like a magic mouth. Victor has never seen it before. He is scared and amazed.

Come on says Tony. Unless you want to walk eleven flights.

The doors shut, chomp. The floor presses up and his feet feel heavy. Then a bell rings and the mouth opens and Tony says All-righty.

The hall is quiet, it has carpet and white paint on the walls. Here we go. Tony opens a door for Victor. The room inside is as big as his room in the dormitory but instead of five beds there is one. There is a potted flower on the windowsill and a flat metal plate plugged into the wall. There is a sink and a toilet. It is peaceful and clean. You can see the bridge from here. Tony points out the window. Isn't this better?

Better than what? Victor gazes down at the ground far below. The people look like peppergrains.

You'll be happy here. There's the phone. When you need something you can call me. This is my number. I'll be by to check on you. If you need something you can ask. Here's some money. I'll send some more every few weeks. You'll be very comfortable, I promise. Is there anything you need? Are you hungry?

They go back in the mouth and Victor observes how to use it. He is learning all the time.

At the store which is called a restaurant Victor asks for eggs. Tony drinks coffee. The woman brings them everything and Victor eats. The eggs taste delicious.

This must be quite an adjustment for you. Tony waits and looks at him. Then he says We're going to make up for everything. You're free to do whatever you want. You can go outside, you can go to the museum or to the park. You can go to the baseball game. You can have anything you want.

Victor asks for another plate of eggs.

As much as you like. Tony sips his coffee. There's shops nearby. What do you need?

Victor thinks. He says Paper.

There's a store right up the way. They're probably closed at this hour but I'll show you the way and you can go buy whatever you'd like, I'll give you some extra money. Do you want some dessert?

They walk to the store. In the street a man sells peanuts from a cart. The smell is wonderful and Victor's mouth waters. He wants some peanuts but he doesn't want to interrupt Tony, who is talking about all the possibilities Victor has open to him. Victor notes the location of the peanut vendor. He notes places that look interesting. He draws a map in his head. He can write it down later.

The stationery store is closed, but in the window Victor sees appealing stacks of paper and pencils. He does not know how much money Tony gave him but he hopes it will be enough.

They walk around the neighborhood. Tony shows him where to buy food. It is getting dark and cold and Victor shivers. Tony says You need a new coat.

After that they walk home. Victor goes to the wrong door and Tony says No, that's not ours. Then Victor understands that the house is like a dormitory, after all. He feels disappointed. He had wanted to see the other rooms.

Tony brings him to the correct room. Victor memorizes the way as best he can. Tomorrow he wants to get pencils and paper and pens and some envelopes so he can write to Freddy.

Are you going to be all right here tonight?

He nods.

I'll be back tomorrow. In the meantime you call me if you need anything.

Victor is alone. He looks out the window and thinks about Freddy. He takes the clothing out of his suitcase and puts it neatly in the bureau. He fills a cup with water and drinks. He is very thirsty so he drinks some more. Then he gets undressed and lies down on the bed. He thinks about Freddy. He touches his privates and then he falls asleep.

Usually his eyes open at sunrise. But the next morning he keeps sleeping until pounding at the door wakes him. He stands up and puts on his pants and his shirt just as a key turns in the lock. It is Tony. He looks worried and he is breathing hard.

You didn't answer the door.

Victor says nothing.

Are you all right?

Victor nods.

You can't frighten me like that Victor.

Victor does not know what he did to frighten Tony.

Under one arm Tony holds a folded coat. Here.

Victor puts on the coat. Its sleeves go past his fingertips.

We'll have to fix that. Have you eaten anything?

They go back to the restaurant. Victor eats eggs. Tony drinks coffee.

I see you like eggs.

Victor does not talk with his mouth full; Mrs Greene taught him. He nods.

You can learn to make eggs at home. That way you can have them whenever you want. Should we teach you?

Tony teaches Victor how to use the hotplate. They make eggs that do not taste as good as the eggs at the restaurant but Victor does not want to be rude. He says Thank you. But he is impatient because he wants to get to the paper store before it closes. He does not want to wait another day.

When you're done you wash the pan. Did they teach you how to do that?

Yes.

But Tony insists on standing there and watching while Victor does it.

Good job he says like Victor is a child. Victor decides he cannot trust Tony. After Tony leaves Victor runs to the store.

In the beginning Tony comes often. He comes with gifts or money or to say hello. He takes Victor to a doctor and the doctor says Cough. Tony takes Victor for clothing and shoes, things that Victor doesn't want. He tells Victor about the interesting things to see in New York City. He takes Victor to see the Statue of Liberty. He takes him to the Museum of Natural History and to the park in Flushing. Victor says Thank you but inside he wishes he could stay at home with his drawings and the quiet and the view of the bridge. Outside there is too much honking, too much banging; it hurts Victor's head and makes him want to shut his eyes. He endures the trips with Tony because he has made a new bargain with God. If he suffers enough, he can bring Freddy sooner. So says nothing; he welcomes the loneliness he feels.

Soon it grows too cold to go outside. Tony comes less often. He says I want you to be independent. Instead he calls on the phone. Their conversations are short. Hello and Hello and Is there anything you need and No thank you.

One time he cannot open his door. There are two locks and you have to turn them in the opposite directions. Though he tries and tries the door will not open. Maybe he went to the wrong room. But no, it is the right one, he remembers the number. He does not know what to do. Finally he gets the locks and goes inside and sits on the bed, so scared that he cannot stop shaking all night long.

But most of the time he is okay. Sometimes he sees other people in the hallway. They look at him strangely. He walks around the neighborhood. He buys pencils and paper. He buys some pens and markers and discovers that he likes those, too. The man behind the counter offers to sell him paints or drawing pads. Victor says No thank you. He likes the paper that comes in huge bunches. He buys five bunches and the man asks if he's writing a book. On the way to and from the store he always stops to buy peanuts.

He goes to the restaurant. He wants to understand why his eggs taste different from the eggs at the restaurant, and so he sits at the counter where he watches the chefs with the paper caps, their foreheads dripping with sweat as they chop onions. He sees that they put milk in the eggs. So he buys some milk and tries to make eggs for himself. But the eggs burn and after a few days the milk stinks. He flushes it down the toilet. He will go to the restaurant instead.

Every two weeks a letter comes from Tony. The man at the front gate gives it to him. Inside is some money. He uses the money to buy what he needs but he has most of it left over. The money grows. He saves it up.

He sends letters to Freddy. He sends drawings. He draws the bridge and the water. He draws birds and flowers. Freddy never writes back but Victor knows that his efforts are not wasted. He can tell the moment Freddy gets a letter, no matter how far away. He hears the envelope tear open in his mind.

The seasons change. Since Mrs Greene no longer sends him books he buys a new one and writes down the weather. He writes down everything so that he can tell Freddy when Freddy comes. He will say Here is what I saw while I waited for you. He prays. He goes to church. He bargains and confesses. A long time passes. Then one day the man at the gate hands him two envelopes. One is the cream-colored paper Tony uses; the other is flimsy and bluish. Victor tears it open.

Dear Vic. I'm coming.

Victor is excited. He decides to buy Freddy a gift. He takes his money and goes to a store. There he stands for a long time, thinking about what Freddy likes. Freddy liked sometimes to throw glass bottles against the trees and listen to them break. What else? Thinking about what to buy Freddy is the most difficult thing he has ever done. The man in the shop says May I help you sir?

Victor says A gift.

The man shows Victor ladies' gloves, handmirrors. He shows Victor some scarves. Victor leaves without buying anything.

For days he wanders around the neighborhood, looking in the shop windows. He is very nervous because he doesn't know when Freddy is coming, he didn't say anything in the letter. He has to find a gift as soon as possible; he wants to be at his apartment when Freddy arrives. He goes from one store to another, running through them, ignoring the shopkeepers when they try to talk to him. He has almost settled on a woolen hat when he sees the best thing yet: a horse made of gold and silver. It glints, its head thrown back with nobility. Victor asks the man for the price. The man looks distrustful. A hundred and fifty dollars he says. Victor pays him and takes the horse and leaves.

When Freddy comes, he whistles. Would you look at this. He sets down his suitcase and walks to the window. Victor is trembling. He wants to reach out and touch Freddy but he does not dare. Holy Toledo Vic. You got it made. He winks at Victor and a spasm travels through Victor's groin.

They said you got a rich cousin or something. You never told me about no rich cousin. What else he get you, you got a car?

Victor shakes his head.

Well still. I think you're a lucky son of a bitch. And lucky me too huh? He laughs. What you look like that for Vic? Huh? You miss me? C'mere. Let me see. Christ amighty you got a hard-on. Freddy laughs. What a fuckin thing is that.

Victor is happier than he has been in his whole life. Every moment he suffered was worth it. He has his own room, he has food and paper and he has Freddy. In the morning he wakes up and watches Freddy's chest going up and down. Freddy has light hair on his chest, Victor's is heavy and black. Sometimes he draws Freddy sleeping. Sometimes Freddy turns over or wakes up and then the drawing is incomplete. When he wakes up he tells Victor to put his mouth on his privates. Sometimes in the middle of the night he wants that too and he wakes Victor up and tells him to get going. Victor doesn't mind. He is in love.

*

TIME PASSES. Freddy stays with Victor although he doesn't stay every night. Sometimes he disappears for two or three days at a time and Victor gets worried. He prays and bargains. Or then sometimes Freddy goes for a week at a time, a month at a time, and Victor plunges into the worst despair he has ever known, worse than before, because now he knows happiness. Freddy refuses to explain where he goes or to warn Victor first. He is there and then he is gone. Victor comes home from the park where he has been drawing trees or from the restaurant or from the shop where he buys bread to make sandwiches for lunch and the apartment is quiet, a quiet different from when Freddy steps out to take a walk or to buy a bottle of beer or whiskey. Then Victor loses his mind. He swears the way he ought not to, he rips the pillows and breaks cups. When it is over he is tired and there is a mess and still no Freddy. Then Victor begins to bargain. He begins to pray.

Whatsit matter where I go? I always come back. The fuck do you care. Stop asking me, you're getting on my fucking nerves. You can be a real pain in the ass you know that? When Freddy's voice sounds this way Victor is frightened. He does not want to make Freddy unhappy. He would gladly cut off his own hands and feet to please Freddy. He would cut off his balls.

Look at this. It's pathetic. Freddy picks up a pillowcase with a dark oily smudge where Victor puts his head every night. Do some fucking laundry.

Victor doesn't know how to do laundry. Freddy takes him to the Laundromat. You put a nickel in, you put the soap in. Now you don't have to live like an animal. Freddy laughs. The sound makes Victor's heart grow. But another part of him doesn't know what to feel. On the one hand he wants Freddy to smile; on the other hand, he was just feeling so low about himself that he now has a hard time feeling happy. He is all ajumbled, as Mrs Greene used to say. Now that they live together all the time – sleeping in the same bed, sharing their meals, breathing the same air for most of the day – Victor sees things about Freddy that he didn't see before. The way his moods change. Long angry speeches. Then compliments dropping out of the clear blue sky. Victor does not understand. He tries to think of another gift to give Freddy. That will make him happy.

Also Freddy refuses to go to church. Victor cannot convince him. He goes alone and prays for the both of them.

Time passes. The seasons dance. Things change. Freddy comes and goes. Victor lives and dies. The strain hurts him. He wants Freddy to stay and never leave. Days become nights become days and Victor's eyes blur.

Stop crying. Stop it.

Victor cannot stop.

You're worse than a broad sometimes. What the hell is wrong with you. I swear to God I ought to knock hell out of you sometimes and you'd get what I mean. You shut your goddamned mouth. Goddammit I will split and you have no idea how fast. I ain't got to stay here one more minute. I got plenty of people I can go see. You think you're the only one I know? Fat fucking chance. You got no idea. You can be really stupid sometimes you know that? How the hell are you so thick. You don't know a thing about the world, you don't know about things happening two feet in front of you. You just sit there like a chimp doodling. Don't gimme no pictures, I don't want any fucking pictures. You really piss me off. You're pissing me off right now. I swear one day I'm going to bash your fucking face in. Give me that fucking thing. Give it back.

Victor throws the bottle out the window. It sails to the earth and explodes.

Oh now I'm going to get you. I'm going to get you for that. You're nothing, if I threw you out the window you'd be a stain on the sidewalk they'd clean you up faster than pigeon shit. You think that's a wiseguy thing to do, I wasn't halfway done with that you son of a bitch. Freddy pins Victor's arms down with his knees. He opens his fly and his privates fall out. Victor tries to put his mouth on the tip but Freddy slaps him. Don't you fucking touch it. Don't you fucking try. Freddy pulls on his privates and says Fuck, fuck. Then Victor is wet. Freddy relaxes, the blood leaves his face. He says All right.

Victor is twenty-seven. It is the week of the Fourth of July, and a summer rainstorm has caused the bunting to run, red and white and blue in the gutters. Victor stands at the window. Freddy has been gone for two days. Victor no longer tries to predict when Freddy will come back, and as rain streaks the glass he prepares himself for a long and lonesome stretch.

The key turns in the door. Freddy stands there dripping. Gimme a towel.

For the next few days Freddy is quieter than usual. He lies on the bed most of the day. Victor thinks it might be the heat, the rain makes the heat worse. He has the weather all written down. He keeps track of every day. He started and he does not intend to stop, it helps him separate one day from another.

The rain lets up. Freddy sits up in bed. I'm going out.

An hour and a half later he returns with newspapers. Victor watches as Freddy reads them. He turns pages impatiently, then throws the paper down and goes to sleep.

The next day he goes out again and comes home with the papers. This time he stops on one page and says Well shit.

Victor looks at the paper. There is a picture of a boy. His name is Henry Strong. He has short spiky hair. He looks sort of like a squirrel.

Freddy says I guess he wasn't too strong after all huh? Then he laughs. He looks at the window. It's raining. I think it'll keep up.

Victor nods.

Freddy sighs deeply, stretches, and lies down.

Victor keeps the picture of the boy.

A month later Freddy comes home with another newspaper. Victor tries to look but Freddy pushes him and says Don't read over my shoulder. Victor doesn't know what the problem is but he obeys. The next morning when Freddy is sleeping Victor goes to look. He sees another boy named Eddie Cardinale. Victor keeps that picture, too.

Summer turns to fall and then to winter. In those months Freddy sometimes brings back papers and Victor reads them. In San Francisco somebody has killed a woman. In Hanoi they drop bombs. Freddy is often in strange moods. He goes out late at night and walks around for hours, returning as the sun comes up over the brick buildings. Often Victor hears him leave and cannot fall back asleep. He sits at the window until he sees Freddy's shape crossing the courtyard. Only then does Victor close his eyes.

He wants to follow Freddy on these walks but he does not dare. He can imagine what Freddy would say. Get back in there. Get back you piece of shit. Freddy's moods make him use bad language, and he does not notice the deep dents he puts in Victor's heart. If anything Victor's sadness makes Freddy angrier. Victor does not have the words to describe what is happening between them. But things have changed. He misses the old days when they lay together for hours and Freddy talked to him about things he'd done, tricks he'd pulled and would pull. Now Victor sees that his body repulses Freddy. He stops trying to touch Freddy, and when Freddy shifts around in the bed and splays his legs greedily across the mattress Victor rolls out and sleeps on the floor.

You dumb piece of shit. You worthless son of a bitch.

Freddy's voice becomes Victor's own, a voice that Victor carries around with him all the time. It tells Victor that he is stupid and it tells him when he is doing something wrong, which is all the time. Though this voice says things that hurt Victor, he still prefers it to silence.

One night Freddy comes home with another man. He is short and has big red lips. Look at what I drug in. Freddy laughs like a horse and the man takes off Freddy's shirt. They begin kissing and Victor sits on the edge of the bed, feeling hot. The man gets on his knees and opens Freddy's pants. Freddy moans. Victor does not watch. The man leaves and Freddy is angry. Whassa matter. Something wrong with me? You got a problem you fuckin faggot? He slaps Victor and then he laughs. He falls on the bed and Victor tucks a pillow behind his head.

A FEW WEEKS LATER Freddy comes home in a rare good mood. He holds up a can of oatmeal. Remember this? We used to eat this shit for breakfast every day. I can't believe how much of that I ate. Well let's have it for old time's sake huh?

Victor hates oatmeal as much as he hates anything in the world; but he loves Freddy more, and so he and Freddy use the hotplate to make oatmeal for breakfast. This happens for a week. Then Freddy says You know what I can't stand this shit. He throws the can out and they don't eat any more oatmeal.

Soon afterward Freddy comes home with another newspaper. He shows Victor a picture of a boy with light blond hair and a square nose. His name is Alexander Jendrzejewski, a name that makes Victor's head hurt to look at it.

Time passes. Freddy comes and goes, Victor lives and dies. Twice more Freddy shows Victor pictures. Victor keeps them all. He wants to ask Freddy what they mean but he understands that they are a gift, they are special and that to ask is to spoil the surprise. He feels jealous of the boys. Freddy spends a lot of time talking about them and about the weather. Who are they? Victor wants to know. But he does not ask.

One day Freddy says I need money.

Victor goes to the box where he keeps the money Tony sends him. He has spent so little that by now he has a bunch as big as his fist. He gives it all to Freddy, who says Christ amighty.

Freddy never comes back. One month passes, two months, six months, a year, two. Victor begs, he pleads, he confesses. He hurts himself. He moans and prays and bargains. If You will, then I will. Time passes. Loneliness settles on him like dust. He is so lonely that he reaches for the phone.

Tony Wexler.

Victor says nothing.

Hello?

Victor hangs up.

Then he makes his most daring offer yet. If You will, then I will. He shakes hands with God and then he takes all his drawings, box by box, down to the basement, where he feeds them into the incinerator. He cries as he does it but he does it all the same. Everything he has drawn in five years goes into the fire until there is nothing left. He takes the elevator to his room and waits for God to fulfill His end of the deal.

But Freddy does not come.

Victor feels lost. He does not eat. He does not leave the apartment. He grows ill. He has dreams, he sees Freddy getting on a bus and driving away. In the dreams Freddy will not look at him. Victor wakes up wet from head to toe. He has the same dream every night for three weeks, and at the end he rises up and takes a shower. He goes to the restaurant. He has eleven dollars left in his pants pocket that he forgot to give to Freddy. He eats slowly, his stomach aches. With the remaining money he goes back to the store and buys a lot of new paper and some new markers and pencils. He carries everything back to his apartment. It is difficult because he is so weak. But he does it and then he sits down and begins to draw himself a new map.

TWENTY-TWO

If I'm still writing a detective story – and I'm not so sure that I am – I believe that we've come to the part of the book where I tie up all the loose ends and reassure you that justice was served. Those of you expecting a bang-up finish might be a little disappointed with me. I apologize. You haven't read this far without the right to expect some sort of fireworks. I wish this final chapter had more guns and explosions; I wish there was a knife fight. I actually thought about making something up. That's how eager I am to please. I'm no novelist, but I could probably spin together an action-packed conclusion. Although – seriously – knowing what you know about me, can you see me rolling through the dirt, both barrels blazing? I didn't think so.

The bottom line is, while I'll do my best to keep you entertained, I'm writing this to get down the unvarnished truth, and even if I've summarized, I haven't flat-out lied.

Now, if I'm keeping track of my story – and really, you have no idea how difficult this is, keeping everything straight – there are several outstanding questions. There's the question of who jumped me and stole my drawings, if not Kristjana. There's the question of how Marilyn and I turned out, what happened to Sam and me, the question of Frederick Gudrais, and finally there's the question of Victor Cracke. Let's go one by one, and let's start with our killer.

HE HAD A RECORD, and not a short one.

'Assault, assault, animal cruelty, loitering, indecency, public drunkenness, sodomy, assault.' Sam looked at me. 'That's just the early work.'

'Before he fell under Monet's influence.'

She smiled sweetly. 'You're a twit, you know that?'

'Where is he now?'

'His last conviction was in' – flipping pages – '1981. Aggravated sexual assault. He served six of a twelve-year sentence. Well, that's a crying shame. These days they'd take a DNA sample, it'd be mandatory. I guess he's either slowed down in the last twenty years or gotten smarter . . . But it's academic. First let's find out if he's even alive. I have a last known address for him out on Staten Island, and the name of his parole officer.'

In his most recent mug shot, Gudrais was smiling mightily, a five-hundred-watt leer that would have creeped me out even if I hadn't known who he was. His date of birth was May 11, 1938, which made him over forty in the photo, yet his skin was surprisingly smooth, like he'd never worried about anything in his life. We scanned the image and sent it to James Jarvis, who once again confirmed that we had the right man.

When we spoke to Gudrais's parole officer, she jumped to his defense, swearing up and down that Freddy had been out of trouble for years, that he was employed and living quietly right where his record indicated. She also told us something surprising: Gudrais had a daughter.

'My understanding of the situation is they aren't on too good terms,' said the PO.

At this point, I assumed we would go storming in like gangbusters. Sam was far more circumspect. To begin with, there was nothing we could do with Jarvis's testimony. At that time, New York had a five-year statute of limitations on rape — one of the shortest in the country and a justifiable source of outrage for feminists, who would manage to get the law changed the following year. But when Sam started building the case, she was forced to admit to Jarvis that he had no recourse; his portion of it was closed and buried. I had an idea that we could call him as a character witness — an anti-character witness, really — but she said that whatever he offered would likely be thrown out as immaterial or speculative.

'So then what good is it?'

'It's good for convincing some important people to get on board with this.'

Staten Island gets a bad rap. In its defense, I would like to point out that the Verrazano is actually quite beautiful, my candidate for the most attractive of all the borough bridges. In certain lights, from certain angles, it resembles the Golden Gate, which is high praise indeed. And if you set aside the landfills and strip malls, a reasonable portion of the island itself is pastoral: quaint brick homes, baseball fields limned in hoarfrost; a Rockwellian vision of Real America. I remarked upon this to Sam, busy angling the heating vents behind the steering wheel to dry-roast her fingers.

'It's Staten Island,' she replied.

Last week of February, half past six on the morning of a vicious cold snap, winter's final twist of the knife. The sun rose on neighborhoods shaking themselves awake. Scarved children waited for schoolbuses. A few joggers tried bravely to keep their footing on icy sidewalks. Windshields needed scraping; dog urine polka-dotted lawns. We headed first to the main police station, near the ferry terminal, where we were met by a lieutenant who shook hands with Sam and said that he knew her dad and was sorry. She nodded politely, though I saw her holding herself in place. That she could still get upset five months later probably comes as no surprise to most people who have lost a parent; but it made me aware of how little sanctity I had in my life.

They gave us an unmarked car and a cop named Jordan Stuckey, and the three of us drove to the neighborhood where Gudrais lived, at the southeastern edge of the island. Gray sand fronted the gray, windswept Atlantic. Along the beach ran a picket fence, most of it rotted or torsioned into oblivion. The local architecture consisted of bungalows. To me, it evoked Breezy Point. Sensing that Sam felt the same shiver of similarity, and that it bothered her, I withheld comment.

At seven thirty A.M. we parked outside a squat apartment building and left the heat running. I had been relegated to the backseat, and as a result had to content myself with secondhand reports from Stuckey, who used a pair of binoculars to keep watch on Gudrais's front door.

It was a waiting game. Acording to his PO, Gudrais worked at a bicycle shop a mile and a quarter up the road, where he fixed broken chains and so forth. Once arrested, he could be forced to give a DNA sample, but in rather a catch-22, we had to have something tangible on him in order to arrest him in the first place. Since the law allowed us to collect whatever he discarded, we hoped that one such item – a cigarette butt, a coffee cup, a tissue – would yield a usable profile. The important thing, Sam said, was maintaining the chain of custody in order to demonstrate that the DNA belonged to Gudrais and not someone else.

By eight thirty, all our coffee was gone. Sam, looking through the binoculars, said, 'He looks good for his age.'

'Let me see.'

'Don't pull.'

I let go of her elbow.

'I think he dyes his hair,' she said. Maliciously, she handed the binoculars to Stuckey, who said in his rumbling baritone, 'He's not just the president, he's a member.'

'Excuse me,' I said from the backseat. 'Hello?'

'Keep your pants on,' Sam said.

I sat back with an angry grunt. From what I had been able to see, Gudrais was tall. He walked at a brisk clip, and although the heavy coat he wore made it impossible to draw firm conclusions, he seemed well proportioned. The tail of a bright blue scarf flew out behind him as he bent into the wind.

'I guess he walks to work,' said Stuckey.

'In the snow,' Sam said. 'Uphill both ways.'

We followed at a distance, Sam on the binoculars as Stuckey crept forward, pulling over when necessary. Gudrais mostly kept his hands in his pockets, according to Sam, who gave me the play-by-play of his twenty-two-minute commute. It was incredibly stultifying: 'Now he's pulling his coat closer. Now he's cricking his neck. Now he's looking across the street. Oooh, there's a sneeze.' She was rooting for him to have a cold, to blow his nose and chuck away the tissue, preferably onto the sidewalk. But other than that first sneeze, he appeared the picture of health, and by the time he arrived at work and disappeared inside, we had gotten exactly nothing.

The morning crept by.

'He might go out for lunch.'

They brought in pizza.

Midway through the afternoon, he stepped out and started across the street before changing his mind and going back to work.

'This is really boring,' I said.

'Yup.'

On his walk home, Gudrais stopped at a corner market, emerging with a single plastic bag. He went straight to his apartment, and we saw the light of a TV come on.

Sam handed me the binoculars. 'Knock yourself out.'

'Thanks so much.'

That was how the next day went, too. If you need to reexperience it, I recommend that you go back two pages and read the foregoing.

At the end of our second day of surveillance we lingered outside his building, I on the binoculars, Sam and Stuckey trying to figure out an easier way.

'Friday's trash day.'

'That might be our best bet.'

'Mm.'

'At least we get tomorrow off.'

'You know what, though. I think—'

'Guys,' I said.

'I think maybe—'

'Guys. He's coming out again.'

The binoculars once again were taken away from me. I swore, but Sam was too busy watching Gudrais lope over to the bus stop.

'All *right*,' she said. 'Now we're talking.'

We tailed the bus up Hylan Boulevard, past Great Kills Park to New Dorp. Gudrais got off and walked three blocks to Mill Road and the movie theater. As soon as he went inside we hurried to the ticket booth, where a blank-faced teenager sat snapping gum. Sam asked for three tickets to whatever the man had bought tickets for, please.

'Thirty dollars.'

Sam said, 'I really hope he picked something good.'

I had to laugh when we got back three adults for the five thirty showing of *Because of Winn-Dixie*.

As we passed the concession stand, I spotted Gudrais at the back of the line, and a jolt of excitement cut through me. It took a concerted effort not to turn and stare at him, or to tackle him right then and there. For a brief moment, I felt intensely possessive of him, as though, having lost Victor Cracke as a medium, I could now vent my creative will through the manipulation and capture of a pedophile. Rage and vengeance, tempered with victory, the thrill of knowing something he did not. It was not a simple emotion, but the best word I can come up with is zealotry. He was mine and I knew it.

And then, just as suddenly as it had come, the feeling passed out of me, replaced by disgust. This night wasn't performance art. It was real. *He* was real. This place – an overheated multiplex – the unglamorous chase – Sam – these things were real. The auditorium was packed with real kids, and I saw the look on Sam's face, and her thoughts jumped into my head. Freddy Gudrais's choice of movie wasn't whimsical or random. It was appallingly true to form. He was here for the crowd. He was as real as he had ever been, real enough to put his hands around someone's throat. I sobered up and did my best to put myself aside.

We wanted to keep an eye on him, so the three of us spread out: I in back, Stuckey toward the middle, and Sam down near the front-left exit. It was an imperfect solution but it would have to do. Our primary goal was still to get Gudrais to relax and enjoy his soda.

He came in as the ads ended and the theater began to darken, and I saw his shape glide into an empty row on the right side of the theater – closest to me. He was slightly behind me, which made it hard for me to look at him without being obvious. I tried to pace myself, glancing back and then away. When he was out of my sight I imagined all sorts of horrible possibilities. Old black-and-white photos of mangled bodies kept filling up my mind.

The movie was a big hit. There was laughter; there were tears. I can't relay the plot because I spent most of its 106 minutes checking my watch, waiting for permission to look back. Gudrais gradually sank down into his seat, until all I could see was the top of his head, his hair so black and glossy with pomade that it reflected the screen's shifting blues and whites. Rationally I knew that I wasn't doing a thing; I couldn't really see him, his hands, anything other than that crescent of hair. But I hoped that my presence would somehow radiate out and encircle the families sitting around him.

The credits rolled; I looked back; he was gone. I waited until I saw Stuckey stand, and then all three of us went up the aisle.

As we'd hoped, he had been a bad citizen, leaving behind a wax cup full of melting ice and an empty container of popcorn with a napkin crumpled inside. Sam let out a happy yelp. Stuckey went out to the car and came back with a forensics kit. He put on gloves and crouched down and began to put things in bags. Then he stopped and sniffed near the popcorn container. He tweezed out the napkin. 'Boy oh boy.'

'What.'

'Smell that?'

I detected corn and salt and artificial butter, but above all something evocative of an overused swimming pool, equal parts sweat and chlorine.

'That,' said Stuckey, 'is semen.'

BY THAT SUMMER I had long given up on my stolen artwork, and so I was pleasantly surprised to get a call from Detective Trueg.

'Well,' he said, 'we found your stuff.'

'Where?'

'eBay.'

Trueg couldn't take all the credit, he confessed. Since his second son went off to school, his wife had had too much free time on her hands; in her boredom, she had become something of an auction junkie. Tired of her blowing money on Smurf mugs and secondhand pashminas, Trueg had put her to work, giving her copies of missing art and telling her to be on the lookout. Just between us, he considered this nothing more than a way to make her feel useful and to prevent her from buying crap. In three years she had never found anything. But lo and behold, she had unearthed some suspiciously Crackean work indexed under Art > Drawings > Contemporary (1950–now).

The seller's handle was pps2764 and he was in New York, New York. The rotating photo gallery showed a half dozen drawings along with assorted close-ups.

Five original drawings by famous artist VICTOR CRACKE. The pages go together. [One of the close-ups displayed a seam between two drawings.] *Cracke's work inhabits the shadowland between Expressionism and abstraction, yet this is no mere recapitulation of shopworn modernisms, rather a deliberate act of stylistic bricolage that incorporates the most striking elements of Pop and contemporary figuration.*

The paragraph continued on in this dreary vein, concluding,

I have more of these for sale if you are interested.

What bothered me most about the description was not its wordiness or its limp bunches of artspeak. What bothered me most is that I had written it. With the exception of the first two and the last sentences, the text had been lifted verbatim from the catalogue copy I'd written for Victor's show.

Also insulting was the price being asked. So far only one person had expressed enough interest to bid, and, as there were only six hours left on the auction, his offer of $150 looked like it would carry the day.

On the bright side, anyone could *Buy It Now* for $500.

I decided that it would be better not to tell Kevin Hollister about this.

Trueg said, 'The first thing I'd like to do is get ahold of the drawings and confirm that they're for real.'

'And that Kristjana didn't draw them.'

'Yeah, well, that's what I mean. It would be pretty dumb of her to keep making copies, though. She sounded pretty scared the last time we talked to her.'

I said that I didn't think she would stoop to eBay to promote herself.

Trueg laughed. 'Bear in mind also that it might be a third party. Can you think of anyone else we should be talking to?'

I almost suggested that he call Jocko Steinberger. But that wasn't his style. He was more the self-pitying type. There were, of course, plenty of other people angry at me, and plenty of those people could draw – not as well as Kristjana, but at this point I made myself no guarantees. 'You really think there might be another forger?'

'Did you think there'd be a first?'

I admitted that he had a point.

'Let's say we check him out and he seems to be for real, enough that we want to get to know him a little better. We make contact with him, make it sound like we're interested in buying a lot more, get to him that way. Failing that, we can go after his account information, although that'll take longer, cause we've got to go through the legal channels.' He paused. 'I hope you realize how lucky this is. Most of what we go after we don't find, ever. You really oughta thank the god of your choosing that this guy is such an idiot.'

I offered to Buy It Now.

'Don't bother,' he said. 'That bid is me.'

THE PARTY THAT SHOWED UP at Freddy Gudrais's door on a late May afternoon included two uniformed Staten Island cops, Sam, detective Richard Soto, and – way in the background – me. I had been allowed to go along for the ride, although it had taken a lot of strenuous lobbying. Nobody wanted an art dealer interfering, it seemed – Sam included.

'It's not safe,' she'd said.

'What's unsafe about it?'

'We're dealing with unknowns.'

'But what, specifically, are you worried about.'

She didn't answer me. Perhaps I should have known then that something was different, that her silence marked the beginning of a new phase of the investigation. At the time I was too excited by the prospect of an arrest to understand that the professionals had begun to take over and that I was slowly being shut out.

THE LOCK TURNED and the door whined and there he was: a skinny old man in a billowing workshirt, his cheeks sunken and unshaven, one gnarled hand on the edge of the door and the other on the jamb, his left thumbnail nearly gone, replaced by a clump of scar tissue. Close-up, he appeared less well preserved. He looked us up and down. Then he smiled, and the change it brought over him was remarkable. He spoke like we were a group of old friends, fishing buddies or a reunited bowling team.

He said, 'Am I gonna need my coat?'

Soto said, 'That depends on how easily you get cold.'

The cops followed Gudrais into the apartment, which was dim and overheated. Sam and Soto and I stepped inside, lingering near the door, as though to go any farther would be to poison ourselves with his air. A television sat opposite a folding chair. On the floor was a tray with a chipped mug and dozens of coffee rings. It was a sad room.

As they led him out, Gudrais said, 'I'll prolly die first. Ever think of that?'

Sam said, 'Next time I have a drink, Freddy, I'll drink to your continued health.'

MARILYN AND I DIDN'T SPEAK for several months following her return from Europe. She made herself so busy with work that it was impossible to get her on the phone, or, at least, impossible for me. I'm sure that relevant people had no difficulty getting through. After sending her that first couple of e-mails, I decided that my prodding was worsening things. She was not afraid to make demands. If she wanted to hear an apology, she'd let me know.

Late that summer – about two weeks after the Gudrais trial hit the papers, deep into a heat wave – my cell phone rang. 'Please hold for Marilyn Wooten,' said the voice on the other end. That's what they do when the president calls you.

It was an inopportune moment for her to invite me to lunch: I was standing in the middle of the gallery, my sleeves rolled up, overseeing the installation of a menacing eight-foot sculpture of a bag of organic lettuce. I wanted to request a postponement, but I understood that if I didn't go now I might never see her again.

Nat had grown into autonomy nicely; lately, in fact, he had begun to chafe under my authority. I put him in charge, hopped in the shower, and taxied to an uptown brasserie, one of the old haunts, far from Chelsea and the possibility of running into anyone.

I got out of the cab feeling drugged, my shower having done little except prime me to sweat again. Marilyn of course was coiffed and polished and dry and svelte and smooth. She kissed me on the cheek and I bathed momentarily in sandalwood and jasmine. I told her I was happy to see her looking good. I was. I could feel happy for her because I no longer desired her – missed her – loved her – you choose. The point is: it was so far gone as to evoke a sense of nostalgia.

For the better part of an hour, we talked about who was up, who was down, the latest *scandale*. As always, she provided most of the fodder. I served as her foil, stippling the narrative with nods and commentary. I hadn't been making the rounds, and so I had a hard time keeping up with her. Between stories she downed a steak and *pommes frites*; over dessert she lit a cigarette that the waiter imperiously commanded her to extinguish. She snorted and ground the butt out on her breadplate.

'Congratulations,' she said.

I looked at her.

'On solving your mystery.'

I shrugged. 'Thanks.'

'Why didn't he just plead guilty?'

'I think he thought they would take pity on him because of his age.'

She snickered. 'Clearly his lawyer forgot that we live in a youth-worshipping culture. Did you go to the trial?'

'All ten days.'

'Really? Then why didn't I read about you?'

'I was in the audience.'

'They didn't call you to the stand?'

'They didn't need to,' I said. 'Actually, my name never came up.'

'Not once?'

'Not once.'

'Well,' she said. 'That's a shame.'

I shrugged. 'It is what it is.'

'You don't get some sort of municipal commendation.'

'Apparently not.'

'Then I guess you'll have to settle for the satisfaction of a job well done.'

I nodded.

'Personally, I never found that worth very much. Was it interesting, at least?'

'It was mostly very technical.'

'Oh *gawd*. That's not interesting at all.'

'Not especially,' I said. Here I lied to her, not out of malice but because I knew that what I considered interesting would likely set her eyes spinning. But I'd learned some very interesting things, to me anyway. I learned that Freddy Gudrais wore a size-eleven shoe, the same size as the cast taken from the scene of Alex Jendrzejewski's abduction. I learned that shortly after the final murder, the murder of Abie Kahn, Freddy Gudrais had been arrested on an unrelated charge; I learned that he had served four years, and that he'd earned his release about eighteen months before the assault on James Jarvis. I learned that our partial fingerprint was intact enough to yield a match, and that your average juror finds DNA evidence remarkably convincing.

I learned that following a brief second prison stint in the mid-70s, Freddy Gudrais had fathered a child. Right around the time I was born, in fact. I found it interesting to note the appearance in court of a tight-lipped, lank-haired woman clutching a Naugahyde purse. She looked considerably like Freddy Gudrais, same pointed chin and wide mouth; aside from the press and me, she was the only person to come every day. Several times Gudrais looked back at her, but her expression never changed, and when they announced his conviction on four counts of homicide, one count not guilty, she stood up and walked out.

One thing that did not emerge at trial – or at any point, for that matter – was the true nature of Victor and Freddy's acquaintance. Soto questioned Freddy about it. He had to consider the possibility, for instance, that Victor had aided and abetted. All Freddy would say is, 'I ain't seen him in years.' Another time he mentioned offhand that he had bought a car with money Victor had given him. Soto asked why Victor had given him money. And Freddy, who never seemed to get upset, not even when the gavel came down, laughed and said, 'Cause I asked for it.'

These were things that interested me, but they would not interest Marilyn. We all have our private causes, and it's the job of the person who loves you to pretend to care. Marilyn wasn't that person anymore.

I said, 'It wasn't like you see on TV.'

'Mm. And the lawyer? She's well?'

'Yes.'

'I'm glad to hear it.'

'I'm glad you're glad.'

She smiled. 'I'm not going to get into a bowing match with you, darlin.'

'We're going to Ireland sometime in the fall.'

She recommended a hotel in Dublin and told me to use her name.

'Thank you.'

'I hope you have a wonderful time.'

I nodded.

She said, 'I'm going on vacation, too, you know.'

'I thought you'd already taken a vacation.'

'A vacation that long demands another vacation. A brief one, anyhow. Kevin and I are going to Vail for a week.'

Now it was my turn to smile. 'Just the two of you?'

'Well, he does have a fairly large *posse*. But yes, I suppose that at certain key moments we will be alone together.'

I couldn't help myself: I started to laugh.

'Be nice,' she said. Then she began to laugh as well. We laughed and laughed and I handed her the remainder of my strawberry zabaglione, which she polished off in three bites. Then she lit another cigarette. 'I've decided to take on Kristjana.'

I looked at her.

She shrugged. 'It was at Kevin's request.'

'I didn't realize they were acquainted.'

'Oh yes. She's been working for him for a while now.'

'Working how.'

'You know, his Great Paintings thing?' She spoke through smoke: 'After Jaime Acosta-Blanca skipped town Kevin had to find someone else and I suggested her. He asked her to make some copies of the Cracke drawings and what she did impressed him, so he hired her. Apparently they've grown quite close. I think he might have fucked her, actually . . . But. That's neither here nor there.'

I said, 'Kristjana's a lesbian.'

'Says you. Anyhow it's all very cordial.'

'*Madam.*' The waiter was strangling on rage, leaning over the table and goggling at her half-finished cigarette. '*Please.*'

'We'll take the check,' she said, handing him her credit card and waving him away. As he stormed off, she took a last drag and dropped the smoldering remains into her water glass. She sighed. 'They're ruining my city, Ethan.'

'I didn't realize they'd given you the keys.'

'Honey,' she said. 'I make the keys.'

*

DETECTIVE TRUEG spent more than three months establishing a rapport with pps2764 in New York, New York, and by that November they had him in custody.

'Sometimes we get our man,' he said. 'You know a Mr Patrick Shaughnessy?'

It took me a moment to place the name. 'From Muller Courts?'

'The very same.'

'But he's the superintendent,' I said, as though that made a difference.

'You should of seen the look on his face when I badged him. Whoo, he looked like he swallowed a sack of rats. At first he claimed he got the drawings from somebody else. Pretty soon, though, he's saying, all right, it was him, but – hey – after all, he was taking back what rightfully belonged to him. He says you ripped him off cause he had the drawings first. I wouldn't be surprised if he tries to come at you with a lawsuit.'

Sure enough, a few weeks later a process server showed up at the gallery. I called Sam, who offered to recommend a real lawyer.

TRAVEL AND ITS ATTENDANT STRESSES provide a good litmus test for the viability of a relationship, and so I suppose it's no surprise that shortly after we got back from Dublin, Samantha and I split up. Apparently my narcissism finally wore her down. Among other things, she told me that I was lost and that I needed to get ahold of who I was.

When my anger subsided I saw that she was on to something. My life had grown somewhat diffuse, aside from our relationship and the case. When both of those had gone I was left with work and little else.

I struggled to get back in the game. For a long time I'd been inventing excuses to stay away, with the result that all my artists were now furious with me. After Jocko's defection several more had followed suit. I couldn't recruit new ones, because the best steered clear of me, having been warned that I could and would desert them at a moment's notice. I spent hours on the phone and over expensive meals trying to restore my hobbled reputation, but by New Year's 2006 I was down to a roster of seven, and quite honestly not my best.

If I learned one thing in my years selling art – if Marilyn taught me nothing else – it's that there's no time like the present. Real estate having caught fire, the price I could get for my space bordered on obscene. I helped Ruby and Nat find new jobs; then I paid them each a year's salary plus bonus and put out the word that I was leaving the business.

'To do what?' people asked. I didn't have an answer for them. I tried to be philosophical. I said that I had run a gallery for nearly five years; my time was up; without knowing what I meant, I told people that I was moving on. I didn't want to reflect. Other than money in the bank, I had a hard time saying what I had to show for myself. I suppose that's something. Marilyn might say that it's everything. You can't argue with her. Anyone can see how happy she is.

I'LL END AS I BEGAN: with a confession: I am not now, nor have I ever been, nor will I ever be, a genius. Odds are, neither are you. I feel obligated to point this out, both because it has taken me a while to understand my own limitations and because these days we've gotten the idea into our heads that every person has infinite potential. The briefest spell of sober reflection reveals this to be a gentle lie, designed to cradle those with low self-esteem.

Ordinariness is nothing to be ashamed of. It carries no moral weight. I don't believe that geniuses are worth more in some cosmic *Blue Book*. They are worthy of more attention, of course, because they're so rare – one in a million, or rarer. What that means for the rest of us is that someone has to be the first of the remaining 999,999 souls; and the higher up you are, the closer you come to genius's vantage point.

To pursue that – to clamber up – to stretch out fingertips in the hopes of grazing the surface – can you imagine a more uniquely modern aspiration? A better metaphor for our oversaturated era than the desire to be president of the fan club? The hero for the age is Boswell.

I was not exempt. I was a devotee of genius; I was drawn to it; and if I had a talent, it was that I could pick genius out of a pile. I built a career out of that talent, and in doing so I came to believe that I might myself achieve genius. I believed that, whether genius lives well or poorly, it lives more deeply. That was what I saw in Victor Cracke's art. That was what I desired. That was what I sought by proxy, what I thought I could have, what I never will.

I NEVER FOUND HIM. Before we ended, Samantha suggested that I continue looking, and with time on my hands, I began to toy with the idea. But I didn't follow up. I left the drawings in storage until the fees started to seem onerous. With nowhere else to put them, I had them delivered back to Muller Courts, telling myself that this was a stopgap, and that I didn't intend to pay the rent on his apartment indefinitely. But I might. I might leave them just the way they are.

INTERLUDE: PRESENT.

At an age when most Manhattan boys of a certain class were primarily interested in lobbing water balloons from the balconies of their parents' high-rise apartments, David Muller could be found most afternoons sitting in the capacious living room of the house on Fifth, quietly reading *The Wall Street Journal* and jogging his ankle triple time to a ticking clock. He didn't have mischievous urges, or at least, he had nobody to scheme with. If you discounted the maids and the manservants, the violin teacher and the French tutor, the barber and the tailor and the elocutionist – and you would have to discount them; they weren't paid to throw water balloons – then he was alone, all the time. He has always been alone. That solitude made him the man he is today.

His parents' decision (it was his mother's decision, strictly speaking) to homeschool him until fourteen has never seemed to him wrong, not per se, although it depends on what you mean by wrong. His education was indisputably top-notch: a physicist to teach him physics; figure-drawing from the dean of the National Academy. If the goal of education is to educate, then Bertha chose wisely, as proven by the fact that by the time he began formal schooling, he was far enough ahead of his peers to skip not one or two but three grades, high school beginning and ending with his senior year. They might have been better off not sending him at all, as that year proved a miserable one, full of solitary walks between classrooms, lunchtimes spent reading. What did his mother suppose would happen? Did she suppose he would emerge with a stable of friends? Fourteen and eighteen are lifetimes apart; and boys are not like girls. Girls form friendships readily and discard them as conditions require. The friendship of boys is slow, suspicious and eternal. By the time David arrived on the scene, everybody knew everybody, who they could trust and who was a gyp, who was good for a dollar and who would put the make on your girl. With all roles taken, none remained for the small, shy interloper who came to school in a limousine – not even that of dedicated outcast. He was invisible.

Perhaps she meant in her strange way to teach him a lesson, one that few people learn, and then only on their deathbeds: you can be surrounded by people and still be alone. Loneliness is man's fundamental state. Created alone, he dies alone; and what comes between is at best a palliative. If her instruction was cruel, we cannot fault her; she taught from experience and believed in her own lessons. Rather than rage against what can't be changed, David has chosen to see his childhood as the crucible that gave him strength.

At Harvard he did not do much better. For much of his freshman year, he spoke to no one. He spoke to professors and to deans, yes; but were professors and deans going to shoot pool with him or punch him for the Porc? No. Roommates might have helped but he had none. The building he lived in, named for his family, had a suite on the third floor that belonged entirely to him. His parents seemed to think that having one's own room was a luxury, but David hated it. He hated, too, the 'man' they sent to mind him. The man's name was Gilbert, and he lived in the second bedroom, in what should have been David's roommate's room. Gilbert accompanied David everywhere: to class, where he would slouch unobtrusively at the back of the room; to the dining hall, where he would carry David's tray for him. Normal conversation was impossible, even at the Widener checkout desk, where the clerk's eyes would drift over David's shoulder to gawk at the silent shadow with the fedora.

The first winter nearly killed him. Mummified in cashmere, he shuttled to and from class, hoping Gilbert would magically evaporate. Desperate for human contact, terrified of it all the same, David took to strolling Mount Auburn in the evenings, pausing outside the finals clubs to listen to their jazz and laughter.

Once in a fit of madness he decided to knock. As the door opened, before he could run away, he suddenly understood the humiliation he was about to bring on himself. He saw for a brief and clear and terrible instant what the person on the other side of the threshold would see: a barely pubescent boy in a necktie, and some creepy son of a bitch standing right behind him. They would think he was somebody's little brother. They would think he was a Boy Scout selling commemorative stamps. He wanted to flee but the light came spilling out and he caught a glimpse of all that he could not have: a room with plush furniture and a half-dozen undergraduates with their jackets off and their sleeves pushed back and another five of them playing poker and cigar smoke and powdery Radcliffe coeds draped over the sofas and girlish peals of delight and a whirling phonograph and paintings of old ships hung askew and glasses of beer and shoes kicked off and carpets rolled up and steps that led to somewhere mysterious and dark and off-limits even to his imagination.

The fellow who answered the door seemed less concerned with David than with Gilbert, whom he evidently took for a police officer or a member of the administration. He began to ask what the idea was, every time they tried to have a good time somebody had to come trample all over it, wasn't there any such thing as a private party anymore. At the sound of his voice, David snapped to and walked away, drawing Gilbert like a duckling and leaving the boy in the middle of his tirade, which came to an abrupt conclusion with a shout of, 'That's right.'

Without math he might have been a goner. He was good at it; its clarity redeemed and soothed him. Plus, all the other students were the tiniest bit off, enough to assure him that he was far from the college's most outstanding freak. He discovered that he wasn't the only one his age. In Introduction to Higher Geometry there was a boy named, bizarrely, Gilbert – no relation – who had a lisp and who lived with his parents, commuting from Newton on the bus. In Potential Theory there was a heavy-lidded boy in horn-rimmed glasses who was, by all appearances, on his own. He and David orbited each other for most of the semester, a formal introduction coming in April when the boy plopped down in the next seat and offered David peanuts from a small wax-paper pack. He said his name was Tony.

THANK GOD FOR HORMONES. His voice leveled out by the middle of his sophomore year; he put on his father's inches and his great-uncle's muscles; his beard started to come in – more heavily than he liked; it became something of a pain in the neck – and, importantly, Gilbert got the boot. David and Tony got thick as thieves, both of them taking up squash, Tony eventually rising to become captain of the Lowell House team. David played with a chamber orchestra and Tony would come sit in the front row. They huddled together at the Game; they ate together in the dining hall. Eventually they did get punched: David by both the Porc and the Fly, Tony by the Fly alone, which effectively made David's decision for him. They even had a few dates. Like finals clubs, once girls figured out that David Muller was David Muller of *those* Mullers, they warmed up to him pretty fast. He tested their mettle by insisting that they bring along someone for Tony. That cleared out roughly half the potential applicants: after learning that they would have to convince some poor girlfriend to spend the evening making conversation with a not-especially-rich eighteen-year-old math-prodigy Jew, a lot of girls found themselves busy with unanticipated homework.

Ironic, because when those double dates did come off, it was not unusual for both girls to end up talking to Tony. He was a natural-born charmer. David, on the other hand, preferred to sit back and reap the fringe benefits.

After graduation Tony went off to Princeton for his PhD. David went back to New York to work for his father. Before parting, David asked if Tony didn't eventually want to come back to the city. The Wexlers lived on the Upper West Side of Manhattan, where she kept house and he was an actuary. One of the first things the boys had learned about each other was that they'd grown up less than three miles apart.

'We'll see,' said Tony. He wanted to be a professor. And why not? He had all the makings of a young academic; his senior tutor had referred to him as 'one of the finest minds of our century'. Even David couldn't keep up. He had to work problems out, whereas Tony would look down at the page and hear the answer shouting at him.

They wrote a few times a week. David wanted to know what Princeton was like; had Tony met Einstein? Tony replied that there were trees and that his general impression of the great man was that he needed a haircut. They saw each other when Tony came home to visit, which happened less frequently as he sank further into his research. Once David took the train out and they had a weekend like old times. Tony said that girls were easier when you were a graduate student; too bad there weren't more of them around. Campus could feel like a monastery.

David withheld comment. In those days, he had no shortage of social engagements. His mother, apparently panicked that she had starved him for friends, had been throwing parties virtually every weekend in an effort to find him a wife. This, he had come to understand, was his mother's fatal flaw, her belief in the quick fix. Ignorant of history, heedless of consequences, she could see nothing but the problem currently occupying her mind; and the smaller that problem was, the more it grew to fill her obsession. David knew from observing his father that the best course of action was silent assent. If she wanted him to be out and about, so be it.

In 1951 Tony received a tenure-track appointment; that same year he served as best man at David's first wedding, a role he would play at the next one, six years later. The third time around, David told Tony that he was bad luck, and besides, little Edgar was nine years old and man enough to do the job.

TONY SAID, 'I WANT OUT.'

'Just like that.'

'It's a terrible life. Susan is going out of her mind. All she does is read magazines, and she's going bonkers for kids.'

'Then have a kid.'

'You say that like that hasn't occurred to me.'

'You could adopt.'

'That's not what I mean.'

'What, then.'

'Give me a job.' Tony sat back in the big leather armchair, crossed his legs, laced his fingers across his stomach. The waiter came by and deposited their drinks, both of which sat untouched, melting ice ruining perfectly good scotch.

Tony said, 'I've been passed over twice now.'

'You're thirty-two.'

Tony shook his head. 'Trust me, David. Not gonna happen. Not for me.'

'You don't know that.'

'I got it from someone who got it from Tucker.'

David said nothing.

'I'm not about to pick up and move to Wisconsin or Texas,' Tony said. 'It's enough already. You've been asking me for years when I was going to come back to New York. Well, here I am. The only thing standing between me there and me here is a job.'

David thought about what it would mean to have Tony working for him. For him? With him. He couldn't expect him to start at the bottom. 'I'll see if—'

'You'll see? Come on, David. Just give me a goddamned job.' He bolted down his scotch. 'I've already tendered my resignation.'

David was surprised. 'That's a hell of a bold thing to do.'

'Well, you're a hell of a friend,' said Tony.

HE EXPECTED TONY to be bored, but on the contrary: his role as fixer and right-hand man seemed to appeal to a primal part of him, the same cheerful and deferential boy who would concede squash matches to David when total slaughter loomed evident. His assistant professor's salary no longer a source of frustration, Tony bought a thirteenth-floor triplex apartment on Park, a quarter-mile from the house on Fifth; with their wives, the two of them went to Miami and to Paris. There was a time, after Tony's divorce and before David met Nadine, when they were both bachelors again, and they spent some exciting weekends in Atlantic City, weekends that left them wrung out and soberly aware of their age.

Gradually Tony assumed responsibility for all the parts of David's job that David didn't enjoy doing; and then he came to do the same for the rest of David's life. It was Tony who did the hiring and the firing. It was Tony who managed the press; it was Tony who picked out a present for Bertha on her sixty-fifth birthday. It was Tony who stood by the graveside when David buried her, and when the terrible surprise came, it was Tony who went to Albany to fetch the secret.

*

DAVID INSISTED ON AUTONOMY. That, he told Tony, was the root of the problem: his parents had considered Victor unable to fend for himself, when it was precisely the institutionalization that had made him dependent in the first place. He had to learn self-reliance, learn to make his own decisions, to take care of his own shopping and to clean his own apartment. At first, of course, they would check on him. But the goal was to make themselves obsolete. Considering himself a liberator, David unconsciously parroted the era's Ken Keseyish ethos; extolling the value of living and dying by one's own choices, he brought the lessons of his searingly lonely childhood to bear on one who, he now realizes, might not have been equipped to handle them. And he chose to ignore the arrangement's built-in contradiction: declaring Victor independent while supplying his apartment and his income and even a safety net, in the form of Tony Wexler, who had been ordered to stay away once he determined that Victor wasn't going to starve to death or run naked in the street.

And there was another contradiction, as well: why go to the trouble of pulling Victor out of seclusion – only to hide him away again? In atoning for his parents' sins, David recapitulated them. For nearly a quarter-century the secret had been a source of shame, the fuel for lies; did he really believe that stashing Victor in Queens would end that cycle? What did he really want, transparency or secrecy?

If, in 1965, you asked David to describe himself, he would have said calm, methodical, the opposite of everything knee-jerk he resented in his mother. But the truth is that in middle age, as he came fully into his wealth, relying more and more on others to handle the nitty-gritty, he had become her son: unable to countenance the notion that his snap judgment might be wrong, unwilling to involve himself in the execution, content to express his will and consider it done. At forty he hated and feared nothing more than 'logistics', and his whole life had contorted to accommodate this fear. If he didn't want to look someone in the eye and tell them they no longer had a job, he didn't have to. If he didn't want to cope with the gymnastics of keeping Victor's identity a secret – even from the Muller Courts management – who would force him? Tony took care of everything, and Tony never complained. In adopting this modus operandi, David had transformed himself into a kind of minor despot; and although generally his edicts went off without a hitch, he never misstepped as badly as he did with Victor Cracke – unless it was in dealing with his youngest son, the one who wouldn't fall into line.

HIS FIRST THREE MARRIAGES had been unmitigated disasters, and he had sworn off a fourth when he met Nadine at a charity event. It was 1968; he was twenty-two years her senior, cranky, misanthropic, known among women as a meat grinder. She was bright, splendid, charming – in all ways wrong for him. She actually intimidated him – him, one of the richest men in New York! – and upon introduction, he was deliberately cold. She made a joke about the cause being feted and picked a piece of lint from his lapel, igniting within him a fierce desire that burned until her oncologist admitted that nothing more could be done.

Unaccustomed to failure, David flew her around the world in search of specialists; and though she played along, when she was gone, he tore himself up for having exhausted her. If he had just let her go in peace . . . He grew surly, snappish, interpreting people's assurances of eventual recovery as a sign that they didn't understand how different she'd been. How could he hope to make them see? It's a feeling no one can contain in words, certainly not David. He didn't want to explain himself to anyone. He didn't need to. The best proof of what she'd meant to him, the living proof, was the boy.

HE HAD NOT WANTED MORE CHILDREN, considering them the downfall of his first three marriages. Supposedly a child expanded your capacity for happiness. But David saw happiness as a zero-sum game. Children threw the entire equation out of balance, and worst of all, they remained once the wives had fled, draining his energy, money and sanity. He had no idea how to talk to them; he felt ridiculous kneeling down and asking questions he knew the answers to. He had been left to raise himself; why couldn't they do the same? When Amelia or Edgar or Larry wanted something, he told them to put it in writing.

But despite his efforts, they grew up soft. Their mothers spoiled them, and by the time he was called on to be a father, it was too late. The boys became yes-men, unimaginative, unable to do anything except take orders given in a stern voice. He made them vice presidents. Amelia didn't do much more than garden. It was good that she lived overseas.

He had enough problems. Why add another into the mix?

'I'm too old.'

Nadine said, 'I'm not.'

'I'm a lousy father.'

'You'll be a better one this time.'

'What makes you think that?'

'I'll help you.'

'I don't want to be a better father,' he said. 'I'm happy being a lousy father.'

'You don't mean that.'

'I do.'

'You don't,' she said.

'Nadine,' he said. 'I have enough experience to know that I am not fit to raise children.'

'What are you so afraid of?'

He wasn't afraid of anything. Fear is what you feel when something bad *might* happen. He knew for a fact that it *would*. What he felt was doomed. He had been here before.

'I love you,' she said. 'This is what I want. Please don't argue with me.'

He said nothing.

'Please,' she said.

HE COULDN'T DENY HER FOREVER. All she had to do was stop asking outright.

At her request he tried to be a better father. Take him out, she said. Take him somewhere fun. David didn't know where to go, and Nadine refused to spoonfeed him. She told him to use his imagination. But at three he had played alone in his room. At three, he had begun to read; he could hold a violin. He had no idea what normal three-year-old children did.

He took him to the office, where he tried to interest him in plastic models of buildings yet to be constructed. He showed him a planned waterfront in Toronto. He showed him two shopping malls in New Jersey. He thought it was going well until his secretary told him that the child was clearly bored to death. At her suggestion David took him instead to the Museum of Natural History. Although he had a seat on the board of directors, he stood in line, like a normal father might, and bought three tickets: one for himself, one for the boy, and one for the nanny who had been tagging along silently all morning. Look, David said to his son. He pointed to a dinosaur skeleton. The boy began to cry. David tried to distract him with other exhibits but the dam had broken. The boy cried; he was inconsolable; he didn't stop until they'd gotten back to the house on Fifth and David handed him off to his mother, saying, Take him, please.

That was the last time he tried to be a better father.

But motherhood became Nadine, very much, too much, and everything he'd known would happen began to happen. He felt her drift away from him and he was powerless to stop it. Hadn't he told her? He had; he'd warned her. She hadn't known any better – but he had, and *he had warned her*. He should have been more firm. He should have told her to wait five years, see if she still felt the same way, if she still wanted to jeopardize everything.

NADINE BROUGHT LIGHT TO THE HOUSE, and when she was gone, the darkness that returned to reclaim its place – the darkness David had so long lived with, if not happily, then at least uncomplainingly – began to suffocate him. The slightest disturbances brought on crushing migraines, so severe that he had to lie down until they passed. Anything could trigger them. A sudden noise, a piece of bad news. The thought of something stressful.

And the boy, of course. He would not sit still. He threw tantrums. He was stubborn, he was willful; he would persist in ridiculous beliefs even after David had pointed out to him, for the billionth time, their glaring flaws. His superstitions irritated David to the point of anger or worse; sometimes, when the boy was asking about his mother, David would simply ignore him, shielding himself with his newspaper and waiting for the questions to stop. He was too old to maintain the charade. He did not want to talk about imaginary things; real life was bad enough. He would grip his forehead and tell the nanny to take him away, take him away.

The headaches faded with time, but the boy's behavior only got worse. They would send him to school and within months he would be expelled. He used drugs. He stole. David didn't want to hear about it; when Tony tried to involve him, he simply said, 'Handle it.' The boy was lost, Tony said. He needed a guiding hand. And David replied that they would do nothing to interfere – believing, as always, in the power of the self to create meaning and pave its own road.

IN HIS SEVENTY-SEVENTH YEAR, he had gotten used to his life, gotten used to the idea that his daughter was frivolous, that his first two sons were milquetoasts, that his third was unmanageable and spiteful. He had accepted it all, without regret or remorse. All he wanted to do was live and work and then die.

Then he sat down to lead an afternoon board meeting and pain laced down his arm and the next thing he knew he'd been steamrolled, whisked high above the room, floating eight feet over the table and staring down at his own limp body, the picture of indignity, some half-wit executive trying to give him CPR and breaking his ribs. He tried to protest but no noise came out. Then he closed his eyes and when he opened them the room was full of doctors and nurses and beeping machinery. Tony was there, too. He offered his hand and David took it. His best and only friend, the only person who had never abandoned him. He squeezed as hard as he could. His hardest was not very hard. His heart had shriveled. He could feel it. Whether from disuse or bad living or bad genes, his heart had remodeled itself, permanently.

They could do a lot for a man his age with his condition, a lot more than they had been able to do for Nadine. Within a month he was walking around as though nothing had ever happened. Physically, he was fine, though he constantly felt glum and anxious. Had he been of a different generation, he might have indulged himself in therapy. That was not the Muller way. He called Tony in and said that they were going to make some changes starting now.

HE CALLED UP HIS DAUGHTER, called up his eldest sons. Amelia was baffled but got on a plane. Edgar and Larry came to the house and brought their own children. When everyone had gathered in his office, he told them he wanted them to know that they all meant a great deal to him. Everyone nodded, but they were all looking in different directions: at the ceiling, at the doodads on the mantel, at the stone carving above the fireplace – anywhere but at him. Nodding into oblivion. Embarrassed by this sudden display of emotion; afraid to offend him. They thought he was going to die, and they wanted to make sure they got their cut.

He said to them, 'I'm not going to die.'

Amelia said, 'I would hope not.'

When did she start talking like that, in that voice? Who were these people? His children, a bunch of strangers.

Larry said, 'We're glad you're feeling better, Dad.'

'Yes,' said Edgar.

David said, 'Don't count me out just yet.'

'We won't.'

'Have any of you talked to your brother?'

No one spoke.

Amelia said, 'I saw him last year.'

'You did.'

She nodded. 'He came to London for the fair.'

'How is he?' David asked.

'Well, I think.'

'Would you tell him to get over here and see me.'

Amelia looked away. 'I can try,' she said softly.

'Tell him. Tell him how bad I look. Exaggerate if you have to.'

Amelia nodded.

But the boy, willful as ever, would not come. David's blood boiled. He wanted to use a stronger hand. In a rare moment of dissent, Tony said, 'He's a grown man.'

David glared at him. *Et tu?*

'I'm just saying,' said Tony. 'At his age you were running the company. He's capable of making his own decisions.'

David said nothing.

Tony said, 'I went to Queens, like you asked.'

'And.'

Tony hesitated. 'He's not good, David.'

'He's sick?'

'I think so. He can't keep living there. It's like a junkyard.' Tony shifted around nervously. 'He recognized me.'

'Are you sure?'

'He called me Mr Wexler.'

David said, 'Jesus.'

Tony nodded.

David said, 'What do you suggest?'

'A nursing home. Someplace where he won't have to look after himself.'

David thought. 'I have a better idea.'

HIS SPINE WAS HOOKED. Skin dangled from his arms. When they took him to the doctor, he weighed in at ninety-two pounds. He might have been David's uncle rather than his nephew. They fed him; they cleaned him up, removed his cataracts, and installed him on the third floor of the house on Fifth, in David's childhood bedroom.

IN THEIR RUSH TO GET HIM out of the apartment, they neglected to look inside the boxes, which Tony assumed were full of junk. Not until he began receiving voicemails from someone who'd spoken to someone who had talked to someone at the Carnelian unit – some fellow named Shaughnessy – did Tony bother to go down and take a good look. When he did, he called David and, following a lengthy discussion, secured permission to call the Muller Gallery.

VICTOR TOOK TO TV QUICKLY. The constant stream of chatter seemed to comfort him. It didn't matter what was on: David would find him watching infomercials, whispering to himself and to the people on the screen, whom he clearly preferred to real company. His weight improved, although he still ate only when food was brought to him. David's attempts to engage him in conversation were silently rebuffed. He did manage to pry out an affinity for checkers. They played once or twice a day, Victor smiling as though remembering a private joke.

WHEN THEY PRINTED THE PIECE in the *Times*, David brought it in to show him. Victor saw the photograph of his drawings and turned pale. He dropped his bowl of soup. He clutched the page, crumpled it, turned on his side and pulled the blanket over his head, refusing to respond to David's questions or to come out. For two days he didn't eat. David, grasping his mistake, made a promise to Victor, one that seemed to reassure him a little. Then David called Tony and told him to get those drawings back at any cost.

THE PAGES WERE OLD AND FRAGILE; they'd been disassembled into individual panels. David stood at the bedside while Victor flipped through them, lingering over a picture of five dancing angels and a rusty star. David asked if Victor was happier now. Instead of answering, Victor got out of bed and limped down across the room to the window overlooking Ninety-second. With difficulty he raised the sash, then took the drawings and, one by one, shredded them out over the sidewalk. It took ten long minutes to get rid of everything, and David had to work not to raise objections. They'd probably be fined for littering. Add a hundred dollars to the two million they'd already spent. But money was just money, and when Victor was done he looked calmer than he ever had. For the first time in weeks he looked David in the face, wheezing slightly as he crawled back into bed and turned on the TV.

*

THAT ISN'T THE ONLY WAY in which Tony's plan has proved a disappointment. It has failed altogether at its primary goal. His youngest son never wrote a thank-you card, never called. David supposes that this is fitting. He reaps what he has sown. Born alone, he will die alone.

At least he has Victor. They are, he supposes, two of a kind.

And he has the house on Fifth. In a way, it has been his most constant companion, if not the most genial one. Since inheriting it, David Muller has had four wives, four children, countless domestics and several lifetimes' worth of headache, both literal and metaphorical. Drafty as ever, it remains a constant source of aggravation: rust-chewed pipes and falling plaster and windows that never seem to stay clean longer than a few days. Only an overgrown sense of filial loyalty has kept him from turning the place into a museum, and when he's gone, that's exactly what he intends to happen.

His doctor likes him to exercise, and so David skips the elevator in favor of the stairs. Three times a day up and down he goes, from the reception rooms and the portrait gallery to the ballroom to Victor's bedroom and then to his own bedroom, his father's former suite. He will sometimes stand in the hallway where as a boy he listened to the sound of breaking glass. He never goes to the fifth floor.

TONY SAYS, 'ETHAN CALLED.'

David looks up from his paper.

'He wants to come by.'

'When.'

'Tomorrow.'

A silence.

David says, 'What does he want?'

'He wants to give the rest of the drawings back.'

401

A silence.

Tony says, 'Your guess is as good as mine.'

THE NEXT DAY DAVID RISES EARLY, showers and dresses and walks downstairs to greet his son, who arrives in a taxi and who seems ambivalent. They shake hands, then stand there reading each other. David is about to suggest that they head upstairs to the study when his son asks to have a look at the portrait gallery.

'By all means.'

There is Solomon Muller, smiling kindly. Beside him, his brothers: Adolph with the crooked nose and Simon with the warts and Bernard with the bushy balloons of hair at either side of his head; Papa Walter, looking like he has eaten too much peppery food; and Father, his long, thin body forced out of joint to keep him within the frame. Bertha's is the only portrait of a Muller woman, and it is slightly bigger than the men's. There is a spot for David's own portrait and two panels that remain undedicated. Leading to the awkward and unstated question of where—

Preemptively: 'I don't want one.'

'You might change your mind.'

'I won't.'

David looks at his son, who is staring angrily at the blank burled maple, and for the first time, he understands how difficult it must be for him to be here.

As they climb to the second floor, David talks about bringing Nadine to see the house, and what she did when she saw the ballroom.

'She screamed.' He smiles. 'She really did.' He opens the door on the vast, dark room, its expanse of unused wood like a frozen sea. Their footsteps echo. Above them the gilt is dumb, and the bandstand seems to be hunkered down and shivering. He really ought to turn up the heat a notch.

He says, 'We danced. There was no music but we were going for an hour or more. Your mother was a terrific dancer, did you know that?'

'I didn't.'

'She was.' Then David has the crazy impulse to grab his son and waltz him around the room, so he says, 'Should we talk turkey?'

THE NEGOTIATIONS LAST less than five minutes; his son will not take any money.

'Something, at least; you've worked hard, they're yours—'

'All I did was put them up on the wall.'

'I understand that you feel a sense of—'

'Please don't argue with me.'

David studies his son, who has grown to look more like Nadine than he ever could have imagined. He could never deny her. And yet he's had no problem denying his son. He could argue with him now; in fact, he wants to argue with him, wants to show him the error of his ways.

'If that's what you want.'

'It is.'

'Okay.'

'They're back at the Courts. Tony can handle it, I presume.'

'Yes.'

'Then that's that.'

A silence.

David says, 'I don't want to keep you.'

'I don't have anywhere I need to be.'

A silence.

'In that case,' David says, 'there's someone I'd like you to meet.'

THE DOOR IS SLIGHTLY AJAR. David knocks anyway. When they enter, the man in the bed is half asleep, almost invisible beneath two heavy comforters. He sits up a little at the sight of visitors. His eyes are watery; they move and search; but as Ethan steps forward – saying to David a word he has not heard in a long time, in a way David can never remember hearing – asking, Dad? – they begin to focus.

ACKNOWLEDGMENTS

Several people made this book possible by providing information, personal references, or both. Many thanks to Ben Mantell, Jonathan Steinberger, Nicole Klagsbrun, Loretta Howard, Stewart Waltzer, Jes Handley, Catherine Laible, Barbara Peters, Jed Resnick and Saul Austerlitz.

As always, I owe a huge debt of gratitude to Liza Dawson and Chris Pepe. Thanks also to Ivan Held, Amy Brosey and everyone at Putnam.

Thanks to my parents and siblings.

I could not write anything without the ideas, support and advice that my wife supplies, selflessly, day after day. Her name belongs on the cover as much as mine.